Jo Watson is the bestselling author of the Destination Love Series, *Love to Hate You* which has sold over 100,000 copies, *Love You, Love You Not*, *You, Me, Forever* and *Truly, Madly, Like Me*. She's a two-time Watty Award winner with over 50 million reads on Wattpad and 85,000 followers. Jo is an Adidas addict and a Depeche Mode devotee. She lives in South Africa with her family.

For more information, visit her website **www.jowatsonwrites.co.uk**, follow her on Twitter and Instagram **@JoWatsonWrites** and find her on Facebook at **/jowatsonwrites**.

Love funny, romantic stories? You don't want to miss Jo Watson!

'A masterclass in character development' *Hannah Reading Books*

'I can't heap any more praise on this book, it just made me feel so happy! I laughed, I cried, I smiled, but most of all I LOVED!!' *Mrs J Tea*

'A perfect read for fans of rom-coms' *Cheryl's Bookworm Reads*

'Jo Watson has found a fan for life in me' *Olive Book Reviews*

'Found myself frequently laughing out loud and grinning like a fool!' *BFF Book Blog*

'Full of pure-joy romance, laugh-out-loud moments and tear-jerkers' *Romantic Times*

'An addictive read, it is heart-breaking at times but ultimately a stunning heart-warming read' *Donna's Book Blog*

'I love a good original love story and Jo Watson managed to surprise me over and over again. Her snappy writing style is refreshing, her main characters are endearing and dazzling and her book sparkles from beginning to end' *With Love For Books*

By Jo Watson

Just The Way I Am

Jo Watson

HEADLINE
ETERNAL

First published in Great Britain in 2021
by HEADLINE ETERNAL
An imprint of HEADLINE PUBLISHING GROUP

2

Cataloguing in Publication Data is available from the British Library

ISBN 978 1 4722 6557 9

Typeset in 11/14.5 pt Granjon LT Std by Jouve (UK), Milton Keynes

Printed and bound in Great Britain by Clays Ltd, Elcograf S.p.A.

HEADLINE PUBLISHING GROUP
An Hachette UK Company
Carmelite House
50 Victoria Embankment
London EC4Y 0DZ

www.headlineeternal.com
www.headline.co.uk
www.hachette.co.uk

Just The Way I Am

CHAPTER 1

I imagined the moment of my death would be different to this.

Firstly, why was it so dark? Where was the bright light that I was supposed to be calmly walking towards? Look, it's not like I was expecting a rotating disco ball or ultraviolet lights or anything that exciting, but there was nothing. I would have settled for flickering candlelight at this stage.

And why wasn't my life flashing before me? Why wasn't I watching all the beautiful, poignant, happy moments playing out on a big screen in front of me while sitting comfortably with God, or whoever, eating popcorn?

And more to the point . . . *why couldn't I even remember my life?* I was sure I'd had a life, right? But in that split second where I'd stood there, balancing precariously between this life and the next, consciousness flicking on and off, on and off . . . there was simply nothing. Not a memory, not an image, not an anything. And then, it stopped flicking altogether and with a loud sound that filled my skull and bashed against the back of my eyeballs, it all went black.

I can't tell you how long I stayed there in the darkness. The only company I had was the deafening thump of absolute silence. Silence that pulled so hard and heavy on me, I knew I must be close now . . .

Death. I could feel it. Dragging me under, pulling, calling me, and then . . .

Halle-bloody-lujah. I was finally hearing a voice.

"Stay with me, stay with me," the voice said.

"Is that you, God?" I said in my head, but for some reason I thought I could hear it too. Wait, had I said that out loud? But dead people can't speak . . . *can they?*

"No, my name is Noah. I'm a paramedic. You've been in an accident."

"Noah? Why are *you* here? Are you finished with the animals?" I asked in a strange, unfamiliar voice.

"What?"

"Two by two by two," someone sang. I think it was me, I'm not sure. "Are we on the boat now? It feels like we're moving. I hope I don't get seasick."

"Um . . ." There was a long pause and I tried to open my eyes to look at Noah. Why wasn't he speaking to me anymore?

"NOAH!" I think I shouted.

"I'm here. What's your name?" He took my hand, and this small action seemed to awaken every single part of my body that had previously not been responding.

My eyes fluttered open, God my head hurt. "A-am . . . I dead?"

"No! You're very much alive."

I think I smiled; I couldn't tell. My lips felt far away from my body, as if they were disconnected. In fact, everything felt disconnected and far away and I got the feeling that in order to be whole again I would need to pull bits of myself back together.

"What's your name?" Noah asked again, squeezing my hand in a manner that made me feel utterly safe. I squeezed back with all the energy I could muster. It wasn't much, but it was enough to feel strangely connected to him. I tried to look at the person attached to the hand, but the images in my field of vision were obscured by a blurry mist.

"What's your name?" the question came at me again.

"Uh . . . it's . . . uh . . ." More strange sounds came out of my mouth. "My name is . . ." I scanned my mind, but it was blank.

"What?" The blurry face leaned in.

"It's ... It's ..." I reached into my mind and grabbed hold of something, but as soon as I tried to pull it towards me, it slipped away. "I ... I ... don't know! I don't know!"

Noah put his other hand over mine and a rush of warmth shot up my arm and momentarily made the pain in my head just a little bit better. "That's alright. Take your time."

I nodded at him and closed my eyes tightly, despite the hot, sharp, bolt of pain that ripped through my skull as I did. I imagined myself climbing into my mind, as if it were a dark cave. I crawled across its cold floor, I scanned its interior, but still, *nothing*.

I stretched my arms out and grabbed at the emptiness, like casting a net into the sea, and then pulled my hands towards me to see if I had caught anything. But the net was empty.

"I DON'T KNOW MY NAME!" I heard myself scream. I tried to sit up again, but felt two hands push me back down.

"Try to be calm. I know it's hard, but I need you to stay calm."

But I couldn't. "I need to get out of here. I need to ... WHY DON'T I KNOW MY NAME?" Pain thumped in my head. Loud, hard, sharp.

"It's okay. I'm with you. Try to keep still," Noah said, but I struggled against him as he put a mask on my face.

"Take some deep breaths. In and out. In and out."

I continued to struggle until I saw two bright blue beacons piercing through the mist in front of my eyes. I grabbed hold of them and stared back. *Blue eyes*. He had blue eyes. His features finally came into focus and his mouth twitched into a small smile.

"I'm right here. Just relax."

I nodded. His smile pulled some of the tension out of me.

"Good, just like that. Deep breaths."

I followed his instruction and started to feel strangely calm.

"A little better now?"

"Yes. Can I ask you a question, Noah?"

"Sure. Anything."

"How did you get the snakes in?"

"The snakes?"

"And the bees, what about the bees? And how did you know which one was male, and which one was female?"

He smiled and I felt him pat my hand. "I'm just a paramedic, ma'am. That's all."

And then I closed my eyes and everything went black again.

CHAPTER 2

*U*nknown *Jane Doe.*

Blunt force trauma to the head.

Confused on the scene with a GCS of 12.

BP 130 over 90.

Pulse 115.

Patient was confused and combative due to hypoxia, settled with a poly mask.

Patient is displaying amnesia and doesn't know her name.

The words swarmed at me through a thick, gooey haze and I felt myself being lifted up. I was airborne for a moment or two: *was I flying?* And then my back came into contact with something hard and everything around me exploded.

Lights.

Voices.

Rushing footsteps.

Beeping machines.

"Noah?" I whispered, clasping at the air in front of me.

"Ma'am, we need you to keep still, please," a woman said, taking my hand in hers. She was wearing a glove and I craved the reassuring warmth of Noah's hand.

"I'm Dr. Bennett." A man shone a light in my eyes. "Pupils equal and responsive," he said to someone over his shoulder. "I'm a neurologist. Can you tell me what your name is?"

"I think my name is Jane Doe."

The man looked at me for a while, an expression on his face I couldn't read. "And do you know what happened to you? Why you're in the hospital?"

"No."

"Can you tell me what day of the week it is?" he asked.

"It's . . . uh . . ." I bit my lip to stop the tears.

"Don't worry." His voice was extra calm and slow now. "Do you know what city we're in?"

"Yes, I think so. Johannesburg."

"Very good. And who is the president?"

"Uh . . ." I scanned my memory again. I felt like I knew this too. Words began echoing in the deepest, darkest, most distant places in my mind and I concentrated hard, trying to listen to them. "CYRIL! Cyril Ramaphosa!" I shouted when the answer finally came to me.

The doctor smiled and I felt an instant bolt of relief. "Excellent. We're going to take you down for an X-ray and a CT scan to see what's going on in your brain."

"Did you know that the X-ray was discovered accidentally by Wilhelm Roentgen in 1895?" I heard myself say, and then everyone stopped what they were doing and stared at me. I waited for someone to say something, but no one did. Instead, the doctor pulled his gloves off and exited the room. I wanted to yell not to leave me alone, and almost did, but then I felt a hand on my arm.

"It's okay, I'm here." I strained my eyes, looking as far left as I could to see who was talking to me.

A smiling face met mine. "I'm Ntethelelo. I'll be taking care of you. So, you mustn't worry, you're safe!"

But I didn't feel *safe.* How did I know who the president was, and about X-rays, but not my own name?

"I'm going to take you to CT and X-ray now," Ntethelelo said sweetly. And then, I was on the move again, being pushed down a long corridor. We arrived at an elevator and, for some reason, it filled me with absolute terror. Ntethelelo pressed the button and we waited for the doors to open. I watched the numbers lighting up as the elevator moved, a sense of impending doom growing inside me as the numbers came closer and closer. I heard a familiar voice and turned. It was Noah. He looked relaxed, leaning against a wall with his phone pressed to his ear. I squinted against the bright light coming from the long railway track of fluorescent bulbs running the length of the corridor.

"Sorry, I was meant to be off today, but I'm not now. You can deliver it tomorrow, if that's okay?" Noah said into his phone. "Yes. Noah Robinson. 19C Edward Drive, Parkmeadows."

Ding! The elevator doors opened and something inside me just snapped. "No! No!" I shouted as I stared into the terrifying empty space behind the open doors.

Ntethelelo put her hands on the side of my face. "You mustn't move your head, darling." She brought her face right up to mine, looking me directly in the eye.

"NO! I can't . . . You mustn't . . . STOOOOP!" I was shocked at the sounds coming out of my mouth; guttural and desperate-sounding. They cut through the air like a sword and made everything around me feel like it was shaking.

"Doctor!" Ntethelelo called out, and soon, someone else was there. And then someone else. Flashes of white coats and arms and a sharp, shiny needle catching the light and then a pain in my arm, a sting, a burn and then . . .

"Hi, it's me, do you remember?" A gentle hand, a friendly voice and those blue eyes.

"Noah!" I whispered, feeling like warm water was flowing through my veins.

"That's right. You must try and keep still, remember?"

Our eyes locked, the blueness drawing me in like calm waters.

"Deep breaths." He inhaled deeply and I copied him.

"Great!" Ntethelelo spoke this time.

"Great," I echoed, my voice sounding more and more like liquid as I talked. "The animals went in two by two by two . . ."

I think I heard a chuckle before it all went dark again.

CHAPTER 3

~

I opened my eyes. My head felt like it was at least ten times bigger than it usually was, and it hurt! The world in front of me was fuzzy and I blinked a few times, trying to bring all the shapes into focus. The air was filled with a smell that hit me in the back of the throat and made me gag. Chemicals, disinfectants and . . .

I sat up as fast as I could. *I was in a hospital room!* I heaved, but nothing came out. The room started spinning and I gripped the sides of the bed to steady myself.

"Take it easy. You've just come out of sedation, it's normal to feel nauseous, I'll give you something for that," a woman's voice said. She was just a brown-and-white blur at this point, but when she came closer my eyes adjusted a little.

I lowered myself back onto the bed.

"I'm Dr. Kgomotso Maluka. Do you know where you are?" she asked.

I nodded. God, my head hurt. "In hospital."

"Good." She looked pleased with my answer and opened the file that she was holding. "Do you know your name yet?"

"It's um, I think it's Jane Doe."

"Jane Doe is what we call someone when we don't know their name," she said kindly.

I looked around the room. "Didn't I come in with anything? A bag or something?"

She turned and indicated the chair in the corner. "Just the clothes you were wearing, a watch and a keyring."

"Was I unconscious?" My throat felt dry as I spoke, and I reached up and touched it.

"You were sedated for some procedures we needed to carry out. Normally, we wouldn't sedate a patient, but you were very panicked." She passed me a cup of water. "Small sip." She gently pushed it towards my lips. The cool water slipped down my throat and the relief was instant.

"Thanks," I murmured.

"So, what about your name?"

I closed my eyes tightly. If my name was not Jane, then what was it? I tried to think of names I knew. *Noah, Ntethelelo, Kgomotso, Jane, Bennett, Cyril.* Those were the only names that existed inside my head.

"No, I don't know. I don't! No!" The words shot up my sore throat and tumbled out of my cracked lips.

"That's okay." She wrote something down in her file and the sound of the pencil against the paper grated against my already shattered nerves, making them feel like they were on fire.

"What are you writing?"

"Just taking some general medical notes." Her tone was casual and placating, and then she wrote something else, as if noting that I was asking about the notes she was taking. I didn't like it, and the panic started to rise again. It felt like it was going to spill out of me and cover the walls and the floors and the ceilings of this sterile, white room. My fingers twitched and I felt like I wanted to grab a hold of something, but didn't know what.

"Why don't I know my name?" My voice shook.

The doctor reached out and put a hand on my arm. "It's common to experience some amnesia after a head injury."

I reached up and touched my head. A big plaster covered my forehead. "What happened?"

"You were in an elevator accident. Do you remember any of that?"

"No. I . . . no!" My heart started to beat faster in my chest and a machine next to me beeped wildly.

"Try to relax. This is probably temporary; your memory should come back soon. The important thing is that we did a CT scan and an X-ray and everything is normal. No brain bleeds, no swelling, no injury. Other than the superficial cut on your forehead, which has been stitched up, some bruising on your arms and legs, and some grazes, you are okay. Your spinal fusion is also intact."

"My what?"

"When we did your X-ray we saw that some of your vertebrae had been fused, and it revealed that you also had a plate and pins in your shoulder. But there's nothing to worry about there either."

"What does that mean?"

"It means that at some stage in your life you had surgery to repair a broken back and shoulder. You have no recollection of that?"

I shook my head and suddenly tears welled up in my eyes. I was feeling an emotion that I couldn't quite name and connect to, and yet it was strong. So strong that it was strangling my throat from the inside.

"I'll give you something to help you relax." She leaned in and pushed a syringe into my IV and a warm feeling washed over me.

"Hello, darhling." Another familiar face came in. It was Ntethelelo, the cheerful nurse who'd attended to me earlier. "How are you feeling?" She walked up to my bed and fluffed my pillow, repositioning my head on it. "This is five-star accommodation here. We want everyone to be as comfortable as possible."

"Thanks," I said, looking up at her.

"I'll be back later. You're in good hands," the doctor said, and then left.

"Excellent hands," Ntethelelo whispered to me. "Right," she chirped, pulling a machine closer. "Time to take your blood pressure and your oxygen saturation." She attached a cuff to my arm and a device to my finger and began taking the readings. I glanced over at the window. I was clearly on a higher floor than before.

"One hundred per cent!" she declared when she was done. "I told you you were going to be alright."

Someone else then came in and put a tray of food on my table. I looked at it and my stomach lurched. I pushed the table away from me, and Ntethelelo glanced down at the food as if she were taking a mental note of it.

"Right, just press the button if you need me." She pointed to a button within my reach. "And try and get some rest."

"Wait," I called after her. "Noah—do you know if he's here?"

"Sorry, who?"

"Noah, the paramedic who brought me here, and then before we went into the elevator, he was there with me."

"Oh, Noah. He brought you in, but I didn't see him before we went to X-ray."

"You did, he came up and helped me. Told me to take deep breaths and relax."

She looked at me sympathetically. "That was me, darling. I was the one who told you to breathe."

"No, it was him. I saw him in the corridor. He was on his phone and then he was by my side and he took my hand and, and . . ." I stopped talking and swallowed. *Had I imagined him?* Had I imagined seeing him in the corridor? Hearing him? What else had I imagined about him?

"It was just me there," Ntethelelo said, with a smile I couldn't interpret. "Get some rest." And then she turned, walked out of the room, closed the door behind her, and I was alone, again.

CHAPTER 4

~

I was surprised to find two policemen in my room when I woke up. A doctor with long red hair who I'd never seen before was also there. I shot up in my bed and pulled the covers towards me.

"It's okay, you're not in any trouble," the doctor said, clearly reading my mind—or whatever mind I had left. It was still blank. I felt it the second I woke up.

"I'm Dr. Cohen, I'm a psychiatrist here, and these two gentlemen are here to see if we can help you find out who you are. Do you still not remember your name?"

"No," I said, glancing from her to the policemen and back again.

I heard a noise at the window, so loud that we all turned to look. A beautiful white dove on the windowsill was pecking on the glass with its beak. *Did it want to come in?* I could think of nothing worse than being "in" right now and I wanted to yell at it that it should fly the hell away.

I turned back and saw Dr. Cohen write something down in her file. So many files. So many notes. I wished I knew what was in them all. It seemed to me that everyone knew more about me than I did.

"And you still don't remember why you're in the hospital?" the doctor asked.

"They said I was in an elevator accident."

"And is there anything you can remember about who you are, or your life?"

"No."

"I'm sorry. I'm sure you're feeling very frustrated and confused right now."

"Yes," I admitted in a tiny voice that was almost inaudible.

"That's perfectly understandable, but we're all here to help you, and because you didn't have any ID on you when you arrived, the police are here to help us find out who you are."

"Hello, I'm Detective Nkanyezi Nleko, and this is our forensics expert, Officer Patrick." The policemen came tentatively closer to me, as if I were a baby bird that had fallen out of a nest. Maybe I was? I knew nothing at this point, so I couldn't rule out that possibility just yet. The dove seemed to agree, as it delivered a loud *thwack* to the window. So loud we all turned and looked at it again.

"Did you know white doves are the symbol of peace and that they choose one mate for life?" I heard myself say, and everyone turned and looked at me once more, the same look I'd gotten when I'd told them about X-rays. *How did I know these random facts?* I changed the subject. "How are you going to find out who I am?"

"Well, Patrick here is going to take your fingerprints and we'll run them through the system and see what comes up."

"Wait, do you think I'm a criminal? Why would you have my prints?" I stiffened as a memory came back to me. "I think I've seen TV shows where people get arrested and then have to have their fingerprints taken."

"Your fingerprints are also on your driver's license and ID card," he said.

"Oh. I don't remember that." I looked over at Dr. Cohen again. "Why do I remember a TV show but nothing about myself?"

"Having these kinds of gaps in your memory is very common with amnesia. The brain remembers some things, but not others."

"So my brain has decided to forget all the important things, like who the hell I am." I lay back down in the bed, hating my brain right now.

"Well, that's why we're here," the detective said. "Patrick is also going to take a photo of you and we'll compare that to any missing person reports and also take it to the building you were found in and show it around. It's a pity we don't know the names of the other two women who were in the elevator with you—"

"There were others in the elevator? Are they okay? Was anyone else injured?" I couldn't believe I didn't remember this. It seemed like such an important detail.

"Both of them left the scene really quickly afterwards, so I think they're fine."

I looked down at my hand as Officer Patrick reached for it but stopped when he saw the bloody-looking grazes on my knuckles. He looked up at me.

"Do you mind? I'll be careful," he said.

I tried to force a smile as he dabbed my fingers in ink, then slowly ran them on a piece of card. I winced slightly as he moved the two worst fingers, the ones I had little movement in, as big scabs had formed around the joints. He immediately stopped and gave me an apologetic look, and the kindness of this gesture made me want to cry. I focused on the window while he fingerprinted me, watching the dove move its head back and forth, as if admiring its own reflection. I turned back reluctantly when a camera was pointed in my face and a photo was taken.

"I think we're all done here," the detective said after what felt like an eternity. Time seemed to move so slowly between these walls, or was that always how time moved? I didn't know. I couldn't think of one example in my life that I could use to measure this concept of time with.

"Thank you," I mumbled as they moved towards the door. "Wait! What if you don't find out who I am?"

"Your fingerprints will be in the database somewhere. It's just a matter of time." The detective gave me a wave before they all exited.

* * *

"Time for blood pressure, oxygen and lunch." A different nurse came into my room.

"Where's Ntethelelo?" I asked, feeling uneasy.

"We've just changed shifts; she'll be here later. But for now, I'll be looking after you. My name is Beauty." She was carrying some food for me, but my stomach lurched at the thought of it.

"I don't want to eat," I said, my tone a little harsher than I'd intended it to be; I could see this because of the look on Beauty's face.

Nevertheless, she smiled at me. "You must try."

I turned my face back to the window and watched my dove friend as he cleaned his feathers with his beak. I felt Beauty attach the blood-pressure cuff. I heard the sound, felt the squeeze and then heard the beep.

"A hundred and twenty-two over eighty-one,' she said. "Perfect."

"Perfect?" I whipped my head around. "How can I be perfect if I don't remember anything?"

Beauty seemed to ignore my outburst, and I felt bad. I don't know why I was lashing out like this. She'd done nothing wrong. I was wrong. Not her. "Sorry," I whispered.

"How's the pain?" she asked.

"Better."

"That's good. You have to eat. I'll be back in an hour to fetch the tray." She left and I looked at the plate of food again. It was covered in a round plastic lid and condensation had formed on it, like it always does . . . .

Wait . . . how did I know that? I lifted the lid and some water droplets fell onto the food and a smell hit me. I knew this smell! And it made me want to be sick. I pushed the plate even further away and tilted my body on the bed so I didn't have to look at it.

I think I must have slept. Because when I opened my eyes again, it was dark. Three trays of untouched food now sat on my table. *How many meals had I missed?* I startled when I heard a noise and saw Dr. Cohen sitting in a chair.

"Sorry, didn't mean to give you a fright," she said. "I was just finishing my rounds and thought I would check on you. How are you feeling?"

"I'm feeling . . . uh . . ." I paused. The words weren't coming to me and, once again, I tried to reach into my mind to find something that I already knew wasn't there.

"Try not to think too hard about it," she urged. "Just say the first thing that comes to you. There's no wrong or right answer."

"Scared," I said, without even checking myself.

"What are you scared of?"

"Everything."

"Can you elaborate?" she asked. For someone who was telling me not to think too hard, she was really making me think.

That blurry, swirly, dark feeling was creeping up on me again. Tapping inside me. Reminding me it was still there. "What if I don't find out who I am? What if I do, and I don't remember? What if there are people out there looking for me, and I don't remember them, or . . ." I swallowed. The spit got stuck in my throat, as if it were a large rock. A thought formed, *the most terrible thought*, the rock seemed to grow. "What if no one is looking for me?"

"I'm sure these concerns feel very real to you," she offered up, "but trust me, they are all very unrealistic. The police *will* find out who you are, they always do. Your memory will come back, maybe not all at once. But in small bursts. I'm sure you must already be experiencing some feelings of familiarity, even if you can't quite place them?"

I nodded. She was right about that. *The hospital food . . .*

"That's a positive sign. And to waylay your other fear, it's very unlikely that no one is looking for you. I'm sure many people are looking for you, and chances are, they'll probably find you before the police figure out who you are."

"How do you know?"

"Believe it or not, this is more common than you'd think. We've had a few patients like you come in with no memory."

"And has everyone's memory come back?"

"Yes. Some people still can't remember the traumatic event, and some can't remember the days leading up to it, some have a few gaps here and there, but all of them regained most, if not all, of their memories. But the important thing is to try not to let this overwhelm you. Don't obsess about not remembering. The more stress you put on yourself, the less likely you are to remember. These things usually resolve themselves naturally, especially because you present with no brain injury. There is no physical reason for you to have forgotten who you are . . ." She paused and looked down at the paper she was holding.

"What?" I leaned towards her, sensing something in her tone.

"Usually, when someone without any physical brain damage presents with amnesia, the reasons for forgetting are more psychological. We call this post-traumatic amnesia."

"What are you saying? That I'm mentally ill?" I asked.

"No. Of course not. But I'm wondering if there's something about your life, your past, or about the accident—perhaps it was just too traumatic to process—that is causing your amnesia."

I glared at her. Her statement had offended me in some way I didn't quite understand. "How would I know that if I can't remember?" I snapped at her, and then looked out of the window.

"And I see that you're also refusing your food."

"I'm not hungry."

"Well, you are physically hungry, but all the anxiety you're experiencing is probably making it hard to eat. And you need to eat." I heard her stand up. "I'll prescribe something to help you relax and I'll be back here to chat in the morning, if that's okay?"

I looked at her for a while. I felt bad for snapping; she was just trying to be nice to me. I kept doing this—lashing out—and I didn't know why. Something inside me was making me feel a level of anger I couldn't account for. "Yes, thank you."

"Great, see you in the morning." She left my room and closed the door behind her. Everyone seemed to walk out of my room. No one really walked in, unless they needed to get something from me, like a blood-pressure reading. It felt like everyone was always leaving me. And then the fear that I'd been feeling moments ago was replaced by something else.

Sadness.

Big, black and all-consuming.

CHAPTER 5

Ntethelelo came into my room the next morning, or was it the morning after? I don't know. I felt like I was losing track of the days in here. I could see she was not her usual chirpy self, and a pile of books and magazines looked heavy in her arms. She placed them on the table with a thump and raised her brows. I turned my head away so as not to meet that penetrating gaze she was busy throwing in my direction. The dove was still there at the window, and its presence felt comforting. It was the only companion I'd had all night, and just knowing that I wasn't totally alone made me feel better in the tiniest way.

"I hear you're still not eating." She was tapping her foot against the floor. "You must eat. Otherwise, you won't get your strength back and then you'll be stuck with us here forever, and you don't want that."

I looked at her briefly, and then back to the window, feeling that dark, heavy ball inside me again.

"Listen, if you don't start eating, they'll send you up the psych ward. And trust me, you won't get a nurse like me up there, since I am Medicare's number-one nurse, and also, it's not five star there. You should feel the pillows . . . terrible!" She nudged me with her arm and I couldn't help the tiny smile on my face. She had a natural way of cheering you up.

"But I don't know who I am. I don't remember anything," I said quietly, a tear sliding down my cheek.

"It will come back to you. You just need to give yourself some time." She said it as if she really believed it, but I wasn't convinced. It had been days now, how many I didn't know, and my mind was still blank, except for those odd flickers of familiarity that I didn't understand.

"But what if it doesn't? What if it never comes back and I never know who I am?"

"The police are running your prints and your photo. You will find out who you are. It's just a matter of time."

"Time. How much time? How long must I stay here? How long have I been here? And what if they do find out who I am but my memory never comes back and then I never remember my life anyway? What the hell good is that?"

"You cannot think of that now. You have to focus on getting out of here."

"I want to get out of here! I really, really do."

"Well, then, you must eat something." She pushed a pudding cup and a spoon towards me.

I hesitated for a second, considering my options—which were few and far between right now—then grasped the cup reluctantly. The second it was in my hands, a feeling of knowing gripped me. I *knew* this cup. I knew its shape, and my fingers automatically went to the flap in the top-left corner and pulled. I dug the spoon in and scooped up a gooey, brown mouthful. I could taste it in my mouth before I put it in, and when I did so, my suspicions were confirmed.

"Well done." Ntethelelo got up and patted the pile of books and magazines on the side table. "I brought you some reading material." She started walking back towards the door, about to leave me again. "And when I come back, that must be finished." She pointed at the cup and I gave her a small nod. I watched her leave the room and then heard her talk to someone else in the corridor. It sounded like Beauty.

"Is she still refusing to eat?" Beauty asked.

"I think I got her to eat one of the puddings."

"Did she snap at you too?"

"Just a little bit."

"She was rude to me," Beauty said and, again, *I felt terrible.*

"I'm sure she's just scared. Don't take it personally."

"I'm so sorry!" I yelled, aiming my voice at the open door. There was a beat and then two shocked-looking faces stuck their heads into the room and stared at me.

"What?" I sat up.

"What were you saying sorry about?" Ntethelelo asked, blinking at me.

"For being rude. I know I've been snappy. And I don't mean to. I am scared."

Ntethelelo and Beauty exchanged a look then slowly brought their eyes back to mine.

"Why are you looking at me like that?"

"Did you understand what we were saying?" Beauty asked.

"Yes."

"But we were speaking isiZulu," Ntethelelo said, as they both walked into the room.

"No, you weren't, you were speaking English."

"No. We were speaking isiZulu," Beauty and Ntethelelo stood by my bed and eyeballed me curiously.

"That's impossible, I don't know how to speak isiZulu. Why would I?"

"Unjani?" Ntethelelo said and, without thinking, I answered and told her how I was.

"Ngikhona, ngiyabonga. Wena unjani?" I gasped. "Oh my God. Did I just speak another language?"

Ntethelelo beamed. "Yes, you did. And I'm fine, too, thanks for asking."

"But . . . how do I know . . . uh, where did I learn . . . uh."

Beauty tutted. "Now we're going to have to stop gossiping about you in the corridors."

"Hey! Why are you gossiping about me?"

"Joking." She grinned. I think the ice had finally broken between us.

I smiled at the two ladies in front of me, feeling better than I'd felt in a while. I couldn't put my finger on it, but hearing them talk in the corridor, hearing the language, those bold, expressive sounds, those clicks that echoed, something about it soothed me.

"*Nawe idla!*" Ntethelelo said, as she and Beauty walked to the door. I picked the pudding cup up and waved it to her.

"Fine, I'll eat it!"

Moments later, with my stomach full, my eyelids heavy, I closed my eyes again.

CHAPTER 6

$\backsim$

$\mathcal{W}$hen I woke up it was dark outside and, much to my relief, my dove friend was still there. I sat up and put on the lights, and as I did, the dove turned his head and looked at me.

"Hello." I waved at him.

He cocked his head to the side, as if he really was looking at me. He probably was; did you know that doves are incredibly intelligent and social animals?

"I would introduce myself, but I don't know my name," I said, and waited for a response from him. And I got one! As if he knew exactly what I was saying, he tapped the window three times. I sat up and swung my legs over the side of the bed.

"Do you know what I'm saying?" I asked.

One tap on the window.

"Okay, one tap for yes, two for no. Do you understand me?"

One tap!

"Oh my God. You do understand." I stood up, but my dove friend startled and opened his wings, as if he were about to fly away.

"Please don't go anywhere." I sat back down and my friend closed his wings. Relief washed over me. "I'll stay here, I promise."

One tap! Either I was going mad, or I was actually communicating with a dove! Or maybe I had developed some kind of psychic powers during my head injury . . .

Two taps.

"You're right, that's crazy. I'm not psychic, or am I?"

Two taps.

"Do you know who I am?"

Two taps.

"Of course you don't. Neither do I." I sighed. "Do you think I'll get my memory back?" I asked. The dove kept silent. "Is someone looking for me?" More silence.

"Hey, why aren't you talking to me?"

Three taps.

"Okay, perhaps I'm asking questions you can't answer." I looked around the room, trying to think of something else to ask.

"Do you have a girlfriend?"

One tap.

"Good for you! I wonder if I have one. Is it tomayto or tomahto? . . . Oh, you can't really answer that, can you?"

One tap.

"Do you eat chicken?"

Two taps.

"No, of course you don't. Is the Earth flat?"

Two taps.

"Duh!"

"Hold on, I've got a good one. Did aliens build the Pyramids?" He paused.

One tap!

"Ha! I knew it! I banged my hand on the bed and my dove friend flew away and I found myself all alone. "Maybe that was too controversial . . ."

I looked at the books and magazines on the table and noticed that Ntethelelo had also left a toothbrush and toothpaste for me. I ran my tongue over my teeth and cringed. I should use that, soon. I grabbed the book on the top of the pile. The striking drawing of an anatomically correct heart on the cover immediately captured my attention. Snippets of rave reviews and a big gold sticker on the front saying that the book was shortlisted for something further drew me in.

The Heart is Just a Muscle by Becca Thorne.

I turned the book over and read the blurb on the back. It sounded morbid and certainly not something I wanted to read at this present juncture in my life. I flipped the cover open to see who would have written such a book and a black-and-white photo of the serious-looking author gazed back at me. She looked intense. Dark hair. Black framed glasses. No smile. She looked intimidating ... *but familiar.* Perhaps this Becca Thorne was my favorite author, perhaps I'd seen her on TV, perhaps she and I had gone to junior school together and had played on the swings as children? I had no idea. I put the book back on the table and picked up a magazine, immediately rolling my eyes at it.

"'Fitness Now,'" I read. As if I was going to jump out of bed and learn to run a marathon in three months, strengthen my core in six easy moves and get a sexy butt before summer. Inside, tanned, toned people stared back at me from the pages. I turned the pages randomly, nothing really grabbing my attention until ...

Frankie's Fitness Protein Shake. I stared at the full-page advert in my hands. A beautiful blonde woman drinking a shake, glowing with sweat from a workout, a towel draped over her shoulder and a skipping rope dangling from one hand. I pulled the magazine away and brought it back up towards my face a few times as that same feeling of familiarity flicked on and off inside.

I'm sure this ad is everywhere. I'd probably seen it a million times before. I closed the magazine and dropped it back onto the table. I was grateful to Ntethelelo for trying, but this really wasn't what I wanted to be doing right now.

I scanned the windowsill, to see if my dove friend had returned but he hadn't. He was gone and I was all alone! That dark, panicky feeling started building inside me and I tried to push it down.

"Shit!" The panic rose faster now. I *needed* to be out of bed and, suddenly, it felt like I couldn't sit in it a second longer. I pulled the sheets back and swung my legs over the side. They felt good on the ground. It made me feel more stable than I'd felt since Noah's hand had held mine.

Noah's hand . . . I longed for it. For something to make me feel less alone. I grabbed my drip bag, attached it to the steel pole then wheeled the pole with me. *Wait* . . . how did I know how to do that? I turned and eyed the drip, feeling as if a memory was about to come to me, only it didn't. I hobbled to the door and pushed it open. The corridor that ran to my left and right was long, cold-looking and empty and . . .

Blood!

Someone covered in blood.

I jerked my head back as something, a memory, a little flash of an image, came back to me. I tried to hold onto it, but it fluttered away like a butterfly being pulled by the wind. The corridor was deserted, and yet I felt too terrified to walk out into it. I pulled the door closed and rushed to the other side of the room. I went to the chair that my clothes were on and picked up the watch that lay on top. The screen lit up. At least I would be able to tell the time now. I slipped the watch back on and the familiarity of the band around my arm made me feel better. I made my way back to the bed and climbed in.

CHAPTER 7

$\mathcal{I}$ couldn't sleep. No matter how hard I tried. I sat up in bed and looked around the room. Feelings like broken, sharp shards of glass, flew at me from all directions. I turned my head and looked at the shiny white basin in the corner. The drip, drip, drip of water, the repetitive motion and sound, pulling on something so deep inside me. A partial fragment of a whiff of a maybe-memory started to come back.

Blood, someone covered in blood.

The image hit me again, and again, and again. I turned my head to the other side and stared at the empty chair. It looked like it was waiting for someone to sit in it. *Who?* Another almost-memory fluttered into my brain, still out of my grasp, but this time so visceral, so real, that it made my skin crawl. I was cold. I pulled the blanket towards myself; the feeling of the hard-pressed cotton dragging over my skin was not comforting.

I looked at the window, and even though it was dark outside I could see he was there. My dove friend.

"Hey!" I sat up in bed and flicked the light on.

One tap!

He was talking to me again!

"I'm glad you're back." I looked around my room. Another plate of food seemed to have appeared and I pulled the lid off.

"You hungry?" I asked.

One tap!

I picked up the sandwich and climbed out of bed slowly, putting my drip bag onto the pole once more. I took a step towards the window and he didn't look like was going to fly off. I walked closer.

"I'm just going to open this and give this to you, okay?" I asked, and almost jumped up and down with happiness when he tapped three times, as if excited to meet me.

I reached for the window and pulled, but it didn't move. I pulled again, and again, and when I pulled even harder and it still didn't move, I stumbled backwards, shaking my head.

"It doesn't open. It doesn't open, it doesn't . . ." I stuttered over the words and grabbed onto the table to steady myself. I was trapped here, in a room with windows that didn't open and, on the other side of me, a terrifying corridor . . .

"Shit!" I dug my fingers into the table as I felt the floor spin. I needed air. Real air. Not this recycled room air. I felt trapped. Caged. A memory of a zoo and a sad black-and-white panda sitting behind steel bars hit me all at once, making me want to cry. I reached for the window and pulled one last time, hoping that by some miracle it would open. It didn't.

The toothbrush! I reached for it and rushed to the window. How did I know how to do this? *How did I know that if you slipped the back of a toothbrush into the mechanism at the top and pushed it to the left, a latch lifted and it opened? How did I know that the modern toothbrush was first mass produced in England in the 1700s but was invented in China in the 1400s?*

But I didn't care that I somehow knew this, all I cared about was getting air. I thrust my entire face out and inhaled deeply. The fresh air rushed into my lungs, and I felt like I could breathe again. I closed my eyes and gulped it in until the floor stopped spinning and the panic evaporated. And when I opened my eyes again, my dove friend was right there, looking at me.

"Hi!" I smiled at him. He cocked his head to the side and, I swear, he opened his beak and smiled back at me. And not since holding Noah's hand, had I felt so good.

"It's nice to meet you, properly." I leaned in and he took a few steps towards me. He was so close now that I could reach out and touch him. Should I?

"Can I touch you?" I asked, and when he took another step forward I stretched my hand out and he opened his beak even more, and I was sure he was going to give me a soft, happy-sounding coo, only he didn't because, suddenly, he was on my face.

"Oh my God," I wailed as his wings beat against my face and his beak pecked my head. "Why are you doing this? Did I do something to offend you?"

But gone was one tap for yes and two for no, now it was one thousand face-piercing taps per second for psychopath. I tried to pull him off me, but his feet were now firmly planted in my hair. I stumbled backwards, grabbing at my head.

"Get off! Get off!" I tripped over the table and tumbled to the floor, taking the steel drip bag with me. I tried to get up, but his flapping wings blinded me. I pulled myself onto my knees and crawled across the floor, finally making it to my feet. I felt a warm, wet, gooey sensation on my face as he let go and flew out of the open window. I stared after him as the wetness dripped down my forehead, ran along the bridge of my nose, and stopped just before my lips. I rushed to the window and stuck my head through it.

"Screw YOU!" I screamed into the night, as the dove flapped away from me after literally shitting on our friendship.

"I hate you!" I yelled and then burst into tears when he disappeared and I could no longer see him. I needed to get away from this place! I needed to be out of this room so badly. If I didn't get out, I was sure I was going to die. I rushed to the basin and washed the crap off my face and then I reached for the drip and quickly, expertly, pulled the sticky plaster aside and then eased the needle out of my hand. I picked up my bag of neatly folded clothes, the ones I'd come here in, and something fell out.

What the hell was this?

Through my tears I saw a large keyring lying on the floor. I examined it. A single key hung from it, but the keyring was huge, made up of various items I didn't remember. A squishy ball of sorts with a fake smiley face on, another ball made of colored elastics, a long string of orange beads and some weird, heavy metallic thing that spun. I put it down on the chair and ripped my gown off and put my clothes on. The urge to leave this hospital was so strong that the passage outside no longer terrified me! I grabbed the strange keyring and then, without a second thought, ran out the door and into the corridor.

Radiology.

Oncology.

Ward B,

Pediatric Ward.

Psychiatric ward—*definitely not there*—I read the signs as I rushed down the long passage. At the end of the corridor, I saw an emergency exit. The red "Exit" sign on the door felt like a beacon of hope right now. I ran for the door and pushed it open. The sound echoed along the stairwell. I hurried down the stairs, feet clanking on the steps, and when I reached the bottom, I burst through the door, into the main hospital reception. I breathed a sigh of relief when I saw those two massive glass doors that led to the parking lot outside.

I tried not to run manically towards the doors. I didn't want to arouse suspicion, but I almost couldn't help it, my feet moved so quickly and desperately towards them, as if they had a mind of their own. And as soon as I'd pushed the doors open, I was finally free. I didn't bother looking back at the hospital as I raced through the parking lot, weaving through the cars until I reached the other side. I ducked under a boom and only stopped running when I was two blocks away. I stood there for a while, trying to catch my breath, and when I had, I looked around and a thought hit me.

Now what?

CHAPTER 8

I stood on the sidewalk, watching the passing cars. They were hypnotizing as they passed me by, one by one, none of them stopping. I was all alone on this street, apart from these ghosts of the road, going past me in a blur. I heard a noise and looked down as a giant rat scuttled by, dragging half a pizza slice with it. Suddenly, it stopped dead in its tracks, let out a strange, high-pitched squeak and dropped the pizza. It stared up at me, squeaked again, showing its big yellow teeth, and then turned and ran back across the road. I watched as it disappeared into a drainpipe, as if it couldn't get away quick enough. I looked down at the pizza slice and wondered what would have made the rat drop it like that. Maybe rats didn't like me either? And then I heard another noise that made me look up at the street again. A car had stopped, a person climbed out of the back seat and I knew exactly what this was. A bolt of excitement lit me up from the inside. This was my escape. I rushed over and knocked on the driver's window frantically. The man sitting inside wound it down.

"Are you a taxi?" I gushed.

"Uber. Yes. Do you need a lift somewhere?" the man asked, and I nodded vigorously, even though I didn't know where on earth he would take me.

The man glanced at his phone and then back up to me. "I don't need to pick anyone up, so I can take you. Where to?"

"I . . . I . . . don't know."

"If you tell me where you want to go, I can take you there," he said, clearly not understanding what I meant. That I had zero idea where to go.

"So?" The man leaned across the seat now and looked at me. I shrugged at him, sighed then hung my head.

"Ma'am, are you okay?"

I shook my head. It rattled, like a single coin at the bottom of a tin might do. And then, there was a small scratching sound inside my head as something seemed to wiggle its way in. I reached out and tried to grab the thought, and this time I did! I flicked my head up and looked at him.

"Noah. Noah Robinson. 19C Edward Drive, Parkmeadows. Does that exist?" I asked, wondering if I had imagined Noah standing there talking on the phone too. The man typed something into his phone and then tilted his head up at me, his glasses slipping down his nose as he did.

"Sure, I can take you there. It's only fifteen minutes away." I jumped, literally—my feet lifted off the ground for a second out of sheer excitement. I couldn't believe my luck. First bit in days.

But as soon as the car started moving, all the excitement I'd felt was gone. I gripped the door handle. I didn't like the feeling of the moving car as much as I didn't like the feeling of being inside the hospital.

"Can I open the window?" I asked, panicked.

"Sure." He eyed me in the rear-view mirror and I could see he was weighing me up, trying to form an opinion of me. He had that same look in his eyes that all the doctors had had when they looked at me and wrote in their charts.

I wound the window down, and as soon as it was open I stuck my face out and the fresh air delivered what I'd been so desperate for. I felt a little better now. But not so much that I was able to loosen the tight hold I had on the door handle. I looked out the window as he drove, studying the buildings around me. Trying to see if there was anything familiar about this place. There wasn't. The buildings and streets were as generic to me as everything had been so far. We turned off the main road into what looked like the suburbs. I knew this because the sidewalks suddenly filled with grass and hedges and trees. Gone was the concrete coldness of before. This place seemed to be filled with a different feeling now, and this was confirmed when we drove past a small park with a red-and-blue merry-go-round in the middle of it. I stared at the merry-go-round and, like with the black-and-white panda, something lit up inside me.

Not so much a memory, but a feeling, in the pit of my stomach as I went around and around and around.

Did you know merry-go-rounds in America tend to turn counterclockwise?

We drove a little more until we finally came to a halt. I was so grateful when the car stopped, I'd been on the edge of my seat since it had started moving. The driver pointed at a house and I looked. It was small, and cute. Tucked behind a pale yellow wall covered in ivy. Big trees rose up from inside the property, and a red tin roof peered at me.

"Here we are," the taxi driver said, turning the engine off. I gazed at the house . . . now what?

"That will be one hundred and fifty Rand," the driver said loudly.

"One hundred and fifty *what*?" His statement hadn't quite landed with me yet. I was finding this with a lot of things. Someone would say something to me and, on some level, I think I understood what they were saying, but it took me a while to register. As if my brain was making sense of the world much more slowly than it should.

At last I clicked. "Oh! Yes. Money!" I looked down at my hand and it was empty. No bag. No money. It hadn't even crossed my mind that I would need to pay this man.

"You do have money, don't you?" he asked, although I got the impression he already knew the answer to this question. I pursed my lips together tightly and shook my head. My head gave a thump, and

I winced, reached up and touched the bandage on my forehead. The man's face seemed to soften slightly.

"I'm going home this way anyway, so it's fine."

"It is?" I was overjoyed. "Thank you. Thank you!" I gushed over my shoulder as I raced towards Noah's door.

CHAPTER 9

~

I hesitated for a second while I tried to gather my thoughts and plan exactly what I was going to say. But I had no idea, and I didn't think standing here any longer would ever furnish me with the answer. So, I just tapped on the door, too softly at first. I knocked again, a little harder this time. But no one in the house stirred. I knocked a little more frantically. The grazes on my fingers hurt and when I looked down at my hand, I had obviously ripped a scab off, because there was blood. But I didn't care. I knocked even harder and even louder. It was dark, except for the low porch light illuminating the space around the outside of the front door. The house seemed completely dead, as if there was no one home, as if it were asleep. *Was no one home?* It hadn't occurred to me that Noah might not be here. And if he wasn't, then what the hell was I meant to do and where was I meant to go? I threw my fists against the door one last time, putting all the effort I had into it, and that's when I saw it. A bell!

A bloody bell! What a brilliant idea to put a bell by a door! Whoever thought of this was really smart, it actually made so much sense to have this here. I wondered if all doors had bells. I rang it. Once, twice and then, on the third time, like dominoes, one light turned on, and then another one, and another one. The lights moved towards the front door like a train until the room behind the front door was illuminated and I was able to make out the shadowy silhouette of a person. I hoped it was Noah. It suddenly occurred to me that he might not live alone. A roommate? A wife and kids? It hadn't crossed my mind, until now, that I might be barging in on more than just Noah.

I heard a chain move and fall, dinging against the wooden frame of the door. I heard a click and then the door swung open and there he was, standing in his pajamas. The look on his face when he saw me was one of utter shock. It clearly took a while for him to register what was happening because he opened and closed his mouth a few times, like he was an actor in a silent movie. Finally, after what felt like forever, some sounds came out.

"Wh-why . . . what are you . . . uh, why . . . what are you doing here?" He moved his head in short, sharp, jerky movements as he stuttered. He looked agitated and nervous. God, this hadn't been the reaction I'd hoped for. But really, if I thought about it, what had I expected? Smiles and open arms?

"I mean . . . it's the middle of the night and, and . . . what are you doing here?" he asked loudly this time.

"I didn't know where else to go . . ." I started.

"What do you mean, you didn't know where to go? You're supposed to be in the hospital. Why are you here? How did you get here?" He walked past me and looked up and down the street, which was now empty. "How do you even know where I live?"

Now I felt bad. My cheeks flushed and it felt like a cold rock fell into my stomach. Clearly this had been a very bad idea, judging by the way he was looking at me now. Arms folded, a scowl on his face. *Was that fear?* Was he afraid of me? Like I was a stalker. Maybe I was.

"I overheard you tell someone your address on the phone," I quickly said, hoping to waylay his fears about me. It didn't.

"You were spying on me?" He took a step back, edging his way into the house.

"I wasn't spying on you, I swear. I was going to X-ray and saw you in the passage and you were speaking to someone on the phone. You said your address and then, tonight, when I left the hospital, it was the only address in the entire world I could think of. I don't even know my own address."

"What are you even doing out of the hospital? Did they discharge you? I'm sure they wouldn't have, so soon. Especially if you still don't have any memories."

"They didn't let me out of the hospital. I kind of escaped." I closed my eyes for a while, not sure I wanted to see his expression. I opened one eye first, and then the other, Noah did *not* look pleased.

"You escaped?"

"Yes," I said faintly.

"Without being discharged? Do you know how risky that is? You have a brain injury! You shouldn't be out of bed, let alone the hospital. Do you know how much danger you're putting yourself in?"

"My brain is fine. They found nothing physically wrong with it. I just can't remember anything."

"Oh!" He sounded surprised and then his eyes moved down to my hand. "You're bleeding."

I looked down. The blood was oozing out of the graze, running down my fingers and had started to drip onto the concrete floor below. "It's from knocking on the door. I knocked for ages."

"Why didn't you ring the bell first?"

"I didn't know it was there, and what a brilliant idea! Who would have thought to put a bell by a door?"

"Uh . . . it's pretty standard."

"Oh."

He looked at me curiously now, like he wasn't so convinced I didn't have a brain injury.

"I'm struggling with my memory still. I remember some things, but other things, it's like I've never seen them before, like a bell by the front door. And some of the things I do remember, I have no idea why I remember them."

Noah raised his hands to his face, placed them on his cheeks and then shook his head. "That's all the more reason you can't be here. This is so, so . . . I don't even know if there's a word for this. You just can't be here."

My stomach tightened so much that I wanted to be sick. "Please, please!" I could hear the sheer, ugly desperation in my voice as I begged. "I had to get out of there. I hated it. And I didn't know where to go. I don't know who I am and where I belong and you— *you*—were the only person I could think of. I *had* to get out of that hospital. I felt like if I stayed there for a second longer I was going to die, or something bad was going to happen to me. And you were so nice to me and made me feel so safe, and I didn't feel safe at the hospital, even though they were nice. And that's why I'm here! Don't send me back. Please!"

He looked at me for a moment or two and I wished I knew what he was thinking. And then, slowly, he opened his door wider and gestured for me to come inside.

CHAPTER 10

"We'd better stop that bleeding on your hand, at least," he said, and I wanted to cry happy tears. I wanted to throw my arms around him and hug him, but didn't.

I walked into a small lounge and glanced around. The floor was almost completely taken up by a huge flat-screen-TV box that had been ripped open. Bubble wrap and bits of cardboard lay scattered across it. I looked up at the wall, where the massive TV had just been mounted. It was enormous, completely disproportionate to the size of the room. A drill lay next to little cement piles on the floor.

"It's . . . it's new," Noah said, sounding self-conscious about it. "I never have time to watch TV. And I'm taking some leave and thought now would be a good time to catch up. I haven't even watched *Game of Thrones* yet."

"*Game of Thrones* . . ." I repeated, and then something hit me. "Dragons. Daenerys Targaryen." I clicked my fingers a few times as images from the show flashed in front of me.

"I much preferred *The Handmaid's Tale*. Wait . . ." I paused. "You see, and how do I know that and not my own name? It makes no sense."

"That's pretty common with amnesia, actually. Fragments of memories come back, and not necessarily in the order you want them to."

"That's what Dr. Cohen said." I looked around the room some more, and that's when I noticed the piece of paper stuck up on the wall. I ran my eyes over the words. All of them familiar.

"My list." Noah came up behind me. "Of TV shows I have to watch while on my break. *The Handmaid's Tale* is down there." I knew all these TV shows, I could see bits and pieces of each of them playing in my head in short bursts.

"I think I've watched these," I said, wishing I could see more than that. *Who had I watched them with? Where had I watched them?*

A cool breeze blew in from the open door and Noah rushed to close it.

"Autumn. Definitely getting colder in Jozi now."

I nodded, even though I had zero idea of how to quantify that. The Johannesburg weather. How did I know what was a cold day, or a warm day? I had no memories of Joburg weather.

"Let me get something for your hand." He disappeared down the passage and I watched him go. I hadn't noticed until now how big he was. Muscular. As if he worked out a lot. He had been a blur of shapes and sounds when I'd last seen him, but now he was high def. He came back moments later with a cloth, some cotton wool, cream and a plaster.

"May I?" he asked, looking down at my hand.

I wanted to scream, *yes*! Please take my hand again, because you holding my hand is the only thing that has felt vaguely normal in days. But that made me sound like a stalker, which at this stage I wasn't altogether sure I wasn't. But I kept that thought to myself and raised my hand slowly.

He took it tentatively at first, and the warmth that came radiating off it was instant. It tingled up my arm, familiar and comforting. I closed my eyes to record this feeling, so I could keep it mentally and conjure it up when I needed to feel better. *God, maybe I was a stalker?* I opened my eyes again and watched as he gently wiped the blood away, put a layer of strong-smelling cream on the grazes, and added a few plasters. When he was done, his hand began to move off but just as his fingertips were about to completely leave, they lingered for a second. I looked up at him. His eyes were locked to my hand. He blinked a few times rapidly, as if something was confusing him, and then he pulled his hand away quickly.

"That should stop any infection." He moved away and we fell silent. It pressed down so hard on us that I wanted to say something to break it. Anything. Why wasn't he saying anything? *Why was he just looking at me like that?*

"I'm sorry I came here so late," I whispered.

He lowered himself into a chair and I did the same. "The thing is, you can't be here. It's inappropriate—you're my patient. And you can't just leave the hospital without being discharged. And I'm sure the whole ward is in a panic right now, looking for you. They might have even called the police in, since you're considered a . . . vulnerable person." He said this last part delicately.

"Because I still don't know who I am?" I asked.

"Yes. I'm going to have to contact the hospital and let them know where you are, and we are going to have to go back."

"You can't take me back!"

Noah started shaking his head at me, and I wanted to reach out and physically stop it. But I couldn't, so I aimed my words at it, hoping they would have that effect.

"Please! I don't want to go back. I feel like I'm going to die if I go back to that place. I can't be there for a second longer. I can't! I'm begging you!"

Noah put his hands together in his lap and squeezed, as if he was really wrestling with this. His knuckles whitened, and I had the urge to hold his hand again.

"I can't. This is highly inappropriate—it could even be illegal. This has never happened to me before, so I don't know what it is. I can't have you here without some kind of permission, I'm going to have to call the hospital."

Tears dammed up, slowly at first. But then they pushed their way out of my eyes, climbed down my lashes and threw themselves onto my cheeks. I was surprised to hear the sound that rose up out of my throat with the tears. And to feel my shoulders shaking backwards and forwards with such force that my whole body seemed to be moving on the sofa. I gripped my knees with my hands, stuck my fingernails into them, trying to stop myself. But I couldn't. It was as if someone had pulled the plug out of the bath and everything that was in it was pouring out, unstoppable. Out of the blurry corner of my eye I saw Noah rise up out of his chair. He rushed towards me, not tentative this time. And the thing I'd longed for the most, the thing that I'd been thinking about, happened. He slipped a hand through mine and gripped it tightly. I squeezed back, as hard as I could, trying to convey everything I was feeling in that one small gesture.

"I'm sure you must be feeling very frightened," he said. "Not knowing who you are. Not having any memory. And I'm sorry this happened to you, I wish it hadn't. But still, I have to contact the hospital and let them know where you are. And I have to take you back." He gave my hand another squeeze, but this time it had a feeling of finality to it, which made me cry even more. He got up and disappeared down the passage once more. It felt like he was gone for an eternity, and when he finally returned, he was holding a phone in his hand.

"I'm sorry," he said again softly and then started dialing the number.

CHAPTER 11

❧

"*T*here you are!" Ntethelelo shouted down the passage. "We were so worried about you. I almost had a heart attack." She raced up to me. "Are you alright?"

"Fine," I said, even though I was anything but.

I looked over her shoulder at the group of people who had gathered at the nurses' station. I recognized all of them: Dr. Cohen, Dr. Maluka and Detective Ndaba.

"I'm sorry, I didn't mean to cause such a scene," I said to Ntethelelo.

"Well, you did! We thought you might have jumped out the window. We didn't know where you were." She took me by the arm and guided me towards the crowd. Everyone was now looking at me. If you could call it looking. It was more scrutinizing. Studying. I felt nervous, and glanced behind to see if Noah was still there. He was, and I didn't want him to leave.

"Are you okay?" Dr. Maluka came up to me and gave me the once-over.

"Yes," I said, now feeling really terrible that I'd caused such a huge international incident. "I'm sorry I left without telling anyone."

Dr. Cohen looked at me and raised her brows. "We were very concerned. We didn't know what to think, especially because there were signs of a struggle."

"Struggle?"

"Yes, in your room." It was the detective who spoke this time. "The window was left open and a table had been knocked over."

"No struggle. Just an argument with a former friend." I looked down at my feet and drew a half-moon across the linoleum floor with my toes.

"I think we can take it from here, Detective," I heard Dr. Cohen say, but I didn't look up. I continued to draw patterns on the floor with my toes as she thanked him for coming. I was just about to add a frown to the face I'd drawn when I stopped.

"Wait!" I called after the detective. "Do you know who I am yet?"

"Not yet. But we're working on it."

"Isn't someone looking for me, though?"

I saw Noah and the two doctors exchange glances and I wanted to know what they were thinking.

"A missing adult is more complicated than a missing child. People often don't realize the adult is even missing for a while. If they live alone, for example, and if they don't show up to work, people might just assume they're sick. We usually only accept an adult is missing if they've been gone for more than forty-eight hours. In your case, it's been seventy-two hours, but it's still not unusual that a missing person report hasn't been filed. And also, we don't know where you live. A missing person report might have been filed in Cape Town. That's why running your prints is the most effective way. But that can take a bit of time. This is South Africa, it's not the US. We don't have the FBI here, so things take a little longer."

"But you will find me, right?" I asked.

He nodded. It was small. I would have hoped for a bigger nod. "We will!" I watched him walk away, filled with a mixture of emotions that was hard to describe.

"Shall we all go and have a chat in your room?" Dr. Cohen said, placing a hand on my arm. Her sudden easy-going tone made me very nervous. It was as if she was deliberately trying to hide something under it. But I followed them into my old hospital room. I turned to see if Noah was coming. He wasn't.

"Can Noah come?" I asked.

"Sure," Dr. Cohen replied. "If Noah is okay with that?"

"Yes, fine," he said, coming into the room.

But as soon as I was inside, I felt that same dark feeling pulling at me. That same anxiety and fear that had made me escape in the first place.

"I think I spent a lot of time in a hospital once," I blurted out, without even thinking. As if that thought had snuck up on me so quickly I wasn't even conscious of it until it came tumbling out of my mouth.

Dr. Cohen nodded. "I concur. The previous surgeries you had would suggest that."

"Surgeries?" Noah stepped forward, looking concerned.

"Yes, but I can't really disclose that information to you—"

"No. Of course you can't, Doctor." Noah held his hand up apologetically. "Sorry, I didn't know." He looked at me with slight relief in his eyes now, as if my escape finally made some sort of sense to him. *Maybe he no longer thought I was a crazed stalker.*

"And that's why I can't stay in this hospital. I get this terrible feeling when I'm here, I just can't stay here."

"That's understandable," Dr. Cohen said, really pushing that calm tone of hers. "If you've had bad experiences in a hospital, your memories of it might not have come back, but the feelings of being there might have resurfaced. Unconsciously. And that's clearly what's making you feel this way. It's very common to have some post-traumatic stress after hospitalizations. And that can stay with you."

"Well, I have some good news for you then," Dr. Maluka said. "Medically, there's no reason to keep you here. But, obviously, since you still have amnesia, we can't just discharge you, so . . ." She pulled a brochure out of a file and passed it to me. "Dr. Cohen and I have already discussed it, and this is a great care home that can look after you while the police figure out who you are. It shouldn't be for very long, but they'll be able to keep you safe."

I unfolded the pamphlet. This place looked similar to a hospital, the only difference was the garden and games room, but it still had those long, terrifying, white-lit corridors, machines by the bed, and it gave me that same feeling. "I . . . I don't want to go to a care home. It looks like a hospital, it's . . ."

"Deep breaths," Dr. Cohen urged. "In and out."

"I'm afraid we can't let you out of here without a guardian to take custody of you," Dr. Maluka said.

"A guardian?" I asked.

"It would usually be a relative, a friend, even a colleague. Someone who can take responsibility for your care while you regain your memory."

"I . . . I don't have anyone like that. How can I, if I don't remember anything about myself?"

"And that's why we can't just discharge you," Dr. Cohen said.

"But there's no one. I don't know . . . there's no one." I sat down on the bed, that darkness in the pit of my stomach radiating outwards, engulfing my whole body. "I don't have a place to go." My words came out strangled as my throat squeezed them. I gripped onto the bed tightly, trying to steady myself on it. Trying not to fall off it and fall into the abyss I felt inside. I felt an arm around me.

"I will come and visit you, eh!" Ntethelelo said, giving me a nudge. "What you say?"

My shoulders started to shake. I was sobbing again. But this time it was a silent, tearless sob. Everything hurt. My ribs, my stomach, my legs.

"Please, I can't go to that place. And I can't stay here. Please . . . please." I don't even think I was begging them anymore. I think I was begging that part deep inside myself that felt so sick and desperate at the idea of being in a hospital, or a care home. That part inside me that told me, if they put me there, I would escape again. And second time around, I really would have nowhere to go.

The sound of a throat being cleared filled the room and we all turned. It had come from Noah.

"She could stay with me for a few days." He said it quickly. "You can sign her over to me. I'll be her guardian until the police work it out."

"Noah, you mustn't feel obliged. There are other options." Dr. Cohen looked concerned about this proposed arrangement.

But Noah stood up straight. "It's alright. I'm off work at the moment, anyway, and I'm sure it will only be for a day or two."

"Seriously?" I stood, but I wasn't sure if my shocked legs would hold me up. But, miraculously, they did.

"Sure." He nodded.

I turned to the doctors. "Is that okay? Can he do that?"

"Uh . . . legally, it's fine. As long as you're going willingly and are not being coerced, and—"

"I am going willingly!" I gushed. "No coercion."

"As long as you bring her to her follow-up appointments?" Dr. Maluka added.

"I will," Noah said.

"Then I have no objection to it. It's unusual, but it's not objectionable." She turned her attention to Dr. Cohen now. "What do you think?"

"I'm fine with that, I would like to see you for a counseling session, though. To check in with you."

"Okay!" I said quickly, and then looked over at Noah. "I mean, if you can. If that's alright, if . . ."

"It's alright," he said, and then gave me a smile that almost made me believe him. *Almost.*

"Wait," Ntethelelo said as I got up to leave. "Take my phone number. Call me if you need something. Or need to talk." She said it to me in isiZulu and everyone stared at us.

"I don't have a phone to put it in," I replied.

She scribbled it on a piece of paper and passed it to me, clasping my hand in hers and holding onto it tightly.

"*Hamba kahle.*"

I squeezed her hand back. "Thank you, friend. And you stay well," I said, and then I left.

CHAPTER 12

‿

"*You* can sleep here in the spare room. It's nothing fancy. I don't usually have guests." He flicked the lights on and a small, pleasant-looking room came into view. "Uh . . . yeah, ignore the duvet cover, it's old. Like I said, I don't get many visitors," he said, sounding a little shy now.

"It must be really old," I commented, looking at the massive Spider-Man print across it. Don't ask me how I knew this was Spider-Man. I just did.

"Well, I won't embarrass myself by saying it's probably not as old as you think it is." He walked over to the cupboard and opened it. "Some towels here, the bathroom is just down the hall. I'm afraid it's a shared bathroom."

"That's okay. More than okay. It's great. Thanks." I smiled at him, feeling so grateful to be out of the hospital. A bed had never looked so inviting in my entire life. Granted, the life I knew had been a pretty short one, and I'd only ever been on one other bed before. If I was a baby, I would only be seventy-two hours old. That is how long my brain had been absorbing and remembering information. It was weird to think that my body was actually older than my mind. I didn't know how old exactly, but it was a lot older than the stuff between my ears. And as for a shared bathroom, well, I might have shared a bathroom with a yeti at this stage, just to be out of the hospital.

Did you know, the yeti originated in Himalayan folklore before the nineteenth century?

Did you know that a British explorer called Eric Shipton searched for it for sixty years?

Did you know—

"Don't worry, though," Noah said, pulling me from my strange, factual thoughts, whose origins remained a mystery. "I definitely put the seat down. My sister trained me well."

"You have a sister!" I was shocked by the concept that someone could have a sibling.

"Yes, she's younger than me, but you would swear she was older." He rolled his eyes and gave his head the tiniest shake, more to himself, though, as if he was remembering something funny. It seemed like he really loved his sister. Did I have a brother or sister that I loved? And if I did, were they worried about me?

"Please, it's your house. Do whatever you like with the seat, use it as a hula-hoop . . . whatever," I said.

Noah's face broke into a smile, now. It was the first time I'd seen him smile since I'd arrived at his house so rudely.

"Uh, I think I'll refrain from that, if that's okay with you?" He was still smiling. He had a nice smile. I'd gotten a glimpse of it in the ambulance, albeit a blurry, somewhat oxygen-deprived glimpse, but now, seeing it in the full, bright, overhead lights of his spare room, I had to admit, it was a *really* nice smile. He had a tiny gap between his two front teeth, ever so small, but it gave his smile a softer quality. It made it seem warmer and friendlier than a normal smile. It wasn't a perfect smile, you wouldn't see it on the side of a toothpaste tube, like the one I'd gotten in the hospital, but it was a smile that you would very much like to see.

Noah looked at his watch. "It's four in the morning already, so we'd better get some sleep."

"Four!" I looked down at my watch too. I'd lost track of time once again. Time seemed to have taken on a strange elastic form since this whole incident. Sometimes it felt like it was stretching out, long and endless in front of me, and other times it felt like it was being flicked back at me. Rushing towards me, bending back on itself in a way that made me feel like it didn't exist at all.

"I'm so sorry again that I woke you. I didn't know where else to go and I just . . . I'm sorry."

He smiled again, but this time it was forced. "It's alright. I offered to help so . . ." He didn't finish that sentence and I wasn't sure I knew what he was trying to say. Maybe if he finished it, he would express regret for the decision he'd made. Because now he had a stranger in his house, about to slip under his Spider-Man covers.

"Well, thanks. Again. It's so kind of you."

"No worries." He made a move for the door and stopped before leaving. "Is there anything else you need to know?"

I sat down on the bed. It was incredibly soft and comfortable. So much better than the hospital bed.

"No. I have everything I need right here," I said, and actually meant it.

He pulled the door closed and I flopped down on the mattress and looked up. For the first time in days, I relaxed. A massive breath of air left my stiff, tense body, and took with it some of the worries and anxiety that had taken up residence in my cells these last few days. I looked up at the ceiling and I honestly, truly, hadn't ever felt this good in my life. The short life I remembered anyway.

I stayed like that for a while, just enjoying the moment. I heard a door close and turned my attention to the wall next to me. Noah was obviously getting ready for bed, and this was confirmed when I heard a cupboard open and close, a light switch being flicked off, followed by creaky steps on the wooden floorboards. There was something so comforting about knowing he was sleeping close to me. It made me feel safe.

"Goodnight!" he called.

"Goodnight," I shouted back.

"GOODNIGHT! GOODNIGHT! GOODNIGHT!" An unexpected shout came from the corner of the room. I screamed and jumped off the bed, scrambling backwards towards the wall.

"What the hell?" My heart thumped as I looked at the corner of the room. A large sheet was draped over something huge. It looked like a giant box. "Wh-wh-wh—?" I scurried backwards toward the door as Noah came bursting in.

"Sorry, I should have mentioned it."

"Mentioned what?"

"Chloe." He pointed into the corner of the room.

"Chloe?"

"Yes, Chloe. She's in her cage."

"Cage?"

"I have to lock her up at night, or she gets into trouble."

"Uh . . . lock her?" I swallowed. It felt like an uneven rock sticking in the back of my throat.

"She's always trying to escape when the lights go off," he said, and then let out a chuckle which chilled me to the bone, like a raging arctic gale had just swept through the house.

"Uh." I inched towards the door. It hadn't occurred to me that Noah might be anything other than a nice, normal guy, but who the hell kept women in cages under sheets in his spare room?

Mind you, doesn't everyone say that about serial killers? He was such a charming man, pillar of the community, instantly likeable . . . *oh my God*, textbook! I could see the vox-pop interviews with the neighbors on TV: *Noah was always so polite, helped me with my groceries, a paramedic, even* . . . and then the documentary filmmaker would cut to old, grainy, smiling photos of Chloe and me as little girls and hard-cut to black-and-white photos of where our bodies were found, police tape outlining the area. *Clearly, I watched a lot of crime shows too!*

"I think that maybe I should . . . uh . . . SHIT!" I pushed past Noah and ran, making a dash down the passage, and practically threw myself on the front door. "Shiiit!" I cursed when the door didn't open. I looked around. I saw another door in the kitchen and I made another mad dash, but it didn't open either. "Oh my Goooood!"

My heart thumped, pouring pure fear into my veins. I was trapped in a house with a man who kept women in cages in his spare room! I was doomed. I was going to die. He was sure to kill me now—

"AAAHHH!"

Noah walked into the kitchen and I grabbed the nearest thing I could find, a spatula.

I held it in the air, "I won't tell anyone that you have a . . . a . . . *wait*, what is that?"

"It's Chloe," Noah said, holding out his arm, where a gray parrot was now happily perching.

"Chloe is a parrot?"

"Yup. Chloe is a parrot."

"Oh." I placed the spatula back onto the kitchen counter. Noah looked at it, and then looked up at me and grinned.

"Who did you think Chloe was?" he asked.

"Um . . ." I was too embarrassed to answer that now.

"Did you think Chloe was a woman?"

I nodded.

"You thought I had a woman in a cage?" His grin grew and all I could do was offer up another feeble nod.

Noah laughed. It was the first time I'd heard him laugh, and it was totally contagious, or maybe I was laughing because I was so relieved to have discovered that I was not in the house with a kidnapping serial killer and the director was not going to cut to old VHS footage of Noah playing a game of soccer in the garden as a child and ask where it all went so wrong!

"I'm sorry you got a fright," Noah said, when his laughter finally tapered off.

"It's okay." I stopped laughing and looked at the parrot on his arm. She was only a little bigger than my *ex*-friend.

"She's very friendly. You want to touch her?" Noah came closer and I stepped back.

"I don't think birds like me. Or rats, for that matter."

"Chloe likes everyone, I've never met anyone that she doesn't like." He stepped closer still.

"You sure?"

"Positive. Scratch her on her head, she loves it."

"Okay." I reached out and Chloe didn't flinch. This was a good start and it filled me with enough confidence to lay a fingertip on her head. Her head felt soft and her little feathers immediately ruffled.

"She's so cute." I smiled, but it was short-lived, because that's when it happened. *Again!*

CHAPTER 13

~

"Get her away! Get her away, get her . . . Aaaahhh!" I wailed, and stumbled about the room as Chloe flew at me, her wings flapping in my face frantically with a sound that was almost deafening.

"I'm so sorry!" Noah said, chasing me and the bird around the room. He kept trying to grab Chloe, but she was relentless. She kept coming for me, over and over again. I ran around the kitchen, waving my arms in the air, trying to fight off this gray, feathered devil. But the kitchen was small, and with me and Chloe and Noah all running around in circles, the crash was fairly inevitable. I ran into the fridge, hit it with a bang, it rocked back and forth once, twice, and then the door popped open and stuff just fell out. Cascaded onto the floor, a cacophony of clinks and pops and bangs, and then a shatter followed by the whoosh of liquid. But this distraction gave Noah a chance to finally grab Chloe. He held onto her tightly, and looked at me, out of breath.

"I'm so sorry. She's never done that before."

"Told you animals hated me!"

"I'll put her back in her cage." Noah left the room and I gave a sigh of relief. I took a step, only to hear a squelching sound and feel the most disgusting sensation I'd ever experienced. I looked down at my foot. A macerated pickle lay squished on the floor beneath it. Mashed into the tiles, mashed through my toes. I cringed at the feel of it and shook my foot. Green-pickle mash flew off and hit the cupboard. I looked around the floor and took in the carnage. Red jam smeared and splattered across the floor, like it had been murdered, pickles, pickle juice and glass shards everywhere. Black olives and more glass and bright pink slices of ham drowning under the brown olive brine. My stomach lurched at the sight.

"Oh," I heard Noah say, and I looked up at him and grimaced.

"Oops. Sorry," I said.

"It's okay. I made you touch her."

We both looked down at the mess together, and I'm sure he was thinking exactly what I was. I took another step.

"Stop! There's glass. You don't have shoes on."

I looked down at my toe, it was a mere centimeter away from a bright shard glinting off the overhead lights, pointing straight up, waiting for the soft, fleshy cushion of a toe to come down on it.

"I think I'm kind of stuck." I shrugged apologetically.

"Lean forward," Noah said, stretching his arms out.

"Lean?" I looked at his outstretched hands. "What are you going to do?"

"Lift you onto the counter, if that's alright?"

"Uh . . ." I looked from his hands, to the counter and back again. "I don't think you'll be able to do that."

"Trust me," he said, and for some strange reason . . . I did, even though only moments ago I'd thought he might potentially be a serial killer! I leaned and he slipped his hands underneath my arms and gripped me. "Now jump."

"Jump?"

"Just a little." He smiled at me and this, coupled with the sensation of his hands under my arms, made me feel strange and floaty. Like, if I did jump, it would be much higher than expected. That I might jump straight up to the roof, or even higher. I looked him in the eye briefly, just a flash of that vibrant blue. It was almost too bright to look at directly and I quickly tilted my head down.

"Okay, I'll jump," I whispered. I bent my knees a little and jumped, and as I did, I felt myself being lifted into the air, as if on a trampoline. My feet and body flew up, and then a small, swinging sensation as he pulled me through the air effortlessly, as if I weighed nothing and gravity didn't exist. I think I heard myself giggle, I'm not sure. And then, touchdown. My bum came into contact with the counter and, the second it did, his hands disappeared. A sudden urge made me want to grab back onto them, but I didn't.

"Thanks," I mumbled, feeling a little breathless now, not from the jump though.

"Sure." He also sounded breathless, I'm sure I wasn't that light to lift. I looked down at my feet and it dawned on me.

"We could have just gotten my shoes from my room." I looked up at Noah and his blue eyes met mine.

"I suppose we could have." He said this in a way that seemed introspective, as if, like me, he was wondering why he'd only thought about that now.

CHAPTER 14

⮑

"Good morning. Good morning. Good morning!" I was awoken by the sounds of Chloe outside my room and, for a moment, when I rolled over and looked around, I didn't know where I was. But it all came back to me quickly when I looked at the Spider-Man duvet that was pulled up around me.

I climbed out of bed. I had slept in my underwear last night, so as not to crease the only clothes I had. I raised my arm and took a sniff. I was going to need deodorant today, and I was also going to need to try and wash out some of the bloodstains around the collar of my shirt, or else I might look like a serial killer.

The only things I owned in the entire world right now were the few clothes I had on my back, the toothbrush and toothpaste and a strange keyring that I'd placed on the bedside table and was currently looking at.

I slipped my clothes back on and strolled out of the room. The smell of coffee hit me and something inside my brain instantly switched on. Like a Dubai skyscraper, switched ON! I smiled. I didn't know much about myself, but I knew I *loved* coffee. I could feel it with every inch of my being right now. I moved a little quicker down that passage to the small kitchen that Noah was busy in, that we had spent half an hour in last night cleaning up.

"Hey," he said when I came in. There was an awkward vibe for a few seconds, had been since that countertop swing, but he broke it with an upbeat offer of coffee.

"Yes! Please! I think I love coffee!"

Noah poured a cup and then paused. "You know how you take it?"

"Um . . ." I stared at the sugar and milk on the table. "I have no idea, actually."

Noah pushed the coffee in front of me and then leaned across the counter. "Well, have fun experimenting."

I sipped the coffee and cringed. "No, definitely not black." I picked up the milk carton and splashed some in, then took another sip and thought about it.

"More?" Noah asked.

"Yes! Definitely!" I tipped more milk into the coffee and sipped again. "Definitely sugar." I picked up a spoon, dropped it in and stirred. "More," I said, after carefully considering the flavor in my mouth. Three spoons later, and it was perfect! Sweet and milky and not too hot.

"Oh my God, mmmmmmmmmm . . ." I moaned as I sipped it, as if this was the thing I'd been waiting for and craving and wanting more than anything. "Mmmmm . . . Sooo good. Aaahhhhh." I moaned longer and louder this time, but stopped immediately when I saw the strange look on Noah's face.

"Was that a bit much?" I asked, feeling embarrassed now.

"Well, you officially know one thing about yourself, so that's positive. You love coffee!"

"Coffee, coffee!" Chloe squawked from her cage by the window, and I jumped.

I eyed her suspiciously for a while, trying to gauge her feelings towards me. She didn't seem to be showing any signs of aggression this morning, but still, I think it was better I remained on the opposite side of the room. "How long have you had her? African Grey parrots can live for sixty years. Don't ask me how I know that, though."

"African Grey. African Grey," Chloe repeated, and Noah laughed.

"Yes, you are." He walked up to her and offered up a slice of apple. "I've only had her for two years." He said that with such a sweet tone in his voice. You could see he really cared for this bird. But there was also something beneath that tone, something a little sadder, and I wondered what it was.

"Where was she before you?"

"Uh . . ." He hesitated.

"You don't have to tell me."

"No, it's not a secret. Two years ago I was called out to an old-age home. When I got there, this guy, Peter was his name, was having a severe heart attack. I was pretty sure he wouldn't make it, he already had a pacemaker and underlying cardiac issues, and I'm sure he knew that too. Just before he died—it must have taken him every last ounce of his strength—he grabbed my arm and told me to make sure Chloe was taken care of. I didn't know what he was talking about until I found out who Chloe was. He didn't have any family. He was all alone, except for her. So . . . I took her. I knew nothing about parrots, didn't even think I liked them, but here we are. Two years later and . . ." He gave Chloe a scratch and she tilted her neck back, almost all the way round. "I love her. She's a cutie. Don't I?"

Chloe whistled and bobbed her head up and down again. "Love you! Love you!"

"That's very sweet of you," I said, slightly in awe of Noah's obvious kindness. "To take her in when she needed it the most." On the surface, I was taking about the parrot, but really, I was talking about myself, and Noah knew it because he turned and met my gaze.

"Pleasure." Our eyes zoned in on each other like arrows to a target and, after what felt like an incredibly awkward second, I went back to sipping my coffee. I walked around the room again, not on Chloe's side, though, noticing for the first time the things I hadn't seen last night.

"What's this?" I pointed at what looked like it had been a pot plant in a previous, more hydrated life. I scanned the room. "And another one. And another."

"I'm not very good at keeping plants alive. People and parrots are far easier."

"But that's because they're in the wrong places." I put my coffee down and started moving them around. "This one needs sun. You can't have it in the shade like this." I moved what looked like it had been a snake plant, once upon a very long time ago, to a sunny spot on the windowsill. "And as for this, too much sun. It needs semi-shade. And as for this succulent, just because it's a water-wise plant doesn't mean it never needs water." I walked to the kitchen, filled a glass up and gave the thirsty plants some water.

"Likes coffee. Likes plants," Noah said, and it took me a moment to realize what he meant.

"Oh! Yes. I guess I do." I stood back and admired my new plant arrangement. Although three plants didn't really make an arrangement, it was more a vague scattering of foliage.

"I'll try and look after them better." Noah walked over to the snake plant and ran his hand up the leaf. He held it up, revealing the dust on his fingers.

"You need to wipe them. They can't photosynthesize with dust on their leaves," I said quickly, as this fact seemed to jump into the conscious part of my brain.

"I'll remember that." He wiped the dust onto his pants, and that's when I noticed what he was wearing: a pair of navy sleep shorts and a plain white T-shirt. And it was also at this time that I noticed what kind of body he had under all of that fabric. I'd vaguely observed his build before, but now I was really registering it. Noah was *very* muscular. I was sure he must be more muscular than other men, except I couldn't really picture many in my head. Other than some actors from TV shows, I didn't have many real-life men to compare him with. I did another "turn about the room", as Jane Austen would say, and then that piece of paper on the wall caught my attention again. I moved towards it and read.

"I can't believe you haven't watched *True Detective*. It's brilliant. Matthew McConaughey gives an amazing performance. He deserved all the awards he got for it."

"I think you watch a lot of TV too," Noah said.

"I think I do." I scanned the list again. "So why do you have time off—to watch all these?"

"I'm changing careers," he said.

I swiveled around. "But you're an amazing paramedic. What will you do?"

"I actually want to study further, I'm doing nursing. I've quit my job, and I start nursing school in a month. I officially have a month off to sit on my ass and catch up on all the shows I've missed because I've worked crazy shifts and hours for the last seven years."

"Wow, that's . . . that's a change."

"My work colleagues can't understand it. Going back to school at this age and changing professions, but I think if you want to do something, something else, why not? You only have one life, right?" He paused for a while and a tiny flash of something moved across his face, so briefly that you might even have missed it. But I hadn't. It was like a tiny cloud sweeping across the sun and disappearing quickly. "Some people don't even get a life to live, or their lives get cut short. You know?"

I nodded. Even if I didn't really know. I knew nothing about life and living it, or not living it. Some of these thoughts must have shown on my face.

"Sorry, I didn't mean to . . . I forgot that you—"

"I forgot too. I *really* forgot," I joked, trying to make light of it.

He smiled. I think it was only for my benefit, going along with me trying to inject some lightness into my situation. I knew this because his smile seemed uncomfortable. As if it didn't quite fit on his face in the same way his other smiles did. The ones where you saw the little gap in his front teeth.

"So . . ." Noah declared, walking into the middle of the room, swinging his arms. "Want to go and have some lunch?"

"Lunch? Isn't it morning?"

Noah pointed at a clock on the kitchen wall. It read twelve. "We both overslept."

"Oh." I felt embarrassed for some reason. Or maybe I felt bad. Maybe Noah had things to do in the mornings and I, with my late-night shenanigans, had caused him to miss those.

"It's cool. I needed it, though. First day of my break." He grabbed his wallet off the kitchen counter and it dawned on me again.

"Uh . . . I don't have any money. I don't know why I didn't have a bag with me when you found me. Who doesn't have a bag?"

"It was pretty chaotic there when I arrived. Maybe one of the other women picked it up . . . *no*, but then they would have returned it." He shrugged. "Do you remember anything about the accident at all?"

"Nothing." I felt that darkness come back, pulling on me, and I swear, I felt a chill in the air that hadn't been there a second ago. I clasped my hands to my body.

"So, lunch. Let's go." He clapped his hands together, changing the mood back to how it was before the darkness reared its head.

"Sure."

"I just need to change and put Chloe outside while we're gone." Noah stuck his finger out and Chloe climbed on. I followed him out of the kitchen into the small back garden, and when I saw what it looked like, I gasped.

"Wow! Is this all for Chloe?" I looked at the massive cage that took up most of the garden. It looked like it had been landscaped to resemble something tropical. Grass on the floor, a little pond, trees and shrubs planted inside and plenty of swings and things for her to climb on. The only other furniture in the garden was a small table and two chairs, but they were completely dwarfed by the cage in front of me.

"I built it for her. I hate the idea of animals in captivity, but she'd been in a cage all her life."

I remembered the panda in the cage at the zoo. I remembered the hospital room and the windows that didn't open, and a strange, anxious feeling gnawed at me once again.

Noah walked into the cage and put Chloe onto a swing. And when he walked back out he looked at me, curiously. "You okay?"

"I don't know. I have this memory—well, I think it is anyway."

"Of what?"

"A panda. In the zoo. I think." I looked at Chloe through her bars. She was happily pulling at the leaves now and jumping from branch to branch. The feeling I got from watching her was nothing like the one I got when I thought of that panda. Or the feeling I got when I thought of hospital windows that didn't open.

"I don't think I like animals in captivity either," I said, although I don't think this was the full truth of the memory I was having. I think the truth was more along the lines of *I* didn't like being in captivity. *Had I been in captivity?*

"Hey!"

I jumped as someone appeared around the corner, seemingly from nowhere.

"Hey," Noah said casually, as if the sight of a woman in his garden with a towel wrapped around her naked body wasn't an issue at all. She was pretty, blonde and had very tanned and muscular legs. The woman registered me briefly, tipped her head and gave me a small hello and then walked towards the house. Who was she?

"Can I use your . . ." She didn't even finish the sentence.

"Shower. Yeah," Noah replied.

"Sorry. The guy is coming tomorrow to fix the tap," the woman said, walking past me in her towel. I turned and looked at Noah with surprise.

"Oh, I forgot to mention, that's Maxine, she rents the garden cottage." He pointed towards the cage and I looked again. And that's when I saw the little building behind it.

"Oh," I said, and suddenly, without making the conscious decision to think about it, I wondered if she and Noah were an item. If they were, they made a really good-looking couple, especially because Noah was so good-looking. But I didn't really have much to compare him with, so how would I know how good-looking he was? And then I started wondering if I was considered good-looking?

CHAPTER 15

"Wat kind of food do you like?" Noah asked as we climbed in his car. He drove a small, understated car, which was exactly the kind of car I would have pictured him driving. Noah was down to earth, there was nothing flashy and showy about him, other than those muscles, mind you.

"I'm not sure," I confessed, and looked down at my feet.

"Oh, sorry, I don't get many—any—visitors in my car. Well, this one, anyway. I'm usually driving a car with flashing lights, and those people don't really care what the car looks like." He reached down, looking somewhat embarrassed—or so the slight pink sheen in his cheeks led me to believe—and grabbed an empty water bottle, a gym bag and two cereal-bar wrappers and tossed them onto the back seat. "I have to eat breakfast on the run a lot," he said, crunching the wrappers up, looking more self-conscious about those than the dirty socks I could see sticking out of the gym bag.

"What about Mexican food?" He started the car and reversed carefully out of the narrow garage.

"Honestly, I have no clue," I said, nervously watching his side mirrors, which came dangerously close to the postbox. I felt very uneasy again, much like I had in the taxi last night, and I didn't know why.

"Sorry. I keep forgetting that you probably don't know that kind of thing." He apologized in that voice he'd apologized with this morning. I wasn't so sure I liked that voice. It made me feel like he thought of me as a weak, fragile bird that couldn't fly. Mind you . . .

was I? I was completely helpless in so many ways. Relying on him for a roof over my head and food in my stomach. Maybe I was fragile after all. I didn't like that thought, and I wished I had some concrete evidence, like a memory, to prove otherwise.

"It's okay. This is a strange situation." I tried to make him, and me, feel a little better about it all.

"Yes, it is," he said quietly.

"I'd like to try Mexican food, though. Maybe, if I eat it, it'll jog a memory. Or if not, I'll discover something else about myself." I gripped the side of the seat as he pulled into the traffic. Sitting in this car didn't make me feel very safe. I needed to open a window, as fast as possible.

"Can I . . ." I didn't even finish that sentence, as I pressed the button and watched the window come down, much to my relief. A taxi cut us off in the traffic and Noah was forced to hit the brakes, hard enough that the car jerked a little. I gasped and straightened in my seat, my heart pounding in my chest, as if it had woken up from a deep sleep.

"You okay?" Noah glanced at me.

"Uh . . . I think so. No. Maybe. I don't know. I don't think I like being in cars." I stuck my face closer to the open window and gulped in the cool air. "Or confined spaces. I don't think I like those either," I added, my finger resting on the window button in case I needed to open it further.

"Totally understandable. Your last experience in a car and a confined space weren't exactly great. Even if you don't entirely remember them. The elevator. The ambulance."

"You're right. I'm sure that's what it is," I said, even though, deep down inside, I knew that wasn't the case at all. I could feel that these fears were deeply ingrained in me, and had been for a very long time, even if I didn't know why.

* * *

The inside of the restaurant was very Mexican-looking and, as we walked in, I felt inundated with facts about Mexico, like:

Mexico has the world's smallest volcano, which stands a cute forty-three feet tall.

Mexico, not Egypt, is actually home to the world's biggest ancient pyramids.

Color TV was invented in Mexico, and so was Caesar salad.

The meteor that caused the extinction of dinosaurs crashed in Mexico.

I tried to turn the facts off as we took our seats at a small table at the back that looked out over a courtyard filled with colorful Mexican tiles and pots and the most incredible green plants.

"So, what appeals to you?" Noah pointed at the menu, which was written on a chalkboard.

"Umm, what do you recommend?"

"Well, guacamole and chips is a classic. So is the spicy bean taco."

The waiter came up to the table, looking very festive in his Mexican-inspired clothing. He placed a big jug of water down on the table and introduced himself. I was too busy studying the blackboard to reply.

"What's that?" I pointed to the poster on the wall next to the chalkboard.

"Oh, that's a competition we run," the waiter replied.

"To get a free meal?" I asked, reading it.

"Yeah, if you can eat a habanero pepper, the hottest pepper in Mexico, then you get your meal free! Not many people have done it, though."

"Habanero peppers score 100,000 to 350,000 on the Scoville heat scale," I said.

Both the waiter and Noah stared at me.

"Scoville is the heat scale you use to measure foods with. For example, a jalapeño only scores 2,500 to 8,000 max on the scale," I qualified.

"I didn't know that," Noah said, and glanced up to the now open-mouthed waiter.

"Yeah, neither did I," he said. "I probably should."

"Cool! I'll do it!" I said, without thinking too hard.

"You will?" The waiter looked taken aback and so did Noah.

"Why not? Free meal. I don't want you to pay for everything."

Noah shook his head. "Really, I don't mind. Especially if you have to eat the world's hottest peppers just to get a free meal. It doesn't seem right."

"Well, technically, the world's hottest pepper is the Carolina Reaper, so at least I'm not eating that!"

"At least," Noah said sarcastically, adding the tiniest head shake to the mix.

"Don't worry, I'll be fine," I assured him, and then banged my hand on the table with enthusiasm. "I'll do it!"

"You sure?" the waiter asked again, eyeing me.

"No, she's not sure," Noah piped up.

"No, I am," I said firmly.

"Cool!" The waiter eyes lit up and he shouted to the rest of the restaurant. "Habanero challenge!"

I heard a few excited whoops come from the direction of the bar and kitchen, and a few patrons also looked up.

Noah leaned across the table. "You don't have to do this. I once got called out to a party where a bunch of teens had dared each other to eat chilis and one guy got so sick he had to be rushed to hospital."

"Lucky for me, then, that I have a trained medical professional here."

I hadn't realized that eating the pepper was such a big deal, though, because soon, the waiter returned with a giant silver cloche, as well as two chefs, the manager and a few other onlookers. The manager put a piece of paper down on the table in front of me and passed me a pen.

"What's this?"

"We need you to sign an indemnity form before eating it," he said.

"Wait. No." Noah covered the paper with his hands. "You don't want to eat something that you have to sign an indemnity form for!" He sounded genuinely concerned, and for some reason, this felt good. It felt good to have him care about my wellbeing. Even though I didn't feel that concerned myself.

"It'll be fine." I felt strangely confident. "I think I like hot food!"

"You do?"

"I do, actually!" I said happily, putting the pen to the paper, but then I hesitated. Shit! I didn't know my name. But I wasn't going to tell them that, they probably wouldn't let me eat a blazing pepper with no name and no memory. I scribbled a signature, making up a name, and then passed the paper back to them. I caught Noah looking down at the paper curiously as I passed it back.

The cloche was put on the table with great ceremony and the lid lifted with a dramatic flourish. I almost expected a drum roll to fill the air. I looked down, and there it was. Tiny and red. The silver plate dwarfed it, which made it look incredibly ominous.

"Is that it?" Noah eyed the small red thing.

"Don't let its size fool you," the waiter said, looking so pleased with himself as he put a glass of milk down for me. "As they say, dynamite comes in small packages."

"The rules are simple," the manager said, also looking like he was enjoying himself very much. "You have to eat and swallow the entire chili in one minute. And if you do, your meal is free and you get your photo on the habanero wall of fame over there." He pointed and I looked at the back of the room, where there was a wall of photos. There were not a lot of photos and—

"No! No!" Noah said. "Look at all those people. Look at their faces, they look like they're about to collapse!"

"I'll be fine," I urged. "Let's do this." I looked up at the manager and gave him a firm, confident nod and then I picked the pepper up and eyeballed it.

"On your marks, get set," the waiter said, holding his cell phone.

"No!" Noah said quickly.

"GO!" The waiter shouted over Noah's protests and a cheer broke out around me, which soon turned into an excited chant, as many of the patrons who'd been previously sitting were up on their feet, coming towards the table.

Without much thought, I shoved the whole thing in my mouth and bit down.

"At least eat it in little bites. Small bites!" Noah said, flapping his hand at me. I thought he might pull the thing out of my mouth if he could.

"No. All at once is better!" the manager assured him.

Everyone leaned in as I bit down and started chewing, eyebrows raised in a kind of mutual question. The question was not hard to guess, and the more I chewed, the higher the eyebrows went and the more they leaned, until all I could see were dozens of eyes and brows looking at me.

"And?" Noah was the first to speak.

"Mmmm," I mumbled as the first rush of heat hit me like a ten-ton truck on my tongue. "Whoa!" I opened my mouth and fanned my tongue with my hand. "Whoa!"

"You okay?" Noah asked.

I nodded my head, fast. I could feel tears dripping down my cheeks as my eyes watered and stung. "WHOOOO!" I fanned my mouth some more. "H.O.T.!"

"Thirty seconds to go!" the manager announced.

"Okay!" I slapped my hands down on the table hard, palms first. And then started bashing the table with each fiery bite. Soon a chant had broken out around me and a countdown had begun.

"Ten, nine, eight . . ."

I chewed faster and faster. I was going to swallow this thing, come hell or high water. I could feel the tears streaming down my face, and my nose was starting to run too.

"Five, four, three—"

"DONE!" I leapt up out of my seat and opened my mouth for

everyone to see, and then I threw my arms in the air and jumped up and down on my feet as fast as I could. The jumping was more to distract me from the feeling of utter agony exploding in my mouth.

"Oh shit! Oh crap, oh . . ." I threw myself back at the table and grabbed the glass of milk, gulping it down so hard and fast that it went everywhere. I could feel it on my chin, running onto my shirt, but I didn't care. I plunged my tongue into the milk and looked up at Noah over the rim of the glass.

"I did it!" I said, the words bubbling into the milk. This time the worry on Noah's face was gone. Instead, he was laughing, and it was utterly contagious. Because soon I was laughing too, and everyone else.

Who knew eating a chili and half burning your tongue off could be so damn fun!

And then I could feel something big and uncomfortable climbing up my throat. I tried to stop it, tried to swallow it down, but there was no fighting it.

"Buuuurpp!" The loud sound came out of my mouth, as well as the red-tinged spit that rolled down my chin and dropped onto my shirt. So *not* dignified.

The burp caused everyone to stop laughing and look at me with concern. But I shot everyone a thumbs-up and then I couldn't help myself. I laughed again.

CHAPTER 16

‿

$\mathcal{W}$e left the Mexican restaurant feeling stuffed and in a mood that can only be described as jovial. We walked towards his car together happily. Swaying from side to side as if guided by some invisible beat.

"So, we know more things about me now," I said, as we reached the car. "That I like spicy food."

"I can't believe you asked them to put more habanero on your taco."

"Once you get over the initial shock of it, it's really very nice."

"Hey, what name did you sign on the indemnity form? Do you remember your name?" he asked.

"No. I don't. I just wrote down the first name I could think of."

"What was that?"

"Becca," I said.

"Becca? Where did you get that from? You think it's your name?"

"No. I got it from this book in the hospital. A writer, Becca Thorne."

"*The Heart is Just a Muscle*," Noah piped up. "That's her book."

"Yes, how do you know?"

"Everyone knows. It was the bestselling book last year, or the year before, I can't remember. Everyone was talking about it, though."

"Oh," I said, suddenly wondering if I'd also read her book, since everyone else had.

"Is it a good book?" I asked.

"I think so. I haven't read it, to be honest. My sister lent me her copy. I'm supposed to read it during this break."

We climbed into the car, and it was already four in the afternoon.

"We have to go past the hospital now. Dr. Maluka wanted to have a look at your wound and maybe take your stitches out."

"Oh, yes!" I reached up and touched my head. I'd almost forgotten about that. Even when I'd seen myself with the plaster on my head in the photo the restaurant had taken of me, I'd barely registered it.

"Thanks," I said to Noah now. "I really appreciate this."

"No problem. Thanks for the lunch!"

"It's my pleasure." I touched the tip of my tongue, which was still tingling and stinging with a sensation that I really liked. It made my mouth feel alive and on fire, in a good way. I liked this feeling of being alive. Out of the hospital, eating chili, laughing and taking risks.

I heard a chuckle and turned to see Noah shaking his head and tutting in an amused fashion. "You really like spicy foods. That's for sure." He reversed out of the parking place. "You're braver than I am. I don't think I could do that." He pulled into the steady flow of traffic and stopped at a red light.

Brave! I mused, running that word over and over in my empty head. I worked the word, kneading it like someone would knead dough. Something about that word sounded strange. Like I'd never heard it before. I repeated it to myself, seeing if it stirred up any kind of memory, only it didn't.

But when Noah began speeding up to join the highway, I didn't feel brave anymore. I grabbed onto the seat again and squeezed.

Did you know that South Africa is one of the most dangerous places in the world to drive in?

I tightened my grip on the seat.

* * *

By the time we got back home it was already dark. I knew that the sun seemed to be slipping away into the darkness sooner now that we were in autumn.

My head was stinging a little. They'd taken the stitches out, and it had not been a very pleasant experience. Being inside the hospital had set me on edge again. Set my teeth chattering and made all the hairs on my arms and neck prick up, as if they were trying to create a barrier between me and the hospital itself. Noah had been with me, though, and when I started freaking as they brought the scissors down towards my forehead, he'd given me a reassuring smile which had calmed my nerves instantly.

We walked into his house and I followed him through to the kitchen. He took out two Cokes and placed them down on the kitchen counter. I stared at the Coke. Obviously, I knew what a Coca Cola was. In the last few days, I'd seen signs for Coca Cola everywhere, but I just couldn't recall what it tasted like.

"Not sure if you like Coke?" he asked.

"I can't remember." I reached for the can. It felt cool and soothing in my hands.

"It's the best," Noah said, taking a sip of his. "I know I should drink less of it, but I swear, it's addictive."

I raised the can to my nose and giggled when the bubbles tickled me. "I wasn't expecting that!"

Noah sat at the counter and watched me.

"What?"

"It's just . . . you don't get to see many people taking their 'first' sip of Coke. Or drinking their first coffee, eating their first chili. I must admit, it's kind of fun to watch."

"Really?"

Noah nodded. "What do they say about when you become a parent? You get to re-live moments from your childhood through your kids when you watch them do things for the first time."

"And you're re-living moments from your childhood through me?" I asked.

He shrugged. "In a way, re-living some first times vicariously through you. So, go on, sip." He crossed his arms across the kitchen counter and looked like he was getting comfortable.

"I can't do it if you're watching me like that!" I stared down at him from my standing position.

He grinned. "Performance anxiety?"

"Well, you *are* staring at me."

"Okay, I'll turn around." He shifted his body in the chair and looked away. He did have the broadest shoulders, and when he crossed his arms like that . . . muscles pulled tightly across his back and bulged through the very fabric of his shirt and—

"And?" he asked after a while.

"Oh!" I stopped looking at his back. "I haven't done it yet."

"Are you distracted?"

"No!" *Yes!*

I put the Coke back up to my lips, trying not to look at those lines on his lower back. Those lines that the shirt was clinging to that seemed to travel down into his pants.

"And?"

"Oh! Um . . . about to do it now."

"Do it. What are you waiting for?"

God, I really needed to stop staring at his back.

"*DO IT! Naughty girl! Naughty girl!*" A squawk filled the room and I turned and shot Chloe a look.

"Talk about pressure!" I put the Coke to my lips and threw it back and, as I did . . .

Sweet, black liquid trickled down my throat. Like syrup. Slippery and refreshing. I closed my eyes and savored the moment, and when I opened them again, Noah had turned around and was staring at me with one raised brow. I had noticed that he could raise one at a time.

"And?" he pressed, looking eager for my reply.

"It's amazing!" I almost squealed in delight as the cool liquid pooled in my stomach. "It's . . . it's better than coffee. Better than chilis, better than, God, I don't know what it's better than, but it's better than all of that . . ."

"Better than sex?"

"What?" I swung around as Maxine walked into the kitchen.

"Better than sex," she repeated.

"Um . . ." I felt my jaw loosen in shock. Sex! I knew what that was all of a sudden. Five seconds ago, sex had not even existed in my head and now, it did, and the thought of it made me blush and flush and I wanted to run and hide my face because I was sure it looked strange. And Noah's face looked just as strange, as he glanced at me and then quickly away.

"What?" Maxine asked. "Tough crowd. You would think I walked in on an Amish convention or something. It's just sex."

I sipped the Coke again to avoid looking at her. *Had I had sex? Did I have sex, and if so, who did I have it with? Was I good at it? Did I like it? Did Noah have it? Who with? How often? And . . .*

"Can I borrow your beater? I'm trying to make these whey protein muffins."

"Sure." Noah pointed at the cupboard and Maxine walked over to it.

"Thanks. If you guys want one, they should be ready in about twenty minutes!" And with that she turned and exited. Leaving this massive, white sex elephant in the room with Noah and me.

"I . . . can't remember having sex," I suddenly said, even though I really hadn't wanted to say anything about it at all.

Noah looked awkward, as if he didn't know how to reply.

"Sorry, was that an overshare? It's just weird, before Maxine said the word 'sex,' I didn't even know it existed, really. And now I do, and that's strange. What else don't I know exists?"

Noah shrugged his big shoulders. "Who knows? You're just going to have to find out."

"When? When am I going to find it all out? And why do I know some things and not others? And surely I should remember something like sex? Or what a Coke tastes like? I mean, who the hell am I?"

Noah looked at me for a while. He seemed thoughtful and then he pushed a piece of paper across the table towards me. "You should start making a list. Write down all the things that you've discovered about yourself in the last few days."

I sat down and looked at the blank piece of paper and imagined filling it with bits and pieces of myself.

"Do it," he urged, passing me a pen now too.

"Right! *Things I know about myself*," I scribbled.

1. I like sweet, milky coffee.
2. I like spicy foods.
3. I like Coke.
4. I like plants.

I glanced behind me at Chloe and then turned back to the list.

5. Parrots and birds don't like me. Possibly rats too.
6. I don't like hospitals.
7. I don't like being inside a car.
8. I don't like closed windows.
9. I don't like animals in zoos.

I considered writing that I may or may not have had sex, but left that one off.

"That's it so far." I looked back up at Noah.

"You should keep it on you and, as you discover more things about yourself, add to it."

"Will do." I folded the paper and stood up, slipping it into my jeans pocket. My entire life so far, and all I knew about myself fitted neatly, with room to spare, into a small pocket in my jeans. What a depressing thought.

CHAPTER 17

I stood in the shower, letting the water rush over my body in warm, steady waves, as if it were washing something away from me. I looked down at my feet and watched the water disappear down the drain, along with whatever it was taking from me. This was the first shower I'd taken in days. I stuck my hand out of the shower and reached for my panties. I only had one pair. In the hospital, I'd worn some awful papery ones, but now I would need to wash these until I found out who I was and went back to my home and got a new pair. I scrubbed them with the soap, and then rinsed and squeezed them out. And when that was done, I turned the shower off and walked out. A full-length mirror on the back of the door—I'd only noticed it now—had completely steamed up. I wiped it with a towel and took a step back. And when I saw my body completely naked for the first time, I stumbled backwards, reaching out for the sink to stop me from falling.

The doctors had told me I'd had a previous surgery, but in my head, it didn't look like this. I ran my hand over my arm and shoulder. This must be where I had a plate and screws in my shoulder. The scar was pale but prominent against my skin, and it was ugly. I turned and looked over my shoulder at my back, and there was the other scar, running down a portion of the length of my spine. It sat right in the middle of my back, dividing it in two equal parts.

These scars unnerved me. They were such a physical reminder that I didn't know who I was. How could I have all these marks on my body and have no idea where they came from? My body was a foreign creature. I might as well be looking at someone else naked. That's how it felt. I turned back to the mirror and continued to look at myself.

My breasts were small and round. Not much more than a handful. They seemed like good enough breasts, though, not that I'd seen many. *Any, actually.* My stomach was flat, but not tight. It was soft, and on my hips, a few white lines. Not scars, though. I didn't know what they were. It didn't look like I had much hair down there, and when I looked a little closer, it soon became obvious I did a lot of grooming. The tops of my thighs were a little dimpled in places, and so was my bum, but all in all, I seemed to have an acceptable figure, if I compared myself to some of the women in the magazines I'd seen in the hospital. I took a step closer and studied my face. Everything seemed okay there too. I wasn't sure if I was what you would call beautiful. I certainly didn't have a face like the girls in the magazines, or a face like Maxine, for instance. But my nose was small, and in proportion to the rest of my face. My lips seemed to be a fairly normal size too, apart from the slight swelling in the bottom lip. My eyes were rather large. That was something very noticeable. Large and round and the color was—what would you call that?—a grayish, khaki green.

Only 2 per cent of the population has green eyes.

Did that make me unique? I wondered.

I ran my hands through my short hair. I'd gauged from an article in one of the magazines at hospital that this was called a pixie cut. Apparently, it was making a comeback. Did that mean I was fashionable? I was *on trend*, as the magazine had said? My eyebrows were pretty perfect, something else I'd gleaned from the magazine, where a whole article, three pages, was dedicated to the art of eyebrow shaping. I shook my head. This not knowing was exhausting. All this thinking and speculating and running things over and over in my brain. And I didn't want to think anymore. I wanted to just *know*.

I turned away from the mirror and bent over to pick my clothes up, just as I heard the door open and felt a rush of cold air on my bottom. I swung around to find Maxine standing there.

"Sorry, I didn't realize you were here," she said casually, looking at my fully naked body as if she didn't even care I was naked.

"Broken collar bone," she said, pointing at my scar.

"Tha-that's what I've been told," I replied, so shocked that she was just standing there that I didn't even bother to bend down and pick up my towel.

"I had elbow surgery last year." She thrust a scarred elbow into my face. "Hurt like a motherfucker. I bet yours hurt too."

"I can't remember," I mumbled, finally bending down to pick up my towel, which I clutched to my body.

"Oh my God!" I looked away quickly as she began taking her clothes off and dropping them to the floor. I tried not to gasp at the sight of her naked breasts, which were suddenly everywhere. And I mean everywhere! I seemed to be standing in a place where the mirror was reflecting her back at me in multiple. Suddenly, Maxine's boobs flooded my field of vision, row after row after row. After the initial shock was over, I found myself staring at them. She did have incredible breasts. Big and round and so damn perky.

"Are you not comfortable with this?" she asked.

"Um, not really," I said, feeling sheepish now, like maybe I should be cool with this. Maybe this is what women did all the time and I just didn't know.

"I sometimes forget I'm not in a gym changing room." She politely wrapped a towel around herself and her perfect breasts disappeared. "Sometimes I just do stuff and blurt stuff out. I don't have a filter. Like that sex thing. Sorry if it made things awkward between you guys. I didn't know Noah was seeing anyone. Fresh relationship, awkward sex talk, I get it."

"No. Noah and I aren't . . . uh . . ."

"Damn, you haven't had sex yet! That's awkward. Unfiltered roommate brings up topic of sex and you guys haven't had it yet."

"No, it's not—"

"Don't worry, I'm sure you guys will have it soon."

"Wait. No, now you really have it wrong, uh—"

"Hey!" Noah somehow chose the absolute worst time to call out from outside the bathroom, and my cheeks immediately went red.

"Hey," Maxine answered him.

"Oh, sorry, I thought someone else was in there."

"I am," I called.

There was a beat of silence. "Oh. You're both in there." His voice sounded a little strange now.

"Yeah," Maxine called, and then she winked at me. "Both of us are totally naked!" She burst out laughing then mouthed something to me that looked like "Now you guys are totally going to have sex." I wanted to die of embarrassment!

"No, we're not naked!" I yelled. "We were. But we're not anymore." This made Maxine laugh even more and she shot me a thumbs-up and nodded.

"Do you need the bathroom too?" Maxine was still laughing. "You can join us if you want!" She gave me several very dramatic and pronounced winks now.

"No! That's . . . I . . . no." Noah seemed to be stumbling over his words and I couldn't help but wonder if he was contemplating this offer. "I was just going to say that I was thinking of starting *Game of Thrones* soon."

"Cool," I shouted through the door. "Coming." At that, Maxine snorted with laughter, and I think I heard Noah clear his throat and shuffle his feet and then scurry down the passage.

"You guys are cute," she said, and then dropped her towel completely and sat down on the toilet. I took this as my cue to leave.

CHAPTER 18

~

$\mathcal{N}$oah and I had gotten comfortable in the lounge, and *Game of Thrones*, season one, episode one, was just about to start, when an advert came on. I immediately sat forward in my chair and stared.

Gooey, brown, melty, warm chocolate being poured onto peanuts and Rice Krispies. Being poured onto nougat, sprinkled with shavings of white chocolate and then wrapped in gold foil and . . .

"Oh my God!" I turned to Noah and looked at him excitedly. "I love chocolate. I mean, I LOVE it! I think it's my favorite thing in the world. Do you have some? Chocolate? Do you?" I mean, of course he had chocolate. Everyone loved chocolate, didn't they? But his face dropped.

"No. I actually don't like it. Sorry," he replied.

"You what? How can you not like it? What's not to like about it? Chocolate is the best!" I declared, nearly jumping out my seat as this almost-memory rushed back at me. For some reason, I could see Easter-egg wrappers on the floor. Warm fingers melting into the chocolate while I held it. Licking the chocolate off my fingers, small fingers. Child's fingers. A half-memory of me as a child eating chocolate filled the void that had been inside my head and I was ecstatic that something so big had finally taken up space in there. I closed my eyes quickly, trying to extract more from the memory, but there was nothing else there. Just the feeling of joy, the taste of sweetness and a feeling of stickiness on my fingertips.

"Sorry. I don't eat it. Bad experience once," he said, looking genuinely disappointed that he didn't have any for me.

"How can you have a bad experience with chocolate?" I asked.

"It's a loooong story," he said. I waited for him to tell me what it was, but he didn't. It looked like it was a story he didn't particularly want to recount, so I didn't push.

"BUT . . ." Noah jumped up. "Maxine will have chocolate." He rushed out of the kitchen door, into the garden. I followed and we made our way to the garden cottage behind the aviary. Noah knocked on the door and, truthfully, I was feeling awkward. My last three interactions with Maxine had been somewhat strange. We heard a "come in" and walked inside. Maxine was in the middle of the floor, her laptop open, and she was doing what looked like some seriously vigorous lunges. The sweat coating her face and hairline was a dead giveaway.

"Hey," Noah said.

She replied, but didn't look up. She was far too engrossed in what was going on on her laptop. I looked over at it, and that's when it hit me.

"Hey, I know her!"

"You do? You remember?" Noah asked, staring at the laptop.

"I saw her when I was at the hospital," I said. At this, Maxine stopped what she was doing.

"You were at the hospital?" she asked, wiping her sweaty brow with a small towel.

I pointed to my head. "I bashed my head," I said, not wanting to elaborate. "I saw her in a magazine."

"Yeah, she's a fitness blogger I follow. Frankie. She and her boyfriend—well, I should say ex-boyfriend—do these great workout videos."

I looked at the screen. Frankie and a Ken of a man were doing exercises, huge smiles plastered across their faces. They looked happy together. Happy and perfect, and they weren't even sweating. He had the biggest, whitest smile I'd ever seen and she, well, she looked every bit the fit, blonde, perfect Barbie.

"They broke up?" I asked. It didn't seem possible. I mean, look at them.

"He broke up with her on Instagram. Can you believe it! And now she's missing."

"What?" I suddenly felt a deep concern for this stranger I didn't actually know.

"Look." Maxine picked her phone up and flicked the screen on, showing me what I recognized as Twitter.

"Hashtag Find Frankie. It's been trending."

"So, where is she?" I asked.

"No one knows. It's a real social media mystery. Anyway . . ." She moved off and picked up a bottle of thick, green liquid and sipped. "What happened to your head? You didn't tell me you were in hospital."

"Apparently I was in an elevator accident, but I don't remember anything."

"What do you mean, you don't remember anything?" She took another massive sip of the gooey green stuff and then held it up. "This is Frankie's protein shake. Want to taste?" She thrust the drink towards me and I shook my head. "How much don't you remember?"

"I remember almost nothing about anything," I replied.

"What, like your name?"

I shook my head. "No."

"No way. This is crazy." She put the drink down and stepped closer to me. "Your age?"

"Nope."

"Where you live?"

I shook my head again.

"Fuuuuuuck, that is seriously weird."

"I know!" I agreed with her.

"Man, I'm sorry. I had no idea, or I wouldn't have been so . . . *wait*, when I was joking about you and Noah having sex—"

"What?" Noah cut her off. "You were what?"

"Chill, I was just pulling her leg, you know. Like I always do."

Noah rolled his eyes. "Yeah, your subtlety is well known."

"Do you even remember sex?" she asked.

I shook my head. "No. I know what it is, obviously. But I don't remember having it."

"Waaaiiit!" Maxine held her hand up now. "You're like a newborn virgin."

"A . . . What!?" I gasped. "I . . . what? Well, that's just . . . um . . ." For some reason, her words made me wildly uncomfortable, made my skin flush and prickle.

"Maxine!" Noah chided her now. "Not everyone is as comfortable with talking about—".

"Oh. Right. Sorry!" She held her hand up and then looked thoughtful for a while. "You know what, you should try and do as many things as possible, to figure out what you're into."

"I've been doing that. I've been making a list of the things I know about myself."

"That's great! I mean, in a way, it's actually quite cool if you think about it. You get the chance to get to know yourself all over again."

Her words made me stop. A real full stop as everything inside me zoned in and focused on her meaning. *Was she right?* That this was in some way an opportunity? Her words seemed to make Noah stop too. He looked over at me curiously, as if trying to gauge my reaction to what had just been said. I shrugged at them both. I was on the fence about it. I still would prefer it if I had my memory back and wasn't bumbling through the world right now, remembering some things and forgetting others.

"Chocolate," Noah suddenly said, breaking what was becoming an awkward silence as I was contemplating the fence I now felt like I was balancing on.

Maxine took a step back, looking uncomfortable for the first time since I'd met her. "What about it?"

"I know you have some," Noah replied.

"NO! No, I don't . . . no . . ." She tutted and her eyes flicked about the room.

"Uh . . . yes, you do. I know you do. In your cheat drawer."

"What? Cheat drawer . . . psssst, what's that? I don't have one. Not me."

Noah smiled at her now. "Yes, you do. I even know where it is." Noah made a move and Maxine jumped in front of him. Noah laughed.

"You totally have a cheat drawer and I have seen you in it! Late at night, scrounging around. Busted!" He pointed at her and she gasped.

"Okay, fine! I have one. But you can't tell anyone. It would ruin my reputation if they knew I ate chocolate late at night when no one is looking!" She looked at me and raised her brows, as if seeking sympathy or affirmation. I nodded back to her as if I knew exactly what she meant. Of course I didn't. She sighed and then walked over to a drawer in the kitchen and pulled it open. I gazed into the drawer of wonder and marvel and then saw it.

"Kit Kat!" I said quickly. "Definitely Kit Kat, if you don't mind."

She reached into the drawer and pulled it out for me. "That'll be two hundred calories. You can come work out with me tomorrow if you want. Frankie does this amazing butt and core workout, it'll burn that right off. Or you can come to the gym with Noah and me in the morning?" She looked at Noah.

"Sure," Noah said quickly. "Of course, if you want?"

"I have no idea whether I exercise or not," I said, wondering if maybe I was a gym girl. I was slim, after all. My stomach was flat, slightly squishy, but it didn't protrude. My arms looked relatively toned. Maybe I went to the gym! Maybe I worked out? Maybe I did marathons and things like that. Okay, maybe that was taking it too far, or was it? I didn't know.

"That's perfect, then. Something to add to your list!" Maxine said, starting to close the drawer, but then she paused. She looked down at it with something that resembled lust. "I'm just going to . . ." She didn't finish the sentence and grabbed some chocolate out of the drawer and then slammed it closed, as if punishing it. "Definitely gym tomorrow!" she said, looking at the chocolate as if she wanted to climb inside it.

"Great!" I chirped. "Sounds fun."

"We leave early, though," Noah added quickly.

"That's fine. Maybe I'm an early riser too!"

"Cool. See you in the morning," Maxine said, as Noah and I left. Strangely enough, I felt pretty excited about the prospect of the gym. I had a feeling that I did go to the gym. In fact, I had a feeling that I *really* liked working out.

CHAPTER 19

"*S*he's cool. Where do you know her from?" I asked, peeling the red paper off the Kit-Kat and exposing the long, sleek chocolate fingers.

"She goes to my gym. I met her there. I was looking for someone to rent my garden cottage, she was looking for a place to stay, so it worked out."

"Why would her reputation be ruined if people knew she ate chocolate?"

Noah chuckled. "She is the most hardcore personal trainer at the gym. People are scared of her. She craps on her clients if they so much as look at sugar."

I shook my head. "She's also a little weird."

"That she is!" Noah now smiled in a way that set me on edge. I didn't mean to ask it, I didn't intend to, but somehow the words floated out of my mouth.

"Have you and her . . . are you guys?"

"Maxine and me?" Noah turned, looking shocked. "No. I am not her type."

"Really? I would have thought you guys were, all muscles and all."

"No, she likes these nerdy small guys that wear glasses and work in IT. The last one ran a bookstore."

"What?" I sat forward in my chair, intrigued. This was not what I imagined.

Noah leaned in too, as if gossiping. "She's on this dating app for guys who like muscular women and want to be tossed around and wrestled a bit."

"Nooo." I gasped now. "I would never have guessed. And she likes to wrestle them then?"

"She must, or she wouldn't be on it."

"A dating app," I mused thoughtfully. "I wonder if I'm on one?"

"Well, if you're not in a relationship, you probably are. Everyone is."

"Are you?" I suddenly heard myself ask, and it seemed like such a personal question I wasn't sure if I had crossed a line with it.

"Sure. Some," he said, sounding deliberately nonchalant, as if he was trying not to put effort into what he was saying.

"Some? How many?"

"Not all of them."

"How many are there?" I asked.

"Too many to count. Most are total crap, though. People just looking for hook-ups, you know?" He looked at me now, blue eyes coming into contact with mine. They almost had a sound to them. Like the sound of lasers cutting through the air, or a jet hurtling into the sky.

"And . . . you're not into, just, hooking up?" I looked away now. This conversation seemed to be veering somewhere else now, and in my entire life, which was short, granted, I'd never had a conversation like this before.

"Well, I mean, it's fine from time to time, I guess. But it's not really what I want. It's hard to find what I'm looking for. I work long, strange hours and I don't get to meet many people in my job."

"People that aren't unconscious," I piped up.

"You were conscious," he said back quickly.

"But I was also a little out of it."

"The animals went in two by two by two," Noah suddenly sang.

"What's that?" I asked.

"You don't remember singing it?" He looked amused now.

"No. When?"

"You kind of thought I was Noah, as in of the ark."

"Noooo! I didn't! Oh wait, I did." I face-palmed. "That is so embarrassing. I asked you about the snakes. You must have thought I had totally lost it! No wonder you got such a shock when I came here. Not only did you probably think I was a stalker, but a crazy one at that."

He laughed. "I didn't think you were crazy. Just confused."

"I'd say. Thinking you were Noah of the ark." I smiled at him, and he smiled back. Those blue eyes met mine again, slightly different sound, this time more of a whip cutting through the air, and I wondered if my eyes also had a sound to him? Or was I the only one hearing things? I looked at my chocolate. I'd almost forgotten I was holding it and it had gone soft where my fingertips were clutching it. I raised it to my mouth and took a bite.

"Oh wow! This is so much better than the Coke!" I crunched down on the chocolate and immediately felt a whole bunch of things flick on in my head. Not memories, but little dopamine circuits zapping back to life and firing on all pistons and sending messages of pure damn joy circulating around my body. It was so much better than I'd anticipated.

Noah was watching me with an amused sort of interest, it seemed. I took another bite and a loud long "Mmmmmmm" sound escaped my lips, which caused Noah to smile. And then, unexpectedly, he rolled his shirt sleeve up and scratched a red mark there on the top of his arm.

"Last of the summer mosquitos zapped me last night," he said, answering my silent question.

"I hate mosquitos," I said, and stopped chewing for a moment. "Mmm, one more thing I know about myself."

"Loves chocolate, hates mosquitos!" he said.

"You obviously work out a lot." I pointed at his arm, my mouth still full of chocolate.

"It's probably a cliché to say this, but I'm a bit of a CrossFit addict.

I like working out, it takes my mind off work. Sometimes, I don't have the best days. You know?" His tone changed now and that smile I'd seen seconds ago was gone. I swallowed and stopped chewing.

"You mean that sometimes the people can't be saved?" I lowered the Kit Kat and watched his body language. He looked down at the floor and shuffled his foot across it.

"Like the man who you got Chloe from," I said.

"Yeah. Like him. And more. So many more . . . *many*." He trailed off and I inhaled sharply. I inhaled this little bolt of pain, or something. A bullet of empathy hitting me between the ribs. Physically experiencing pain on someone else's behalf was new.

"It must be hard." I put the Kit Kat down on the table. It didn't seem right, eating chocolate at a time like this.

"It can be. Sometimes it's great, though. Other times . . . it's tough. Working out takes my mind off it. Besides, I need to keep relatively fit for my job. I've had to drag people out of cars, out of pools, climb over walls to get into a house, and once, climb to the first floor of an apartment. So, it's important to keep fit."

I observed Noah. He didn't seem as composed as he usually was. There was an undercurrent of restlessness to him now. The way he was now tapping his foot on the floor, the way he'd interlaced his fingers and was twisting them around ever so slightly. I leaned forward, wanting to suddenly take him by the hand and make him feel better, as he'd made me feel better, but I didn't. He looked up at me and I gave him a smile, one that I hoped conveyed I was here and listening to him.

"I think what you do is amazing," I said.

"Thanks." He held my gaze and, this time, I held it back. Even though it felt difficult, as if holding his gaze was physically heavy, it was weighed down with something invisible.

"You wake up each morning and go out and save lives. How many people can say that? I bet not that many. But that's what you do! And you do it well." I carried on talking and Noah kept smiling and hold-ing my gaze.

"I try to do it well, every time." He broke the heavy eye contact. "There's a lot of pressure, though. You have to get it right, make the right decisions quickly, sometimes so fast you don't even know you're making decisions. And each one is so important, because if you mess up, or make the wrong choice in a moment, it could mean death . . . sorry, I'm ram-bling now. I'm just talking. You probably don't want to hear all this."

"I do!" I said, so emphatically that it caused him to look up at me again and, this time, he graced me with one of his big smiles. The full, little-gap smile that seemed to have the ability to lighten every-thing around it. Like a lighthouse on a dark night.

"Thanks. You're a good listener." He paused for a while and looked at me. "And now we know another thing about you."

"What?" I reached for my Kit Kat again as the mood in the room lifted.

"Well, you're obviously a really good friend, and listener."

"You think?" I asked, perking up. I liked the sound of that.

"I'm pretty sure you're a good friend to a lot of people."

And then a thought hit me. An uncomfortable one. "But if I am, then why hasn't anyone come looking for me yet?"

"I'm sure it won't be long now," he said, ignoring my actual ques-tion. On purpose, no doubt.

I sat back in my chair and took another bite of my chocolate. But as much as I was enjoying it, it wasn't enough to drown out a voice in the back of my head that kept asking, why had I not been found yet? Who was looking for me?

"I bet that by this time tomorrow, you'll be home." Noah picked up the remote and pointed it back at the TV. The last frame of the chocolate commercial was still frozen there.

I wanted to believe him, I really did, but something inside was finding it hard to do so.

"Right, *Game of Thrones*, season one, episode one!" Noah

announced, pressing play and getting comfortable in the seat. The anthemic theme music blasted into the room and we both jumped in fright as Noah scrambled to turn the volume down.

"The sound is huge on here!" Noah shouted.

"Well, it is the world's biggest TV," I replied.

"Are you mocking my TV?"

"Yes!" I replied playfully.

Noah gave me a teasing eye roll followed by a disapproving head shake, and a bolt of something shot through me. I'd never experienced such a bolt before. This was new. This strange feeling that zapped through me, from the center of my chest, all the way to my toes and fingers. It wasn't unpleasant, but it was wildly uncomfortable. On one hand, I didn't want it to stop, but on the other hand, I did. Like when something is ticklish for too long and it becomes painful. The music continued to blare, despite it being turned down.

"Did you know that a man named Ramin Djawadi wrote the music, and that sound you're hearing is a cello?" I gushed, pointing at the screen. It was the only thing I could think of doing to dissipate the way the bolt seemed to be churning in my stomach now. It was no longer a bolt, more of a wave.

"Ha! Another thing we know about you," Noah pointed back at me.

"What?"

"Facts! You know millions of random facts!"

"Yes, I do! Like I know that the language Dothraki in the show is a real language. It was created by a linguist called David Peterson. You can actually learn it!"

Noah laughed at this. "Take out your list, write it down."

"Cool. I will." I took my list out and wrote down the other things I knew about myself:

Hate mosquitos.

Good listener and good friend.

I know facts!

LOVE chocolate. Especially Kit Kat.

I picked my chocolate up, took another bite and then placed it back down on the table.

"And another one," Noah said sounding excited. "Definitely not OCD!"

"Why?

"Look how you're eating your Kit Kat, you've bitten through the fingers. That would completely trigger someone with OCD!"

I looked down at my Kit Kat for confirmation. I had indeed bitten into it, leaving what looked like a large shark bite through the four fingers.

I took another bite, quite pleased with Noah's assessment of me so far and with the things I was finding out about myself. Maybe Maxine had been right, that figuring out who I was could be fun and exciting. Because, so far, I was a coffee- and plant-loving, spicy-food-devouring, chocolate-obsessed, fact-knowing, non-OCD good friend.

CHAPTER 20

"*W*akey, wakey, rise and shine!" I felt my body lift off the seat as the loud voice ripped me back to reality. I opened my eyes and blinked several times as the voice seemed to ring out around me, coming from all directions at once.

"Wh-What . . . uh . . . WHAT?"

I looked to my right when I heard the series of "what"s ringing out. It was in a familiar-sounding voice, although I had no idea who the voice belonged to just yet. But when the shock of the loud wake-up washed away, I realized it was Noah. We were both slumped in the chairs that we'd fallen asleep in last night, watching *Game of Thrones* together, at around three in the morning. We kept saying, "Last one, last one," but after saying that at least five times, we both passed out at some stage.

"Gym, guys," Maxine said, with so much damn enthusiasm, as if she'd been drinking straight out of the enthusiasm chalice and was now drunk and giddy on the stuff.

I dragged my eyes to where she was standing and gave her the once-over, top to bottom. She looked perky as hell in her luminous gym gear and big smile, protein shake in one hand, gym bag in the other. I blinked at my watch a few times and then moaned.

"It's waaay too early," I said.

"I caaaan't," Noah moaned next to me, his voice deep and croaky.

"Me neither," I said, massaging the base of my neck. It felt stiff. Not surprising. I'd fallen asleep in some awkward position, my neck hanging over the back of the chair, my leg over an arm, slight drool pooling in the corner of my mouth.

"You're not getting out of it," Maxine said, looking full of the joys of early mornings and protein shakes.

I rolled over and covered my face. "I don't have any gym clothes," I said, hoping this would end the conversation. Of course, it didn't, because twenty minutes, one borrowed set of gym clothes and two cups of coffee to wake up later, I found myself standing inside a gym. I'd walked around aimlessly at first, while Noah and Maxine had started doing regimental boot-camp-like exercises that almost looked inhuman. Vigorous jumping, and lunging and lifting and . . .

My goodness, Noah looked like he could bench-press an entire ship, he was that strong. A cruise ship, full of thousands of people, who weighed extra because they'd all been eating five complimentary meals a day and having free soft drinks . . .

A cruise ship?

An image of a cruise-ship brochure flashed through my mind, and then disappeared back out again before I could even inspect the memory. After following Maxine and Noah around for a while, orientating myself with everything, we found ourselves standing in front of an interesting-looking contraption.

I looked up at the pyramid-shaped rope climber. A big steel structure with a spiderweb mesh of ropes crisscrossing it. A man had just scaled it all the way to the top, like bloody Spider-Man. And then, he'd turned around and come back down, face first, crawling on it as if crawling down the side of a building. He made it look so effortless.

"Wow!" I said as he disembarked. "That looks like fun."

"That's actually pretty advanced," Maxine said.

"Nooooo, it looks so easy." I walked up to it and pushed the web of ropes with my hands. It wasn't as tight as I thought it would be and moved around much more than I'd anticipated.

"Don't let it fool you, just because you see those in children's playgrounds. This is an adult version."

"Psssshhh!" I tsked and flipped my head back. I knew I could do this. Much like I knew I could eat a chili. I knew I could climb.

"Well, go for it," Maxine said, "you'll never know until you try."

"Exactly!" I gripped the ropes in my hands.

"Are you going to do that?" Noah asked, coming around the corner. I only turned around to reply to him briefly. That had been the intention, anyway. But it didn't pan out that way, because when my eyes caught sight of him I found it a little hard to prise them away.

He was sweaty. Wet shirt clinging to him like a second skin. His muscles looked bigger and bulgier than before. Probably from all those jumpy, lungey whatevers he'd been doing. He had these sexy lines of veins that ran up his arms and into the back of his hands and . . .

Look away! I turned my head quickly and focused my attention on the ropes, trying to hide the smile that had swept across my face, quite against my will, I might add. I had not given that smile permission to take up residence on my face like that, but it had. And it was very inconvenient.

I felt a kind of hot flutter in my stomach, another completely new sensation to me. In all my few days of consciousness, I'd never experienced anything like it. It was a little like the bolt that had turned into the wave, but this time it wasn't residing in my chest so much as residing a little more south of it. *I made a quick mental note to secretly add to my list later that I clearly liked men, and muscular ones at that.*

"It's a lot harder than it looks," Noah said from behind me.

"Don't worry," I called over my shoulder, not looking back at him because I was still trying to swallow away the smile that had consumed my face. "I think I'm a climber!" I put my foot onto the first rope and tried to climb, but the thing swung wildly.

"Whoooo!" I hung on and tried to stop it from swinging.

"It doesn't really keep very still," Maxine pointed out. "You need a strong core."

Core? What was a core? I didn't know what it was, but I was sure I had one.

"It's okay! I have one of those!" I called, and this time I think I heard Noah chuckle. But I wasn't going to let that stop me. In fact, it only spurred me on. It took me a while to get the hang of it, but eventually I was managing. Although it was starting to hurt like hell. My arms and legs and stomach were burning as if on fire. I'd never experienced such bodily, fiery feelings before. Until this moment, I hadn't known they existed. Pain, I understood. But this burning, just below the skin, as if my muscles had been set alight, *well*, that was a new one. But I persisted. Resisting the burn and climbing higher. But when the burn turned into a twitch, a shake, that I could actually see happening in my arms and legs . . .

"OH MY . . . AAAAH!" I yelled as I lost my footing on the rope and disaster struck.

CHAPTER 21

$\mathcal{M}$y feet slipped into the mesh and the force of my body drove my legs all the way through, the ropes climbing my thighs until they finally stopped right at the top. The force of it threw me backwards and I reached out to stop myself, closing my eyes tightly, not wanting to see the ground rushing towards me. Only there was no way I was falling, not with my legs so tightly knotted into the rope mesh. So instead of tumbling out of the thing, which would have actually been preferable, my arms and shoulders slipped into two mesh holes and the force of my fall pushed me right in there. Deep, until I felt the ropes cutting into my shoulders. But it didn't stop there.

My body shook violently, and with each move the ropes kept tightening around me like nooses. And when it was all over, when everything no longer moved, I opened my eyes and looked at the world. I was upside down. Stretched out on my back, my legs wedged in, my arms wedged in, and I was just hanging there.

"Are you alright?" Noah shouted from down below.

"NO! Help!"

"Oh my God!" The usually calm Noah sounded panicked, which unsettled me greatly. Blood rushed into my face and pooled somewhere in my forehead.

"I'm coming," Noah called, and even though all the blood was making my head feel bigger than I think it really was, it didn't stop me having the thought that this was rather gallant of him. Coming to my upside-down rescue.

I watched as Noah started climbing the mesh ropes, followed by Maxine, who was rushing up it like a pro. The shaking of the ropes as they climbed, only seemed to wedge me in even tighter. A small crowd had gathered below, most of them large muscle-bound men, some with their shirts off. Some looked shocked. Some were shaking their head. Some were smiling. Finally, Noah and Maxine reached me. It felt like it took two forevers just to get to me.

"Can you unstick yourself?" Noah asked.

I pulled against the ropes, but my arms and legs were so wedged in there that I couldn't move.

"No," I squeaked in a small voice.

"Right, how are we going to do this?" Noah asked Maxine, who was on my left, while Noah was on my right. I turned and looked at Maxine. She tilted her head as she looked me over.

"Honestly, I'm not sure," she said.

This did not make me feel better.

"Should we try to get her legs out first, or her arms?" Noah asked.

"Mmmm, legs first," she replied after some thought.

Noah looked like he was considering this. "But if we do that, she could flip over and damage her shoulders, unless you can support her weight and stop that?"

"Mmmm, difficult, because the ropes move so much."

"And if we take the arms out first?" he proposed.

"Mmmm, her legs could come loose and then she falls."

"Mmmm." Again, Noah seemed to consider this, and I wondered why they were both saying "mmmm" so much. It was not a sound that filled me with great confidence.

"Maybe someone can catch her at the bottom?" Maxine suggested.

"No! NO! No falling. No catching." I spoke for the first time.

"What if two more people come up and it's done all at the same time? Legs and arms!" someone yelled from down below.

"Yes," someone else replied.

"Yes," someone echoed.

"For sure."

"Let's do that."

"Totally."

Affirmatives rang out in abundance from the small crowd below.

"No!" someone else said, breaking it. "I think the ropes come loose at the top. We could loosen it and catch her as she comes down."

"They don't loosen," someone else confirmed.

"Shit," someone moaned. There was a momentary silence from the crowd, as well as from Noah and Maxine.

"Maybe we should cut her down?" someone offered.

"NO CUTTING!" A man wearing a shirt with the gym logo on came running up. He looked like the manager here. "No cutting."

Another long silence. So loooooong.

Really, very bloody long.

"Where's Mikey?" someone asked.

And then the huge murmur broke out. It was loud and consistent, and the volume of it increased as the seconds passed.

"Yes!"

"Yes, Mikey!"

"He'll do it?"

"Mikey!"

"Him!"

"Yes!"

Everyone seemed to be in agreement now that this Mikey person would be able to fix my upside-down, stuck predicament. I should never have climbed this in the first place. Oh, regrets! Deep ones.

"Call him," someone yelled.

"Call Mikey!" another person echoed.

"Yes, Mikey!"

And then a chorus of "Mikey"s rang out followed by a loud and booming, "I'm here!"

Oooh, now that sound gave me confidence. That was the sound of someone who seemed like he could get me off a rope.

I tried to turn my head, to see who this Mikey was. And when I did, I couldn't stop the shocked sound that flew from my lips.

Mikey was the biggest man I'd ever seen in my like. Granted, my life so far had consisted of the ambulance, to now. But still, I was sure that if I knew what more men looked like, I would still be quite convinced that this Mikey fellow was indeed the largest man in the universe. He was huge, he was shirtless, he was bulging and he was indeed very, very orange. Mikey made his way across the floor, stomping towards me. And even though the floor was made of sponge, I swear his feet made loud thumping sounds as they went.

"Come down," Mikey bellowed to Noah and Maxine, and they obeyed and scurried down. I closed my eyes tightly now. Maybe if they were closed, this whole ordeal wouldn't feel as bad. And then the ropes gave an almighty shake as Mikey began climbing. The ropes shook like they had never shaken before, and then stopped when he finally reached me. I felt what I think was one of his hands, although it was so big it was hard to imagine this as a mere mortal's body part. I felt first my legs untangle, and then my arms, and then a strange and frightening sensation as I felt my body being lifted and tossed! I yelped in fright and heard Noah shout an "It's okay!" from the floor. With my eyes still closed, I had no idea what was happening to me, but when the strange swinging sensation stopped at last, I opened them. And that's when I realized I'd been slung over this mammoth orange man's shoulder.

A big cheer rose up from the gym as Mikey walked with me like that for a while, and I didn't know if I should give one of those waves that the Queen does. It seemed appropriate, for some reason. So, I did. This caused a huge burst of laughter to ring out from the crowd around me. Noah and Maxine were also laughing now. The mood in the room lifted and soon this big muscle-bound man stopped walking. And then, ever so gently, he lifted me off his shoulder and placed me down on a chair. It was almost elegant, the way he'd done it. Like that scene from *Dirty Dancing* when Patrick Swayze lifts Jennifer Grey into the air while they're both having the time of their lives. This, in contrast, though, was not the time of my life.

CHAPTER 22

⌒

"*B*rave and fearless," Noah said as we started walking out of the gym after my ordeal was over.

"What?" I asked.

"Your list. Brave and fearless. Sure, clumsy and bad at climbing, but fearless nonetheless."

"You think?" I asked, trying to decide whether he was right.

"Definitely," Maxine echoed. "I bet you're always doing things like that in life. Trying new things, being fearless."

"I like that," I said with a smile.

We were just about to exit into the parking lot when Maxine poked me on the shoulder. "That's him!" she said.

Noah and I both turned.

"Kyle. @TheKyleWhite101. The guy. The one who broke up with Frankie!"

At that, my eyes zoned in on him and, I must say, for a guy whose girlfriend, or ex-girlfriend, was missing, he looked entirely unperturbed as he drank a green smoothie and flexed his sun-kissed calf muscles in the gym mirror.

"What a douche," Maxine murmured.

I had to concur. Only a total asshole breaks up with someone on social media and then flexes his calves like that.

"I have to get back inside, I have a training session now. But see you guys later." And then Maxine did something unexpected. She pulled me into a hug, as if the two of us were actual friends, and I liked it more than I could say. She ran off and Noah and I walked into the parking lot.

"Brave and fearless," I echoed as we ambled towards our car. "You know." I stopped walking and swung around to face Noah, leaning my hand against a cement pillar. "Maxine was right, this getting to know myself is actually fun. I'm really starting to get a better picture of myself, and now that I think about it, I . . . WHAT THE HELL?" I pulled my hand off the pillar and flung my arm into the air. "Get it off me, get it off me! GEEET!" I yelled as a lizard ran up my arm towards my face. "NOAH! Noah, stop it! Stop it!" I swung my arm in the air in massive circles, jumping and running in an attempt to fling it off.

"It's in my shirt! It's in my . . . NOAH!" I shrieked, as I felt the toe-curling, nauseating sensation of the lizard running into my shirt sleeve and onto my chest. "Nooooo!" I ripped at my shirt, sticking my arms inside and trying to catch it. "Where is it? Where is it?" I jumped around in front of Noah, not caring that we were in a parking lot and some of the people from inside that had stopped to watch me on the rope contraption had stopped to watch me now. I looked down and saw the lizard dart out of my shirt and onto my leg.

"Keep still!" Noah reached for the lizard, which was running around my thigh in circles.

"It's going to go into my paaaaannnntss," I wailed. A wail that was so loud it echoed through the cement chamber of the underground parking lot we were in.

"Stand still. I've almost got it! I've got it!" Noah said, triumphantly holding the creature in the air.

"Oh. My. God!" I was panting from the sheer terror of it all, bent over at the waist, trying to catch my breath.

"Where did it come from?" Noah asked.

"From the pillar. It must have been on it when I put my hand there."

Noah walked over to the pillar and put the lizard back down on it. "There you go," he said.

I ran my hands over my lizard-free body, just to make sure there was nothing on it. I looked at the pillar and noticed that another lizard had joined it.

"There are two now." I pointed. "Wait, three . . ." I watched as another lizard crawled down the pillar. It stopped and raised its head and, I swear, its eyes met mine. *A lizard locked eyes with me!* I took a step back.

"Noah, what's going on?"

"What do you mean?"

"Are they staring at me?" I inched backwards as Noah turned to the pillar. "There are four now!" I pointed a shaking finger at them.

"They're not staring at you," he said.

"They are, and I don't like this. I don't like this at alllll . . . NO!" I turned and ran as two of the lizards leapt off the pillar and started running towards me across the floor. "They're coming for me." I ran across the parking lot, as fast as I could. "Press the button, press the button!" I yelled over my shoulder as I reached the car. I heard a beep, saw the flash of lights, jumped in and slammed the door behind me. I swiveled in my seat and looked out of the rear-view window as Noah walked towards it.

"Hurry!" I shouted, and waved my arm. He seemed to be walking towards the car without a care in the world, as if reptiles had not just been chasing me. He climbed in casually, shut the door and then turned to me and smiled.

"Why are you smiling? Did you see that? They were chasing me!"

Noah laughed. "They were not chasing you, they were just running across the floor."

"Towards me! *Me!* They were looking at me funny, didn't you see that?"

He laughed even more. "I promise you, they were not chasing you."

"Animals hate me! What's wrong with me? Is there something about me, something on me that makes them want to attack me, or run away from me?"

"They don't want to attack you, I'm sure you're just imagin—"

Noah stopped talking and stared at the windshield, his eyes widening.

"What?" I turned and . . . "*Oh my God!* I told you. I told you," I hissed at him, as two lizards clung to the windscreen and glared at me. "They *are* looking at me, can you see it?" I gasped as another one suddenly scuttled up the bonnet and joined them.

"What the hell?" Noah leaned forward and looked at them.

"Quickly, get rid of them!"

"How?"

"Windscreen wiper! Swipe them off!"

Noah reached for the wipers and first a spray of water blitzed the windscreen and then the arm came out and, with a slow, loud, squeaking sound, it moved the lizards off the windshield.

"Thank God," I inhaled sharply with relief.

"NO! They're coming back!" Noah pointed at the ground as the three lizards started running towards us. "Let's get out of here!"

"Quick!" I shouted at Noah as he started the car and then we flew out of the parking lot. When we were a little way away, we stopped the car and both looked out the rear-view window.

"What the hell was with them?" Noah asked.

"I told you, animals hate me."

Noah looked at me and this time he seemed to actually consider it. "Better add it to the list."

"Brave, fearless, bad at climbing and hated by animals, reptiles and birds," I repeated, and Noah burst out laughing.

"It's not funny," I insisted.

"It kind of is, actually," Noah said, and pulled off onto the road again. "We just got swarmed by a group of lizards."

"It's actually a lounge of lizards, by the way," I said, and this made Noah laugh even more, and soon I was also laughing. He looked at me over his shoulder as he drove and flashed me a smile that gave me that same feeling that I'd had before. Warm, and fuzzy and tingly in places that I'm not sure I should even tingle in!

CHAPTER 23

When Noah and I got home, the day passed in a daze of *Game of Thrones*, popcorn and chocolate on the couch. He ate the popcorn while I tucked into the chocolate. The marathon lasted almost all night, and finally, at around 2 a.m., the two of us said our goodnights and retired to our bedrooms. I lay there with a smile on my face. We'd had such fun that day, even the gym incident and the lizard incident had become something to laugh about together. I wondered if this was what friendship was like. You met someone, and from the start, just clicked. You felt so comfortable with them that you could spend an entire day and night with them without getting bored or feeling like you needed your own space.

I closed my eyes, that happy thought filling the space between my ears. I rolled over on my pillow and then . . .

"Oh God." I shot up when I caught a whiff of my armpit, and almost gagged. I needed to give my clothes another wash. I couldn't keep wearing the same clothes over and over again like this, but I didn't have a choice. I wasn't going to ask Noah if I could borrow some of his. I tiptoed out the bedroom and into the bathroom, careful not to wake him. I didn't want to draw attention to the fact I was still wearing the same clothes. Gross.

I stripped naked and wrapped a towel around me, and then, with a bar of soap, I washed all my clothes and hung them up to dry in the shower. I stuck my head around the corner again, to make sure Noah wasn't around, and then scurried back to the room. I climbed into bed and set the alarm on my watch for six. That would give me enough time to wake up before Noah did, I didn't want him to find my undies hanging in his shower.

* * *

In the morning I crept down the hall in my towel. It was still dark and Noah was, thankfully, fast asleep. But when I pulled my clothes out the shower I was dismayed to find them still dripping. I squeezed the pants and shirt as hard as I could. A few drops of water emerged, but not enough to rid them of their dampness. The panties and bra were also moist. I slipped them both on and cringed at the feel of the wet fabric against my skin. It felt disgusting. Like I'd peed myself and my boobs had leaked.

Shit! I had nothing to wear! I mean, I guess I could wear the gym clothes from yesterday, only they were covered in orange-tinged sweat from where Mikey had thrown me over his shoulder.

I grabbed my clothes and waved them around in the air as fast as I could, like a lasso. If only there was something in the world that could spin clothes around like this that wasn't my arm.

Wait! A semi-thought grabbed hold of me. An image, like the merry-go-round, of something else going around.

"Tumble dryer!" I said out loud, thrilled that the word and the image had come to me. And better than that, I actually knew where one was! With a towel around me, I raced through to the scullery off the kitchen, where I'd seen a tumble dryer. I put my clothes in and then looked at all the buttons.

"Mmmm," I mumbled, trying to decide what kind of a spin cycle was right for these clothes of mine. "Thirty minutes . . . I think!"

I looked at the clock on the wall. Hopefully Noah would still be asleep then. I pressed the big "On" button and the dryer sprang to life. The clothes started whirling about, round and round. It was quite a silent dryer, which I was deeply grateful for. I climbed onto the kitchen counter, making sure my towel was covering my lower half—a naked bum on a kitchen counter was not a hygienic thing, I imagined—and watched the clothes through the glass door. The dryer was fairly empty, so when the clothes reached the top they tumbled down to the bottom, where they were then swept up again by the drum. I felt I could draw quite a parallel here to the inside of my brain, which was about as empty as the dryer itself. Only a few thoughts and memories filled it, leaving it largely empty. I wondered if it would ever be filled. And with what stuff?

I must have stared and thought for longer than I'd anticipated, because soon there were only three minutes left on the spin cycle. But just as I was on the home stretch, I heard a door open and close in the passage. I froze, towel clutched to my naked body, and peered down the passage. Noah's bedroom door was open and the bathroom door was closed and the light was on.

"Shhhhiiiit!" I looked at my bedroom door, I could make a run for it, but I might bump into Noah coming out. I rushed to the tumble dryer with the kind of speed I didn't know I possessed, pulled the dryer open, dropped my towel on the floor and then started scrambling into my clothes. The underwear and the pants went on okay. But *not* the shirt, which was now a short-sleeved one with buttons that didn't close. I heard a flush, the taps turned on and off, the door started to open, and still my shirt did not close. I heard footsteps coming towards me and I glanced around frantically.

"Hey," Noah called, obviously aware that I was up.

"Uhh . . . Uh . . ." I flung myself against the wall. Chest first, arms outstretched, as if I was hugging it. It was all I could think to do. I didn't want Noah seeing my boobs! No man had ever seen my boobs—well, not that I remembered anyway!

"You're up early . . . uh, what are you doing?" he asked, coming into the kitchen.

"Nothing," I said, face and chest pressed into the wall.

"What's wrong?"

"Nothing." I tried to put on the most normal-sounding voice, which, ironically, sounded so far from normal it was frightening.

"Uh, it doesn't look that way."

"I'm just stretching." I made a stretching sound and lifted my legs up as well, one at a time, while I kept my chest flat to the wall. "Oooh, feels good. So streeetched."

"Mmmm." Noah sounded amused now.

"It does, feels really, um, stretchy."

"If you want, we can do a stretch session together. I have some mats. We can take this into the lounge. It might be more comfortable there."

"NO! I'm good, all gooooooddd," I said, and then started to slither along the wall. The wall curved now, and I slithered around the curve and into the passage. I heard Noah's steps behind me and saw him watching me out of the corner of my eye.

"What are you doing now?" he asked, sounding more amused by the second.

"Just sliding." I continued to slide down the wall towards my bedroom.

"Sliding? Really?"

"Yup. You know . . . sliiiiding." My bedroom door was in my sights now, but Noah was still following me.

"What exactly is it doing for you?"

"Mmmm, stretching out the chest, you know."

"Interesting technique." He sounded like he was teasing me now. Obviously, he wasn't buying my ridiculous stretching act at all. Who would? And why hadn't I just wrapped the towel around myself? Why had I thrown myself against the wall like an idiot? I could only conclude that my desperate lack of life experiences had caused me to choose this particular course of action, which was, to say the least, utterly absurd!

"What are you going to do when you get to the open bathroom door there?"

"Oh." I stopped slithering and looked at the door.

"Are you going to stop there, or slither into the bathroom and around, pop out on the other side of the door or . . ." I swear I could hear a laugh bubbling up in him, just under his words, and I couldn't take it anymore. So, I stopped my slither and I spun around. I should have done this ages ago!

"Alright, I'm not stretching or sliding." I pointed to my chest, where my cleavage was spilling out and over.

Noah's eyes travelled down to my chest, then they enlarged.

"What happened?" He quickly looked away.

"Apparently, this shirt shrinks in a tumble dryer," I said, feeling defeated.

Noah looked like he was holding down a laugh.

"It's not funny. I don't have any other clothes. This is it. This little quarter of a shirt is all I have left."

Noah looked back at me, his face serious now. "Oh yeah, that's right. I'm sorry, I didn't even think about that. You only have the clothes you went to the hospital in. You must have been wearing them for days."

Sudden mortification hit me. "I washed them! A lot. Especially my underwear. I did wash them! They're clean."

"I should have realized."

I relaxed slightly when I saw that he wasn't looking at my chest at all but right into my eyes.

"It's not your job to think about those kinds of things," I said.

"You should have said something," he added.

I shrugged. "I guess I was embarrassed. I mean, whose clothes would I have worn? It's a bit awkward to ask for clothes. Besides, it's not like I can wear yours."

"I can ask Maxine, I'm sure she won't mind."

I shook my head. "No. I can't. She gave me chocolate and lent me her gym clothes and . . ."

"Wait! I can't believe I didn't think of this!" Noah's eyes lit up excitedly.

"What?"

"I know the perfect place for you to get clothes from."

"Where?" I asked, perking up, but then instantly lost the perk when a thought came to me. "I don't have any money."

His smile grew. "No, these are free."

"Really?" I raised my brows at him.

"Yup!"

CHAPTER 24

~⌒~

A few hours later, when it was a decent hour to call on people, we found ourselves standing outside an apartment building back in downtown Joburg. I'd borrowed one of Noah's T-shirts; it hung to my knees it was so big. I looked around. This place was obviously very cool. This was the kind of apartment that oozed coolness and trendiness. The kind of apartment that artists and other creatives would live in. A brightly colored mural covered the entire side of the building. The painted faces that stared down at me looked familiar, but I didn't quite recognize them until . . .

"Nelson Mandela." I pointed excitedly when one of the smiling faces leapt out at me.

"Yes," Noah said.

"First democratically elected president, jailed for twenty-seven years, recipient of the Nobel Peace Prize, called Madiba, which means father of the nation."

"That would be him," Noah said with a smile.

I smiled back at him, still amazed by the strange way my brain worked. How it was remembering some things in crystal-clear detail, but others were just a blur, and others were still totally out of my reach. I glanced to my left, where a big blue sculpture rose up out of the sidewalk. It was abstract and I liked it very much, even though I had no idea what it was meant to be. I scanned the buildings and started noticing more and more sculptures and pops of color.

Something about the art and the sculptures and the way it seemed so laid back and casual here resonated with me. I couldn't put my finger on it, but it made me flutter inside. Maybe I was an artist? A sculptor. Some creative person? The idea made me happy.

"Who lives here?" I asked.

"My sister."

"Wait, no. I can't borrow clothes from your sister. I don't even know her."

"It's okay, you won't be borrowing *her* clothes."

"Hello!" A voice came through the intercom.

"Hey. It's me!" Noah replied.

"Come up," the voice said, and then the gate buzzed open.

We walked inside and Noah went straight for the staircase and started walking up it. "If it's not *her* clothes I'm borrowing, then whose?"

He looked back at me over his shoulder. "My sister's a stylist for TV and theatre. She has a whole wardrobe of clothes left over from productions, or clothes she made for productions. And she loves dressing people up, so you're in luck!"

"Really," I said, taking the stairs two at a time to keep up with Noah. The man was fit. That's for sure.

"We're here," Noah said, stopping outside a bright yellow door. I looked down the passage. All the other doors were brown or gray, but hers was like sunshine. It made me feel warm from the inside out, as if I'd just swallowed the sun.

"Hey." I heard a voice and then the door opened. Noah and his sister fell into a big hug and, when she pulled away, I found myself looking at the coolest person I'd ever seen. I stared at her for a while, trying to take her all in, but not wanting to be rude.

"Hey there," she said, and also pulled me into a hug.

"Oh. Hi. Thanks." I patted her on the back awkwardly, not sure how to respond.

"Oh, we're a family of huggers," she said quickly, pulling away. "Sooooo. Wow! I mean, wow. Noah told me what happened to you . . . unbelievable!"

I nodded. "I know."

"It's like a storyline from a soapie," she said.

"Sindi!" Noah scolded her.

"It's okay, it does sound like a storyline from a soapie," I said with a smile of genuine amusement, as memories came rushing back to me from soapies that I'd watched. "But it's not as unbelievable as the time Marlena was possessed by the devil on *Days of our Lives*."

"She remembers TV shows more than anything else," Noah explained to Sindi.

"I don't remember that," Sindi said. "I think that was before our time . . . wait, how old are you?"

"I don't know," I replied.

She stepped back and looked me up and down. "You can't be older than thirty, unless you have some seriously good genes or know the secret to eternal youth."

I reached up and touched my face, concentrating on the skin around my eyes, and then looked at the backs of my hands for a while. "Honestly, I have no idea. I could be fifty, for all I know."

"Wow. That's crazy." She looked at me with wide brown eyes.

"It's not crazy," Noah quickly corrected.

"Sorry, I didn't mean it like that," Sindi added.

"Don't worry. I know what you mean. It is crazy that I don't remember things like that."

"It's fairly common after a traumatic event. It's the brain's way of coping," Noah said.

"Oh, stop being all medical for a moment." She gave him a swat. "You're cool to talk about it like this, aren't you?" she asked me.

"I am. I've kind of gotten used to it these last few days, not knowing things. Not that it doesn't freak me out sometimes, but I expect it now. And it's quite nice to talk about it casually."

"Great! Come inside and then we'll see what we have for you." She pulled the door open and gestured for me to come in. I followed her in and let out a happy gasp when I looked around.

"Wow! I love your place," I said, running my hand over a bright green wall and then moving to run a hand over the yellow-and-green Shweshwe wallpaper.

"Thanks. I like color," she replied.

"I think I do too," I said and looked at her again. She wore a bright pink T-shirt tied at the midriff, exposing a flat stomach with a belly ring. Cut-off jeans exposed a big tattoo on her upper thigh and she was barefoot, except for the ring around her toe. Her dark hair was natural, almost a small Afro, and of course I'd noticed she was black and Noah was white, but for some reason this hadn't struck me as being as different as the fact Noah was dressed so plainly, and his house was just as plain, whereas hers was vibrant and bursting with color. I looked from her to Noah and then back again.

"Yes, my brother and I have very different aesthetic sensibilities," she said. "And he will never let me style him." She huffed, as if this was something they argued about often.

He ran his eyes up and down her then gave her a stern, playful look. "That's because you'll probably make me grow a beard and get a topknot!"

"I would never do that to you. Give me some credit. I know what I'm doing."

Noah smiled at her affectionately. "I don't know, I still don't trust you. Not after the way you dressed me up when we were young."

Sindi reached forward and squeezed Noah's cheeks. "But you made such a cute fairy princess." She looked at me. "He really did. Want to see the photos?"

"WAIT. No!" Noah said.

"Yes!" I nodded.

"God, no. Please can you not do this, again?" Noah sounded defeated and he shook his head.

Sindi tsked and pulled a framed photo off the wall and handed it to me. A much younger version of Noah stared back at me. He was dressed in a pink dress, a tiara had been placed on top of his head and his face was smeared with pink makeup. Sitting next to him was a younger version of Sindi. She looked a lot younger than Noah in the photo, but despite that I could see she wore the pants in the family. Literally, she was dressed in a camo army outfit.

"GI Jane and the Fairy Princess," Sindi pointed at the photo. "It's a game we used to play."

"*We*? Correction, a game you used to force me to play!"

Sindi laughed. "It's true. I did hold him hostage."

"And I still bear the psychological scars of that," Noah said on a long sigh.

"Oh, you turned out just fine," she said, then turned to me. "Don't you think?"

I looked at Noah, and a strange, warm feeling fluttered ever so slightly inside my belly. Suddenly I felt desperately shy. I wanted to look away and not answer, but Sindi seemed to be waiting for a response from me.

"Uh. Yes. He's . . . great." The word "great" came out sounding a little peculiar. In a tone I'd never heard myself use before. The tone was soft and breathy-sounding, with a slight lilt to it that made me sound younger than I was, although I had no idea what age I was. But Sindi looked pleased and gave her brother a pat on the back.

"See! I've trained you well. Right . . . give me a moment and then we'll get you some clothes." She scuttled down the passage and disappeared.

I turned to Noah. "Thank you. For having me. For feeding me. For not sending me to a care home, for thinking about the fact I might need clothes and then coming all this way to get some for me."

"I don't mind. Honestly."

I felt my insides warm up even more. The fact that he didn't mind made his gesture even more meaningful. It was such an act of kindness and compassion and I felt I could never take this for granted.

"I . . . I'll find a way to repay you, when I figure out who I am," I promised.

"No need. Really, I'm happy to help."

I was about to open my mouth and protest when his sister returned, this time wearing a pair of bright pink sunglasses and neon-yellow sneakers.

"Where are we going?" I asked.

"The roof. All the apartments have storerooms up there. That's where I keep the clothes. No space for them here."

I followed Noah and Sindi up the stairs and onto the roof. The view was incredible from up here. You could see the treed suburbs below, awash in the brightest hues of reds and orange.

"Did you know that Johannesburg is one of the most treed cities in the entire world?" I heard myself say.

Noah and Sindi both turned and looked at me curiously.

"Don't ask me how I know that, though, or why." I gave a shrug. "But I can also tell you that Pretoria is known as Jacaranda City and has over 70,000 Jacaranda there. I can also tell you that the Jacaranda tree was brought to South Africa in the 1800s from Argentina. They are actually not indigenous."

"I didn't know that," Noah said, shielding his eyes from the sun with his hand. It was directly above us, and it was making the autumn air warm and pleasant.

"Neither did I," I said, "until one second ago ."

"I wonder what other interesting facts you'll suddenly remember," Sindi said, walking to one of the storage lockers on the roof.

"Don't know." I tried to reach inside my brain again for something to grab onto. But once more, I was faced with the same dilemma: the blank nothingness stretching out in front of me. It seemed that I wasn't able to find anything when I looked for it, but rather that it found me when it wanted to. Dr. Cohen had been right: trying too hard to remember anything didn't work. We reached the storeroom and Sindi slipped the key into the lock and turned. And then, she bent down and lifted the door up with a loud whooshing sound. I peered inside. It was dark at first, and then something flew at me out of the darkness.

"Don't worry. Sometimes I get bats in here," Sindi said. "They usually just fly away."

But of course, it didn't fly away . . .

CHAPTER 25

✎

"$\mathcal{U}$h . . . guys," I said, turning in circles as the bat flew around me over and over again.

"That's weird," Sindi said. "They usually can't get out of here fast enough."

"Guuuyys!" I started to feel panicked as it seemed to swoosh towards me, do a full circle around my body and then fly off into the air, only to come straight back for me and repeat the action. I flapped my arms and it darted away from me again, only to turn around once more and fly at me. I fell to my knees with a squeal and crawled as fast as I could into the storeroom, where I hid behind a rail of clothes.

"What is it with me?" I threw my arms into the air when Sindi and Noah came inside. "I've got this weird thing with animals. They all seem to hate me."

"I'm sure it's nothing," Sindi said, flicking the lights on.

"Trust me, it's not. In the last few days I've been attacked by two birds, a rat ran away from me, lizards tried to eat my face and now I've been dive-bombed by a bat!"

"It's true! I can vouch for it," Noah said.

Sindi put her hand on her hip and looked at me. "Maybe you're a pet psychic."

"A what?"

"This chick that lives next door to me hired one when her dog started peeing on the floor. The psychic reckoned that a dog had died in the flat before they moved in and its spirit was still there haunting the place so her dog was marking its territory." We all looked at each other then, as if timed, burst out laughing.

"She paid three hundred Rand a session for it," Sindi said, which made us laugh even more. Once our laughter tapered off I took in my surroundings.

"This is . . . I wasn't expecting so much!" I stared at the racks of clothes in front of me, tightly packed together in rows with a small path down the side that looked like only one person could squeeze down. Sindi walked up to the first rack of clothing and pulled it towards me. All the racks were on wheels, making it easier to move them around in the tight space.

"This is what I was thinking for you," she said, as I walked up to the clothes and looked at them. I ran my hand over them: jeans, T-shirts, some cardigans and pullovers. White, blue, gray, black and beige.

"These are some essentials I keep for shoots. You always need a pair of jeans and a white tee. Try on whatever you like," she said.

"I don't know my size."

Sindi looked me up and down a few times. "You're a small in T-shirts, and I would say a twelve in jeans. You've got a great figure, actually." She took some things off the rack and handed them to me. "There's a makeshift change room at the back, and a mirror, if you want to try these on."

I looked at the clothes in my hands, and back at the clothes on the rack. They all seemed to blur into one another. None of the colors popped or shouted at me. None of the shapes and lines spoke to me like the art on the walls outside had, or Sindi's bright green wall, or the blue abstract sculpture.

"Is this all you have? I don't want to sound ungrateful or anything, but, I don't know. These are all so . . . plain?"

"You don't think these are you?"

"Well, I'm not sure I know what me is, but these don't really seem to be me. If that makes sense." I looked at Noah and he nodded.

"It does," he said.

"I know these are similar to the clothes I went to the hospital in, but those clothes don't feel like me either. Maybe I was going to a smart meeting, maybe those were work clothes or . . . I don't know how to explain it. But blue jeans and beige tops just don't feel like me."

"I have other clothes at the back," Sindi said, "but those aren't ordinary clothes. They're more like costumes that I made for shows . . . stuff like that."

"Let's see," I said, as she led me past the racks to the back of the storeroom. A smallish space had been cleared there and a full-length mirror was attached to one of the walls and, in the corner, a sheet had been draped on a wooden frame to create a changing area.

"I have these." She pointed to the last few racks.

I cast my eye over them and smiled: yellow and blue and green. Bright and bold and twirling together. Twists and pops of color shouting and screaming at me. I reached out and touched one of the items, a long dress, and as soon as my fingertips came into contact with the dress, I knew.

"These. I like these." Excitement made my voice loud and high-pitched. "What are they?"

Sindi laughed. "Those are costumes from the musical *Hair* I did a few years back. I tie-dyed them myself. Very sixties."

"I love them!" I pulled the dress from the rack and held it in front of me. I could feel myself smiling at the piece, as if it was out of my control. As if this unique blend of colors was forcing the smile onto my face. I saw Noah and Sindi exchange a look.

"What?" I turned to Noah. "You think it doesn't suit me?"

"With a smile like that, you'll suit anything," Sindi said, then she looked over at her brother and raised her brows.

"Yes," he said. "With a smile like that . . ." His voice tapered off and I got that rising hot feeling on my skin again.

"Do you want to try it on?" Sindi pulled the curtain aside.

"Okay!" I rushed in, eager to rid myself of the clothes I was wearing and put something on that was more me. The dress in my hand was the most vibrant thing I'd ever touched. The yellow color was in the center of a big circle, like the sun, and from it radiated this bright teal and lime that faded into the surrounding white of the dress.

"Here." Sindi said as a swath of fabric come over the top of the changing-room wall. "This is a headband that goes with the dress, but it's probably waaaay too much."

I took the fabric in my hands: bright yellow sequins and beads and bells hung from it. "I love it."

I whipped my clothes off and then climbed into the dress. It was a maxi, almost touching the floor, and it fell in a way that when you moved from side to side, it swished like water might do. The fabric looked alive. Like it was its own living, breathing creature. The sleeves were long and bell-bottom shaped, gaping open at the elbows and hanging down in long wisps. I wrapped the headband around the top of my head and, when I was happy with it, I pulled the curtain aside and burst back into the room with a flourish, my dress flapping against my legs as if it was being blown by the wind.

"Ta-da!" I announced. I felt like a glowing kaleidoscope of colors. "I love it!"

Noah and Sindi's eyes were fixed on me.

"What?" I asked, incredulously.

But they didn't say anything. Instead they shared a look.

"What?" I pressed.

"It looks great," Noah finally said.

"Amazing!" Sindi echoed. "I love it."

"You guys mean it?" I asked. But the big, warm smiles on their faces as they looked at me made me realize they did.

"It's totally nuts. And only you could pull that off," Sindi said.

"What do you mean?" I asked, intrigued by this statement, which seemed to imply a level of knowing.

"Well, you're clearly really fashionable," she said.

"I am?"

"Well, I'm assuming. You've got great eyebrows, and your

haircut—not many women would wear it so short like that. You're obviously a creative of some kind. And your eyes, so big. You've got this whole fun pixie thing going on."

"Fun pixie? A creative?" I loved the way it sounded. I looked at myself in the mirror again, swooshing from side to side, watching the skirt move rhythmically back and forth.

"Or, maybe you're actually a hippie, arrived on a time machine from the sixties," Sindi said, coming up behind me, adjusting the dress. "Or maybe you grew up in a commune in the forest somewhere, which sort of weirdly makes sense because you know so much about trees."

"You think?" I swung around and looked at her and then Noah, excited by all these sudden theories about me and my possible origins. This was the first time that someone was actually suggesting concrete explanations for who I might be.

"That kind of makes sense, right? Why else would I know about trees? I love that, that maybe I was raised in some wild and free hippie camp. All tie-dye and barefoot. Maybe we lived in treehouses; close to nature. Lots of birds, a babbling brook."

I glanced at Noah, and he was smiling from ear to ear now. That big, tiny-gap smile. "What do you think?"

"I mean, it does sort of make some sense. You were adamant about watering my pot plants and you knew which one should go where."

"I did, right?" I turned back to the mirror. Was this who I was? Some free-spirited hippie? Or maybe a fashionable creative? I swished from side to side again, and the colors all blurred into one then came apart again as the dress stopped moving, I couldn't help myself. I laughed.

"I never thought I would ever hear myself say this," Sindi said, "but this look totally works on you, and in real life, not on stage."

I looked over at Noah again now for additional confirmation and I found it when he started nodding.

"It's you," he said, in such a matter-of-fact tone that I believed him. This was me, obviously!

"And now you have some more things to add to your list," he said.

CHAPTER 26

～

$\mathcal{N}$oah and I climbed back into the car. We'd spent a few hours at Sindi's drinking coffee and talking. I liked her very much. She was certainly the coolest person I'd ever met and I was thrilled when, at the end of the visit, she gave me her phone number and told me to call her whenever I wanted to—as soon as I got a phone.

"You know what's just around the corner?" Noah said to me, as he slipped the key into the ignition.

"What?"

"The building where you had the accident."

"Oh." There was a pause. A moment of epic silence in the car.

"Do you want to go and see it, in case some of your memories come back? I mean, but if it will be too traumatic . . ."

"No! I'd actually like that. I want to see where it happened."

Moments later we pulled up to the building. It was another cool-looking building, much like Sindi's.

"Do you recognize anything?" Noah asked.

"No." I walked towards the entrance and Noah followed. "Nothing about this is even vaguely familiar." I stopped to look at the façade, hoping that something would come back to me. And then I scanned the list of businesses and offices on the wall outside.

A film company. A talent management agency. Bookstore. Gallery. An interiors shop. Clothing store. A lawyer. An investment firm. A cake shop. Even a pharmacy and hairdresser, and so, *so* many more. The list went on forever, and of course there were all the apartments and restaurants too. I could have been here for any reason. I could work here. I could live here. I could have been here because I worked in film. I could have been having my hair done.

I walked towards the elevator. It still had red-and-white danger tape cordoning it off. The doors were open, the shaft was empty and a huge orange cone told people not to go anywhere near it.

"This is it!" I said.

"Yes." Noah came up behind me, speaking to me over my shoulder. He was close. If I took a step back, I would be able to touch his chest.

"Is anything coming to you?"

I shivered and clutched my arms to my body as a cold sensation clawed its way over my skin and made the hairs on my arms stand up. "No. Just a feeling." I clutched myself tighter and the feeling intensified. "I . . . I don't like it," I whispered. "It frightens me."

I felt a hand on my shoulder. Firm. Big. Reassuring. I didn't realize until that moment how much I'd missed the feel of his hand. It had been a day since I'd felt it.

"Let's go. It's not worth it." He turned my body away from the elevator and then looped his arm through mine and walked us out of the building together. People looking at us might think we were great friends. Or even husband and wife. That's how comfortable I felt with Noah. How comfortable his arm felt looped through mine like that.

When we got home, I changed into one of the bikinis that Sindi had given me. She'd bought some for a swimwear shoot, and they'd never been used, so I was going to use them as underwear. I was feeling so much better in my new clothes, and certainly with my new undies. We'd fallen into another *Game of Thrones* marathon and, this time, we talked the entire way through. We kept having to pause the TV to finish what we were saying to each other. But when I started feeling a pain in my abdomen, went to the bathroom and came back out, I was unable to sit down again. Something Noah seemed to notice straight away.

"What?" He looked up at me.

"Um . . ." I started, and then stopped. This was not an easy conversation to have.

"Soooo," I stretched the word out, buying myself time to think.

"Yeeees." He imitated me with an amused smile, as if I was starting some sort of game.

"The thing is . . ." I hesitated.

"Yessss." He stretched out the "s" sound like a snake might do.

"I need tampons!" I blurted out.

Noah's eyes widened. "Oh. OH! Aaaahhh!"

"Overshare. I know. Awkward. But I need them," I gushed.

"Of course." Noah stood up.

"Or pads. Or tampons, or pads, or those little cups, or . . ." I scanned my mind again, looking into the nothingness once more. "I don't know, actually. I don't know what I use." I shrugged.

Weird thought, that. You lose your memory and can't remember what kind of sanitary wear you use. I bet no one had ever thought of that. Those tiny things that go with losing your memory. I wondered what other small things I might encounter along the way like this.

CHAPTER 27

⌒

$\mathcal{I}$ stood in the sanitary-wear aisle at the pharmacy. Noah was hanging back. I didn't blame him. I scanned the row. So, so many different things to choose from. I walked the aisle once, looking carefully at everything as I went, hoping that something would look familiar, but it didn't.

"I'm Andi. Can I help you?" a young-looking girl with bleached hair and a nose stud asked.

"I like that." I pointed to my own nose. She seemed confused for a moment and then smiled.

"Thanks."

"Did it hurt?" I carried on looking at the pink stone glinting from the side of her nose.

Andi shook her head. "Not really. Maybe like a bee sting." And then she gestured to the products behind me. "Anything specific you're looking for?"

"I don't know," I said, wondering what I would look like with a nose ring.

"Are you looking for sanitary wear?"

"I am."

"Well, which brand do you use? If we don't have it, I can go and check in the back. Some of the stock hasn't been unpacked yet."

"I actually don't know," I confessed. This seemed to elicit a really strange look from her. She dragged her eyes over me, up and down, and then up and down again.

"How? I mean . . . sorry, I don't mean to offend you or anything, but you seem to be in your mid-twenties so . . . how do you not know what brand you use?"

"I lost my memory," I said.

"You what?"

"I was in an accident a few days ago." I pointed to my head and her eyes followed my finger there. "And I've lost my memory."

"Wait . . ." She took a step forward, looking intrigued. "You have no memory? Of anything?"

I shook my head. "Nope."

"Seriously? That's . . . hectic." She stepped closer to me and eyed the wound on my head.

"I don't even know my name," I added.

"That's so weird." Her face lit up, as if this was the most interesting thing she'd ever heard. And then she turned to Noah. "Are you her boyfriend or husband who is trying to make her fall back in love with you or something, like in that movie?"

I felt my cheeks go a little red at the mention of Noah as my boyfriend, and I was sure Noah's went a little red too.

"Noah is the paramedic who saved me," I said quickly, in case he was also feeling uncomfortable.

"That's even better," she gushed. "You save her life, and she has no memory, but she falls in love with you, even though she actually has a husband or fiancé or whatever in her life."

"I don't have a husband, or a fiancé," I said, and held my hand up. "No ring."

"True!" she said, looking me up and down. "And you don't have kids either . . . although those are on the horizon pretty damn soon! Sooner than you know, actually!" She smiled at me and then looked at Noah then back to me.

"Wait, how do you know that?"

"I'm psychic."

"Really?" I flashed Noah a look.

"Yeah, but I work here. Obviously, card reading doesn't really pay the bills . . . I KNOW!" she suddenly gasped.

"What?"

"Let me do a reading for you!" She rushed to the counter and skidded back seconds later carrying a dirty, well-thumbed pile of cards. She held them in the air with a kind of reverence that made Noah and I both stop and stare. "These were my grandmother's. She was also psychic. That's where I got my gift from. Here . . ." She thrust them at me. "Think of a question, really focus on it and then shuffle the deck and split it into three parts."

I looked at Noah for some kind of reassurance and he gave me a shrug. "Okay." I closed my eyes as I held the cards and I asked the question. It really was the only question to ask right now anyway.

Who am I?

I repeated it over and over again as I let the cards move through my hands. When I was finished, I opened my eyes and looked at her.

"So, three piles, lay them here." She patted the top of one of the counters. I laid the piles down and then she slowly reached out and turned each card over. Noah and I leaned in as she stared at them. A sense of anticipation rose up in the air around us.

"This is your past, this is your present, and this is your future." She tapped each one with her finger and Noah and I stared at her as she zoned out while squinting at the cards, as if they were conjuring images in her brain. "Mmmm, interesting. Very interesting."

"What? What?" I asked, totally caught up in this moment now. The door of the pharmacy suddenly opened, and we all looked up.

"Sorry, closed," Andi shouted at the woman in the doorway.

"You look open," she said, looking confused.

"Nope!" Andi waved her hand at the woman. She didn't seem convinced, though. "Stock-take!" Andi pointed at the shelf and the woman gave one more confused look and then left.

"And?" I asked. The anticipation was killing me.

"When the Six of Swords is reversed like this, it means that you may be going through a personal or spiritual transition. You're in the process of leaving behind and ridding yourself of a relationship, belief, or behavioral pattern that is no longer good for you. This is a very, very personal and private journey for you, but it doesn't mean you have to take it on your own. Be open to the new people in your life that can help you. Embrace your new way of thinking and living."

"Mmmm," Noah and I both mumbled together.

"And this one, this is your present. The fool."

"The fool? That sounds terrible."

"Not at all, the fool is a joyful card. He shows up at the beginning of a journey as well. One filled with optimism and courage and freedom from the usual constraints in life. He approaches each day as an adventure, in an almost childlike, naïve way. He believes anything is possible and opportunities are just ahead. The world is waiting to be explored and he is excited to uncover it all."

"That sounds exactly like you," Noah said.

"I know!" I couldn't believe how accurate this was all sounding. "And my future?" I asked.

"Filled with love," Andi replied straight away. "These are the lovers, and they mean that your soul mate is just around the corner. True love is coming. It might be closer than you think."

"Wow!" I looked around excitedly.

"Oh, and those are the tampons you should take." She turned and pointed at a bright pink box. "Pink is your spiritual color."

"It is?"

"Yup! Pink is romance and sensuality and femininity."

"Really . . . ?" I took the box, feeling very introspective.

"Yeah, so now you know some things about yourself," she said.

I nodded at her and then pulled my piece of paper out. I put the box back on the shelf momentarily and flattened the paper out.

"What are you doing?" she asked.

"Writing down the things I know about myself."

Romantic.

Sensual.

Feminine.

I wrote those after the other things I'd discovered about myself today.

Fashionable.

Creative.

Maybe a hippie!

I sighed happily and was just about to put the list back when Andi told me to take her number. I scribbled it down, and I was told to call it whenever I needed to. It sounded vaguely cryptic, but apparently, I would know when I needed to call her, and she would be expecting it too.

A while later Noah and I walked out of the shop. I almost skipped across the parking lot, swinging my shopping bag from side to side. I was excited. I knew more about myself than I had in days, and all of it felt right for some reason that I couldn't explain.

CHAPTER 28

*T*here was a long, slow knock on the front door and Noah and I both spun around. There was something about that knock that made us both sit up a little straighter. We'd gone from relaxing and slouching in front of *Game of Thrones* to both looking at the door with suspicion.

Noah glanced at his watch. "It's almost seven. No one comes around this late." He got up off the couch and walked towards the door. It was a slow, deliberate walk and when I followed so was mine. It was as if we could both sense something coming. Something important lurking behind that door. But what?

He looked at me and raised his brows before pulling the door open, a gesture that kind of conveyed an *"are you ready?"* sentiment. As if he already knew that whatever, or whoever, was behind that door, pertained to me. I nodded at him, and he inched the door open. As soon as he did, I knew exactly what this was about.

"Detective!" I looked down at the file in his hands. "You know who I am!"

"I do." He smiled at me, as if this really mattered to him.

"Well, tell me!" I declared enthusiastically.

"Your name is Zenobia."

"Zzzz—what?"

"Zenobia," he repeated.

"I'm sorry, I don't think I heard you right. Did you say Zenobia?" I repeated the name. I didn't feel like a Zenobia at all.

He nodded and I looked to Noah in horror.

"I think people call you Zen for short, because we found your Facebook page."

"I have a Facebook page?"

"You do. You haven't actually posted anything there, though. Just a profile picture."

"Oh," I said flatly, my enthusiasm starting to wane.

"You haven't really friended anyone there either," he added.

"You're probably not into social media," Noah offered.

I nodded. This was probably true. "What's my surname?"

"Small," he said.

"Small? Zenobia Small?" I said, trying to take this in. Trying to take in these two names that seemed so incongruous to the person I thought I was. These would not be the names I would have chosen for myself. I thought my name would be big, not, literally, small.

"How old am I? Where am I from? Where do I work?"

"You're twenty-nine, turning thirty in a month. You live thirty minutes away from here. In an apartment in Fourways. The Main. Apartment 3C," he continued to explain, reading from the file now.

"The Main," I said, letting the words roll over my tongue, hoping that they would sound familiar in some way. But they didn't. They were as foreign to me as Zenobia Small.

"Where do I work?"

"You work at an advertising agency."

At this I perked up. I worked in a creative field. I knew it. I was a creative. I shot Noah a huge smile and he smiled back. I was a creative! Just like I thought.

"And am I . . . I—" I looked over at Noah and for some reason felt a rising warmth in my cheeks. "Married?"

The detective shook his head. "Not that we can find."

"No kids?"

He shook his head again.

"Parents?"

"Yes, you have two parents. They live in KwaZulu Natal."

"Wow! That's great. I'm sure they've been really worried about me, wondering where I am. I'll phone them as soon as I can. And do I have any siblings?"

"No."

"I'm an only child, I must be close to my parents," I said, feeling thrilled by this information.

"All the information you need is in here." Detective Ndaba handed me the file. There wasn't a lot of information in there at all, though. "It's very thin," I said. "Is this my life?"

"We only looked for the basics. I'm sure when you start remembering and learning about your life you'll find it to be much fuller than this," he said with a warm smile. And of course, he was right. My file was certainly going to be much fuller than this. Thirty years on this planet would make for a very full file indeed.

"Thank you so much, Detective." Noah stepped forward and shook the detective's hand, and I threw my arms around him and gave him a hug before he turned to go.

"Wait, how did you find me in the end?" I called after him.

"Well, we ran your prints and got a hit, but we also found a missing person report. It was filed today."

"By who?"

"His name is in the file. I can't remember it. But he lives in the same building you do. Apartment 4C, right above you."

I flipped the file open and scanned the words on the page until I found it. "Eugene Bester," I read.

"That's the one."

"Eugene," I repeated. "He must be a friend of mine. Shame, he must have been worried," I said to Noah as the detective walked back to his car. I clutched the file to my chest, a sense of building exhilaration made me feel like I could grow wings and fly, but then that feeling quickly disappeared. "I'm going to be honest, though, I don't really like my name."

"It's not that bad," Noah insisted. "It could be a lot worse."

I eyed him incredulously. "How could it possibly be worse than that?"

"It could be . . ." He paused and thought about it. "X A 12, or something."

I smiled. "Who would name their child that? You just made that up."

"I didn't. I'm sure my sister told me that Elon Musk named his kid that."

I scrunched my face up. "But Zen. Zen Small. If you'd asked me to choose any name for myself ten minutes ago, it would not have been that."

"Let me see the file." Noah held out his hand and I passed it to him. He walked over to the coffee table and placed it down. He grabbed a pencil and started drawing on one of the pages.

"What are you doing?" I asked.

"Hang on." He held his hand up, silencing me, as if he was deep in concentration. And then when he was done, he pushed the paper towards me and I bent in to read it.

"Zoe?" I read out loud.

"It's a partial anagram."

"Zoe," I repeated. "Zo-eee. I kind of love that."

"Zoe," Noah said, and this time, something about the way he said it, about the way it sounded coming out of his mouth, I knew! I just knew it was right!

"ZOE! That should be my name. My name should be Zoe!" I said excitedly. "My name is Zoe and I'm a graphic designer, or a copy-writer, or something cool like that!"

Noah smiled. "Makes sense, Zoe."

"Oh my God. That is the first time you've said my name—well, the name I've just given myself, which is so much better than Zen. So maybe my parents didn't have the most up-to-date ideas when it came to naming, but I love this. Zoe!"

"It suits you," Noah said, his face so bright with that smile spread across it. "So, shall we go to your apartment?"

"Now?" I asked.

"Aren't you desperate to see what Zoe's life looks like?"

"I am, but are you okay with that? I mean, it's seven and it's getting late and—"

"I'd love to!" He reached for his car keys, and a thought came to me.

"Wait, I bet that key on my keyring is for my apartment." I rushed back to the room and picked up the strange keyring with the small, single key on.

I was about to discover who I was, and I couldn't wait!

CHAPTER 29

~

*T*he detective was right. I lived exactly thirty minutes away from Noah. The suburb we drove into was very different to Noah's, though. His had trees and green sidewalks; this was a built-up suburb that contained row after row of apartment developments and hardly any greenery. This struck me as odd. *Why would I choose to live in such a place?* But maybe there were other reasons I hadn't considered. Maybe this was close to my work? Maybe this was all I could afford? So many questions that were surely about to be answered. We parked in the visitors' parking lot and walked into the building. I was just minutes away from putting the last pieces together and finding out who I was. I'd solved much of that mystery already. I was just waiting for the final pieces to fall into place. I saw a doorman and quickly made a beeline for him.

"Hey," I called out happily, sure he would know me.

And he did! I could see it the second his eyes met mine. His eyes widened as a look of recognition swept over his face. He'd probably been wondering where I was this last week. I smiled, hoping to match his smile, the one that was surely about to come. Only it didn't. He didn't smile. At all. Not even vaguely. Not even a little twitch of one on the corner of his lips. The shadow of a twitch even. Instead, he looked down and picked up a pencil and paper. He tapped the pen against the desk, as if . . . *he was avoiding me?*

"Hey," I said again, and this time he mumbled something that I couldn't quite hear. This would be the first person I'd met that knew me. The *real* me.

"Sorry, what? I didn't hear you," I said.

"Good evening, Miss Small," he said, not making eye contact.

"Good evening!" I looked behind at Noah and shot him a thumbs-up. "Did you hear that? He called me Miss Small!"

"How are you today?" I asked, turning back to him. At that, his eyes flicked up quickly, he scrunched his face, crinkled his brow and then he looked over my shoulder at Noah. He seemed to stare at Noah, and I wasn't sure why. Finally, after what felt like forever, he looked up at me briefly and then back down at his pencil.

"Fine," he said flatly, as if he was putting as little effort as possible into his answer. It didn't sound like a warm "fine" or a happy "fine." In fact, it didn't sound *fine* at all.

"That's great," I declared, waiting for him to ask me if I was also fine. But he didn't. He started tapping his pencil against the paper instead and then, with his other hand, reached for his phone. Well, maybe we weren't so close. Maybe we didn't know each other that well. Maybe he hadn't worked here for that long. Maybe our paths hardly crossed. Maybe we didn't have conversations at all. He was a doorman—maybe he liked to maintain a level of professionalism. I could respect that.

Noah walked up to me and I felt a hand on my shoulder. It was a very brief squeeze, but I could feel he was trying to convey something in it.

"Let's go," he said softly. His tone had taken on a cadence that I hadn't really heard before. There was something in his voice. An anticipation of something. *Of what?*

We walked to the other side of the hall, where the elevators were, and when I reached out and pressed the button I wondered how many times I'd done this. But when the elevator doors opened . . . *I froze.*

"Let's take the stairs," Noah said, reading my body language.

"It's okay. I think I can do it."

"Are you sure? I mean, there's no pressure. If you're afraid of something, it's fine. It can take a while to get over it. When I was five, my parents got a clown for my birthday party and I was so terrified of it that I screamed and ran away and I've never been able to look at one again. So I get it."

"No. I can do this. Besides, I'm too excited to see the inside of my apartment. I can do this." I must have said this with a little more confidence than I was feeling inside, because Noah didn't look convinced. But he gave me a warm, supportive smile as we walked into the elevator together. The last time we'd been in an elevator together, the circumstances had been totally different. I walked to the far end and leaned my back against the cool steel wall and watched as the door started closing in front of us. I saw some people coming for the elevator and I rushed to stop the doors closing.

"Hey, come in," I said to the two women standing by the lift, arms weighed down with shopping bags.

"Uh . . . hey," one stuttered, and avoided eye contact with me, while changing the hands holding the heavy-looking bags.

"Come in, your bags look heavy," I said, with an encouraging smile. The two women looked at each other for a moment and then turned back to me.

"We'll take the next one," one said, taking a step backwards.

"There's plenty of space," I offered.

"It's fine," the other one said, also taking a step back.

"Oh." These two women were looking at me like they knew exactly who I was. I felt a hand pull mine off the door button gently.

"They'll get the next one," Noah said, and the doors started to close again.

I gripped the railing that ran the length of the wall and held on tightly as it started to move. I tried to steady myself when it gave the tiniest shudder.

"Are you sure you're alright?" Noah asked.

"Are you really afraid of clowns?"

"Yes. It's nothing to be ashamed of, or so my old therapist told me once. Apparently, a fear of clowns is a common thing."

I chuckled as he put his hand on his hip. It looked like an attempt to make himself a little more manly.

"I wonder if I'm afraid of anything?" I mused.

"Nah. I doubt it. You're afraid of nothing. Look at you riding the elevator like nothing happened. Eating the hottest chili in the world, and climbing that thing at the gym . . ."

"Yeah," I said, "I'm badass that way, aren't I?" The elevator continued to rise until it stopped with a ding.

"*You have arrived at floor three. Floor three,*" a stilted-sounding American voice said. I looked around to see where it was coming from.

"*Doors closing in ten seconds. Depart now. Depart now,*" it said in that deadpan tone.

I flicked my eyes in Noah's direction and we both laughed.

"Well, that was completely unnecessary."

"Totally."

We stepped out of the elevator and surveyed the area. This was it. This was where I lived.

CHAPTER 30

⟋

A corridor to our left, a corridor to our right. I looked up at the numbering on the wall and then pointed.

"This way." I was so excited I almost skipped down the corridor. I was only seconds away from seeing it all. My life. No doubt there would be color and maybe even patterned wallpaper like at Sindi's. The walls were sure to be pink, or maybe purple. There would be lots of plants. *Oh God! Who had watered them in my absence, poor things?* Feathers and fluff and sequins and shine and sparkle and romantic rose-pink whimsy. All the things that I'd come to understand about myself in the last week. As I got closer to my apartment, the excitement felt like it would explode out of me. Like a fizz of champagne following a cork into the air. And I was almost there. Only a few doors to go, and then . . .

"Hello! Hey!" I put my arm in the air and waved at an old lady standing in the corridor. I gave her a huge smile—this was my neighbor, after all—but she didn't smile back. She turned her back on me quickly and started making her way back inside.

"Wait!" I called out and picked up my pace. "Sorry, didn't you hear me?" Poor dear, maybe she was hard of hearing.

The woman stopped, but she didn't turn around to look at me.

"It's me," I said. "Your neighbor." Maybe her eyesight wasn't that good either.

The woman's shoulders slumped and she turned to face me, her eyes firmly fixed to the floor.

"I know who you are," she said. "We've been neighbors for six years."

"Wow! My neighbor." I extended my hand for her to shake. I'm sure she was a little confused by this, I mean, we must have met hundreds of times and now I was reintroducing myself to her. And we probably hugged after six years.

"You probably think it's quite odd that I'm wanting to shake your hand, don't you? The thing is, I've been missing for almost a week. I'm sure you noticed. And I had an accident, so I've lost my memory. I know that sounds odd, but it's true. So hello, again! Even though we've met a million times before. Should we hug instead? Maybe we hug?"

The lady looked down at my hand coldly. "We don't hug. And we've never *really* met."

"What do you mean? I've been your neighbor for six years. How have we never met when we live next door to each other? And for so long?"

She gave me a small smile. But it wasn't a warm smile, it was a sarcastic one. "You keep to yourself a lot. You could say."

I shook my head at this information. It seemed completely at odds with who I was. I was a good friend, after all. It was on the list. "What do you mean, I keep to myself?"

"Well, for the past six years, I've barely seen you. You've barely said a word to me. I did try. In the beginning, when you moved in. I came to visit, I brought cookies and a casserole, but you told me you didn't eat sugar and beef."

"What! Of course I eat sugar. I love sugar. And beef. I had the best beef taco the other day, didn't I?" I looked at Noah for confirmation, but he didn't give me what I was looking for, other than a strange look. "Right, Noah?" I asked again. "Beef! Sugar!" And then I turned to my neighbor again. "I eat them. I do."

"That's not what you told me." Her lips were pursed together tightly and her tone was acerbic. "You seemed to have no interest in eating my gifts or in getting to know me. In fact, you go out of your way to avoid me in the corridor every time you see me. And it's a narrow corridor. I've gotten very used to you turning your back on me when you see me and walking in the opposite direction."

"That's . . . impossible! I'm sure you must have just misinterpreted it?" I sounded desperate now.

"No misinterpretation, dear. In fact, when you told me never to bring you baked goods and casseroles anymore, I think I got the message pretty loud and clear." She sounded hurt. "And when I invited you to the Christmas party that we were all having here in the garden, you said you would rather be alone and Christmas held no meaning for you and I should not invite you to things like that ever again."

"What?" I stood there open-mouthed. This information was in no way at all, even vaguely, compatible with the person I thought I was, or the list I had, or the things that Andi had said to me. And then she turned and slipped her keys into her door and opened it. A cat came out of the door to greet her. It twisted around her ankles and then stopped when it saw me. It gave me a loud hiss and then ran back inside, as my neighbor walked in and closed the door behind her. I blinked a few times as I tried to take this in, but I couldn't. It was just too bizarre. I turned to face Noah. The look on his face had changed. He looked . . . *concerned?*

He moved closer to me and laid that hand on my shoulder again. That calming hand. That hand that had held mine in the ambulance, that hand that I can't explain why, but it gave me so much comfort. The hand that felt vaguely familiar in the strangest way that I wasn't able to put my finger on at all. But it felt none of those things now.

"What's going on?" I asked, salty tears itching in the corners of my eyes. "People are not greeting me warmly. People haven't noticed I've been gone. People don't seem to like me."

"Maybe . . ." he said really slowly, dragging out the word in a way that made me know he was about to say something serious that might offend me. "Maybe you're really busy. A high-powered creative at an ad agency. You don't have time for chatting."

"Maybe?" I was struggling to wrap my head around this. "No. This is all a misunderstanding. Maybe the doorman is new and doesn't really know me. Maybe my neighbor misinterpreted what I said. I mean, why wouldn't I want to go to a Christmas party? Everyone likes Christmas, right?"

"Not everyone," Noah said softly, almost sadly.

"What do you mean?"

"Oh, nothing. Just thinking out loud."

"No! This is all a misunderstanding, and I'll prove it to you." I stomped to my door, took the key in my hand and then slid it into the lock. It was hard to get in, even though it fitted perfectly, and that was because I was shaking. Shaking from a mixture of excitement and nerves. But also shaking from something else. A sense of foreboding, looming behind that door.

"Wait." I turned.

"What?"

"I'm not sure. I don't know, but I have this feeling that I can't explain," I said.

"Maybe it's the start of a memory," Noah offered.

I nodded. "Maybe. Maybe not."

"You can do this." But he didn't sound entirely sure, and this unnerved me.

I went back to the door and turned the key. It clicked, I paused and then pushed . . .

CHAPTER 31

*T*he door swung open, revealing a dark passage in front of me. It was so dark, it seemed abandoned and dead. I shivered as I took my first step inside. It was cold in here too. Instinctively, I reached for a spot on the wall and found the light switch. I flicked it on and the passage brightened, but it didn't spring to life. Those were two very different things, as I quickly discovered.

The passage still looked dead; the only difference was that now that death was lit up. I walked down the dead passage and scanned the walls as I went. Their emptiness and starkness not only struck me as odd but left me feeling utterly cold. The walls lacked life, color, clutter or any mark that told you that a person lived here. I looked down at my feet. Two white envelopes with my name on the front lay there. I bent down and picked them up.

"*Where are you? Get hold of me. Eugene,*" the first one read. And the second: "*Where are you? I can't find you, I need to speak to you. Eugene.*"

I looked up at Noah and waved the letters. "From Eugene, the guy that filed the missing person report." I stood up and walked down the passage. It ended in a small living room. I reached up and laid my fingertips on the light switch. The act had a familiarity to it, as if my muscles remembered doing it, even if my head didn't. But when the lights went on, when everything in front of me was illuminated, I took a step back in shock as I stared into the space in front of me.

Beige.

That was the only way to describe it. Not white, not brown, not even cream. But this strange in-between nothing color that covered absolutely everything. Covered the floor. The curtains, the furniture. *Surely this wasn't where I lived?* I could not live here. There was no way I lived here. I liked pink and purple and shine and pattern, and everything about this place was the antithesis of that. It was cold, boring, clinical even. Which surprised me even more, because it had become clear to me that I hated hospitals.

"This can't be where I live," I said.

Noah shook his head in what could only be disbelief. He ran his eyes over me, looking at my clothes and then at the room. He glanced between me and the room and back again.

"The key fits in the lock, right?" I asked the question even though it was a stupid one and, clearly, I knew the answer to it already or else we wouldn't be standing here inside the strange beige dead place. I took a few steps into the living room. I'd never seen anything so neat, so precise, so perfect, so surgical in my entire life. Even more so than the hospital. There was hardly any furniture in the room either. Other than the beige couch and a small coffee table. Oh look, a pop of color! A single brown scatter cushion on the couch. All the remote controls were lined up perfectly on the table, a couple of magazines, a book, all in a straight line. As if someone had taken a ruler and made sure everything was just so!

I couldn't live here, could I?

I started scanning the walls again for pictures, photos to confirm that I was indeed the owner of this place, but again, nothing. No evidence pointing towards the fact that I was the person that lived here. Who didn't have any photos on their walls? Any pictures?

I walked into the open plan kitchen area. White countertops sparkled and gleamed back at me, as if they had been recently cleaned. A long row of cleaning products, anti-bacterial wipes and anti-bacterial sprays were the only flashes of color in the entire place. Bottles of blue, pink, orange and green were the only things that looked alive around here. How ironic that the only living-looking things were the things designed to kill.

"You're neat," Noah commented.

"Apparently," I mumbled.

"I . . . would never have guessed," he said quietly.

"Me neither." Noah was staring at the cleaning products, and I could see he was trying to reconcile these things with the person in front of him. Hell, I was. Up until ten minutes ago I was sure I was the girl that left the lid off the toothpaste and a dirty dish or two in the sink. I made a mess in the kitchen when I tried to cook. That was me, not this . . .

I picked up one of the bottles of disinfectant. "*Kills 99% of all known bacteria and germs.*" I put it back down on the countertop and walked over to the fridge, wondering what surprises would greet me there. I was expecting spices and chilis, coffee, chocolate and Coke and all those things that burst with flavor that I *knew* I loved. But there was nothing in the fridge other than a row of neat water bottles. One carton of soy milk, seven green apples and half a bag of sugar-free gummies. I opened the freezer and there, to my absolute surprise, were rows and rows of neatly stacked ready meals. I pulled one out and looked at it. Chicken breast. Brown rice. Broccoli. Organic, antibiotic free, allergen free, Non-GMO and dairy-free. I turned the box over and read the ingredients; there were no spices in this whatsoever. Nothing to give this plain lump of chicken meat and veg any flavor whatsoever. I reached in and took out another frozen meal . . . chicken. I took out another one, chicken again. And another one . . . also chicken!

"This is all I eat?" It was a question that I was posing to myself. To a myself that I didn't know at all. "Is this what I eat every single day?" This looked like the blandest meal on the planet. This looked like, if someone had to deliberately go out of their way and intentionally try to create the world's most tasteless meal, this would be it. And I ate it. And clearly I ate a lot of it.

I dropped the frozen boxes on the counter. They hit it with a loud bang. One dropped to the floor and I kicked it out the way with my foot, a spark of anger igniting in me. I grabbed at the other kitchen cupboards and started flinging them open. Two boxes of All Bran Flakes—that was it. I opened another cupboard and found four sugar-free protein bars. Vanilla flavor.

"What's . . . what's . . . how . . ." I stuttered, and slammed the kitchen cupboards and rushed out of the kitchen to the door I'd seen at the other end of the lounge. I opened it, flicked the lights on and as soon as it was all illuminated my fears were yet again confirmed and a terrible feeling started growing deep inside my belly.

CHAPTER 32

ᕲ

Beige. White. Only a bed. Single bed. One pillow. A side table with a bottle of disinfectant spray. I scanned the walls again for something, anything, that told me there was life here. That anyone with any kind of life had once been here. But the walls were as dead and cold as a mortician's slab. I walked inside and pushed open the door to the en suite bathroom. And once again, I walked into a white tomb. This was a place where people came to die. Where personalities came to die. This place was like a vortex that sucked life out of things. I looked at myself in the bathroom mirror. This colorful thing reflected back at me in this clinical room. The two pictures side by side like this were a complete oxymoron.

That feeling in my belly grew . . .

The colorful version of myself had no place here. The version Andi had told me about, and I was convinced I was. It didn't belong here. It *couldn't* belong here. *I* couldn't belong here. I caught Noah looking at me in the mirror. He had a look smeared across his face. The look was hard to truly understand. It seemed to be a mixture of so many things that it would take me ages to pull it all apart. But at the very top of it, the core, the one I could see most clearly, was concern.

This was confirmed seconds later when he asked me how I was feeling. I spun around and faced him in the small, white bathroom. I shook my head. That was all I could do. I don't think I was able to put words to the feelings I was experiencing right now. *How could I*

have been so wrong about something like this? Something so funda-
mental, like who I really was. I'd been convinced that in the last few
days I'd managed to piece parts of myself together, but it was clear
from this place that I'd been sorely mistaken. The picture I'd had of
myself had been utterly incorrect. Fundamentally wrong.

The feeling in my belly twisted and thrashed as if it were alive . . .

I pushed past Noah and rushed back into my bedroom. I put my
hands on my hips and glared at the bed, glared at the walls, empty
and dead, glared at the bottles of germ killer. I raced back into the
lounge and did the same thing, scanning everything around me
angrily. As if it all offended me. Which it did. I scanned the corners
of all the rooms again to make sure I hadn't missed anything—a pot
plant, some greenery, something alive to tell me that a zombie didn't
live here. But there was nothing. A crushing feeling in my throat as
the monster in my belly rose up into it, forcing tears into my eyes as
well. I collapsed onto the couch, utterly defeated. Everything that
had made me feel alive and buoyant only a short while ago had been
sucked out of me by this place and the realization that I was *nothing*
like the person I thought I was. My head fell forward and I put my
elbows on my knees, unable to hold up the weight of this realization
on my own. I felt Noah sit on the couch next to me.

"This is who I am," I said, hanging my head even lower, as the
invisible weight pushed down on me. "I'm not the person on my list."

There was a pause, as if Noah was gathering his thoughts. I could
almost feel him pulling them towards him, as if they had been scattered across the room itself.

"This is *not* who you are." He reached over and wrapped his big
hand over my tightly clasped ones.

"It is. Look around, Noah." I raised my head and started pointing
at things. "I'm not pink. Or purple, or sequined and bright." I shook
my head. "I am beige and brown and dry, spiceless chicken breasts in
little frozen containers." As I said this, I could feel all the previous
ideas about myself being painfully ripped away from me, dissolving

into the bland, muted tones of my surroundings. The once-bright colors swallowed up by the insipid.

"You are pink!" he said firmly, squeezing my hand. "And you're not spiceless chicken breasts. You're chilis that are too hot for mere mortals to eat and that get you a photo on a wall of fame!"

I shook my head. "I'm not. Can't you see, nothing about this place is even vaguely pink and chili-ish." I pushed Noah's hand away and stood up. I walked into the middle of the room, and threw my hands in the air. The feeling in my belly had grown so big that it had pushed itself out into the world and into this room, and I wasn't able to control it or swallow it back down.

"Look! There are no plants here. There is not a single sign of life in this place. Not even a fresh bloody head of lettuce, or a real vegetable in the fridge. Even those are dead and frozen and boxed and packaged. And this room! Look at it. It's as if someone—*me, apparently*—went out of their way to find the most boring, muted tones to paint the walls. And these surfaces, de-cluttered, de-contaminated, de-germed, de-everything! Like a hospital. This place is a bloody hospital. And I hate hospitals. So why would I live here?"

I rushed into my bedroom again, Noah followed and I took up a position in the middle of the room. I repeated my action, throwing my arms into the air. "And look at this. A bedroom is meant to be a person's sanctuary. Look around. What the hell does this say about me if this is my supposed sanctuary!" I flung the wardrobe open now, my feelings running away with me. "Look! Look! What do you see?"

Noah came up next to me and peered over my shoulder, I turned to face him and raised my brows. He didn't say anything. "Well, what do you see?" I pressed.

Noah ran his hand over the clothes inside the cupboard. "I see the same thing."

"Exactly. You see the same thing over and over again. Repeated. Slight color variations, but the same thing. I must wear the same clothes every single day. Beige, gray, navy or black slacks. White, gray, navy or black button-up shirt. And look at these shoes, they're utterly hideous. I clearly choose comfort over looks, that's for sure."

"Well, maybe you need to be . . . practical? For your job? Perhaps you're on your feet a lot."

"Practical? I'm a graphic designer or a copywriter, I'm sure I sit all day and I . . ." I paused. "Wait, I'm not a creative. I can't be." I face-palmed and held my head in my hands. "Oh God. How is this possible? That I got everything so wrong?"

"Hey, hey." Noah reached up for my shoulder again, but this time I sought no comfort from it at all. I pulled away.

"No. I got it all wrong. This is who I am." I walked back into the lounge and pulled the list out. "And as for this!" I held it in the air. "It's all crap. Made-up stuff. Imaginary stuff, I'm not . . . *a good friend*." I read off the list. "My neighbors don't think so, any-way. In fact, you could go as far as saying that my neighbor hates me!"

"I'm sure she doesn't ha—" Noah tried to interject, but I cut him off.

"And I'm certainly not creative and fashionable, you've seen my wardrobe. No hippies in sight. And I don't like colors! The only color I like is beige, apparently. I don't like plants, or pictures or pho-tos or anything like that!" I looked back at the list and huffed. "Feminine?! HA! Nothing feminine about that wardrobe or this apartment. And I'm not brave—look at me, I can't even handle a germ, it seems. Who owns that many disinfectants? Me, apparently. Zen Small. Non-adventurous Zen Small."

"Stop!" Noah said, coming towards me. But I backed away. I was overcome by a new feeling now. The one that had started in my belly had morphed into something else now. *Rage.* Rage and hurt, and it wanted to lash out. I looked at the list once more before ripping it up. I shredded it and let the little pieces fall to the floor, as all the things I had thought about myself fell away too.

"Don't do that," Noah said.

"Why? None of it is me." I walked backwards, my shoulder blades hitting the cold, hard beige wall. I slid down onto the floor, pulling my knees towards me and gripping them tightly.

"I got it so wrong," I hissed.

Noah put his arm over my shoulder and pulled me towards him. This was the closest we had ever been.

"You don't have to have got it wrong," he said softly.

But something about that statement made me furious. It was hard to say what. I flicked my head up and glared at him.

"What does that mean?" I asked.

"It means that you don't have to be this. You can be the person you thought you were, that I know you to be. This doesn't have to be you."

"But it is me!" I said, getting riled up.

He shook his head. "No. It's not."

"Yes. It is," I shot back.

"Well, I don't know you like this. And I think I've gotten to know you a little over the past four days—"

"No! What you got to know was not me! You got to know some strange, amnesiac version of me. Maybe I was a little mad this last week. I'd just lost my memory, clearly. I wasn't myself. Clearly something came over me and I was acting out. Making stuff up. Playing some fantastical game of pretend in my empty head. And that's who you think you know. That person. Some fictitious, make-believe version of myself that isn't real. It was all imaginary. It was made up!" I was rambling, jumping from thought to thought. It was a strange feeling to suddenly have so many thoughts in my head, but I did, and they filled my head up until it felt like it might explode.

"No." He continued to shake his head.

"What are you not getting about this, Noah?" I snapped, and the sound of my voice and tone shocked me as much as I could see it had shocked him. I could see it in the way his face contorted and the way his body began to lean back, away from me. A part of me wanted to reach back out and pull him closer, but this other part of me told me to push him away. And that part was so much stronger than the part that wanted to pull him closer. And although I didn't have any memories yet, this feeling of pushing someone away felt very familiar. So I did it. I stood up and loomed over him.

"Noah, you don't know me. At all." I put my hands on my hips.

Noah stood up too. "That's where you're wrong."

"I'm not wrong," I snapped.

"Okay, fair enough. Let's say you are this person." He waved his hands around the room. "Where does it say that you have to continue being this person?"

"What do you mean?"

"Well, clearly, you don't like this version of yourself. So change it. Be the person you were this last week. Isn't that what Andi said in the cards, anyway? A journey, a new way of life, leaving behind and ridding yourself of a relationship, belief or behavioral pattern that is no longer good for you."

I laughed. "And you're going to listen to some psychic pharmacist who gave me a card reading on top of a shelf of sanitary wear?" These words came out sounding so much harsher than I imagined they would, and they took me by surprise. No! This was the most ludicrous, naïve thing I'd ever heard. I rolled my eyes at him. "Noah, I'm almost thirty years old. Clearly this is who I am, and have been forever. And now I must just change it? Swish a magic wand and change everything about who I am? That's . . . it's . . . impossible. It's ridiculous. Stupid."

I saw Noah take a step back from me. "I'm changing who I am. I'm changing my career. I'm starting something new. Is that stupid? Ridiculous?"

"I didn't mean it like that."

"How did you mean it?" he asked.

"I . . . I . . ." I stuttered, feeling so out of my depth right now. So uncomfortable. Teetering on something thin that I could fall off at any second.

Pull or push?

Two different sides to this thing I was standing on. Each side totally different. Each side totally opposed.

Pull or push?

I took a deep breath. Perhaps the deepest I'd ever taken in all the time I'd had a memory of breathing.

"Noah, thank you for everything you've done for me this last week. I will always be grateful for what you did. For saving my life. For taking care of me when I couldn't . . ." I stopped.

"Why does that sound like a goodbye?" he asked, his eyes widening.

I hung my head, unable to look into those eyes of his.

"Because it is," I whispered. "I want you to go now."

There was a long pause, and I heard Noah take a breath too. Also long like mine, inhaling and then exhaling. I felt him letting go of something on that exhale. Something that made me want to cry.

"I'm glad I could help," he finally said, and then I heard his footsteps to the door.

Pull or push?

"I wish you all the best, Zoe."

"Zen," I quickly corrected. "My name is Zen."

Another pause, then I heard him open the door and, before he walked out and closed it, I heard him murmur something, almost under his breath.

"Goodbye, Zoe."

CHAPTER 33

I was alone.

Alone with this life and this apartment that seemed so foreign to me. Noah had walked out the door only ten minutes ago, and already I missed him more than I could fathom. I had searched my apartment for a handbag and a cell phone, but had found nothing. And now I wondered if it had been stolen or lost somehow in the elevator accident.

I walked over to the TV, picked up one of the remotes and turned it on. I was greeted by a menu that I scrolled through. Netflix, Showmax, Hulu, DSTV . . . the list went on. It looked like I'd subscribed to every single streaming platform possible. I went into Netflix and explored it, and then Showmax and then others. I had watched a lot of TV. I mean, *a lot*. In fact, it looked like that might be all I did. Sat here and watch TV. I dropped the remote on the couch and then turned my attention to the books on the side table.

The Massive Book of Random Facts.

10,000 Amazing Facts.

Know it All.

So, this was Zenobia Small. Who watched TV and read books about facts. Something about that picture felt so depressing and bleak, and it made me miss Noah even more. I walked through to my bedroom again and into the bathroom. I opened the mirrored cabinet and looked inside. A bottle of hair-removal cream, a bottle of natural tranquilizer pills, and then I found myself reaching into the cupboard automatically and picking up a pair of tweezers and then closing the mirrored cabinet behind me and raising the tweezers to my eyebrows. I did this. I plucked my eyebrows often and obsessively because . . .

Did you know, thousands of insects are secretly living in your eyebrows. They're eating, mating and laying eggs all over our faces.

I leaned in and looked closely at my eyebrows, trying to see if I could find any. I couldn't. And then I remembered something else as I looked at the razor blade and hair-removal cream.

Did you know, mites can live in your underarm and pubic hair?

A sudden sense of rising panic flooded me as I thought about germs and mites that could infect and infest your body and stay there without your permission. I opened another drawer and saw a white box there and pulled it out. Tampons!

"Wrong again, Andi!" I guess pink is not my spiritual color after all.

I walked back into the bedroom and sat at the foot of the bed, staring into the open wardrobe of clothes in front of me, and the more I stared, the more they felt familiar to me.

I walked up to the full-length mirror and stared at myself. The tie-dye clothes and bright colors all seemed so silly now, ridiculous in this new environment. They didn't belong here. *I didn't belong in them.* I pulled the dress off and tossed it to the floor, reaching for the first thing I could find in the cupboard.

Beige pants, a white button-up top and a gray cardigan. I slipped the clothes on and stood back to look at myself. My short hair no longer looked cool and pixie-ish in this outfit, it looked old and boring. It looked like I didn't care. Like I didn't even have a hairstyle. I bent down to get a pair of shoes to complete the outfit, but just as I reached in something caught my attention. I pulled the old-looking shoebox out, sat cross-legged on the floor and opened it. It took me a few moments to register what I was seeing. The first *real* bursts of color, other than the disinfectant bottles, since I'd walked into this apartment.

I ran my eyes over the brightly colored crayons and pencils and pieces of paper. I turned the pieces of paper over in my hands. None of them had been drawn on, but the crayons and pencils had definitely been used. Their varying sizes told me so. Some had been sharpened much smaller than the others. The ones that were the shortest were the bright colors; the ones that looked like they'd never been used were the brown and dull colors. I put everything back into the box and pushed it into the wardrobe again. Why was that there? Stashed away like it was a secret. And what was it?

I tried to reach into my mind again, to force a memory to come forward . . . *nothing came*. I had no idea what these pencils were for, and if I was even the one who used them. I gave up on the shoes and stood up again, pulling the clothes off as I went. I wanted out of them. I stood there in my underwear for a while, surveying my surroundings, trying to decide what to do next. I walked over to the bed and sat down. I looked at my side table. A charging device lay there as well and I instinctively took my watch off and placed it in the holder. The watch lit up as I did and its name flashed across the screen. I'd never seen its name before—*ULTRAGO Watch. Ultrasonic Mosquito Repellent*.

Was I so afraid of insects that I had a watch that repelled them too? I opened the bedside-table drawer and a brochure for the watch greeted me. I picked it up and started reading.

This ultrasonic mosquito repellent repels mosquitos and other pests by emitting a high-frequency sound too high for humans to hear . . .

I scanned the words on the page until I came to the tiny print at the bottom, so small that I had to lean in to read it.

Warning: The ultrasonic waves might also affect other animals, including bats, birds, small reptiles, dogs and cats.

Waaaiiiit . . . I put the pamphlet down and stared at the watch. Was this the reason animals hated me? It was my watch, and not me? The thought made the tiniest flicker of a smile grace my lips. I would have to try my theory out in the morning. I closed this drawer and opened the one beneath it. There were two things in it.

The first was a book that looked like it had been read a million times over. I picked it up. The cover was torn and barely clinging onto the spine. The pages were brown with age and the corners were soft and bent. I turned it over again and stared at the cover. I flicked my bedside lamp on and the full picture came into view.

A Windsor and Swoon Royal Romance.

A woman lying tussled in red and gold sheets in a Bedouin tent in the middle of the desert, a man with a big, bare chest and long, flowing black hair cradling her with big, bulging, masculine arms.

Heat of the Desert, Heart of the Sheik.

Why would I have this next to my bed, and why would I have read it so many times? I opened the front cover and read the blurb.

When intrepid archaeologist Amanda Stone goes fossil hunting in the Arabian Desert, little does she know that a sandstorm will change the course of her life. The last thing Sheik Khalifa needs is to be forced to rescue a damsel in distress and have her stay at his Desert Palace oasis. But when the two are trapped inside by the sandstorm, a storm of another kind rages inside both of them, as they succumb to lust and love in each other's arms.

I held the book in my hands and it fell open at the place that looked like it had been read the most. My eyes drifted over the pages and instinctively honed in on a specific part, as if they'd gone there a million times before.

The sand raged and beat against the glass, almost drowning out the sound of her thumping heart as he leaned in and pulled her into his smooth, muscular arms. His hot masculinity was like an intoxicating drug to her, and she felt dizzy in his arms. His smell set her skin ablaze and a fire now burned deep in her sensual, hot core. He gripped her leg with his long fingers and moisture blossomed between her legs. She ached for him. She needed him in a way that she had never needed a man before. His hand moved up her leg, sending shock waves into her pulsating center, where the need blazed out of control like the wild storm itself. And then, she let out a cry of ecstasy as his fingers sought out her innermost, womanly sanctuary. The place that no man had ever been, until now. He slipped inside her and she embraced him with her hot slickness, wrapping around him tightly as her muscles contracted in pure, unabated pleasure.

"Oh my God!" I slammed the book shut and threw it into the drawer. What the hell would I be doing with that, and why was there a single lipstick in the drawer next to it? I opened the lipstick; it was bright pink.

That was so unlike the me I'd been introduced to so far. I raised the lipstick to my lips. It looked strange, like it wasn't real. I turned it over in my hands to examine it further and a button on the underside caught my attention, so I pressed it.

"Oh my God!" I jumped in shock as the lipstick began to shake and vibrate so wildly that it dropped out my hands and hit the floor. It began moving across the floor as if it were alive. What the hell?

And then I gasped when I realized what this was. I watched in horror as the thing crawled across the floor, making a terrible noise as it vibrated against the hard tiles. I was in too much shock to pick it up or touch it. So I simply sat on the edge of my bed and watched as it began to go round and round in a small, tight circle. Finally, when I couldn't take the noise any longer, I reached down, turned it off, threw it back into the drawer and slammed it closed. I stared at the drawer for a while, my mind racing. Trying to connect the dots of all that I was seeing.

This was me.

A woman that no one knew, or liked, for that matter. Who lived in an apartment that looked like a morgue, ate bland and boring foods, spent most of her evenings, it seemed, at home on the couch watching Netflix and reading books about facts and then, at night, coming in here to read from her favorite book and . . .

I cringed.

But the picture I got of it all was so depressing and sad that I wanted to cry. I could see myself, even if I couldn't remember it clearly, as a lonely someone, reading romances that only other people got to live and pleasuring myself because, clearly, I didn't really get it anywhere else. The vibrator in my drawer was not a sign that I was sexually awakened, or kinky, this was a sign rather that I was all alone. I did push. I pushed away, I never pulled. And I was sure, looking down at my bed, that I'd probably never pulled anyone into it.

Ever.

CHAPTER 34

I woke up drenched in sweat. My pillow was wet and my hair was stuck to my face in tentacle-like strands. I sat up on a loud inhalation, sucking air in as if I hadn't been breathing for a while. Lightning bolts in my head. Flashes of light illuminating pictures and memories and . . .

I jumped out of bed. I felt unsteady on my feet as memory after memory hit me like flying debris. They were chaotic and random. Out of order. And not all there. I ran into the kitchen and flung open a cupboard, reaching inside for a bag of tea and . . .

I knew where I kept the tea.

I knew where I kept the sweetener that I put into the tea.

I knew that the button on the kettle stuck so I had to give it a shake before I turned it on.

I knew a lot of things.

I held onto the kitchen counter as the kettle boiled and I waited for the memory flashes and pictures to stop flying at me, so I could pick them up and order them into something that looked like a time-line of my life. But they kept coming. Each time it was something new, something I didn't know about myself. Finally, it was over and I stood there, catching my breath.

I remembered. Not everything. I could still feel gaps everywhere in the fabric of my memory. But large chunks had been filled in, like a tapestry in progress. I mentally picked all the memory shards and fragments up and began sticking them back together like a puzzle, and when I was done, I knew so much more.

I worked at an ad agency, but not as a creative.

I had worked there for seven years.

I had lived in this apartment for seven years.

I lived in this apartment because it was across the road from my office, and I walked there. I did not own a car. I did not have my driver's license. I was afraid of driving. That much I already knew.

I had studied online, I was too scared to go to a university, I had studied isiZulu and Arabic. Two languages. Arabic because I'd always dreamed of going into the Arabian desert like Amanda Stone in my book, and isi-Zulu, because, for some reason, I understood it. Although I couldn't remember why.

I had lived in my parents' house in Durban while I was studying.

Then I'd come up to Joburg when I'd been offered a job as a primary-school teacher.

I had lasted one day. The kids were all too dirty. They sniffed. Their hands were filthy and all I could see when I looked at them was germs. I had decided teaching wasn't for me. And a job with less contact with people would be better.

I got the job at the agency through my landlord, whose son owned the agency and knew about the job opening. I think he only told me about it because he thought I wouldn't be able to pay my rent.

But now I owned this apartment.

I hadn't had a housewarming, though.

I didn't have anyone to invite to a housewarming.

I didn't have any friends.

I think I had a friend once, a good friend. But I don't really know where I know him from and why we're no longer friends.

I closed my eyes and tried to reach further into my memory banks.

I ate the same meal every night. I did this because I knew what was inside it. What ingredients had been used. I was afraid of strange foods and strange ingredients and allergic reactions to them.

For lunch I ate an apple and a protein bar. To keep my sugar levels up, but balancing them with protein. I was afraid of sugar-level spikes, and diabetes. But I wasn't a diabetic. I was also afraid of nuts, in case I went into anaphylactic shock.

I was afraid of lots of things.

I reached further into my memories, but kept hitting a blank at certain points. I could remember parts of my life from the age of nineteen upwards, but there were still gaps. And then I could remember nothing in the weeks leading up to the elevator accident. I strained, I tried to pull more memories out, but nothing else was coming.

My head spun and I held onto the kitchen counter even tighter. It felt like I was caught in the middle of a hurricane of memories, swirling around me, fast. It felt like I had to hold on so that I didn't get swept up in the rush of them and fall over. I thought about Noah suddenly, and the desire to call him and tell him about what I knew was overwhelming, only I didn't have his number, and then I remembered how I'd pushed him away and that made me feel like crying.

I poured myself a cup of green tea. It's the only tea I drink. It's rich in antioxidants and has been proven to lower your risk of getting certain cancers. But only two cups a day, too much caffeine otherwise, and never coffee. I moved back over to the couch and sat down again, sipping on my tea as I watched the rest of my memories play out in my head. Flipping from one to the other. And as they flipped, it became more and more clear to me that in the last several years nothing of any significance or importance had happened to me. And for some reason, that was the way I wanted it. But I didn't know why. Why would I want to lead such a routine, boring and regimented life? Where every aspect of my day was planned and controlled.

I finished my tea and looked around the room again. *This was my life.* This one here, in front of me that I could touch and feel and see and drink. Last week had been some fantasy role play in how things might have been, but now I knew that they couldn't ever be like that, no matter what Noah or some stupid drugstore psychic said. I had such a desire to phone Andi and tell her it was a good thing that she had never bloody quit her day job, because clearly she had gotten me so wrong . . .

And I had gotten me so wrong too.

CHAPTER 35

*

"$\mathcal{H}$i, hi," I said, walking into the open-plan section of the office. It had taken exactly ten minutes to walk to work. It could have taken five if I'd wanted, but I preferred taking the long way round so I didn't have to cross at the busy intersection that cars often went racing through without paying attention.

I stood there and looked out over the desks filled with cool-looking people. I knew each and every one of them. The copywriters were on one side of the office and the designers on the other. The creative directors had their own offices, but they all looked out over the open-plan section, so I was in their sights. I was in everybody's sights, but no one looked up at me.

"Okay, cool, nice to see you too . . ." I mumbled and then walked towards my office. I remembered exactly where it was. Through the cool industrial open-plan with the exposed electrical cabling and copper piping on the walls and ceiling. I walked all the way through to where the kitchen and bar for after-work functions was. A few people were milling around in the kitchen, drinking coffee. The barista with the twisty moustache was there, serving coffees with little flowers and hearts sculpted into the foam. A group of my co-workers were standing around laughing and talking as they sipped their artisanal coffees. I moved closer to listen to the conversation.

"Yeah, we should totally do something for Gareth's birthday. He's turning thirty," Ash, a blonde-haired girl with big, black-framed glasses, said. She always wore these seriously oversized glasses. A couple of months ago they were pink, but she'd accidentally stood on them at the office party to celebrate the company's win at the SA Advert Awards.

"Totally," Dave, the guy who was wearing purple eye shadow, said. He always wore eye shadow, and now that I was looking, he really did pull it off.

"We should do a surprise party!" Nonhlanhla piped up. I noticed that her braids were now blue. Last week she'd had red braids. The blue was really cool against her dark skin.

"Oh my God, we should do a nineties-themed party, cos he was born in the nineties!" Ash said.

"OMG, that's brilliant," Nonhlanhla, or Nonnie as everyone called her, replied. "I'll come as Beyoncé, but Destiny's Child Beyoncé."

"I'll come as Britney. 'Slave for You' vibe. With a snake!"

"Oh, that would be awesome if you got a fucking snake!" Dave said, jumping up and down.

"That's a nice idea," I said, "Gareth deserves a party. He works really hard. He clocks more working hours a month than anyone else."

Silence. A weird one as everyone turned and looked at me. Their eyes swept over me, up and down. Left to right. Up and down again.

"Uh . . . yeah. He does," Nonnie mumbled, looking a little confused.

"Also, 'Slave for You' came out in 2001, so either you must have a noughties party, or choose to come as someone else," I said, smiling at all my co-workers. And then I turned and started walking towards my office. They must have thought I was out of earshot, but I wasn't.

"Uh . . . who was that?" Dave asked.

"No idea," Ash replied.

"Like, literally, who is that?" Nonnie added.

"And did you see what she was wearing?" Dave said, and then they all laughed.

A pit formed in my stomach and knotted so tightly that it made me want to be sick.

"Hey, I wonder if Gareth will get a mystery birthday card this year?" Nonnie asked.

"I'm sure, everyone in the office does," I heard Dave say as I pushed the door open behind the kitchen and raced downstairs to the basement, where my office was. On the way down Cynthia rushed past me. She worked on the same floor I did, on the good side, though. The side that wasn't next to the hot server room and storeroom.

"Hey," I said.

"Hey, Zen." She stopped and looked at me.

Finally, someone that knew me! Cynthia was in charge of accounts here. She did all the billing, sending of quotes, getting purchase orders and then invoicing. It was a long, tedious job. Especially at the end of tax year, she often pulled all-nighters around that time.

"So much work to do today," she said. "What with all the load shedding this week, I am so behind. You probably have a lot to catch up on too."

"Probably," I said. "But not because of the power outages. Obviously, I was away this last week."

Cynthia's face scrunched up. "You were?"

"Yes," I said flatly. "I was away the whole week. Didn't you notice?"

"No. But I mean, you never really come out of your office during the day and your door is always shut so . . . Did you go on holiday?"

"No. I was in an accident," I said, starting to feel hurt and offended.

"Oh no, shame." She said it, but I could hear there was no real concern in her voice.

I pointed up at the mark on my forehead. "I'm sure you noticed this."

"Oh, wasn't that there before?"

"No." I couldn't hide the anger in my tone now. "It wasn't."

Cynthia shrugged casually. "Okay. Coooool. Have a good day." And then she trotted back up the stairs and out of the door. I stood there for a while, holding onto the staircase railing. I felt like I was in that elevator again, falling. Only I wasn't. Had I really worked here for so long and no one had noticed I was gone, or worse, even knew me? The thought made me feel like crying again. I rushed down the rest of the stairs to my office. I opened the door and slipped in. It was dark and I flipped on the lights. The room illuminated the shelves and shelves and cupboards and cupboards of files that filled it. I moved over to my desk, a small wooden table with a chair, nothing personal on it to tell you that a human had sat here for seven years. I looked out of the slot in the wall that allowed my co-workers to push the job bags into the room without even seeing me. Or throwing through their hand-scribbled timesheets, the ones that I was meant to make sense of and input into the computer software program that calculated everyone's working hours so we knew how much to bill each client.

I looked at the massive pile of job bags that had been pushed through in my absence. There were at least a hundred lying there. Maybe more. Papers had fallen out of them too, strewn across the floor like bits of litter. Hundreds of scraps of badly scribbled bits of paper, like dead butterfly wings, also lay spread out across the floor. I reached down and started picking up the endless job bags. The big brown envelopes that are stuffed to breaking point with the creative work and endlessly changing briefs for each client and job. It was my responsibility to file these bags in an order that made some sort of sense in case they needed to be pulled out again. And with over fifty creatives working in the building, each one of them working on as many as seven different jobs at a time, the amount of job bags that came through that hole in the wall was endless. Not to mention the hand-written scraps of paper, or sometimes, if I was lucky, typed pieces of paper. If you'd asked me what my job was yesterday, this would *not* have been it. Sitting in what was essentially a basement

with a small single window close to the ceiling that looked out over
the parking lot and hardly let any natural light in. Sometimes I got
so panicky and claustrophobic in here that I had to pull a chair up to
the wall, open the window, stick my head out and gulp in the fresh
air. I was forced to do this pretty regularly. Everyone else in this
office had space and air and light; I had none of those things.

"Here. It's the latest bag for Craft Cola." Suddenly a job bag
slipped through the hole in the wall and fell onto the table below. I
took it between my hands and looked down at it.

So, this was . . .

My job?

I looked over at the phone on my desk. I'd intended to call my
parents the night before, but the strange lack of phone in my apartment had rendered it impossible. I dialed their number now, rather
excited that I would soon speak to someone who had missed me,
who had been worried about me and had noticed I was gone. Only,
I was sorely mistaken . . .

* * *

I slipped the key into my apartment door. It was ten o'clock at night.
It had taken hours and hours to get the job bags sorted and input all
the numbers, and I wasn't even finished yet. I walked into the apartment that still didn't feel like mine, from a job that *really* didn't feel
like mine. The lights flicked on; the beige didn't come to life. It sort
of whisper-murmured with boring insipidness. I tossed my bag onto
the sofa, but it was so hard that the bag bounced and hit the floor. It
wasn't even a comfortable sofa. I was starved, so went to the freezer
and grabbed one of the meals inside it. *Maybe it wasn't as bad as it
sounded. Maybe it would surprise me.*

I popped it into the microwave and then made my way to the sofa
and sat down. I turned the TV on and scanned my "To Watch" lists.
Series after series after series stared back at me. They seemed to be a

mix of two things. Shows about dating, and shows about murder. I had no idea what that said about me, but I think it definitely said something. There were no movies really; clearly, I preferred TV shows. I sat back on the uncomfortable couch and pressed play randomly on something, anything to help take me away from this reality. A TV show about people on the autism spectrum trying to date filled the screen and I immediately thought of Noah when I saw two people at a restaurant eating together. In fact, Noah had been on my mind a lot that day. I didn't want him on my mind, though. Noah was from a time in my life that wasn't real.

The microwave dinged and I walked over to it and changed the settings to "cook" for four minutes. Which is one minute and thirty seconds more than it should be, but with chicken I prefer to overcook it. There are things like salmonella, E.coli and, of course, listeria . . . you just never know!

"What?" I said out loud. The person of two days ago would never have been afraid of chicken. Never been afraid of catching some invisible disease from it. But I was no longer Zoe, I was Zen. Zenobia and, apparently, she was full of phobia. I briefly smiled at the alliteration, and then it faded when I realized how sad that actually was.

The microwave gave another ding and I pulled out the hot chicken, rice and broccoli and dropped it onto a plate. It certainly didn't look appetizing. The bright white breast stared blandly and featurelessly back at me. You could see it hadn't been seasoned at all. It lay on a small bed of brown rice that looked just as unappealing without some kind of sauce on it.

I walked my food back to the sofa and sat again, changing the channels and trying to decide between two shows. I flicked between the channels. A show on Indian matchmaking, or a show on the worst murders in America? I chose the dating show. I liked watching dating shows, even though it was clear I never went on dates. In fact, the closest thing to a date that I had been on for years were these past few days with Noah.

Noah.

I chastised myself for thinking about him again and sliced into the chicken breast and put it into my mouth. It was disgusting. More disgusting than I'd imagined, and I was forced to spit it out.

I put the plate on the table and walked to my bedroom, I wanted sleep. I wanted to block this all out. I pulled the covers back and climbed into bed. At least my bed and the linen on it was comfortable. I lay on the bed, looking up at the ceiling, hoping that sleep would draw me in soon. But it didn't. Instead this anxious feeling gnawed inside me and my heart started pounding so hard and fast that it made me feel light-headed and woozy. I sat up as I remembered something and raced through to the kitchen to get it. I picked up my keyring and it finally all made sense. Why all these things were on it.

Therapeutic tools, I could hear a woman's voice say. I didn't know who she was, but I knew that she was the one who'd suggested I get it.

I lay back in bed and pulled on the elastic bands of the ball and then squeezed the stress ball over and over again. And when I was done, I twirled the fidget spinner between my fingers. These were for my anxiety, a feeling that hit me hard and cold and sticky day and night. But the therapeutic tools weren't working to quell the growing feeling inside. I needed a distraction, so I opened the drawer, grabbed my book and let it fall open randomly.

He burned for her. His loins, his skin, his entire being. His fingertips ached to trace that soft skin on the nape of her neck. His lips throbbed, desperate to devour her with his mouth. To explore her every inch with his hungry tongue and make her cry out for him. But he couldn't. She was forbidden to him, because he was promised to someone else. It had been arranged since his birth, that he would unite two great royal families by marrying Sheika Aisha. But he'd never felt for Sheika Aisha anything like what he'd felt for this strange woman who'd accidentally tumbled into his palace, much like the raging sand in the storm, pushing its way underneath his doors, an unwanted guest forcing its way through. And much like the sand itself, she had done nothing but rub him up the wrong way since she'd arrived. His attraction to her was a total mystery, and yet he had never been more attracted to and drawn to another creature in his entire life.

I slammed the book shut and stared at the ceiling again. I had no idea what I was meant to do next, how I was meant to transition back into this life that seemed so foreign to me now. I made a note to go and call on Eugene Bester soon, when I had caught up on all my work, my neighbor who'd filed the missing person report, and clearly my only friend in the entire world. I rolled over onto my side, clutching the book until I finally fell asleep.

And so it went like that for another day, and another day. *Work. Home. Chicken. Alone. (Think of Noah.)*

But on the fourth night back, when a feeling of utter restlessness had me cleaning an already spotless apartment until two in the morning, I found two things. The first was Andi the psychic's number, which I'd scribbled onto my list that I'd ripped up, and the second was another number crunched and tossed into the wastepaper bin. I pulled it out and the address made the hairs on the back of my neck prickle. This was from the building where I'd had the accident! That is why I was there.

VAST INVEST FINANCIAL SERVICES AND WEALTH PLANNING.

Why would I have been there?

I turned the card over in my hand, and there it was. A scribbled note for a meeting with Johan Visser an hour before my accident.

CHAPTER 36

~

I went into work before anyone else was there and phoned Johan. He'd sounded so thrilled to hear from me, the first and only person who'd sounded happy to hear from Zenobia. I'd asked for a meeting and he'd said he would shuffle his day around for me. *For me?* He was more excited that I'd called than my parents were. They hadn't even noticed I was missing. Apparently, we only spoke "every so often." They'd been shocked and upset by the accident, and had offered to come to Joburg and help me, but I'd said no. I got the feeling our relationship was strained, but I didn't really know why either.

I caught a taxi to Vast Investments, and when I arrived, like the last time, nothing about this place looked familiar. The accident, and my childhood, all those years before the age of nineteen, were still a blur to me, and no matter how far or hard I reached inside my head I wasn't able to access any of it. It was strange how my mind was cherry-picking the things it wanted to remember, and the things it wanted to forget. There was no logic to the way it was organizing my memories, it was completely out of my control.

I walked into the building again, but this time Noah wasn't with me. I walked past the coffee shop, the bank and then past the bookstore and . . .

I stopped when the table display caught my eye. *The Heart is Just a Muscle.* Becca Thorne. The books were adorned with big red stickers that read "Signed Copies." Maybe I should buy one and read it, since for some strange reason I kept bumping into it. I walked a little more, past another shop, a small art gallery and then a pharmacy. Something caught my eye there too. "Frankie's Fitness Protein Shake." That was what Maxine drank, and I suddenly found myself thinking about poor Frankie and where she was, and Kyle and how he looked like he didn't care she was gone. He looked like he cared more about his calves than the fact his ex was missing. I felt a sudden kinship with her. People hadn't seemed to care that I was missing either. I walked right past the elevator this time and went straight for the staircase. I climbed the two floors and soon found myself standing outside the rather lavish-looking offices of Vast Investments. I walked the red carpet outside and pushed the big, gold doors open. A white marble floor gleamed up at me, shone as if it had been hand-polished with hundred-rand bills. I walked up to the reception and had to push my way past the huge bunches of white flowers in crystal vases to even find the receptionist. This place was so fancy and over the top, why the hell would I have a meeting here? I couldn't be more different to this place than if I was . . .

"Zenobia." I heard a voice and turned.

"Uh . . . Johan," I said, looking at the man, whose face seemed vaguely familiar to me.

"Have you changed your mind then? I knew you would." He sounded so upbeat. So bright-eyed and bushy-tailed in his glossy suit that glinted in the warm chandelier lighting.

"Um . . . maybe," I replied, playing along, even though I had no idea why I was here and what he was talking about.

"Please, come through. Can I get you something to drink? Some champagne? Moët, maybe? Or would you like some Dom Perignon?"

"Champagne? It's so early in the morning!"

"We can add some orange juice to it if you like? It's obviously hand-squeezed," he said seriously. As if the kinds of people that came to this place drank champagne in the morning, because it was perfectly normal to drink champagne in the morning, especially if it came with orange juice. That made it a breakfast drink, after all. One of your "five a day."

"Uh . . . sure," I said, still going along with everything around me. "Either is fine."

"Martha. Martha!" Johan clicked his fingers at the receptionist. "Can you bring Miss Small a mimosa. And use the Baccarat crystal glasses, please. Bring it to boardroom five. Thanks."

He said my name, Miss Small, with such meaning, as if my name represented something to him. No one had said my name with meaning before and I wasn't sure how to take it. Johan led me through to another gold, opulent-looking room. This company obviously wanted to impress its clients. *Was I someone to impress, though?*

"Please sit." Johan pulled the chair out for me and I slid into it.

"Thanks," I mumbled as the champagne appeared in the shiniest glass I'd ever seen. I reached for it and took a small sip. My throat was dry anyway, mainly from the nerves, and it was rather delicious actually! I usually never drank alcohol; it increases your chances of certain cancers, after all. Except on a Friday. I have one glass of red wine on Fridays. It contains flavonoids which are antioxidants that are good for you.

"I can't tell you how happy I am that you came back," he said. "I didn't like the way our last meeting ended, with you leaving so abruptly. I think that maybe our suggestions were a little too . . . uh, how shall I say this? You like a much more conservative investment, even if the returns aren't as good as some of our other more, uh, 'risky' ones." He gestured air quotes. "Not that any are at all risky—our fiduciary experts are very sure to balance risk and stability carefully. But I think you would prefer something a lot more stable. Most of our other clients like a portfolio that delivers more returns, often offshore, like we discussed, but we at Vast pride ourselves on understanding each unique client and what their particular needs are. So, I'd like to suggest something completely different to you today. Something much more conservative. Which is what I think you are looking for?"

"Uh . . . yes,' I said. I was sure this was the correct answer, because what I'd come to learn about myself in the last few days was that I was certainly a very risk-averse person.

"Great, that's excellent to know. And again, I can't tell you how happy I am that you came to see us again."

"Uh . . . me too." I took another sip of the champagne, and then another one, and another: *very delicious, actually*. There was something decadent about drinking champagne in the morning, and just a tiny bit thrilling.

"If you are happy with our 'Market First Portfolio,' which delivers a little more than a money-market account at very stable interest rates, then I have all the paperwork here if you are ready to sign with us."

"Uh . . . that sounds . . . good." I finished the last sip of champagne and put the glass down.

"Martha, Martha! Get Miss Small a top-up, please."

"Wait, no." I held my hand over the glass and looked from Johan to Martha and back again. They both seemed to be looking at me with a great sense of anticipation. "Uh . . . okay. Why not?"

"Why not indeed?" Johan clapped his hands together happily now. Did he want me drunk? "Oh, Martha, and please bring Miss Small her handbag too." He turned to me. "You left it here last time. I was sure you'd come in for it, but I guess you have so many handbags you probably didn't even notice it was missing. We were going to call you about it today. But you called us! So it's working out perfectly." He smiled and I wondered why he thought I had so many handbags.

Johan left the room then came back in with a bunch of papers just as Martha came in with my handbag and more champagne. I opened the bag and peered inside. There was my wallet with all my IDs in, and there at the bottom was my cell phone. I reached into the bag and pulled it out.

"My cell phone was in here." I held it up for Johan to see.

"Well, it didn't ring. I suppose you must have used your other one."

I looked down at my phone. What did he mean, my other one?

"So, this is the paperwork to say that you're joining Vast Investments as a client, and then also paperwork indicating which investment portfolio you want your funds to be transferred into, and then the last is just that you are giving us permission to transfer all your funds, the total of fifteen million, three hundred and sixteen thousand Rand and ninety-seven cents, to be specific.

"Sorry . . . WHAT?" I choked on the bubbles of champagne. "That must be a mistake, I don't . . . why would I . . . um, that's . . . no!"

Johan looked panicked and then scanned the papers in front of him. "Oh I sincerely apologize. You're absolutely right. Your money is currently in two separate accounts—there is that other two million in your transactional account—but I understood you wanted to leave that there, as you regularly draw on the interest. Have I misunderstood, do you want the full seventeen million transferred across?"

"Uh . . ." I blinked at this man a few times in shock. "Can I . . . see those?"

"Sure." He pushed the papers across the desk and I cast my eyes down. And there it was, in black and white. All those digits, so many digits, belonged to me and I had no idea why the hell I had so much money. I downed my glass of champagne and, this time, I asked Martha for another one.

Who the hell was I?

CHAPTER 37

I swayed tipsily across the open-plan office, my feet zigzagging across the floor, and still no one looked up at me. Even when I stopped in the middle of the floor and hiccupped loudly, no one looked up at me. I pushed the door to the stairwell open and thundered down the stairs, three at a time, almost losing my footing as I went.

"Heeeyaa, Cynth—" I slurred as I passed her on the stairwell yet again.

"Zen!" she said, but didn't look up at me, even though I was now sliding down the stairs with my back pressed into the wall, hiccupping as I went. I barged into my office and looked around once more. If coffin-chic was a decorating trend, this room would win an award. I looked at the phone on my desk and a desire to make a call suddenly consumed me. I dug in my pocket for the number, slumped down onto the desk and dialed. It only rang once before Andi picked it up.

"Hello," she said.

"It's me." My voice stuck on the "s" sound. "I know who I am. My name is Zenobia and you and your cards were totally wrong about me! And I just wanted to let you know that. Wanted to let you know that you sold me a pack of lies and gave me false hopes and made me think things that were not real, and made me wish for things that I can never have, which is super-mean of you, if you think about it!"

There was a long silence on the phone, and when I couldn't take it anymore I whistled into it like Chloe might do.

"Helllloo?" I called.

"I've been expecting your call," she said, and I burst out laughing. Without me meaning to do it, the laughter started to sound strange, as if it were bordering on crying. I slapped my hand over my mouth to stop the sounds.

"Why have you been expecting my call?" I asked, rolling my eyes.

"I had a dream about you," she said.

I tutted loudly and then hiccupped.

"Are you okay?"

"NO! No, I'm not okay. How can I be okay when I thought I was one thing and it turns out I'm something else entirely? What did you say? Adventurous, approaches each day as if it's an adventure, opportunities and love ahead! Romantic, sensual, spiritual pinkness! Oh please! You should see what my life looks like. There's no pink in it, the only pink in it are the tampons you sold me!" I threw my free hand in the air. "How the hell can I be okay?" And then I laughed again, and soon I was teetering on the edge of tears again.

"I'm sorry," Andi said softly. "But if you remember what the first card said? That you are in the process of going on a journey to rid yourself of a belief, or behavioral pattern that is no longer good for you, and embrace a new way of thinking and being."

I shook my head, hard. I could almost feel the alcohol swishing back and forth in my brain. "No! No, I'm not going anywhere. No journey. This is me, just the way I am. Right here in this office that smells like a damp shoe and then back to my beige apartment that smells like a disinfectant wipe."

"Just the way you are?" she asked. Her voice sounded strange and faraway. It sounded like how she'd looked when she'd zoned in on the cards, as if she was pulling something from somewhere that no one else could see. "You don't have to be this way. In fact, the person I met the other day wouldn't settle for that."

"The person you met the other day was fake. Much like your fake reading." I pulled the phone away from my ear and was about to slam it down in anger, but I had one last thing to say to her. "And as for romance being on the horizon, pppssst! That—*that*—was the thing you were most wrong about. No romance on the horizon for me, other than Sheik Khalifa's paper arms and a lipstick shade I wouldn't even wear!" I shouted that last part and then dramatically slammed the phone down, missing the cradle completely and bashing it on my desk. I lifted it to my ear and listened.

"I'm still here," Andi said.

"Oh! Well! BYE!" I slammed the phone again, and missed once more. This time it tumbled to the floor, bounced and then hung there. I grabbed it and put it to my ear once more.

"Ja, still here!" the voice on the other end said.

"Dammit," I cursed. I couldn't even slam a phone down properly, so I reached for the electrical cord and pulled as hard as I could. It came flying out of the wall, whipped through the air and hit me across the face.

"Fuck!" I winced as a fiery sting radiated across my face. *I give up!* Officially! I give up on slamming phones and trying to make sense of anything around me, I just . . . *give up!* I slunk down onto the floor and sat there for a while, staring at the grime-encrusted carpet that looked like it had been laid in the seventies, back when orange was a thing.

"Work! Must work!" I took a breath and grabbed for the nearest crunched-up piece of paper. I could tell whose this was immediately. I had become so familiar with everyone's handwriting over the years, I could recognize it instantly, even if none of them recognized me. But I didn't feel like working, so I crunched the paper right back up and tossed it across the room. It hit the wall and then fell to the floor like a dead thing, disturbing a line of ants that were scurrying across the floor, crumbs on their backs.

I burped and hit my chest as some acid crept up my throat. God, one should *not* drink champagne on an empty stomach, and certainly not in the morning before work. Without thinking, I reached for my bottom drawer and opened it. I took out the paper and colored pencils that I kept in there and laid them on the floor in front of me. I was just about to pick a pencil up and start drawing when it dawned on me.

I made cards for people!

I was the person who made secret birthday cards, and baby-shower cards, and wedding cards and congratulations cards for everyone in the office, even though I'd never been invited to any of those events. I thought about the colored pencils in the bottom of my cupboards. It was all coming back to me. I made cards for everyone. Random strangers. My neighbors—when Mr. Burns from 309 lost his cat, I'd made him a condolence card and slipped it under his door. When the doorman had his first child, I'd made him a card and left it secretly on the counter, and when I didn't go to the Christmas party that I'd been invited to, I'd made everyone I knew in the building Christmas cards and put them in their post boxes.

I sat up straight and looked down at the card I was busy making Gareth for his birthday. I put a lot of effort into these cards, into the fine, detailed illustrations that went on the outside and the unique, hand-drawn typography that went inside. *Why did I do these?* I had an inkling I'd been doing them for years, almost all my life, further back than I could remember, and I got a feeling that there was something very significant about the cards. I ran my hand over the card I was currently making and wondered why I didn't just give it to the person directly? Why did I secretly leave these cards lying around for people, and never walk up to the person and put it directly in their hands?

Pull or push?

A part of me wanted to pull, a part of me wanted to make connections with others, but for some reason, I didn't. I kept people on the outside, while I only peeped in. I peeped in while others lived their lives and I didn't. And when someone did want to connect, more than just over a card, I pushed them away. Like I'd done with Noah. I had a feeling that my strange relationship with connections started way before I had a memory of it. I lowered the pencil to the card and started drawing. This was the only way that Zenobia knew how to connect, from a distance, pencil lines on a page. But if I was truly honest with myself right now, I wished that I could go beyond the card, like I had with Noah. But that was over. The one real connection that I'd had was gone. Except for Eugene. He and I were clearly friends. I would try and see him again. I'd knocked on his door a day ago and he hadn't been home. I would try again later.

I heard footsteps echo down the corridor. It was Jeff and Loyiso, the two maintenance guys, who also worked here in this shitty little basement area. They were always running around carting furniture back and forth whenever the creatives upstairs decided to move things around, which was at least once a month.

"So, what are you doing this weekend?" Loyiso asked. I know for a fact he's hardly been able to do anything lately. His wife, Zama, has just had a baby and he hasn't had a boys' night in ages. That's what he's always saying to Jeff anyway.

"Don't know. Me and Vuyo were thinking of going to The Keg."

"Damn, wish I could come. But Mandla is teething and I think Zama will kill me if I go out."

"Dude, that's why I'm in no hurry to settle down." Jeff laughed. This is the other thing Jeff always said, but if you asked me, he was turning forty next month and I was starting to wonder if he would ever be ready to settle down.

"Shit, this cabinet is getting heavy!" Jeff heaved and I heard something wobble.

"Why the fuck are they always rearranging the furniture upstairs?" Loyiso was also heaving now. He shouldn't push it too much. He'd missed a few days of work recently to go to some doctor's appointments. I'd overheard him on the phone to his wife talking about having a heart murmur!

The footsteps grew closer, as did the huffing and puffing, until they were both right outside my office door. I could see the shadows of their feet. I jumped in fright as a loud alarm started blaring throughout the building. It was so loud that I momentarily covered my ears until I got used to the sound, and then I looked around. The red fire-alarm light was flashing at me.

"Shit, another fire drill," I heard Loyiso say.

"I am so sick of these," Jeff said. "Unless it really is a fire?"

"God, that would be great. We could go home early."

"Let's hope," Loyiso replied. "We'd better go to the assembly point." And then I heard a loud thud, the sound of the filing cabinet being put down, I was guessing. I jumped up. The thought that there might actually be a *real* fire here was terrifying. Although I did have a memory of doing fire drills, now that I thought about it. I grabbed the laptop and my handbag, raced for the door and pushed it. It didn't open.

"What the . . ." I pushed again, but the door banged against something hard. ". . . hell?" I banged it over and over again, trying to push whatever was there . . . *the filing cabinet!* They had put the filing cabinet right outside my door, as if they didn't know that someone was in here. Was I that invisible to everyone?

"Help! Help!" I shouted, banging on the door. I could hear my banging and my shouting echoing down the hall, but no one shouted back. No one came for me.

"No, no, no!" I looked around the room in a total panic. What if there was a real fire? What if this wasn't a drill and I was trapped and I was going to burn alive? Do you know how painful being burnt alive is? I called out for help again, but still didn't get a response. I finally looked up at the tiny window at the top of the wall. It was my only escape. But how the hell was I going to squeeze through it?

CHAPTER 38

⌒

"Zenobia? Zenobia?" my boss called, looking out over the crowd assembled in front of him in the parking lot. "Zenobia?" He said the name as if he'd never heard it before. The way his mouth formed and wrapped around the letters sounded strange. As if this specific group of letters and syllables was totally foreign to him and this was the first time his mouth was making them.

"Zeeenobiaaaaa," he said again, stretching all the letters out as his mouth began getting comfortable with the sounds. I watched as people started looking at each other, shaking their heads. A murmur started. I could make out snippets of what was being said as I hung halfway out the window. I'd had to pull boxes of files out and make a tower in order to get high enough to reach it and climb through.

"I don't think a Zenobia works here?" Angi said. How the hell did Angi not know who I was? I knew almost everything about her. I had read her personal file. She was twenty-five; this was her first job out of college, where she'd come top of her class in animation graphics!

"Didn't she work here once, and then leave?" Ed from the IT department said, which I could *not* believe. He'd come around only a month ago to fix my computer! How did he not know who I was? We'd even had a conversation while he was there in which we'd established that he hated rainy weather and would rather it be sunny.

Someone must know who the fuck I was! Someone. Anyone.

And then, to my relief, Cynthia stepped forward. "Zen works in the room at the end of the basement passage. She does our timesheets," she said. Everyone turned around and looked at her blankly.

"Well, I think she does. I know she does the job bags, though. I just assumed she does the timesheets because that's where we hand them in."

"Aaaaahhh!" Another murmur rose up from the crowd, as people suddenly started to click. "I don't think I've ever seen who works in there," someone else said. I craned my neck to see who was talking, while still trying to pull my body fully through the window. It was Sello. The cool strategist. The guy that everyone looked up to and wanted to be, even though he was always the last one in the office in the morning and the first one to leave in the evenings and probably did the least amount of work.

A few "me neither"s rang out, a lot of head-shaking and general face-scrunching took place, and that's when it happened. Like something uncontrollable. Something inside me snapped. I could simplify this all by saying it must have been the champagne, I mean, who drinks three glasses of champagne before coming to work? That was surely the reason it happened. I could maybe even say that being psychosomatically burnt alive might have also contributed to this. But that would all be a lie. That explanation would be far too simplistic for what happened next. Because I knew that this had nothing to do with the champagne or the imagined flames. This was a feeling that had been much, much, much longer in the making. This was a feeling that I'd been sitting with inside me for years and years. A feeling that had been weighing on me for so long that today it was just too much to take and I finally crumpled under its weight. I could no longer be this invisible ghost that worked downstairs in a crappy, damp, musty basement filing room that no one seemed to know, or care about. I pulled myself fully out the window, and then, teetering on the small windowsill, I jumped down and hit the floor with an audible thud. And then I screamed.

"IT'S ME! I AM ZENOBIA!" My voice came out high-pitched, and everyone turned and looked at me. I rushed forward and stared at all my co-workers. "I am the person that no one bothered to look for or think about when a fire might have started. The person that no one even noticed was missing after an almost fatal fucking accident in an elevator that landed me up in hospital for daaaaayyys! And YES, I am also the person who does the fucking timesheets every single bloody day! Did no one ever wonder how all those crappy hand-scribbled bits of torn, flappy paper that you shove through that hole in the wall then get translated into something that actually makes sense and then finds its way into your . . ." I pointed at the MD now. "Your inbox! Did you not realize that someone called Zenobia did that for you? Did the email address Zen.Small@creativehub.co.za not alert you to the fact that someone called Zen might work for you? That someone called Zen trawled through all those crappy bits and pieces and things that aren't even written on paper sometimes." I pointed at someone in the third row, "Like you, Andile! Stop writing your fucking hours on scraps of chocolate paper. Do you know how many ants that brings into my 'office'?" I made very large and dramatic air commas. "Office!" I scoffed. "As if! You know how cold it gets in there in winter? It's like a bloody icebox, but none of you would know that, now would you, because none of you have ever set foot in it. It's probably not even legal to have someone work in there. I bet that room is a safety hazard, hardly any fresh air. Almost zero light. Only a really crappy person would stick another human being into a damp, dingy icebox." I turned to the MD and scowled at him, and his eyes widened in shock, and then anger. "And while I am at it, just a general note, please can you all try to write a little better. Most of you look like you didn't even make it past Grade Two with your bloody writing. Like you, Eric!" I pointed at Eric, who was one of the illustrators. "You might be able to draw, but let me tell you, you can't write! I can't tell your 'l's' from your 'f's'! And that becomes a problem when one of your clients is called 'Lucky

Loo Clothing.'" I paused and looked around to gauge the effects of my rant. People were still looking at me as if they had never seen me before in their lives.

"You still don't know who I am, do you?" I looked around the floor and then saw something. Two pieces of cardboard lay strewn there. I grabbed them and held them up to my face, cutting it in half, so only my eyes and forehead were visible. "Well!" I screeched. "Does this ring any bells yet? HUH? HUH?" I peered through the small hole I'd just created with the pieces of cardboard and everyone suddenly started to nod in acknowledgment. I dropped the pieces of cardboard, now feeling totally gutted. I had worked there for seven years and the only way these people recognized me was when I peered at them through a hole that only showed my eyes and forehead. I felt tears well up. But I was not going to cry! I wasn't going to cry!

"And you know what else?" I said, and despite not wanting to cry, I could hear my voice was shaky now. "*I* am the one that makes you all the cards. That's me. The one who puts the birthday and congratulations cards on your desks, because the thing is, I know so much about each and every single one of you that I feel like I know you, and you have no idea who I am. Do you?" I put my hands on my hips and stared out over the crowd. I might as well be a ghost to everyone here. And I knew this wasn't entirely their fault either; I had deliberately made myself into a ghost. Like I had with my neighbor. I waited for someone to say something to me. Anything. For someone to step forward and say, "Oh yes, I know you! I see you!" But no one did. Not even Cynthia. Everyone just stared at me in wide-eyed, gaping shock. So I turned my back on all the people I had "shared" my life with for seven years and I ran. Ran to the one person in the world who probably cared about me.

CHAPTER 39

I banged on the door, tears running down my face, I couldn't keep them down; they had been pouring out of my eyes the entire way here. And when the door opened, the relief washed over me in waves and I couldn't hold back.

"I'm here," I said, wiping tears from my eyes and looking at this man that I didn't recognize but knew I knew.

"Where have you been? I've been looking for you," he said.

"I know! I know!" I nodded my head and then rushed towards him for a hug.

"Whoa, whoa . . . what are you doing?" He stepped back and held his hands up, blocking me.

"I was trying to hug you." I was still smiling at him.

"We don't hug," he said flatly.

"So I've heard. And I'm sorry. I don't remember how long we've been friends, because I can't really remember— Long story, I'll tell you soon, but I swear I'm going to start hugging you. I want to change. I know I probably haven't been the best of friends towards you, but I'm ready to start now." I stepped forward and tried to hug Eugene again. And he took a big step back.

"Uh . . . we're not friends," he said.

"What? We are!"

"No. We're not."

I blinked. "But you left me all those notes. You filed a missing person report? Of course we're friends."

"I only left you those notes and filed the missing person report because I thought you had done a runner on me."

"A what?"

"When I gave you the bill."

"What bill?" I asked.

Eugene folded his arms now and glared at me. "Oh my God, are you actually going to do this . . . *what bill*? *What bill*? Are you kidding me?"

"I've lost my memory. I really don't know what you're talking about. What bill?"

"The vet's bill! For my dog!" He sounded like he was getting worked up and I shook my head. I still had no idea what he was saying to me.

Eugene looked over his shoulder and then whistled. I watched as a shadow began to emerge from behind him, and when it was fully in the light, I gasped.

"What happened?" I stared at the dog with the cone around his neck and the patch over his eye.

"You—you happened! You approached Rex a few weeks ago and he ran into the road and was hit by a car. Don't you remember that?"

I looked down at poor Rex. "No, I don't. I'm sorry."

"He had to have his eye removed!"

"Noooo!" My hands flew up and covered my mouth in shock.

"And he had to have pins put in his leg. It's broken in three places."

"What! I'm so sorry, I didn't know. I was wearing this watch. It gives off ultrasonic waves that humans can't hear and that insects and animals can, and it's meant to repel insects but it also affects animals and I didn't know it did, I just thought animals hated me and—"

"I don't really care what you were wearing. You said you would pay for his vet's bill. And then the day I gave it to you, you disappeared."

My stomach dropped. "You filed the missing person report because of that? Not because we're friends?" That cold, clammy, sweaty feeling washed over me again.

"Friends!" And now he smiled. It was smug and awful and made me feel worse about myself than I already did. "Darling, I don't think you have friends. That's what everyone in the building says anyway."

"People in the building talk about me?"

"Well, you come up every now and then . . . sometimes rather colorfully," he said, trying to stop a smile.

"Wh-what do you mean?" I asked, but he didn't answer. "Please. What do people say about me? I need to know."

"Some people call you the B in 3C." He said this a little smugly now. "I never called you that, though. In fact, I always thought it was a little unjustified, until you pulled the runner when I gave you the bill. Rex could have died, you know. I've had him for sixteen years!"

"I'm so sorry. Please send me the bill again. I'll definitely pay it."

"It's twenty thousand Rand! I had to put it on my credit card. My electricity bill bounced this month." He turned and pointed back into his apartment, "I have no lights, so you'd better pay it. The lawyer said I could sue you if you don't."

"A lawyer?"

"Yes. I consulted one. He suggested I file the missing person report."

I pulled my bag off my shoulder and took out my checkbook and a pen.

"How much did you say it was?" I asked.

"What's that?" Eugene took a step closer to me.

"I'm going to write you a check."

"A check? Do the banks still take those?"

I looked up at him, feeling a little irritated this time, but I took a deep breath and looked back down at the check. "How much?"

"Twenty thousand, three hundred and fifty Rand."

I scribbled the numbers down, wrote my name and signed. And then I pulled it out and handed it over to him. He took it like he had never seen one before.

"This is for twenty-two thousand," he said.

"I added extra. For the inconvenience. Your lights, and anything else Rex might need, or for anything you might need, and . . . and . . ." Eugene turned around and my throat tightened so much that I don't think I was able to talk anymore. Without a thank you or a smile or anything, he just walked back in and closed the door loudly. I stared at the door in front of me.

No one liked me. In fact, it was clear that some people vehemently disliked me, and why wouldn't they, I guess. I was unfriendly, I scared animals—I probably scared babies and children too! I was a monster of a person that no one knew or cared about and that realization was so painful I felt like I needed to get as far away from it as I possibly could. I hurried down the staircase. The tears came in buckets now, and my shoulders were shaking by the time I got to my floor. In fact, I could hardly see through the veil of water covering my eyes as I raced in the direction of my door. I bumped into something and, when I saw what it was, I cried even more.

CHAPTER 40

"I'm so sorry . . ." I bent down and tried to pick up the groceries that I'd just knocked out of my neighbor's hands. "I didn't see you there." I reached for a tin of baked beans, an onion, a packet of crisps and a loose chocolate, pulling them towards me, trying to balance them in my arms but dropping them all because my arms were shaking too much. Or was it my shoulders that were shaking? Or all of me?

"Don't worry. I can get them," I heard my neighbor say from above me.

"No! No! I will." I could barely see a thing through the veil of water dripping down my face.

"Stop. Please," my neighbor said, but I kept on going, unable to stop, crawling around the floor, reaching for things I could no longer find and see and hold.

"PLEASE!" she said firmly, and I felt a hand grip my shoulder.

I stopped what I was doing and sat down, pulling my knees towards me and leaning my back against the wall. I wrapped my arms around my knees and lowered my face into them and hung on for dear life. Hung on while all the emotions pulled at me so strongly and from so many different directions I wasn't sure gravity would hold me in place.

"Are you okay?" my neighbor asked, in a voice filled with genuine concern. I could hear it, and it made me want to cry even more.

"No!" I said.

"Would you like to come inside for some tea?"

I whipped my head up and looked at her. "Me? Tea?"

"Yes."

"But you hate me. Like Eugene hates me. You sent me food that I threw away and invitations that I turned down, and apparently, I ignore you in the corridors and scare your cat. I seem to scare everyone."

"That's true. You do scare my cat," she said. "But I don't hate you."

"You don't?" I asked, wiping my face with the collar of my shirt, not really caring what it looked like. "Why? Everyone else seems to hate me. God, I think I hate me."

"I don't know you well enough to hate you. I don't know you at all. I can't hate someone that I don't know."

She looked down at me and smiled. It seemed like the kind you give someone you actually care about. The kind of smile that I hadn't seen in days, not since I'd kicked Noah out my apartment.

"So, what say we get to know each other a little? I could do with a cup of tea, and it looks like you could do with an ear to listen."

We walked inside together. Her flat was a mirror image of mine in shape and size, but that was the only thing it mirrored. While mine was spartan and beige, hers was full and bursting with color. Porcelain dogs and swans and printer's tray displays chock-a-block with trinkets. Spoons and thimbles and tiny jugs and miniature things and bright plates hanging on the walls. Coffee tables full of old tea sets and tins and just about every single bright thing a human could collect.

"I love what you've done with the place," I said, reaching out and running a finger over the slippery head of a bright pink porcelain dog.

"Thank you, dear," she said from the open-plan kitchen, pulling down equally bright mugs and turning on the kettle.

"It's so bright." I wiped my hand over the floral couch before I sat down on it, moving one of the lace pink embroidered cushions out of the way.

"Oh, don't sit there, dear. That's where the cat sits, and since she's not that fond of you——"

"Ppprrrr." With a strange sound, the cat jumped up onto the couch next to me, as if she knew we were talking about her, and just as I was about to get up, the cat jumped onto my lap. I froze, and didn't move again until she looked like she'd settled.

"She . . . she . . . oh, she likes me!" I looked up at my neighbor and beamed. An actual beam that burst out of my lips, and that I could feel throughout my entire body. I winced as the cat started kneading my thighs, her little claws digging into me ever so slightly, and purring like a machine. I reached out and touched the top of her head, and she nuzzled into my hand and wrist, the wrist where my watch was not. It was the watch! It wasn't me.

My neighbor walked into the lounge carrying two cups of tea and placed them down on the coffee table in front of me.

"I just realized, I don't know your name!" I said, taking the warm cup of tea and sipping it.

"Betty," she said. "I did tell you that once, but . . ."

"Sorry, I've kind of lost my memory—well, not kind of, I have. Not all of it, but a lot. I had an accident in an elevator over a week ago." I reached up and touched my head and her eyes went there. "I only remember parts of my life, and they're not exactly the parts I particularly want to. In fact, everything I remember is not really something I care to."

"What do you mean?" Betty looked at me over the rim of her teacup. She was really listening, I could see it, and I liked it. It reminded me of Noah.

"When I didn't have any memories of who I was I built up this idea of the kind of person I was, and then when I got my memories back and realized who I actually was . . ." I shook my head and placed the teacup down, my hands shaking now. I laced my fingers together to stop them.

"Go on," she urged me in the kindest tone, which broke my heart a little. I had been so cruel to her over the years and here she was showing me nothing but kindness.

"I don't like the person I see. And I wasn't this person a few days ago. I was the complete opposite. And then I came here, and I saw my apartment, and saw how people didn't like me, saw how the people I've worked with for seven years didn't even know me. That's not the person I thought I was, and I can't understand how I got it so wrong."

"Maybe you didn't get it wrong," she offered.

"What do you mean?"

"Maybe the person you thought you were when you couldn't remember is actually the person you're meant to be."

I chuckled now and wrung my fingers together even more. "Funny, you're not the first person to say that."

"Well, maybe it's true then."

"Maybe. But what if it's not? What if I am this person, the one that lives in a beige apartment and is mean to her neighbors and doesn't like Christmas parties?"

"So change it." She reached over and took my hand. The gesture caught me off guard, but I didn't pull away. Instead, I squeezed back.

"Also not the first person to say that to me," I said.

"It's never too late to change who you are."

"You think?" I let go of her hand and stroked the cat when it lifted its head and rubbed it against my arm.

"I know so," she said.

I thought about it for a while. Maybe Noah had been right. I didn't have to be this person, but I was almost thirty now and it was clear that I had been Zenobia-Phobia for so long already.

"Sounds like this other person who said the same things to you cares a great deal," she said.

"I pushed him away."

"You can pull him back."

"What if I pushed him too far away?"

"Nothing is ever out of our reach if we just put in a bit of effort," she said, then took a long, slow sip of her tea in a way that made her seem very wise and worldly. "Perhaps you could start with an apology? I find those, when sincere, go a long way."

I looked down at the cat for a while. Its fur felt good beneath my fingers. Soft to the touch and fluffy enough that your fingers completely disappeared into it.

"I'm sorry." I looked up at her. "For being so rude to you and for not accepting your invitations and your food and for not being the neighbor you deserve to have."

"Thank you, dear. Apology accepted," she said, with that warm smile again.

"I'd better go. I think I have another apology to deliver."

I placed the cat down gently and got up. "Thank you."

"Wait, before you go, take my phone number, in case you need it." She scribbled her number out and passed me the piece of paper. I raised it to my nose and sniffed. "Rose-scented?"

"I have lavender if you would prefer?" She laughed at this and then I did something that I hadn't done as Zenobia yet. I pulled her into a small hug. And this time, she didn't stop me.

CHAPTER 41

"Noah! Noah!" I yelled, holding my finger down on the bell until he opened the door.

"You were right!" I gushed as soon as I saw him. "And I am so sorry for the way I treated you. Because you were totally right and I was wrong."

"About what?" he asked, sounding not so friendly.

"Everything!"

"Can you narrow that down?" He folded his arms and rested his body against the doorframe.

"That I am *not* this person!" I pulled the gray jacket off and tossed it to the floor by his feet. Okay, that was dramatic. But fuck it, I was feeling very bloody dramatic now. "The person who wears these clothes. These gray, bland clothes. I am not this person. I am more than this! I am more than invisible Zenobia-Phobia that no one knows and cares about. That no one notices in a fire!"

"A fire? What happened?" He pushed himself off the doorframe and moved towards me.

"Nothing. Well, something could have happened, and no one would have noticed and that is the point! No one noticed me. I'm a ghost that haunts the dark, damp basement that no one notices, except for Eugene, but he only did because he was trying to sue me."

Noah shook his head. "You're not a ghost. I see you. I notice you."

"No! You notice the person I was a few days ago, because that person is noticeable. But this one . . ." I ran my hands up and down my body, displaying my bland plumage. "You would not have noticed this person. And it wouldn't have totally been your fault either, because this person, this Zen, makes herself invisible. She's terrified of everything, and I mean everything. Cars, germs, salmonella, spicy food and clothes with color, vitamin deficiencies and not flossing, and insects living in her eyebrow hairs!"

"What?"

"Loooong story. Point is, she's terrified of life and everything in it. And people too. She is—no, *I am*—scared of getting close to people, and I don't really know why. I know I've been doing it for the last ten years or so, but I know it started before that, and I can't remember that far back."

"Wait, you remember? Your memory's come back?"

I nodded and then shook my head. "Sort of. I remember a lot from the age of nineteen upwards, but nothing else."

"Nothing about your childhood?"

"Nothing."

"I just know who I am now."

"But I told you, you don't ha—"

"Have to be this person. I know! I know now. I didn't know that a few days ago, but now I know it. And I don't want to be the person who is only seen through a slot in the wall. I don't want to eat bland chicken and wear clothes like this! I want to be someone else."

"No. Not someone else," he said, sounding emphatic.

I paused. "What do you mean, not someone else?"

"Well, what if the person of last week . . . Zoe! What if Zoe is really who you are and this person is not. What if the life you were living before is not meant to be the life you're supposed to be living, and never was."

"How would that have happened, though?"

Noah shook his head. "I don't know, but I'm sure there are two people who could give you a clue."

"Who?"

"Your parents."

I nodded. "Yes. My parents. Them. I don't think we're very close. They didn't notice I was gone either."

"Oh." He sounded surprised. "I'm sorry, that must have been . . ."

"It was," I agreed. He didn't need to say what it was; the meaning was clearly implied.

"But even if you're not close, they'd be able to tell you about your childhood. Maybe that will give you some greater understanding of who you are."

"Or why I'm like this," I added.

Noah nodded at me and I pulled my phone out of my bag. "I'll call them and ask."

"Wait," Noah stopped me. "Why don't you go and see them? This seems too important to talk about over the phone."

"You're right. I should."

"I'll come," Noah said.

"What? No, you don't have to."

"I want to. Besides, watching TV is getting boring and I'm off for another few weeks and . . . *wait*, but if you don't want me to come. If this is something you want to do alone?"

Alone . . . ?

'When the Six of Swords is reversed," I blurted out.

"What?"

"It's what Andi said," I mumbled to myself, and now felt terrible for phoning her like that. I could hear her words ringing in my head . . . my journey is personal, but it doesn't mean I have to take it alone. I looked up at Noah. "I would love you to come, if you still want to?"

"I want to. If that's okay with you?"

"Yes! It is!" And then, I didn't plan it at all, but I threw my arms around him and hugged him. It felt good to hug; I should do this more often. I pulled away.

"But before we go, I have to phone Andi."

"The psychic pharmacist?"

"Yes, I sort of need to apologize to her for something I said earlier today."

"Hey, look." Noah pointed at the ivy-covered wall next to me. I turned.

"What?"

"A lizard, and it's not chasing you," he said.

"Oh, that's right! Can you introduce me to Chloe again," I said, holding my arm out.

"Why?"

"I'll tell you in the car, but in the meantime, please can you introduce us."

"You sure?" he asked, raising one of his brows at me. "I thought you said that animals hated you."

"Nope! I was totally wrong about that, like I've been totally wrong about a whole lot of other things. Animals love me!"

CHAPTER 42

❧

Only a few hours later, Noah and I were in his car, heading out onto the open road. He'd dropped Chloe off with Maxine, who was only too happy to have her, and I'd finally gotten to meet her properly too. She'd climbed all over me and nibbled on my earlobe in a way that made me laugh. We'd gone back to Sindi's and borrowed a few more of her clothes, stocked up on chocolate and then hit the road. It was strange how the idea had only crystalized a few moments ago, and yet, here we were, actioning it already. I had called my parents and told them I wanted to talk about my childhood. They were only too happy to have me there, they said. But I also had this strange feeling inside that was growing with every kilometer we drove. *What if I didn't like what I found out?* This feeling had been nagging at me for the last two hours in the car as Noah and I had sat in almost total silence.

"You okay?" he finally asked.

"I don't know," I said. "What if I hear something I'm not going to like? What if I have something in my past that is so terrible and painful, that's why I've forgotten it? What if I learn something about myself, or my childhood, that I don't really want to learn? What if there's something in my past that is so bad, so terrible, that I'm deeply ashamed of it, or regret it? What if I am actually better off not knowing?"

Noah paused for the longest time. The pause was heavy. Like there was something inside it waiting to come out.

"There's nothing in your past that is not worth remembering, no matter how painful it is. There's nothing in your past to regret, because everything that's happened is what made you the person you are."

"Yes, but I don't know the person I am. I thought I did, but I don't."

Noah turned and smiled at me. "I know the person you are."

"Who?"

He looked back down at my clothing. "You're the kind of person who wears clothes like that and totally pulls them off. You're this person sitting here. Right now. Just the way you are."

I looked down and ran my hands over my leggings. I was wearing a pair of leopard-print leggings with fluff around the ankles. They were a costume from the stage show *Cats*. I'd paired this with a pink tie-dye T-shirt and a glittery handbag which had been a prop from a soap opera Sindi had worked on some years back.

"Thank you." I smiled at Noah, but then felt it falter as I thought about what I was possibly about to uncover. This didn't go unnoticed and he looked at me meaningfully for a moment, before turning his attention back to the road.

"I want to tell you something." He sounded solemn.

"Yes." I turned in my chair to face him. His eyes were fixed on the road ahead and it looked like nothing would pull them away. Like he'd deliberately locked them there.

"What is it?" I pressed.

"It's about my childhood. My past. I guess you could say it's something that one might wish to forget. But I'm glad I haven't forgotten it, because it changed the course of my entire life."

I leaned closer to him. His tone was so serious now. Soft, yet purposeful. I hadn't heard anyone talk to me like that, not that I remembered, anyway. Someone was about to open their mouths and share something of great importance with me. The very notion humbled me.

"When I was eight years old, my mom was pregnant with my

baby sister. We were all so excited about it and I couldn't wait to be a big brother. And then one day my mom and I were home alone and she slipped down the stairs."

"Oh God!" I gasped.

"There was so much blood, that's what I remember the most. And she was in such pain, she couldn't talk. She could barely breathe, and it was . . ." He shook his head and I could see he was gripping the steering wheel even tighter now. "I have never experienced fear like that before. And loneliness. She was there, but she wasn't. She wasn't there to tell me what to do and to comfort me and take away the fear."

"What *did* you do?"

"I dialed the police. I remembered their number from a class we'd had in school. But I was terrified to call, and I couldn't remember our address either, we had just moved to that house. A three-bedroom house for my sister. I had to find a letter with our address on. My mom had lost consciousness, I was terrified and in shock and trying to read this address. The police were asking me to describe my surroundings . . . it was so chaotic. And our new house was on a smallholding just outside Joburg, so I couldn't even run to my neighbors and we were at least an hour to the nearest hospital."

"That must have been horrific."

"It was. Finally, the police figured out where we were and called an ambulance. It arrived after what felt like years. The whole time I was there alone with my mom, I had no idea what to do. She was in so much pain, she was going in and out of consciousness, she was losing so much blood, all I could do was hold her hand and tell her it would be okay. Which in my heart, even at that age, I knew it wouldn't. I knew there was no way this would ever be okay and I just knew that this moment was going to change everything."

"Is she alright now?"

"She is." He smiled. "And actually, despite how terrible the incident was, everything worked out the way it was meant to, I guess you could say."

"I didn't know you had another sister, other than Sindi," I said.

Noah turned and looked at me. It was the first time he'd looked at me since he'd begun his story. "I don't. My other sister died that day."

I inhaled, and tears stung my eyes. "I'm so sorry. Your mom and dad must have been devastated. And you."

He looked back to the road. "They were. When we finally got my mom to the hospital, they were able to save her, but not the baby. She had to be rushed into emergency surgery, but there was nothing they could do . . . she had to have a hysterectomy. Severe obstetric hemorrhage."

I reached over and put my hand on his shoulder. "I'm so sorry that happened to you."

"I am too. And I'm also not."

"What do you mean?"

"Well, two things came out of that moment. The first one was me realizing that all I wanted to do when I grew up was help people like that. I wanted to be that man who had scooped me up in his arms and carried me into the ambulance and held my hand and told me not to be afraid. I knew that I wanted to do that for someone one day,"

"You did for me. You were the only thing, the only voice, the only hand that made me feel better."

"I'm glad."

"And what was the other thing?" I asked.

"Sindi," he said. "Because my mom could no longer have biological children, my parents adopted Sindi. And it's weird, you know. The moment she came into our lives we all knew she was meant to be in our family. She was already one year old and had been waiting for an entire year for a family. Just waiting for us to find her. And if you ask my mom today, she'll tell you that Maggie—that was going to be my biological sister's name—however much she was wanted and is missed, just wasn't meant to be. Because Sindi was meant to be in our family. She was the sister and daughter we had all been waiting for."

Tears made my chest tight. The first one fell and I wiped it away with my fingers and looked down at the wet tips.

"So, you can't say that things that have happened in the past are worth forgetting. Or regrettable. Because they just can't be."

"Thanks for telling me that," I said. No one had spoken to me like that before and I realized how much I wanted this. A *real* human connection. A connection beyond the cards. "I don't think anyone has ever told me something so personal."

"I find that hard to believe. You're so easy to talk to. People must talk to you all the time."

I hung my head. "I worked at that company for seven years, and no one knew who I was. I was, quite patently, invisible. I don't think I've had a single conversation with any of them in seven years."

Noah turned again and gave me that smile. A dazzling bloody smile it was. "Well, now you have someone to talk to."

I felt that little rush of warmth in my body again. "You're so nice. That's why you make such a brilliant paramedic. You get people. Even if I don't get myself."

"I've actually been feeling these past few years that it's not enough for me anymore, being a paramedic. When you're a paramedic, you only help people for a short period of time. You get them to where they need to be and then leave. You don't get to watch them on their journey of recovery, and that's why I want to go to nursing school. A few of my colleagues have been teasing me for wanting to go into such a female-dominated profession, but I don't care. Besides, I'm not afraid to admit that I'm not academic enough to become a doctor. Nurse it is. I just want to do more for the patient. I want my journey with them not to end at an emergency room."

"Kind of like me," I said. "You're seeing me all the way through. In fact, you could say that I'm your first real patient."

"You're not a patient." His words came out in a strange tone. It felt like it was laced with something, I don't know what. I didn't think I was that good at conversations with undertones like this. I didn't think I had the social skills for tone interpretation.

"What am I?" I asked.

"Well, I'd like to think we've become friends?"

I smiled to myself and looked at the road in front of us. "Friends. That sounds nice. I like that. I don't have many friends." "Many" was downplaying it. I didn't have any friends. Although, in the last few days, I'd collected four phone numbers of people, and my phone was the fullest it had ever been. "Friends," I repeated to myself, and then, as if the universe was punctuating that statement, a massive sound made us both jump.

"What the hell was that?" I asked, looking around as an explosion rocked us.

Noah and I leaned forward and looked up at the sky. Thick, rolling black clouds had almost swallowed it up. We'd been talking so much, we hadn't noticed this blackness sweeping across the once-blue sky. I couldn't believe it.

"Thunder," Noah said. "Very close. But it's still blue in front of us." He pointed at the light sky on the horizon. "If we keep driving, we'll probably miss it."

I looked up again. "I think you're right. It's right above us. If we just keep moooo— *what was that*?" I asked, grabbing onto the dashboard as the car seemed to rock back and forth.

"Wind!"

"Wind that moves cars?" I let go of the dashboard when the car stopped rocking. "What kind of wind moves cars?"

"That kind!" Noah pointed to the sky ahead. The dark clouds above seemed to be rushing to fill the blue space there. They reached out with wild, black twisting arms, like those inflatable people with the arms that move around like crazy outside tire stores.

The wind raged and the entire sky soon turned black as the last of the sun disappeared. It reminded me of the storm that had raged outside Sheik Khalifa's oasis which Amanda Stone had gotten caught in. She'd looked up to the sky to see the sun finally swallowed up by the red dust that twisted up from the dunes. *A shadow fell across the once-illuminated landscape and Amanda knew that she was in serious trouble.* Were we in serious trouble?

Noah pulled the car over on the side of the road as the clouds ripped open and rain poured out of them. It thumped down on us relentlessly; it sounded as if giants were jumping up and down on the roof, and we both looked up at it. I was petrified the whole thing might buckle and bend.

"Will it hold?" I shouted at Noah over the deafening sound.

"Yes," Noah assured me. "I mean . . . I think so. It should . . . probably." Okay, so now he wasn't sounding as self-assured.

"Now what?" I shouted even louder.

"We'll have to wait it out. I don't want to drive in this."

I looked at the window. The rain was pouring over it as if we were behind the curtain of a waterfall and I could no longer see the landscape outside.

CHAPTER 43

"So how much longer do you think we'll have to wait?" The rain had not abated at all; in fact, it was coming down harder than it had been a while ago, if that was even possible. Huge pools of water were rippling across the surface of the road, and where the road was a little higher than the ground it was built on, waterfalls rushed off the edge, creating a river on the side of the road that raged down the slope.

"It looks like it's really settled in. We might have to do the same," Noah said, undoing his seatbelt and moving his chair back into a more comfortable position.

I looked around the car and wondered just how long we would need to settle in for. We'd left Johannesburg late, and it had already been getting darker when the storm hit. We sat in silence for a while. I too had pulled my chair back and stretched my legs out, my feet on the dashboard.

"I spy with my little eye something beginning with 'R,'" Noah said, and I laughed.

"Rain. Obvious!"

"I spy with my little eye something beginning with 'L.'"

"Lightning. Even lamer!" I laughed even more.

"You're good at this game." He turned in his seat to face me, and I turned too.

"No, you're just bad at it."

"That's a matter of opinion. I spy with my little eye something beginning with 'W.'"

"Water! You *are* bad at this!"

"Fine. I'll try harder this time. I spy with my little eye something beginning with . . ."

I watched Noah, amused as his eyes flicked around the car.

"Stop looking at me, that's cheating!"

"And you clearly need all the help you can get." I put my hands over my eyes and let him continue.

"I spy with my little eye something beginning with, with . . . uh, with . . ." He paused, and I smiled as I imagined his eyes working overtime, scanning every inch of the car for something to grab a hold of. "Uh . . . 'D,'" he finally said.

"'D'?" I pulled my hands off my eyes.

"Yes. 'D.' Right next to us. Pointing at us."

"Huh?" I looked out the window to where he was pointing.

"Double cab. Winding down its window." Noah and I both leaned across the seat in an attempt to look through the blanket of water coating the window. And there it was, a big double cab with an elderly lady who looked like she barely peeked over the steering wheel, pointing at us and indicating that we wind our window down too. Noah cracked the window ever so slightly, and the rain took the opportunity to burst into the car.

"Helloooo!" she shouted at us. "You alright?"

"Thanks, we're just waiting the storm out!"

"Here? On the road?"

I leaned over Noah to get a closer look at her and a spray of water hit me on the face.

"Oh no, look, you're getting wet," she said.

"Hi!" I waved.

"Ag, no. You cannot wait here on the road. Come with me. My farm is just down that road. You can dry off, have some nice warm coffee and a rusk and then leave when the storm is over."

"That's so sweet of you, but we wouldn't want to be an imposition," the ever-polite Noah said.

"Nee, man, no imposition."

Noah shook his head. "Really, that's very kind. But we're okay."

"Come. I insist." She sounded determined.

"Uh . . ." Noah looked a little stumped now.

"I can't leave you two out in the rain like this. Besides, we don't get any visitors out here, Tiaan will be so happy to see someone other than me! Follow me, it's just down here. I'll drive slowly. I absolutely insist!" She wound her window up and began to drive.

"She seems to be insisting. Shall we go?" Noah asked.

"I mean, she seems nice. She doesn't seem like—"

"She keeps a woman called Chloe tied up in a cage in the corner of her room?" He laughed at this.

"No! She doesn't seem the type. And . . . I kind of need the toilet too . . ." I felt utterly embarrassed saying this, but was relieved when Noah agreed with me.

We followed her down a dirt road that had turned to mud. Huge puddles of dirty brown water flew up at us as we drove. After another muddy five minutes, we arrived at a small farmhouse in the middle of nowhere.

"Wow, this is amazing," I said, gazing at the old sandstone farmhouse in front of us. "D" for double cab indicated for us to park under the car port with her, and when we finally did, I realized just how loud the rain had been.

"Come inside!" She climbed out of the car. "It's warm and I'll put the kettle on. TIAAANNN!" she screamed, so loudly that I flinched.

"LIEFIE!" An equally loud shout came from what looked like a workshop at the back of the car port. "What's wrong?" Tiaan emerged from the workshop. He was portly and wide, holding an equally wide and portly-looking knife. His other hand was covered in a dark liquid and he wiped it across his blue overalls.

"Shame, these poor people were sitting on the road in the car, waiting for the rain to pass."

"Ag, shame, man. They must come inside, for some coffee, liefie!" It was strange to hear such a large man—really, he was huge, well over six feet, calling his wife "lovie."

"Yes, that's what I said!" And then she turned to us and smiled. "I'm Mienkie, by the way. And this is Tiaan."

"I'm Noah, and this is Zoe," Noah said quickly.

"Come now, let's get you inside and warmed up," Mienkie said.

"Give me a minute," Tiaan shouted. "I have to finish Susie off." And with that he disappeared back into the workshop with his knife . . . *a knife?*

I looked at Noah and my eyes widened. "Finish Susie off?" I mouthed.

"Come! Come! No point in staying out in this terrible weather." Mienkie waved her arm at us and then disappeared into the house.

"Who's Susie?" I hissed at Noah. "What does he mean, finish her off?"

THWAK! A loud sound, so loud that we heard it over the rain, came from the workshop and Noah and I both jumped.

"Um . . . what's going on here?" I asked.

"I don't know . . ." Noah looked around the place, and so did I. And that's when I noticed all the chainsaws lined up against the wall.

"Why do you need so many chainsaws?"

"I don't know," Noah whispered back to me.

THWAK! And another sound, followed by another.

"Noah, I don't know about this place." I took a step back towards the car.

"Me neither." Noah also took a backward step.

"I'm getting a weird feeling here." A shiver ran down my spine, into my feet and toes.

"And she was so insistent we come here . . ." Noah sounded thoughtful. As if he was connecting dots in his head. I knew what those dots were, and scarily, the picture was starting to come into focus.

"Maybe we should get out of here." I shuffled further away from the house.

And just when the feeling couldn't get any worse, Mienkie stuck her head out the door and held a box in the air.

"Tiiiaaan!"

"Yes, liefie!" Tiaan stuck his head out the workshop again.

"What's in here?" She waved the box at him.

"It arrived for you when you were out!"

Mienkie looked at the box excitedly. "Oooh! I think it's Lucy's eyes! I've been waiting so long for these."

"That's nice, liefie," Tiaan shouted. "I'll be in soon, I've just peeled Susie's leg." And with that, both their heads disappeared around their respective doors and Noah and I were left blinking at each other.

"That's it! Let's get the hell out of here. GO!" I ran for the car, Noah close behind me, we flung the doors open and jumped in.

"Oh my God!" I grabbed at the seatbelt but pulled too fast and it jerked. "Did you see that knife he had! And why is he peeling someone's leg? And why are there so many chainsaws? And who is Lucy and why are her eyes in a box? Oh. My. God. Where the hell are we? I've watched enough crime shows to know what happens next. Why did we come here?"

Noah turned the engine on. "Who are these people?"

"Let's not find out. Go! Go! Go!" I patted him on the shoulder frantically as he plunged the keys in and the engine sprang to life.

"And was that . . . dried blood on his hands?" I gasped.

Noah slammed the car into reverse and swung around in his seat. I was looking forward to our speedy getaway. The car lurched back, but then stopped so hard my head hit the back of the seat.

"Shit! How did he get there?"

"Where?" I swung around, only to see Tiaan standing behind the car. I squinted to get a better look at him, and when I did . . .

"GOOOOO!" I smacked Noah on the leg. "He's wearing a

mask! A mask! Like in *Friday the Thirteenth*, and he has a knife in his hand. Go! Go!" *This was the documentary, right here!* And at this moment, the director was busy cutting between the scenes of a dramatic re-enactment of Noah and I desperately trying to escape the scene of the crime.

"Shittttt!" Noah looked at me with the widest eyes I'd ever seen.

"Reverse!"

"We'll run him over!"

"Do it!" I wailed in panic. "Before he kills us and they do God knows what with our legs and eyes!"

"Uh . . . I don't think I can run someone over!"

"He's coming towards the door! Go forward and through there!" I pointed at the gap between the workshop and the house. "DRIVE!" With all my might, I pushed Noah's leg down on the accelerator. The tires spun and tossed water into the air before we flew forward through the gap and onto another dirt road.

"We're FREEEE!" I yelled, looking over my shoulder at Tiaan. And then, the car stopped.

"Why are you stopping?"

"We're stuck!" Noah's voice trembled.

"What?"

"In this muddy puddle!"

"Reverse!"

Noah ground the gears into reverse and we both looked behind us. The wheels spun again, throwing an avalanche of brown mud into the air.

"Forward!" I shouted when we didn't move. Noah repeated the action, and more mud flew into the air. With each wheelspin I could feel us sinking deeper and deeper into the mud and our hopes of escape sinking deeper and deeper and deeper, until a knock on the window confirmed that all hope was officially gone.

"What are you doing?" Tiaan's voice was a little muffled through his mask.

Another knock made us look to the other window. "Where are you going?" It was Mienkie.

I was going to die. This was it. I was sandwiched between two lunatics and, right now, the director was showing side-by-side photos of them. Then and now. Smiling on their wedding day, and then manically in their mug shots. I closed my eyes for a second and a strange calm descended on me and, when I opened them again, I knew what to do.

"Noah, it was really nice meeting you, and I've had such fun with you, and I wanted to thank you for everything you've done for me." I reached over and took Noah by the hand. If I was going to die at the hands of some old-age serial killers, it was at least with Noah's comforting hand in mine.

CHAPTER 44

"$\mathcal{T}$his is not where our story ends!" Noah hissed at me, placing his hands on my shoulders. "I am not dying today. Not here. I refuse!"

"What do you suggest?"

"Helllloooo." Mienkie tapped on the window again and a flash of silver made me turn.

"Oh God, she also has a knife, and she's knocking on the window with it!"

"I think you're stuck in this puddle," Tiaan said at the other window, pointing at the puddle with his massive knife.

"Smile at them," Noah said under his breath. "Smiiiile."

"Okay." I plastered the biggest smile across my face that I could muster.

"Natural smile!" Noah snapped.

"I'm trying!"

"So, this is what we are going to do, Zoe—" Noah started.

"The kettle has boiled!" Mienkie cut him off, leaning down and looking straight at us through the window.

"We're going to climb out of this car and we're going to act normal and natural and then we're going to run!" Noah continued.

"Run where? You know how long it would take to get to the road?" I said through the toothy grin that was starting to hurt my face.

"No, we're going to run into that workshop of his, find something to block the door with and phone the police!"

"But Susie is in there, and whatever may or may not be left of her leg."

"Exactly, and I'm sure we'll find many things in there to defend ourselves with!"

"I hate this idea." My smile was starting to falter. It was just too hard to maintain it under the circumstances.

"Well, I hate the idea of dying!" Noah said. "Where's your phone?"

"Right here, in my handbag."

"Bring it with you. Mine is in a bag on the back seat." He reached for the door handle. "Ready?"

"Nooot really." I picked up my handbag and also reached for the door handle.

"Climb out first, acting normal and natural, wait for my signal, and then run! Okay?"

"Okay!" I started pushing the door open, and Mienkie moved back. I kept my eyes glued on the knife she was wielding and, oh my God, there were red smears all over it. It was smeared red from top to bottom, as if she had just sawed through an arm.

"Where were you going?" Tiaan asked.

"Uh, we were just, we remembered that we actually had to be, uh, somewhere," Noah stuttered. He was a terrible liar.

"Oh, that's such a pity!" Mienkie said. "We were so looking forward to having guests. People seldom come round here." She smiled at me and I nearly fainted at the sight of her red-smeared teeth. *Like a fucking cannibal!* It was bad enough that they peeled legs—did they also eat them?

"NOW!" Noah screamed, and I didn't hesitate. My feet hit the floor and mud flew as I raced through the puddles. Noah grabbed me by the hand and pulled me into the workshop. I blinked when I entered, my eyes trying to adjust to the total blackness.

"We need something to block the door," Noah said in between gulps for air.

"I can't see a thing," I shouted.

"Grab your phone torch!"

"Okay, okay." I scrambled for my phone but dropped my bag. "Shit!"

"Find it!" I could hear he was bumping into things. I fell to my hands and knees and crawled across the floor, hands reaching out in front of me, looking for the familiar feel of my phone.

"I can't find it!" I wailed at Noah.

"I can't find anything to block the door with," Noah wailed back at me with the exact same-sounding voice I had, one laced with terror. "I can't see a damn thi—"

We paused in horror as the lights flicked on.

"Nooooo," I whispered, closing my eyes tightly because I just couldn't face what was coming. Maybe it wouldn't hurt as badly if my eyes were closed?

"What are you guys doing?" Mienkie asked.

"Why are you crawling on the floor like that?" Tiaan asked.

Well, this was it, wasn't it? The end of it. The end of my life, and I couldn't even remember that much of it anyway. What a waste, that I could only account for a few short years and now it would all be over. I turned slowly, catching Noah's eye on the way. We both looked towards the door just as a lightning bolt ripped through the sky. We screamed and reached for each other as Tiaan and Mienkie stood silhouetted against the doorway, knives in hand.

"Please don't kill us. I don't want to die!" I howled at the top of my lungs.

"Wait! Wait!" Noah stood up and walked in front of me. "Take me and let her go. You can kill me, but you have to let her go."

"Kill you?" Mienkie asked, coming forward.

"Why would we kill you?" Tiaan also stepped forward.

"You have knives! You have Lucy's eyes and you're peeling Susie's leg!" I shouted at them, peering around Noah, who was now completely blocking me. They shared a look, and then when they glanced back at us, they burst out laughing. Their laughter was so wild and loud and unrestrained. Mienkie was even bent over at the waist and Tiaan rested his hand on a nearby bench to support himself.

"You thought we were killers!" Mienkie howled.

"Well, aren't you?" Noah asked. "Who are Lucy and Suzy and what are you doing with them?"

"Look around," Mienkie said.

"Look arou—" I repeated as I turned my head and took in the illuminated room for the first time.

"This is Susie." Tiaan walked up to a bench and picked up what looked like a ball of fur.

"I do taxidermy. This is the little squirrel that lived in the tree in front of our house for years. We called her Susie, after one of my favorite songs, 'Susie Q.' You know it? I used to go out every morning and feed her. And then, one day, she wasn't there. I went to look for her, and she was dead. I couldn't bear to bury her, she had been part of our lives here for years, so I thought I would memorialize her."

"You . . . taxidermy . . . squirrel . . . Susie?" I muttered, trying to make sense of things.

"You know, I get so attached to my animals as a farmer I name them all, and one day, I just thought I'd like to be able to keep them with me when they die. So I learned how to do taxidermy."

"That's not weird at all," I whispered to Noah.

"And Lucy's eyes?" Noah asked.

Mienkie pointed at a workstation behind us and we both turned. "I'm a reborner."

"A what?" I asked, staring at a table full of miniature body parts, still not sure what I was looking at.

"I make reborn babies. I make them from scratch, but the eyes are the only thing I can't make, so I have to order them."

"But the knife," I pointed at Mienkie. "It's covered in blood."

"Cutting up some red velvet cake! For tea!" She gave me a massive smile with those red-smeared teeth of hers then nudged Tiaan.

"Why do you have so many chainsaws?" Noah asked.

"I rent them out to the farmers close by for some extra money, and I rent out other tools too." He pointed to the other side of the work-shop, and there it was, a whole wall of various power tools. There was a beat in the conversation and everything suddenly went very quiet.

"Can you believe it, liefie, they thought we were serial killers." And then she and Tiaan laughed again, and Noah and I looked at each other and, this time, our cheeks went as red as the cake on Mienkie's teeth.

CHAPTER 45

～

"Well, we simply cannot let you go now that it's dark," Mienkie said, looking through the curtains at the world outside. It had stopped raining about an hour ago, but now it was night-time. With the homicidal misunderstanding cleared up, we'd all sat in the lounge together and enjoyed far too many slices of cake and koeksisters. Tiaan and Mienkie had told us their life story, how they'd met at a diner that Mienkie was working at, skating around on roller-skates serving food. That actually happened, not just in movies. How she'd been the prettiest girl he'd ever seen and he'd told her that very night that he was going to marry her! How they had moved to this farm fifty years ago and raised two boys and more sheep than they could remember. I'd told them my story, and they had listened, fascinated by it all.

"You're just going to have to stay the night then!" Mienkie declared, straightening the pink crocheted tablecloth in front of her. I had quickly discovered that pink doilies and crochet were very popular fixtures in this house; even the toilet had one of those pink crocheted seat covers with lace frills around the edges. I just couldn't get it out of my mind the entire time I was weeing: what if someone missed just a little? Next time you sat down you would sit on a wet, woolly seat. And of course, the spare toilet paper was kept tucked up the crocheted pink skirt of a Barbie doll standing on the cistern looking at you!

Their farmhouse was an absolute visual feast, because in amongst all of that were taxidermy sheep heads on the wall, and little taxidermy calves, rolled up in a ball, set on a bed of fake grass, looking like they were sleeping angels. Tiaan was very proud of his taxidermy animals and could name every single one of them and tell me the story of how they lived and how they died. And still, if that wasn't enough, rows and rows of reborn baby dolls. Freakishly realistic looking, staring down at you with massive eyes that never blinked. And in one corner, rather disturbingly, a lamb and a baby were curled up together.

But what they lacked in decorating taste—not that I should pass judgement—they made up for in warmth and hospitality and conversation. And after a huge home-cooked meal, which I was almost too full to eat after all the cake, a nightcap on the veranda looking up at the stars, and a mug of warm milk in case we needed anything else in our bellies, Mienkie showed us to the spare bedroom.

"Now, just because we seem old-fashioned and live in the middle of nowhere, it doesn't mean I don't know what's going on in the world around us," Mienkie said, holding onto the bedroom door and leaning towards us conspiratorially.

"Huh?" Noah and I exchanged a confused look.

"S.E.X." She whisper-spelled that.

"Beg your pardon?" Noah raised his brows at her.

"Now, in my day, when Tiaan and I got married, it was frowned on to have it before marriage, or even to talk about it. I mean, no one said a word about it, no one told you anything at all. You had to figure it all out yourself when you got married. For the first three months I don't even think we knew if we were having it!" she said in a very serious whisper now.

Noah and I glanced at each other, and I could see he was biting back a smile. If he continued to do that, I would soon be biting one down too.

"And when I think we finally did get it right, it was very quick, you know." She leaned in a little closer. "Let's just say, we weren't very good at it. But we got better, we managed to have two boys, so we must have got it right at least twice." She laughed now and then smacked me on the arm. "I'm just teasing. Tiaan is a very giving lover."

"Uh . . . happy to hear it," I said, and nodded over at Noah. "Don't you think?"

"Mmm, yes," he said, his hidden smile growing.

"Anyway, my point is, I know what the kids are up to these days. My God, I raised two teenage boys. You could not wash the sheets fast enough, if you know what I mean." She looked at Noah directly now and raised her brows at him.

"Uh . . . yes, I do know what you mean. Unfortunately," Noah whispered that last part.

"Anyway, I know you young people are having S.E.X. before marriage now, before you even get to know each other on all these computer things and the things on your phone, doing that, whatever it's called where you send those sexy messages. Anyway . . ."

Where the hell was this conversation going?

"So you can sleep in the same room, I don't see any wedding bands, but that's okay. Tiaan and I are very modern here. I didn't even make up another room for you, so I really mean it."

"Oh . . ." I started.

"No . . ." Noah said.

"We're not . . . uh . . ."

"Not." Noah added.

"Together," I clarified.

She looked from Noah to me and back again.

"Well, that's okay too. Like I said, I know what goes on these days—friends with benefits. That's what my son said he had with the girl two farms away. Friends for years, they used to play together in the sprinklers naked as toddlers, and then, you know, the hormones hit and next thing you're catching them in the sheep barn, but as much as he protested they were just friends, they're now married and I have my first grandchild on the way." She clapped her hands at this. "I don't think that friends with benefits thing works."

"But we really are just friends," I said, pointing at the space between Noah and me.

"Really?" She looked confused now. "But he was willing to sacrifice his life for you back when you thought Tiaan and I were South Africa's most wanted."

"He's just a nice guy," I offered.

"Did you tell them, liefie?" Tiaan's voice boomed down the passage.

"Yeees!" Mienkie shouted back.

"Good! We're very progressive here, we even watched that movie . . . *what's it called, liefie*?"

"*Fifty Shades*," she shouted back down the corridor, and then whispered, "Although, not really for us, all that stuff. We tried it, but no."

"Not for us!" Tiaan shouted down the corridor.

And then Noah surprised me when he agreed. "Me neither."

"Oh?" I turned and looked at Noah.

"Very dangerous. You won't believe how many *Fifty Shades*-related injuries we get called out to. Whenever a new movie comes out, new injuries."

"Really?" Mienkie and I said at the same time.

"Realllyyyy!" Noah dragged the word out and raised one brow at us, for added dramatic tension, no doubt. We all looked at each other for a while. I could tell Mienkie was doing exactly what I was, letting her imagination run away with her. Only I was trying to remember exactly what *Fifty Shades* was about. I think I'd heard about it, but I couldn't remember watching it. Besides, I didn't watch that many movies.

"Fascinating!" Mienkie finally said, once she looked like she'd concluded the painting of her mental image. "So, anyway, like we said, it's all good. You guys can share the room, not a problem for us." And with that she opened the door and practically pushed us through it.

"Goodnight," she called, and closed the door behind us.

Noah and I looked at the bed, and hundreds of pairs of reborn-baby eyes stared back at us. I shivered. Being so close to them in this small, confined space was making me feel nervous. But was it the dolls? Or was it the look on Noah's face as he stared at the bed?

"Let me get another room," he said, walking towards the door.

"Wait! No. She hasn't made it up, don't want to inconvenience her . . ." I looked back at the bed. "I mean, we can share. Can't we?"

Noah stared at the bed again, as if weighing up some complex equation, and then he smiled at me. It looked forced. "Sure we can."

CHAPTER 46

~

Moments later, the two of us were awkwardly deposited in the bed. It had taken ages ridding the bed of all the newborn babies in order to be able to even get to anything that resembled a duvet. And when we'd finally navigated our way in, we lay there on our backs, looking at the ceiling, shoulders touching. I was acutely aware of the feeling of his shoulder touching mine. How could I not be? It was making my entire arm hot. I tried to ignore the feeling, but it was taking so much concentration that I was now lying dead still, like one of the stuffed baby lambs, or one of the dolls themselves. God knows, I wasn't even blinking.

"So that was a weird conversation." Noah finally broke the ceiling-staring silence.

"I know." I turned my head to look at him, but he had turned his too and, as a result, our noses missed each other's by millimeters. It was a small double bed, and Noah was so large and broad that it made it even smaller. We both turned back to the ceiling again. Safer, that was. Less chance of nose-bumping.

"What's *Fifty Shades*?" I asked.

"You can't remember it?"

"I think I do. I'm not sure."

"It's probably one of the most famous books and films of our time."

"Well, I didn't remember that Becca Thorne book. My memory is still weird and sketchy. So, what is it? And why are you and Mienkie not into it? Into what? And what injuries?"

Noah turned his head again, and I did the same. His cheeks seemed a little rosier this time. "You really don't remember it?"

I shook my head.

"The characters in the book and film sort of engage in—oh, I don't know what the right term is—practice! Yes, they practice bondage. You know?"

I blinked. "Bondage?"

He cleared his throat again. "Tying each other up, spanking, that sort of thing."

"OH! Oh, yes. I've, um . . . read about that," I said, remembering a moment in *Heat of the Desert, Heart of the Sheik* when Sheik Khalifa binds Amanda Stone's hands with a silken cloth and blindfolds her eyes and . . .

Amanda had never felt anything like it. With her eyesight now gone, she could smell and feel and taste him so much more as he brought himself down on her, his heavy muscular chest pressing into her pink, peaked nipples. And because she couldn't lay a hand on him, as he had bound hers, it made her want to touch him even more. To feel his swollen sword and unsheathe it.

"Okay, goodnight," I said, and quickly turned over, feeling too hot and awkward to continue the conversation. I felt Noah turn and, because of the size limitations of the bed, his entire back now pressed into mine.

"Goodnight," he said. And then we lay in silence again.

"What kind of injuries?" I asked.

"Uh . . . you know, this and that."

"Like what?"

I heard Noah take a breath and felt his back expand against mine. "Well, there are a few we need to rush to the ER for, um . . . foreign-body removal, if you get what I mean."

"Foreign . . . OH! Oh. Right!" I thought about my lipstick and melted into the mattress with embarrassment.

"And then the odd mishap with ropes, and once, a guy got electrocuted because his girlfriend tied him up with an electrical wire and the massage oil acted like a conductor."

I laughed at this. Although I did feel a little bad doing it. "Poor guy!"

Noah laughed too and the bed wobbled ever so slightly as he did, forcing our bodies into each other's a little more.

"Can I ask you something else, Noah?"

"You're already asking me questions."

"Would you really have let them kill you over me?"

"I guess that is what I said in the moment, isn't it? Out of instinct, when my adrenalin was pumping, so I suppose yes!"

"Wait." I turned around and Noah did the same, and now we were face to face again. "Are you saying that now you wouldn't? Now that your adrenalin isn't pumping?"

Noah smiled. "I kind of like living."

"So if they burst through the door again with knives, what would you do?"

"Tell them to take you first." He burst out laughing again and I hit him on the shoulder. It was like hitting concrete.

"Ow!" I winced, pulling my hand away.

"Sorry." He took my hand and looked at it in a way that made my fingers feel like they were on fire.

"You have very big muscles," I heard myself say without thinking, and then, because it was such an odd thing to say, I started to laugh. "Sorry, I didn't mean to say that. But they are very big! And hard."

Noah smiled at me, but this time the smile seemed different and it stopped my laughter immediately. "What?"

"I'm having fun," he suddenly said, and it caught me off guard.

"Me too."

"I haven't had fun in a while," he continued.

"Well, I don't think I've had fun in at least seven years, or so it seems."

"Maybe you broke a mirror seven years ago and you're finally coming out of it."

"What?"

"Seven years' bad luck?" He raised his brows at me.

I shook my head.

"It's this thing my gran said to me when I was small. If you break a mirror, you get seven years' bad luck."

"That's awful!" I said.

"But I've never broken a mirror. I always handle them with extra care."

"Huh?" I thought about it for a while. I kind of liked that thought. That maybe I had done something like that, and now, I was finally coming out of it. I smiled at Noah and suddenly wanted to lean in and kiss him on the cheek. But I didn't.

"Goodnight, Noah," I said, and turned again.

I felt him move again and, this time, I didn't try and pull my body away. Instead, I just let it settle where it was, leaning against his big back, and it felt good.

"Night, Zoe."

God, I loved it when he called me by that name.

CHAPTER 47

"*H*ere we go." Mienkie passed us two brown paper packets through the car window.

"What's this?" I asked.

"Padkos," she replied.

"Food for the road," I repeated, translating the Afrikaans into English. I peered inside one of the bags and saw a sandwich, a juice box and some chocolates and biscuits. I smiled up at her and Tiaan, feeling like we were their kids, going off to school with a thoughtfully packed school lunch. "Thank you so much for your hospitality."

"And for not killing you," Tiaan joked, and we all laughed.

"Especially for that!" I said.

"We're going to miss you. If you are ever in the area again, you must pop in."

"We definitely will," Noah said as he started the car.

"Wait, here. Take our phone number. We don't have a cell phone. Our sons are always telling us to get one, but I just don't know how to use them."

I pulled my phone out and added her number. I paused before saving it: this was my fifth number in only a few days and this made me smile.

"Goodbye!" Tiaan and Mienkie said together as we pulled off down the road.

I turned around in my seat and waved until they disappeared over the rise.

"That was a really nice, unexpected surprise," I said, as we joined the main road.

"It was. I really liked them."

"Me too," I mumbled thoughtfully, thinking about all the strange ways that life had thrown people into my path recently. If it hadn't been for the elevator accident, I wouldn't have met Noah. If it hadn't been for the storm, I wouldn't have met Tiaan and Mienkie.

I looked at the road in front of us. The storm had definitely left its mark. Little streams and dams seemed to have popped up all over the place, as well as . . . *something else.* I sat up straight as a feeling gripped me.

"Stop the car!" I suddenly heard myself say. "Stop it."

Noah pulled over.

"What is it?" he asked, looking through the windshield. Only, it wasn't what was on the road that I was looking at; it was what was on the sides of the road that had caught my attention.

"There." I pointed into the vast fields that lay to the left and right of us. I reached for the door handle and began pushing it open.

"The flowers," I said, as I climbed out of the car to survey my surroundings. Because there, spreading out from the sides of the road on both sides, all the way into the distance, into the open fields and up to the faraway mountains that dotted the horizon, were pink and white flowers. Pops of color on the otherwise muted background. A colorful carpet stretching out as far as the eye could see.

"Cosmos," I said.

"Yes," Noah replied. "That's how you know it's autumn in South Africa. The cosmos comes out, and soon it's chocolate Easter eggs."

I walked up to the first flower I saw. Pink, with a bright yellow center looking straight at me. A darker, brilliant pink in the center radiated outwards to a soft pastel pink that you just wanted to somehow capture and use it to paint all your walls with. Because it was the kind of color that could only be associated with happiness . . . but . . .

But, what?

I moved deeper into the field, touching the cosmos as I went, running my hands over the flowers, picking up pollen like a bee making honey. Making something sweet . . . but . . .

But what was this feeling?

Walking through this field of sunshiney brightness, two very different emotions started growing inside me. I could feel one coming from one part of my brain and the other coming from a very different part. A hidden part. Both feelings rose up inside me, and their crashing together felt inevitable and imminent. One feeling: freedom, happiness, the best and most beautiful happiness ever; and the other feeling . . .

Darkness. Pain. Tragedy. Everything that was bad about the world.

How could these two feelings coexist, let alone both be building up in me at the same time, rushing towards each other, about to collide? God only knew what they would form when they met in the middle of my consciousness. I looked back at Noah. He was standing by the roadside watching me as I walked deeper and deeper into the fields of flowers.

And then, like the eruption of a rumbling volcano shaking the ground beneath your feet, they collided. My body physically jolted. The sensation took my breath away and a sensation of physical pain wracked my body. It was so overwhelming that I felt my knees going weak. I couldn't stop it. My legs wobbled. My head spun and I couldn't stop myself from falling.

My knees collided with the ground. Hard. My head disappeared into the flowers, until all I saw around me were stems. Green stems, as I kneeled down in the field for a reason I just didn't understand.

"Zoe! Zoe!" I heard Noah shout from behind me, and even in that moment a small smile flicked across my face.

Zoe! I liked that name so much. But I stayed like that, looking at the stems in front of me, until I felt those two great, comforting hands slip under my arms and pull me up to my feet. I don't know why I was on the ground. Why my legs had buckled under me and made it impossible to stand up. Why the earth below had reached up and grabbed me and pulled me down to it, as if it wanted to show me something from a different perspective. As if it wanted me to look at the world from my knees?

"Zoe? You okay?" Noah spun me around until I was facing him. I looked at him, into his eyes, but it was as if I wasn't really seeing anything. I still wasn't present in this moment. Something had severed me from it.

"Zoe?" He shook me and I snapped out of it.

"I . . ." I mumbled.

"Come on, let's get you to the car. When last did you eat or drink anything? It could be your blood sugar. Do you feel any chest pain? Any breathlessness? What about any tingling sensations? Can you smile for me, please? Smile." His words came at me like a steam train. One after the other after the other. "Zoe, I need you to smile."

I smiled at him and his shoulders seemed to relax a little. He took his smart watch and strapped it around my wrist. He pressed the screen and looked down at the heart graphic as a number popped up next to it.

"Ninety bpm. A bit high. But fine. Do you feel any numbn—"

"Shhh," I put my finger over his lips. "Shhh. I'm fine—well, physically. There was . . . I had . . . I can't explain it. It was like a memory. Well, not a memory, but this overwhelming feeling of a memory. Or a feeling from a memory. Two feelings, and they kind of just—I don't know how to explain it—overwhelmed me."

Even though he'd stopped talking, I hadn't moved my finger from his lips. It had not been my intention to keep it there for so long, and I stared down at it. His lips were lovely. He had a little mole next to them, like a Cindy Crawford mole, but so, *sooo* much more masculine. There was a bit of stubble surrounding his lips, as if he'd missed a day of shaving. They looked smooth, and pink, and so kissable, kind of like how Amanda Stone's had looked to the sheik in chapter five where he was tempted to just lean in and kiss her, right there and then . . .

But I would never just kiss a guy, would I?

Well, Zenobia wouldn't. She hadn't kissed a guy in years. Zenobia hadn't been on a date in years.

But Zoe . . . *she was different.* She was the kind of girl who would just kiss a guy because she felt like it. She was brave. She had balls. She threw caution to the wind and she . . .

I moved my finger off his lips, and he seemed to part them slightly, as if inviting me to kiss them. And so, I leaned in and softly, slowly, planted the smallest of kisses on his lips. But I didn't pull away entirely afterwards. I stayed there, only an inch away from his lips, to let him know that I was going to kiss him again, or let him know that it was alright if he wanted to kiss me. But he didn't. Instead, he took a step back.

"Zoe, uh . . . I . . . we can't." He reached up and ran his hand through his hair.

"Oh." I said, feeling utterly shocked. "Oh, uh . . . okay." I took a step back too. Mortification and embarrassment gripped me, and I felt so, so stupid. Damn, why had I listened to Zoe?

"It's not ethical. I'm the paramedic who saved you, and you don't have all your memories back, so I feel that it would be inappropriate and, uh . . ." He took another step back.

"Oh. I see." I also took a step backwards. We were two magnets repelling each other, not pulling together.

Push or pull?

"I'm sorry if I gave you the wrong impression and—"

"No! No!" I cut him off. "You didn't, I was just . . ." I felt like I wanted to cry. This was the most embarrassing thing that had ever happened to me. And I was the girl who'd had a meltdown in front of one hundred people at work and gotten stuck in a piece of gym equipment. So, I should be able to take humiliation. But this was, *wow*. There were no words for this, as I watched Noah back away from me.

"I understand," I said quickly. "I just got, I was . . . overwhelmed. There was so much, in my head, so many strange emotions, and it was all just confusing and, and . . ."

"I understand." Noah sounded sympathetic, which made me feel even worse. And even though he said he understood, I knew he didn't. And I also knew that Zoe was clearly very bad when it came to reading signals. What did I expect? She had almost zero experience in it. I wasn't listening to her again, certainly not when it came to men.

"We should get back on the road." Noah looked back at the car. "Unless you want to stay here a little more?"

"No." I shook my head then looked back at the field. "I don't want to stay here anymore." In fact, I wanted to be as far away from this field as possible, not to mention as far away from this moment as possible too.

CHAPTER 48

~

$\mathcal{W}$e pulled up to my parents' house about two awkward hours later. The drive, after the field, had been a silent one, for the most part. Other than the forced small talk that we'd made to try and fill the endless silences. There were the terribly uncomfortable glances too, the restless finger tapping on the steering wheel—by Noah—and on the dashboard, by me. All in all, I'd felt like I'd wanted to crawl out of my skin and slither out through the vents in the air-conditioning system to escape the confines of the car. And every now and then, when Noah thought I was looking out of the window, I could see him staring at me in the reflection in the glass. He had this look like he was about to open his mouth and say something, but he never did.

"We're here," he said, when we pulled up to the house. It was evening, and the sun was setting. I looked up at the small house set back in the tropical garden of palm trees and overgrown shrubs.

"Do you recognize it?" he asked.

"I do." I climbed out of the car and walked up to the front door. I remembered so much about this house now. I'd lived here and studied for a few years, but I couldn't really tell you much about this part of the world. Driving here, things had seemed vaguely familiar, but not so much that I could stick a concrete memory to anything. It was as if I'd lived here, but only stayed inside this house and never ventured out. I knocked on the door. I wasn't sure what to expect from my parents. I knew that we weren't that close, and I had a feeling that we'd had a big fight once, but I had no idea what it was about.

My parents came to the door, and their faces were almost exactly how I'd pictured them in my head. Only a little older, which made me think I hadn't seen them in a while. And the hug that they both gave me seemed to imply that too. They drew me into their arms and hugged me so hard and long that I wasn't sure if I was able to breathe. And when my mother started crying against my shoulder, I started crying too, even though I wasn't really sure why.

They led us into the small sitting room at the front of the house, and when we were all seated, introductions had been made and we had looked at each other self-consciously for a while, my father spoke.

"You say you don't remember anything about your childhood?"

"No. I don't." When I'd phoned them earlier, I'd explained everything. My parents shared a sideways glance now. They both looked concerned.

"What?" I sat up straighter in my chair.

"You don't remember *anything* from your childhood?" my mom asked now, even though my father had just covered that. "Nothing?"

I shook my head and my parents exchanged yet another look. A look that was quite obviously loaded with something.

"What? Tell me. Just tell me. I need to know."

"Well," my father said, moving forward in his chair and lacing his fingers together. I looked over at Noah. He too had sat forward, as if he was waiting to hear a really important thing. Because you knew it was important. The air in the room, the way it hummed and buzzed, told you what was about to be said was important. Everything in the room seemed to know that too, because soon the room felt smaller, as if the walls were also leaning in to listen.

"There was an accident, when you were young," my dad said solemnly.

"What kind of accident?" Along with the walls, the space around me shrank.

"A car accident," my dad said, glancing at my mother; she was crying again.

"Where? How?"

"We were on our way to a game reserve to spend Easter with your aunt and uncle. We were almost there, and you saw this field of cosmos on the side of the road."

"What?" I looked over at Noah and my eyes widened, as did his.

"You wanted to pick your aunt some flowers. So, we all stopped and got out of the car. You ran around, picking flowers for her."

"They were such beautiful flowers," my mother added, wiping a tear away from her eyes. "And you were so happy and excited to take them to her."

"And then what happened?" I asked.

"You had finished picking the flowers and we were all walking back to the car together, and then . . ." My father clenched his jaw and his fists, as if he wanted to hit someone.

"It happened so quickly," my mom jumped in.

"It did. It happened so fast. He just came out of nowhere. No one saw him. We didn't see him." He sounded desperate while saying this.

"All we saw was this flash of red, and then we heard the sound. The sound . . ." My mother buried her face in her hands and shook her head. "I'll never forget it."

Noah looked at me. My mouth felt dry and my throat tight, but I managed a whispered "And then what happened?"

My mom looked like her throat was as tight as mine. She could barely get the words out and she too whispered. "A car lost control going around the corner and he just, he slammed into us. You were just about to climb back into the car, and the force of his car against ours . . . you just, you went flying."

"It happened so fast," my dad said again, that same air of intense desperation in his voice. "I didn't see it coming. If I had, I would have grabbed you and pulled you out of the way. But I didn't see it. It happened so quickly."

"So quickly," my mother echoed again, as if this was the thing that they still couldn't wrap their heads around, and then . . .

Bam!

Like the car crashing into me, the memory crashed into me too.

I saw it. Me holding onto a bunch of flowers. Me flying through the air. The flowers flying through the air. Me landing on the ground . . . *all I could see were stems.* Green stems and then sky and then flowers falling from the sky onto me. I grabbed at my shoulder as a pain wracked my body.

"You broke your shoulder," my dad said. "And your arm. Some ribs. Your back. You had to learn to do so many things all over again."

My mom stifled a little cry, and I looked at her.

"We rushed you to the hospital and they immediately took you into surgery. You had to have a lot of surgeries. But when they were over, and they had repaired the damage, we thought that was it. That they had fixed you, that you were out of the woods and you would be able to recover now . . ." My dad stopped talking. He wrung his fingers together and his knuckles went red.

"I was very sick," I suddenly heard myself say, as image after image after image of hospital rooms flashed through my mind.

My mom nodded. "A year after your accident, just when we thought all those hospitals were behind us, on a checkup, they found out you had leukemia."

"I was very sick," I said again. I looked at Noah. This was starting to make sense. The pieces were drawing themselves together and forming a picture in front of me. It was not a picture that I wanted to see. But it was a picture nonetheless, and I was looking at it.

"I spent years in and out of hospital."

"You did." My mom's voice was even softer this time. "From the age of eight until around eighteen you were in and out of hospitals. First with the damage from the accident, then all the rehab you had to do for your back, and then with the leukemia. You went into remission for a while, but then it came back."

"And we started treatment all over again," I filled in the blanks and my mom nodded. "Birthdays, and Christmas and . . . I never went to school again. I did homeschooling. Even after the cancer was gone." I was remembering more and more by the second now. The white, sterile loneliness that the four walls of the hospital provided me with. Day after day, year after year.

"I had a lot of complications from the treatment," I said, almost whispering that to myself. "The hospital became my prison." I looked up at Noah, and he gave me a sympathetic smile. The smile was warm and I wished I could reach out and grab it and put it in my pocket. Keep it close.

"But I was cured," I said, finally looking at my parents.

"Yes. You were very lucky. We were very lucky."

"I might not be able to have kids one day though," I said thoughtfully.

"No," my mother said sounding solemn. "The chemo, all the radiation . . . you might not be able to." I heard her swallow from across the room. As if swallowing down a ball of pain that was too big for her throat. "But you are alive," she whispered.

"A lot of my friends aren't alive. Many of them died." I had an image of getting close to people, only for them to die and leave me. *Push or pull?*

"Yes, they did. But you survived. You were lucky," he reiterated.

I nodded, but I didn't feel lucky. "You two were always so scared. When I was at home, you disinfected everything. I was never allowed to go outside and play with other children, because of that time I caught flu and landed up in the hospital with double pneumonia. The doctor said it was 'touch and go.'" *Touch and go.* The words echoed in my head. I'd heard them a lot as a child. More times than a child should.

"Your immune system was so compromised," my mom said.

"I used to . . ." I turned and looked at the window behind me. I got up, walked over to it, pulled the curtain aside and felt the tears flood my throat as I looked at the park. "I used to sit here and watch the other kids playing, but I couldn't play with them. One germ, just one little germ could kill me." I stared at the playground and could almost hear the excited screams and laughter as they went around and around on the merry-go-round, making themselves dizzy.

"We had to take such precautions." My mom's voice quivered now.

"You overcooked all the food. You were always so scared of me getting sick from it. From anything. You would make people who came to visit wear masks and wash their hands. We even moved to Durban because the air quality was better here than in Joburg. And sometimes, you and Dad weren't allowed to hug me."

My mom nodded and inhaled sharply. "Yes. Sometimes you had to be isolated in the hospital, to prevent infections. And when you were home, we did everything to keep you as safe as possible. We didn't want to lose you."

I turned away from the window, back to everyone in the room. All eyes were fixed on me. "I was so scared too. I was scared of dying and catching an illness and getting sick and going to hospital and . . . *I'm still so scared*. Of everything." A tear escaped my eye. Hospital was not my only prison. I'd gone from one prison into another one. A self-imposed prison. I'd locked myself away in that clean, disinfected apartment eating the same foods day after day, wearing a watch that repelled mosquitos because I was scared of malaria, removing body hair because I was scared of mites and other disease-carrying insects, scared of driving, of crossing the road, scared of people and their germs, just scared. Terrified.

I walked back to the couch and sat down. I put my head in my hands then shook it from side to side. "The last time I felt truly free and happy was in that field." I felt a hand come out and grab mine. I looked up to see whose it was. It was my mother's.

"Before the accident, we couldn't get you out of the garden in the evening to come in for supper. Always playing, climbing trees, planting flowers—I was sure you were going to become a florist. You loved being outside."

"And then, one day, I never was." The painful realization of this loss hit me hard.

"We made some mistakes," my mom suddenly said. "We wrapped you up and kept you away from life because we were scared, but I'm afraid the way we handled it made you so afraid of life and living. If we could go back and do it all again, we would do things differently. We would be more balanced." My mother started crying now, not like before. Not small tears. My father reached out and squeezed her hand. His lip was trembling, as if he too was fighting back the waterworks.

I felt Noah tense up next to me, and then he spoke for the first time since this conversation had begun. "You did what any parent would. To keep their child safe," he said firmly. "You did what you thought was right." I gazed over at him. He looked almost as broken as my parents did. I didn't feel broken, though. I felt detached. Like I was sitting outside of myself and this conversation.

"Why do I have so much money?" I asked, changing the subject.

"The man who was driving lost control because the road was cracked and damaged. We both sued city roads for their negligence, and the road accident fund paid out a lot of money, to you and him. He's in a wheelchair now. He's a quadriplegic."

"Oh God," I gasped.

"We used a lot for your medical bills, and the rest you wanted to put into a retirement fund. So we did."

"That's very sensible," I said, in a mocking way.

"We always thought you should spend some of that money. Quit that job you hate so much and go and do things with it. Get out of your apartment and travel the world. Live life. Live your dream . . . but you never wanted to. You wanted to keep it safe for 'one day.'"

"One day." I remembered that phrase so well now. And then I remembered something else. "We had a fight about that."

My mom and dad exchanged glances again. "Yes, two years ago. And we've hardly seen or heard from you since then."

"You were trying to push me to do something with the money. A cruise! That's right. I remember. You showed me all these pamphlets. You kept saying that I needed to go out and experience the world and explore. I said no."

"So much of your life was stolen from you, with the accident, the cancer. And when you got better, we always imagined that you would go on to have this big, full, wonderful life. But you didn't."

"I might as well have died in that car accident," I whispered softly, to myself, really. I didn't need anyone to acknowledge that statement. Because I knew it to be true. The accident happened, and then the illness, which robbed me of so much of my life. But when that was all over—*well,* then I went right ahead and continued robbing myself. All my memories flooded me now. Each and every one was back with full, bright glaringness. And those two feelings were back again too.

Fear! I was afraid of everything.

Anxiety! So much that it kept me awake at night.

And so I wrapped myself up in a bubble of cotton wool and hardly ventured out into the world. Hardly deviated from my routines. From the things I ate, to the way I spent my evenings, to the way I worked and got to work and the way I scrubbed everything clean and neat and shiny until there was not a sign of life left. And the way I pushed people away. The truth was that, in many ways, the illness had killed me.

I stood up. I felt shaky.

"I should go now," I said, taking a step away from everyone.

"Wait, Zen." My mom and dad stood up at the same time.

"My name is Zoe now. I'm going to change it," I blurted out.

My mom and dad smiled at me. "You never liked your name. When you were young you always said it was too old-fashioned and you wanted to change it one day."

"You shouldn't have named me after Great-aunt Zenobia," I said, and smiled back. We stood there smiling at each other for a little while, and I'm sure we were all thinking the same thing: that this felt nice. Being here, with them, felt good and right.

"We didn't know about the accident. No one told us. If we'd known, we would have come to Joburg immediately," my mom said, breaking the moment.

"I know," I said, because I did know. My mom and dad had been there with me every single step of the way. Every test, every scan, every day I had spent in hospital, they came to visit. But still, they were unable to take away the loneliness I felt when they left and I was there all alone at night. Listening to the machines and the nurses' chatter. They were not able to take that away. "You were always there for me."

"I'm sorry we fought," my dad said. "We just want the best for you."

"I know you do." I walked over to my parents and drew them both into a hug. "I love you guys," I whispered. "And I want our relationship to be different. Better."

"Us too." My mom held onto me so tightly that I thought she might never let go.

"Let's put this all behind us and start again." I pulled away and looked at them.

"A fresh, new start," my dad echoed. "With your new name, Zoe."

"It suits you," my mom said.

"Noah came up with it." I said this part with a bigger smile than I'd intended to. My mom and dad nodded, both smiling truly happy smiles, and I found myself smiling back at them too, feeling this sense of relief wash over me.

"I think I want to go now, though. I have a lot to think about."

"Of course. Why don't you come and have dinner with us before you go back to Joburg?"

"I'd like that a lot." I gave them both one last hug before walking straight out of the house and into the park across the road I hadn't been allowed to play in as a child.

CHAPTER 49

⌁

I sat on the swing and moved it back and forth gently with my feet on the ground. Noah was on the swing next to me. He hadn't said a word since we'd left the house, which felt like hours ago. Instead, he sat in silence next to me and, his toes on the ground too, pushed himself back and forth in time to my slow rhythm. A few guys in their late teens were the only other people in the park. It was dark now, and they were skateboarding down a flight of stairs and falling each time. One had made it down the banister once on his skateboard, only to crash into the dustbin at the bottom, much to the mirth of his friends. They were swigging something from a bottle and laughing like they didn't have a care in the world. They didn't seem to mind that anyone else was in the park either, and I found myself quite engrossed by what they were doing. Noah looked like he was too, because we both made an out-loud cringing sound when the one fell backwards off the wall and landed on his ass.

We both turned and smiled at each other. This was the first time in ages that we'd actually connected.

"Idiots," Noah said, with an air of affection and knowing in his voice. Like he too had once been an idiot like that. It dawned on me that I never had. I'd been in hospital while I was meant to be out and about being an idiot with my friends in a park at night.

"You okay?" he asked quietly.

"No," I said, walking myself backwards on the swing and then lifting my legs up and swinging forward. Noah did the same thing, matching my height, which wasn't very high.

"You know," I started, looking at the kids, who were now filming each other in what appeared to be fits of hysterics over something. "I've never done that before." I pointed at them.

"What? Skateboard? Or fall off walls?"

"Both." I straightened my legs and the swing moved higher. Noah did the same. "I sat in that window and watched everyone else do them. I never did. I was either in my house, or in the hospital."

"You never got to be a teen," Noah said, straightening and pulling his legs back with more force now, making his swing go even higher. I looked over and copied his movements, thrusting mine into the air too.

"I never got to be stupid and wild and a drunk idiot who tries to skateboard down a staircase." I kicked my legs and the swing went higher still.

"I did a bit of that in my youth," Noah confessed.

"See," I said, going higher still as Noah followed suit. "I never did. Ever."

"I'm sorry." Noah looked over at me, his hair moving back and forth with the motion of his swing. Our eyes locked. He was swinging higher than me now, and I leaned back further in my seat to match him. Noah laughed and did the same, making his swing shoot up into the air. I laughed as I tried to catch up to him.

"I'm going to beat you!" he shouted as he got higher.

I squealed in excited terror as I threw my body back and forth, making the swing go so high that I got an actual fright when the chains made a little jolt on my way back down.

"No, you're not!" I screamed, and kicked my legs with abandon.

"TRY ME!" Noah shouted back, reaching new heights now that I just couldn't match, no matter how much I tried. We were laughing so loudly that my ribs hurt. The laughter made it impossible to kick our legs anymore and we both stopped, simply enjoying the feeling of our swings beginning to slow down and then finally, finally, stop. I kicked my shoes in the dust below, sending a little puff of it flying, and watched it as it settled back down. This dust had been kicked and moved by so many laughing children over the years, but not me. I turned to Noah. He was resting his head against one of the chains, watching me.

"No wonder . . ." I said, as something dawned on me.

"No wonder what?" Noah asked.

"No wonder Zen is the way she is."

"You didn't get to experience life, growing up."

"No."

"You watched life pass you by through a pane of glass."

"Yes. Everything always happened out there." I kicked up the red dust again, and it went everywhere. "No wonder I have no personality."

"That's not true. You do have a personality."

I looked up at him and rolled my eyes. "Yes, beige, bland, chicken-eating, no-one-ever-notices, gray-cardigan-wearing, no-date-going me. That's a real sparkling personality. No, it's hard to develop a personality from a hospital bed, or behind a sheet of glass. I feel like I lost who I was in the field that day."

Noah looked thoughtful for a while. "So, let's go out and find it. Let's go out and re-live it all."

"Re-live what?" I asked.

"Let's go and be dumb teens! Let's get into trouble and stay out late and be wild and crazy and get grounded because we snuck in after curfew and threw up on our mom's carpet."

"Eeew."

"Yes, it wasn't one of my finest moments," Noah said. "So, let's go!"

"Where?"

"To a cool party!"

"Wha— how? I mean, how and where would we even go?" I shook my head.

Noah looked around, and then, as if a lightbulb had gone off inside him. "I know exactly who to talk to about that!"

. . . *And that's how we found ourselves driving to a club ten minutes later with a back seat full of eighteen-year-old skater boys with black hoodies, purple hair and more piercings than I'd ever seen on anyone's face before.*

CHAPTER 50

"*W*here the hell are we going?" I whispered at Noah as we started driving into the dimly lit downtown area. Honestly, this did not look like a great place. This did not look like the kind of place you wanted to be when the lights went down. This looked like the kind of place where tomorrow's gruesome headlines would be made. "I don't like it here," I whispered even lower, casting my eyes into the rear-view mirror, looking at our three traveling companions in the back seat. They all looked a little darker and more dangerous sitting in a row like that, illuminated only by the flickering lights from the dashboard, or when a rare street light actually worked and shot a faint beam of light through the window. In fact, with their hoodies pulled down like that, those chains around their necks, those piercings, I began to wonder if these were not in fact the people who helped generate those headlines.

"I have no idea," Noah whispered back, with the same trepidation in his voice that I was clearly feeling. Noah looked into the rear-view mirror too, acting cool and casual.

"So, uh . . . like where are we going . . . dudes?" he asked.

I tried to stifle a giggle at Noah's attempt at acting cool. The "dude" sounded so odd coming from his mouth.

"Uh, yeah, we're, like, going to this really underground club tonight. Like, not a lot of people know about it," the one with the eyebrow rings said.

"Yeah . . . it's kind of like, exclusive," one of the others said, the one whose face I hadn't seen yet, since his hoodie was so low.

"Like, if you weren't coming with us, you'd like not be able to get in," said the third one, the one who, for some strange reason, wore his jeans around his knees, exposing a massive section of his underwear.

"Coooool," Noah said, forcing a smile. He looked at me and raised his brows, as if trying to communicate something.

"Oh. Yes. Cool," I quickly added. Trying to play along. Trying to be this cool person who was down for whatever and all good with late-night excursions into dark and dingy places in the city.

"Yeah, there it is." Hoodie One pointed. I'd had to start calling them Hoodies One, Two and Three in my head to differentiate them, since I was unable to see their facial features. Noah slowed the car down and the two of us looked in the direction he was pointing.

"Where?" Noah asked. All I could see was a row of dumpsters.

"There. You can park around the corner," Hoodie Two said.

I flashed Noah a look, a question. A "*do you think the car will be okay here? Or do you think it will be stolen a minute after we park it?*" I think they got wind of what we were thinking, because Hoodie One quickly spoke.

"Don't worry, there are car guards," he said.

"Although, like, I wouldn't steal this car, man. It's not cool." The Hoodies all laughed. "Like, if I was an adult, I would not drive a car like this."

"What?" I swung around. "There's nothing wrong with a Toyota sedan. It's a very reliable and comfortable car."

"Exactly," Hoodie Three piped up. "Boring."

"It is not boring. It's sensible, it's—"

"A rental," Noah cut me off. "It was all they had. I would have gotten a mustang if I could, but you know. Last-minute trip. You take what they have." Noah winked at me discreetly, and I knew what to do.

"That's right. This was the only car. I mean, if it were up to me, I would have taken a . . . a . . ." My mind was blank. I looked at Noah and raised my brows.

"Porsche. You love the Porsche," he said to me.

I nodded. "Yes. I do. Especially the red ones."

"Cooool." There was a murmur from the back seat. "I bet they are, like, fuck-off fast!" one of the Hoodies said. I was really starting to get them somewhat confused. If they'd just had the sense to wear different-color hoodies, it would have made identifying them a whole lot easier. But they had all insisted on black.

"Totally. Fuck off," I added, getting the swing of this cool thing.

"Park here." One of them pointed. I think he was Hoodie Three.

Around the corner, we saw a row of parked cars and bikes. Most of them were black and mean-looking with tinted windows, so when we pulled our pale blue Toyota into the mix, I got what they had been saying. This would be the last car that anyone would steal here, even though it did stick out like a sore thumb. We climbed out of the car, and that's when I noticed the huge man emerge from the shadows.

"Oh God!" I jumped back and grabbed onto Noah's arm.

"Dude, it's okay, that's the car guard." One of our hooded friends waved at him, and then shot him a very nonchalant "Yo," the kind of "Yo" that seemed to take so little effort to say. The kind of "Yo" you hardly opened your mouth for and barely made any sounds.

The shadow-lurker gave a half-hearted head-shake. I guess that was meant to act as some sort of acknowledgement that he would, indeed, look after our car. We followed behind the three skaters as they walked up the very dimly lit street that was quite literally on the wrong side of the tracks. Running parallel to this road, under the dark and dodgy-looking bridge, was in fact, a railway track. We carried on walking until we came to the collection of dumpsters. Most of them were covered in graffiti. Bright colors, rude words, but most interesting of all was the rather crudely sprayed lettering "Worm Sheep Head!" I stopped and looked at it for a while, trying to figure this out. Was it code for something? I hardly knew.

"Are you sure we're safe?" I nudged Noah. I was still clutching onto him.

"Honestly." He looked at me. "I don't know."

I nudged him again, a little harder this time. "Don't say that."

"Well, what do you want me to say? We are being led by strangers into a bunch of dumpsters in the middle of the night."

"Oh shit," I said.

"This way," they said, walking behind one of the dumpsters now.

Noah and I followed, a little slower now, keeping a wider gap and a greater distance. We walked around the dumpster and were met by a discarded shipping container.

"Oh dear," I mumbled, thinking about Dexter and his affinity for murdering people inside shipping containers.

But, regardless of all these thoughts, we followed them around the container anyway. I could hear the growing sound of music and chatter now, which made me feel a little safer. And when we turned the corner and got around the other side, I stared at the sight in front of me.

CHAPTER 51

"*L*ook," I said, turning to Noah.

"I can see!" he said, blinking a few times.

"Do we *not* fit in here, or what?" I whispered to him.

"You can say that again," he replied. I looked around me. There was a queue of people waiting in line to get through a small door in the wall. The door was so small you had to duck to get in. At the front of the queue were a group of girls. I'd never seen so many fishnet stockings in my life, and who knew you could wear them as a top. No bra needed, it seemed. Just some star-shaped leather bits stuck over your nipples. And who knew you could get your hair standing so high up off your head? And that girl with the luminous lime-green dreads down to the back of her knees! Who knew?

"Oh God!" I grabbed onto Noah as she turned and looked at us. Her eyes were completely white, and against her dark skin, they made her look like a demon that had crawled up from somewhere deep, dark and distinctly evil.

"Contact lenses," Noah mumbled. "Must be contact lenses."

"Yes!" I said, hoping that was the case.

I continued to scan the crowd. There were a few normal-looking folk, just in leather jackets with metal studs sticking out. But then, in amongst those, punctuating the line, were the extravagant ones. Like birds of paradise, they were so bright with their pink mohawk hair, or bright orange laces that crept up purple knee-high boots. And then there was that guy wearing a red kilt with the black fishnet stockings underneath and all those chains, so many chains, dangling off the kilt and hanging to the floor. A girl with a purple jacket that said "Born Dead" on the back, and another guy with the words "Fuck the system" across the back of his jacket.

"Um . . ." We definitely did not fit in there, or so I thought.

"Heeeyyyyy." A girl with a lip ring stopped in front of me. "Nice clothes, like totally retro, you know."

"Uh . . . you talking to me?"

"Yeah, like all tie-dye shit and all," she said, putting a cigarette between her lips and inhaling. She cast her eyes to Noah and then burst out laughing.

"Dude, that is so cooolll." She was pointing to the Polo logo on his white T-shirt.

"This?" Noah pointed at himself.

"Like, fuck fashion, right! Screw Polo and Calvin Klein and those Kardashians, or whatever. That's, like, so ironic."

Noah looked down at his shirt and then looked back up and nodded. "That's exactly what I was going for," he said, playing along. "Fuck fashion!"

"Coooool, see you inside," she said, and then walked away in a cloud of smoke and mirrors. Literally. She had broken shards of mirror on the back of her purple leather jacket.

"Did you hear that?" Noah draped an arm around me. "We're cool. You are retro and I am totally screwing fashion and being ironic!"

"I had no idea that's what you were going for," I teased.

"You guys coming?" Our skating traveling companions waved at us from the front of the queue, and Noah and I nudged each other.

"To being wild and crazy," I said. His eyes looked unusual in this light. The pink light emanating from the club had turned his blue eyes a shade of purple.

"To being wild and crazy!" he repeated, and we made our way to the front. Our skater friends were clearly familiar with the big bouncer with the tattoos on his face.

We walked into the club, ducking under the doorframe. When I got inside, I was even more shocked by what I saw. There was a bar to my left that looked like it had been made with corrugated-iron roofing sheets and a small stage in front of us, which was currently empty, and then, hanging from the ceiling . . . cages! With gyrating women in them wearing red leather bikinis. In the far corner, a small skateboard ramp had been set up and a few people were skateboarding on it.

"Wow!" I said. I had never been to a club before, and if this was what clubs were like, I had seriously missed out on what was clearly a mind-blowing, eye-opening experience.

"Are all clubs like this?" I asked Noah, who was watching one of the girls in the cage. A tiny stab of jealousy hit me in the ribs.

He shook his head, still staring at the woman in the cage. "I've never been to one like this before." His voice had taken on a tone that sounded full of awe. And then he pointed at the cage and my heart dropped. *What was he thinking?* Look how hot she is? Look how sexy she is in her little leather get-up, all swishing her hips and shaking her ass and bumping and grinding against the poles.

"Do you think those are custom made?" he asked.

"Uh . . . the women?"

"No." He laughed. "The cages! I must try and get one that big for Chloe. She would love it!"

"The cage! Oh, right, the cage!" I burst out laughing. "You were looking at the cage, for your parrot. Of course."

"Well, what else did you think I was looking at?"

I shot him an incredulous look. "I kind of thought you were looking at what was inside the cage."

He looked back up and cocked his head from side to side, as if he had only noticed the dancing girls now. And then he looked back at me and scrunched his face up. "Nah, not really my thing."

"Oh! Okay!" I tried not to sound thrilled. Not that I was his thing either, considering that fact he hadn't kissed me back in the field, which was probably the most mortifying experience of my life. I wondered what his thing was.

"Let's go and have a drink," he said, moving off to the bar area.

"A drink?" I mused. The old Zenobia hardly ever drank. But I had already broken that rule when I'd woken up and downed all that champagne and called my boss a crappy human! I might as well continue. Besides, I was all about new experiences now. And the new me would bloody drink in a strange, dark and dingy club filled with people who looked more like they had stepped off the set of a futuristic sci-fi film. What was the name for this subculture anyway? I made a mental note to Google it at some stage.

"Sure, a drink! Why not?" I declared, and followed Noah to the bar. It was busy, a flourish of black leather and spikes and colored hair, and we stood waiting our turn, only to realize it didn't work like that around here. Elbowing and jostling were the name of the game, and pushing your way to the front was the only way to get anywhere, it seemed. Noah took me by the arm and shot me a "you ready?" look over his shoulder. I gave him a firm nod, and then, joining in the general vibe of the place, we jostled our way to the front, pushing aside a variety of characters who didn't even look pissed off, as if this was the thing to do.

Finally, a little out of breath from the effort, and with a scratch on my arm from walking past a man with a spiky cuff around his wrist, we had arrived at the front. It took Noah another five minutes to catch the bartender's eye, and when we did and Noah asked for two glasses of wine, the guy burst out laughing.

"Good one, man," he said, looking at Noah. "No, seriously. What do you want?"

I glanced at the wall behind the bartender, after watching Noah stumble and stutter a few times.

The rows behind were stacked with only a few things: whisky, tequila, vodka and a few craft beers by the names of Nuclear Waste, Happy Bastard, Satan's Drool and Panty Dropper. I blinked a few times, making sure I was reading correctly. I was.

"Two shots of tequila!" I said quickly, getting the idea from that girl who'd complimented my outfit earlier and was now standing opposite us ordering drinks.

The guy behind the bar nodded and walked away, as if this was the correct answer.

"You sure you want to start with tequila?" Noah asked.

"Sure, why not?"

"Uh . . . have you ever drunk tequila before?"

"Nope."

Noah smiled at me. "Okay, if you're sure."

A few moments later the tequila arrived in small shot glasses. And not only had I never drunk tequila before, I'd also never drunk anything out of a shot glass. This all felt very exhilarating, if not nerve-wracking as hell. But when I looked across at Noah, he gave me this inexplicable calm feeling, and I couldn't help believing that there was nothing I couldn't do if he was standing next to me.

"Ready?" he asked, lifting his shot glass into the air and holding it in front of me.

I picked mine up too and we locked eyes over the glass. In this light, those blue eyes were transformed again. This time, it was the overhead green light from the bar that was doing it.

"What are we drinking to?" Noah asked.

"I have no idea. What does one usually drink to?"

He looked thoughtful for a moment. And then a small smile broke out across his face. "New friends, new experiences and seeing where the night takes us."

CHAPTER 52

❧

"*O*h my God!" I screamed at Noah from the middle of the dancefloor. Four shots of tequila later, some strange, delirious courage that saw all my inhibitions tossed out the window and the most awful music known to mankind now had me front and center on the dancefloor, watching the band play.

"This is the worst music I have ever heard," I shouted, and laughed. "I mean, it's AWFUL! What would you call it?"

Noah laughed and put his hands over his ears. "I think they call it death metal?"

"Death metal?" I looked back at the four people jumping around on the stage, the singer was screaming into the microphone, and I couldn't make out one word. On the drums, a skull logo with horns read "Worm Sheep Head", the name of the band. The random graffiti out front finally made "*some sense*," although I saw little point in naming your band that. The screaming intensified and the people in the crowd began jumping up and down and bashing their heads back and forth. Was this the dancing that everyone was doing? If so, it was bloody terrible. Like nothing I'd ever seen on *Dancing with the Stars* or that dance program with J.Lo.

"Is this dancing?" I asked Noah, having to scream over the noise of the other people screaming.

"Headbanging!" he yelled back. "Here," Noah said, passing me another tequila.

I took it and threw it back, the hot liquid slipping down my throat and igniting something in my veins that felt a lot like wild abandon.

"When in Rome, right?" I screeched.

And so, with that last shot running rampant through me, firing all sorts of neurons and transmitters that until now I don't think I'd ever had in my brain, I started jumping up and down too. Noah burst out laughing and soon joined me. We grabbed hands and, just like that, started jumping up and down in a small circle, as if this was a game of Ring a Ring o' Rosie. Which, if you think about it, is rather apt; *Did you know that "Ring a Ring o' Rosie" is actually a song about death?* You couldn't get more appropriate than that right now, because for the first time I think I heard what the singer was shouting about. Something along the lines of "Blood, fire, death" or was it "Mud, tire, death," or maybe it was something else entirely.

But despite that, I seemed to lose myself in the "music." The screaming, growling music, the piercing, shrieking vocals, the impossibly fast drumming and the chaotic guitar. I lost myself in the crowd too. In the sweating, jumping bodies around me and the hair that regularly whacked me on the face as someone tossed their head back. We all got into a strange rhythm of jumping and bumping into each other. But this didn't seem to be a problem. In fact, it was almost encouraged. On several occasions I got bumped and fell all the way into Noah, and each time he caught me in his arms, laughing. I could see he was just as caught up in the strange moment as I was. And then . . .

OMG! I covered my head and bent down as a sweaty body came flying through the air towards me. I hadn't seen it launch itself off the stage, but it had. The body seemed to move in slow motion. I felt a scurry of people and feet around me and then looked up to see the body now suspended above me on a sea of hands. Even Noah was holding the body up above me. But then, the hands started to slip against the sweatiness and soon, the body was tumbling down and coming straight for me.

"Oh NO!" The body landed on top of me with a thud. And then, it slid off me like a wet slug and I was too shocked to think about how grossed out I was that someone's sweaty body fluids were now on me. The body, which belonged to the singer, crawled to his knees and carried on screaming into the microphone. And then he turned and looked at me, aware for the first time probably, that someone was actually there. He thrust the microphone into my face, and without knowing what to do, really, I also screamed. This seemed to be the correct response, though, because the crowd around me erupted. So I screamed some more, and some more, and I continued screaming when the man dragged me onto the stage and gave me the microphone. It didn't matter that I didn't know the "words" to this "musical" "song," or couldn't pick up on a "beat" or "melody." It didn't matter as I jumped up and down on the stage, screaming random words into a microphone in front of a crowd of screaming, jumping people.

"Dog! Sheep! Baby lamb doll! Chainsaw death, and Lucy's eyeballllllsssss! Peel my leg and call me Chloeeee!" I groaned and screamed.

And then, the guitar came to a grinding halt, the drums reached a hectic crescendo and the music stopped. There was a moment of silence, where I looked down at the crowd below me, and they looked back at me, and then, like I was some rock god, they erupted into applause.

So, without thinking, I brought the mic back up to my mouth and screamed.

"It's my birthday soon. Shooters on me!" I jumped off the stage with a thud and Noah immediately pulled me into his arms, putting his mouth up to my ear.

"You can't buy everyone here shooters!" he whispered into my ear.

I pulled away from him and screamed. "Yes, I caaaaann!"

He looked around nervously and seemed to placate everyone with a smile and a wink, as if letting them know I was a little nuts, or something. He pulled me towards him again. "You can't. There must be at least a hundred people here. You can't buy everyone drinks. I know I said let loose, but I can't let you do that. You know how much that will cost?"

I pulled away from him, putting my hands on his shoulders and looking straight into his face, which seemed to be spinning slightly. "NOAH, do you know how much money I have!"

"SSSHHHHH!" He put his finger over my lips and looked around. People had gathered in a circle around me and a chant of "Shooters, shooters, shooters!" had started to build. The "Happy Birthday" song had also been thrown into the mix.

"Whisper," Noah insisted, putting his ear to my lips.

"Noah, I am, like, literally, a millionaire. No! Like, not even a millionaire, a multi-multi-multi-millionaire. A few times over. And you know what is crazy . . . I've never spent a cent of it! Not a cent. It's all in some low-risk, bland-chicken-breast retirement policy and I've never done anything silly and wild with it. And I deserve to. At least once in my life, so . . ." I pulled away from him again and screamed. "Shooters on MEEE!"

I rushed through the crowd to the bar and smacked my hand down on it, hard. I looked at the bartender, who was definitely looking in my direction now. No need to fight for his attention this time. "Well, what are you waiting for?" I said to him.

He looked at me very skeptically and raised his brows. "Uh . . . you sure you can . . . uh, it's just no one has ever bought everyone drinks before. This is very . . ."

"Wild! Crazy!" I jumped a little in excitement. "I know! And I'm loving it. Wwwwhhhoooo-hooooooo!" I threw my hands in the air and looked at the crowd around me. They all gave a loud "whoo-hoo" too!

I turned back to the barman. "Well, you'd better get pouring!"

"Okay, but I think I'll need your credit card first, you understand," he said, still looking very skeptical.

"Totally!" I whipped my card out of my bag and slapped it on the bar counter with a dramatic flourish.

"Are you sure about this?" Noah asked one last time.

"Noah, I have never been more sure about anything in my life." The crowd around me let out a massive shout. They were all on me now, high-fiving me, pulling me into hugs, telling me how cool I was, *dude,* and wishing me a happy birthday!

No one had ever called me cool before. I looked at Noah. He was sitting on a bar stool watching me with a massive smile on his face. I smiled back and he shook his head in an amused fashion.

"Aren't you going to have one?" I asked, as I saw him push the shot the barman had given him aside.

He took his car keys out his pocket and waved them at me. "One is enough."

"Now look who's the sensible one!" And for some reason I blew him a kiss before I was dragged back onto the dancefloor by the girl with white eyes.

CHAPTER 53

~

$\mathcal{T}$wenty minutes later, drenched in sweat and out of breath, I stumbled back over to Noah, who was seated at the bar. He'd been watching me with amusement while I'd been jumping up and down on the dancefloor. Every now and then I would look back over my shoulder and find him smiling at me indulgently. I can only think that my dancing was probably terrible and he was finding it very funny. I stretched my arms out over the bar and collapsed forward onto a chair.

"I'm exhausted," I said. "Is this what being young is like? I don't think I could keep up."

"Looks like you're keeping up rather well!" he said.

I fanned my face with my hands. "I think I could do with some fresh air. Should we get out of here soon?"

"Heeeyyyy." Noah and I turned when we heard a smooth, slippery-sounding voice. It was the lead singer of the band, and his voice sounded very different to that raspy-groan-shriek-moan that he sang with. He was shirtless, bare-chested, except for those large nipple rings that glinted in the lights. His black hair was long and wet-looking, sticking to his pale shoulders like masses of thin black snakes. His skin seemed to be an unnatural shade of white, like he had just emerged from a decade-long sunless hibernation. His pants were tight, black and leathery with long chains that hung from his pockets. His hands were covered in silver skull rings and his fingernails were painted green.

"Hey," I replied.

"I'm Klaw." He ran his hand through his wet hair and I noticed, like bees to honey, a small flock of women suddenly appear by his side. They seemed transfixed by the movement of his fingers through his wet hair and then even more transfixed when he leaned across the bar and moved closer to me.

"Zoe," I said to him. I think I was slightly transfixed too, not so much by him but by those tattoos on the back of his fingers, especially that Hello Kitty one. It seemed on one hand not to suit him at all, but on another hand to suit him perfectly. I wondered if I should get a tattoo.

"Uh . . . NOAH!" Suddenly Noah's head popped over Klaw's shoulder. He had slid in between Noah and me, partially blocking Noah from my sight.

"Hey, dude." Klaw threw a very half-hearted non-committal mumble at Noah and then oozed even closer to me.

"Interesting name," Noah said, his head bobbing up and down. "How do you spell that?"

"With a 'K.'" Klaw angled his body to completely block Noah now, and he slithered even closer to me. "It's really sick to meet a fan like you."

"A fan?"

"Yeah, someone who knows all the lyrics to our songs."

"Wait!" I stifled a laugh-gasp. "Those were the lyrics? The actual ones? I got them right?"

"Yeah, man, the lyrics are whatever the lyrics are. And you sang them so passionately. I've never met such a passionate fan before."

"Aaaah," I mumbled. If only he knew the truth. And then he reached out and placed his hand on my shoulder and squeezed. I looked down at it and then back up to him.

"It means such a lot to me and my band." His dark eyes zoned in on mine now and, when he found them, he held onto them tightly in an intense, dark stare that made me shiver. "I love your style." Klaw removed his hand from my shoulder and ran his fingers over one of the tie-dye tassels hanging from my shirt. "So unbelievably retro and cool." He slithered closer to me and I admit, for the first time since his arrival, I was finding him startlingly, oddly, alluring. That dark black eyeliner really brought out the coffin shape of his eyes.

"Thanks," I muttered, feeling a little flutter inside. Noah's head popped up and he rolled his eyes before it disappeared behind Klaw's shoulder again.

"You're so beautiful," the slippery singer continued.

"Th-thanks," and now I giggled. It felt very undignified, but it happened anyway, and I heard a chorus of breathy sighs coming from the girls standing close by. I looked over at them and the girl with the white eyes caught my attention.

"Kiss him!" she mouthed to me, and I immediately felt my cheeks go red. I shook my head at her, but she countered my shake with a very vigorous nod. And then the girl next to her nodded, and soon they were all nodding. I looked back at Klaw. He was definitely increasing his lean. A long, languid lean, like a thick liquid slowly dripping down the side of a wall.

"Sooooo," the word oozed from his lips, "you want to like, hang out or . . . *something*?" He made that "something" sound like a loaded gun.

"Um, I mean, sure," I replied.

"Well, actually." Noah's head was back again. "We were just leaving."

"I'm sure she can stay a little longer, can't she?" Klaw came closer to me, his body almost touching mine now. I looked over at the group of girls, and White Eyes caught my attention. She stuck her tongue out and flicked it about in the air. *Oh my God, she had a tongue like a snake!* Everyone around her laughed and I quickly looked away.

"We *were* actually about to leave," I said.

"Noooooo." He pushed his lower lip out into a pout, revealing a tattoo on the inside of his lip that looked like a finger engaged in a zap sign. "Such a pity, but here." Klaw took my arm and pulled a Sharpie out of the front of his pants. He raised the lid to his mouth and then, with this sexy casualness, he pulled the lid off with his teeth and spat it to the floor. He lowered the Sharpie to my arm, still making this uncomfortably intense eye contact, and then scribbled his number all the way down it. When he was done, he tossed the Sharpie over his shoulder nonchalantly. Noah protested and swatted it as it connected with his forehead, and I think I heard him mutter something that sounded like "douchebag."

Klaw pointed to my arm. "My number. Like, call me. Anytime. We can hang out. Commune. Whenever."

"We live in Joburg!" Noah piped up, rubbing his forehead.

"Cool. I'm often there for gigs. With my band." He ran his eyes up and down me and I shivered a little. "Cool meeting you." And then he leaned forward and planted a very unexpected kiss on my cheek. I looked over at the girls again. One of them seemed to have picked up the Sharpie lid and was smelling it. White Eyes threw her hands in the air, as if frustrated with me.

Oh well, what the hell, right. So I did it. I leaned in and kissed him on the lips. Our lips remained closed for a while, pressed into each other's, but when his parted and I felt a little wet slug begin to emerge and try to wiggle its way into my mouth, I pulled away, laughing.

"Cool! Nice to meet you too!" I looked down at my arm. "I'll call you sometime." Klaw blew me a kiss and then slither-walked away. I stared after him for a while until Noah leaned into my field of vision.

"Did you see that? I just kissed a rock star. The lead singer of a band. I just kissed him!"

"I think everyone saw that," Noah said flatly, and then looked over at the crowd of girls. I looked too and several of them shot me the thumbs-up. "Besides, I wouldn't exactly call him a singer, and I'm not sure that three people screaming on stage makes a band. But hey, that's just me."

I totally ignored Noah. He wasn't going to rain on my rockstar-kissing parade. "I, Zoe, am the kisser of rock stars. I am the cool kisser of rock stars."

"Yeah, yeah, we know." Noah sounded even flatter now.

"Hey, we're, like, kicking it. We're going to this beach party now. You wanna come?" one of the Hoodies asked as all three of them came sauntering up to us.

"Oooh. I've never been to a beach party before," I said excitedly. "Where is it?"

"It's on the main beach, by the pier."

"Cool, see you there," I said, and turned.

"Uh, actually . . ." Hoodie Two stopped me. "You're kind of our lift there!"

"Oh! Of course. Let's go then." I started walking towards the exit and stopped when I realized Noah wasn't behind me. "Noah, aren't you coming?" I asked.

He looked at me blankly for a while, as if a little sullen and put out. "Sure, I'll come *commune*." He pushed himself off the bar and walked reluctantly after us.

And that is how we found ourselves back in the car for the second time that night on our way to a party with our travel companions, as well as three more. The white-eyed girl, the one wearing the mirror jacket and someone else who was wearing a purple cloak, so it was hard to tell anything about them.

CHAPTER 54

"I can't believe you kissed Klaw," the girl with the white eyes, whose name was Zamantha, with a "Z," said as we drove.

"Wait! You kissed Klaw? Lead singer of Worm Sheep Head and only the hottest guy on the planet?" Mirror Jacket, whose name was Lila, almost launched herself out of the back seat at this news.

"She has his phone number on her arm! On her arm!" Zamantha grabbed my arm and showed it to Lila, who was now giddy. She reminded me of the girl who looked like she had gotten high from sniffing Klaw's Sharpie lid.

"Well, it was more a long kiss on the lips than an actual real kiss," I said.

"From where I was standing, it kind of looked like a real kiss," Zamantha added.

"Me too." Noah spoke for the first time since we'd gotten in the car and started driving.

"Definitely! I saw tongue!" Zamantha said.

"Tongue!" Noah whipped his head around and looked at me.

"There was very little tongue, I assure you. It was just a teeny bit of tongue," I said, and burst out laughing.

"Teeny tongue, not big tongue!" Zamantha said, and also laughed.

"I would take a teeny bit of tongue from Klaw any day of the week," Lila said, and sighed.

"Me too," one of the Hoodies said, also on a sigh.

"Do you think we can stop talking about Klaw's tongue." Noah looked around the car pointedly.

"Oooh, someone sounds jealous," Zamantha almost sang that.

"I doubt that," I said back to her, thinking about the kiss that actually hadn't happened today. No way was Noah jealous, otherwise he would have kissed me back. At least Klaw had kissed me back. I touched my lips when I realized something.

"Oh God, I can still taste him a little."

"I'll just pretend I didn't hear that," Noah mumbled, and tapped the steering wheel.

"Really?" Lila leaned forward. "Can I taste?"

"What?" Noah and I both said at the same time.

And then, without asking, Lila leaned forward and kissed me. It was gentle and, I must admit, once the initial shock wore off, it was rather nice. Her lips were so soft and silky and, without looking up, I could feel that everyone in the car was watching us. And then, she opened her mouth a little and I felt the tiniest touch of tongue and, without thinking, I did the same thing. And for a second there, I was kissing a girl. Really kissing a girl. I heard some loud whoops and cheers coming from the Hoodies in the back, and then, as quickly as it started, it stopped. Lila pulled away and sat back in her seat. She touched her hand to her lips and looked at me.

"If you're not going to use that phone number on your arm, you mind giving it to me?" She had a faraway, distant, smitten look in her eyes, and I don't think it came from kissing me but rather from thinking of kissing Klaw.

"S-sure," I stuttered, also touching my lips, now only tasting her. Which was much more delicious than him. She was clearly wearing a strawberry-flavored lip balm. After letting her copy the number on my arm, I sat back down in my seat and stared forward. What a night! Two kisses. I smiled to myself and then stopped smiling when I caught Noah looking at me.

"What?" I asked, feeling defensive for some reason.

"Nothing," he said, and then shook his head.

* * *

The beach looked amazing at night. The flickering lights from the city cast a golden glow across the sand and what made it look even better was the big bonfire in the middle of it all. People I'd never seen before were either relaxing on towels around the fire or sitting on chairs. Someone had a portable speaker and was playing music on their iPhone, and a few people were swaying to the beat of the relaxed music. This was not how I'd imagined a beach party. I had been expecting something much wilder, and instead I was greeted by this chilled, loungey atmosphere, which, after the chaos of the club, was a welcome relief.

"These are our new friends," Hoodie Two said, after giving a guy who was also wearing a hoodie a rather complicated handshake, one that ended with an elbow bump and a snap of the fingers. Hoodie Two turned and looked at us and then tilted his head from side to side, as if thinking.

"Our names are Noah and Zoe," Noah said.

"Rigght," Hoodie Two said. "Zoah and Noe."

"Close enough," Noah said with a smile.

"Cool, man, welcome. Grab a seat, man, or a patch of sand. Like, whatever, it's all good." Hoodie Four, I guess I'd have to call him, indicated the fire and the floor.

Noah and I glanced at each other, gave a brief shrug and then climbed down onto the floor next to the most gorgeous-looking twins with purple dreadlocks.

"Hey," they both said to us at once. I shook my head to make sure I wasn't seeing double. I wasn't. They were identical.

"Hi," I said, not really knowing which one to respond to.

"I'm Ebony and I'm Harmony," they chorused. I nodded, even though I knew there was no way I was going to remember who was who in a million years and wondered if I was going to have to resort to Twin One and Twin Two? Which I hoped not, because between them and the Hoodies, too many numbers.

"I'm Zoe, this is my friend Noah," I replied, pointing back at Noah, who had been drawn into a conversation with someone else already.

They turned their attention to Noah, and then looked at each other and smiled.

"Noah's kind of cute," they said at the same time. "Although he is old enough to, like, be our dad," the other one added.

"How old are you guys?" I asked.

"Nineteen," they said at the same time.

"I think it's highly unlikely he could be your father then," I replied.

"Oh." They both looked back at Noah. "Well, we were never that good at math," they said simultaneously, and looked at Noah again. I also turned and looked at him. Clearly, his conversation had ended, and judging by the flush in his cheeks and the fact that he was looking in our direction, my guess was that he'd heard what we'd been saying. The fire blazed as someone tossed another log onto it. Small bright orange sparks like fairies flew up into the air around us and the orange blast from the fire made a color flicker across Noah's blue eyes, as if they were merely mirrors reflecting the world around him. They weren't so much a color as a canvas that was constantly changing.

I blushed, turned away quickly and looked back at the twins.

"Oooh, looks like he's totally into you," one said, leaning in with a conspiratorial smile.

The other one leaned in too, also lowering her voice to an almost-whisper. "Totally."

I shook my head, and then hung it a little.

"What?" They moved closer to me.

"I can't say," I whispered. "Not here anyway."

They looked over my shoulder and then overly loudly announced it. "We're just going to the loo." They stood up and one of them held their hand out for me.

"Want to come?" they asked, and one of them winked at me.

"Okay, sure." I stood up and they immediately laced arms with me and marched me across the sand. They stopped as soon as we were out of Noah's earshot.

"Tell us, what's the vibe?" they asked.

"The vibe?"

"Yeah, with you and Noah?"

"Uh . . . I'm not sure," I confessed.

"Tell us everything," they said, at the same time again.

Hang on, was I having girl talk? Was this what it looked like? All those nights I'd missed sleepovers at my friends' houses because I was in the hospital, was this it? If it was, I was going to go with it.

"It's embarrassing," I said.

"Babe, you can tell us."

"Anything," the other echoed.

"Well, earlier today, I thought he wanted to kiss me, but I don't know, maybe I misinterpreted it, so I leaned in and tried to kiss him, but he kind of pulled away."

"Harsh!" they chorused.

"What, you never told us that." I turned when I heard a familiar voice. Zamantha and Lila were walking towards us with drinks in their hands.

I introduced everybody and soon we were all talking. I explained every single detail of the incident to them, and each one asked me for more and more details and posed more questions. The five of us did an entire post-mortem on the event, and when I was done, they stood there looking at me.

"I think he's into you," Zamantha concluded. "He sounded jealous when we were talking about you kissing Klaw!"

"Whoooaaa!" The twins held their hands up and blinked at me. "You kissed Klaw. *The* Klaw?"

"Only with a teeny bit of tongue," Zamantha quickly added, and laughed.

The twins looked at each other and then back at me. "We'd take teeny tongue."

"That's what I said." Lila echoed their sentiments and soon we were all laughing.

"We need to go to another party now," Zamantha said. "You want to come?"

I looked around and then back to them. "I kind of like the beach."

Zamantha and Lila took their phones out. "Cool, exchange numbers then?"

They looked up at me and I pulled my phone out and we swapped numbers. They gave me a hug goodbye and made me promise to tell them if anything happened with Noah and me. I slipped my phone back into my bag. It felt heavier, filled with another two numbers. I turned back to the twins, who now looked like they were in deep discussion.

"What?"

"Well, we think there's only one thing to do now," one said.

"What?" I said again.

"Go and find out from Noah. You wait here!" They both started walking off.

"Wait! No! You can't." I flushed with embarrassment. I couldn't watch this. This was crazy. What were they going to do, walk up there and ask Noah if he was into me? And how was that going to work? Last time I was at school, if the boy liked you, he chased you on the playground or threw a ball at your head.

Do you like me?

Do you like me *like* me?

But I was sure things had changed since then, I just wasn't sure what they'd changed to. I covered my eyes and looked away. I had no idea how any of this worked and I couldn't bear to watch. This was all just so. . . .

I couldn't stop the smile that swept across my face. Yes, this was wildly embarrassing but this was also something I'd never done before. I'd only ever dreamed of doing this kind of stuff from my hospital bed. Going to parties, being cool, talking to guys, flirting, hanging with my girlfriends. All of those were things I'd never done, and now, I was doing them. Regardless of how this turned out, what truly mortifying consequences this had, I was finally doing it.

"Sooooo." The twins slid up to me again, after what felt like hours chatting to Noah.

"What did he say?" I could hardly contain my excitement and I knew that I sounded about twelve years younger than I really was.

"Sooo, like the vibe I get from him is that he is totally interested in you," one said.

"Did he say that?"

"No."

"Then how do you know?"

"Well, we asked him if he was single and then told him that our mom was looking to date and showed him her photo."

"Huh?"

One took her cell phone out, pressed a few buttons on the screen and then showed me.

"Wait . . . that's your mom?!" The most gorgeous woman filled the screen.

"Yes," they both said at the same time. "She's a model." Also at the same time.

"But when we showed Noah the picture, he didn't seem interested. At all. And then we asked if he was seeing someone, and he said no, but he's not really looking right now either. And then I asked if he wasn't looking because he had already met someone he was into, or whether he wasn't interested because he wasn't dating."

"And?" I pressed.

"Well, that's when he went all silent and his cheeks flushed and he started blushing and saying stuff like, maybe he's met someone, but it was complicated, and he wasn't sure, and . . ."

"Wait. He said he wasn't sure?"

"Yes," they replied.

"Really?" I thought for a while. What exactly did that mean, though? That he wasn't sure about me? Wasn't sure about kissing me? And why was it complicated? And did he even mean me? I mean . . .

I felt a lot like Sheik Khalifa when Amanda Stone accidentally walked into his bedroom in the middle of the night, looking for the kitchen. How tormented he was with thoughts that he couldn't make sense of.

"Well, thanks."

They nodded. "Cool. We got your back, girl."

I smiled. Wow, no one had ever said that to me before, and I wanted to hug these two girls in front of me who I didn't even know, but suddenly felt close to. Felt some sisterly bond with. Some "girls must stick together" feeling that, until this moment, had never existed in my life. And then a loud shout cut through the air.

"SWIM!" someone yelled.

"Oh my God, yes!" The twins clapped their hands excitedly and started rushing towards the sea.

"Aren't you coming?" they shouted at me as they sprinted forward.

"Uh . . . now? In the dark? The sea?" I stared at the mass of black water in front of me.

"Yes," they shrieked. "Come!"

"Okay!" I shouted, and then looked for Noah. I scanned the crowd of people and, finally, a pair of blue eyes caught my attention.

"Meet you there," he shouted across the beach as we ran towards the water. I looked in front of me. The twins had started peeling their clothes off, exposing bikinis underneath. I certainly wasn't going to peel any of my clothes off. Never. And I was sure Noah felt the same way. I looked back at him to have this confirmed, only it wasn't. And that's when it happened . . .

CHAPTER 55

$\mathcal{I}$n slow motion, the whole world went silent, everyone else disappeared and a light broke through the dark sky above and illuminated Noah from the heavens. I stood dead still, digging my toes into the sand, gripping at it, in case I was going to fall over as Noah peeled—and I mean, that was the only way to describe it—a long, slow, deliberate peeeeeel of his shirt from his muscled torso. I watched, fairly bloody gobsmacked, as he shook his head, his hair flopping from side to side, and then he turned, scrunched the T-shirt up into a ball, which made all the muscles in his arms and torso ripple, and then tossed it across the sand. My jaw sort of dangled open and I realized precisely what I was doing: drooling over a man. I hope Noah didn't turn around and see me . . .

"Shit!" I slapped my hands over my eyes and started running back towards the sea as Noah turned and his eyes zoned in on mine, as if he knew exactly what I'd been doing. Mortified, I kept on running towards the sea, swept up in the flurry of feet and excitement, but all I really wanted to do was turn around and look at him again, and so I did. I think I caught a one-second glimpse of a shirtless, running Noah before I was no longer running. I was flying. Or maybe it was falling. It was definitely falling, as my foot caught on some driftwood, and I started to tumble. If I hadn't been craning my neck backwards to perv at Noah, I would have been looking at the ground in front of me and would not now be lying face down in the sand.

"Crap!" I said, regretting it instantly as little bits of sand went into my mouth and crunched between my teeth.

"You okay?" I looked up to find Noah standing over me.

"Yes. Cool. Just, you know, slipped." I turned around to face him. He held his hand out for mine and, as if I was nothing but a wisp of air, he pulled me to my feet.

"Sure you're okay?" he asked again and then did something that rendered it impossible to answer him. He brushed some sand from my cheek.

"Aahhm mmmm . . . nnnn." Ridiculous sounds came out of my mouth. They were an attempt to answer his question, but it no longer felt like my lips worked enough to form words, not since his fingertips had brushed them.

He smiled. It was that one where that tiny gap showed and made him look so warm and approachable. The smile caused me to smile, although I don't think mine was as cool as his; I think mine was more of a starstruck, awe-inspired smile, which I felt a little embarrassed about. Me, an almost-thirty-year-old woman, acting like a teenage girl with a crush . . .

Mind you, this was something I'd missed growing up. So, I guess my maturity level for such things was probably on par with a teenage girl crushing over the hot guy with the big muscles and no shirt.

And then I think my whole body forgot how to work as he pushed a strand of hair behind my ear, which was totally unnecessary, as my hair was so short it didn't even stay behind my ear.

"So, shall we go?" He took a step back and held his hand out once more. I looked down at it. I'd held it a few times already, a few seconds ago, but why did it feel different this time? Like there was an underlying question implied in the holding out of his hand that made it different. And when I slipped my fingers through his, it *did* feel different. The way he looked down at my hand before slowly closing his fingers around it, and then giving them a squeeze that felt different to the squeezes of before. It wasn't a reassuring squeeze like it had been with the stitches, or the ambulance. This squeeze was different. *But what makes a squeeze feel so different?* I didn't quite know, but I knew it had nothing to do with the physical squeeze itself, and everything to do with the intention behind it. I shivered. Yes, it was slightly chilly. A slight autumn chill in the air and the breeze coming off the sea added to this. But that's not why I shivered.

"Come," he said, his voice a whisper now.

I nodded. I couldn't speak. It was as if his words had stolen my tongue right out of my mouth.

And then we ran together, holding hands, right for the sea.

CHAPTER 56

The fire blazed, warming us up from the cold sea. And who knew that running around splashing and jumping through the waves at night on the beach could be so much fun? Who knew that having water splashed into my face by the giggling twins would have caused me to laugh as much as I did? Who knew that Noah grabbing me by the waist and trying to fully drag me under a wave with him would have produced the kind of laughter that I don't think I'd ever heard coming out of my mouth before? It was this laughter that felt utterly free and unrestrained. As if there was nothing in this world that was worrying me. And how could I be worried, with this night, this sea, the stars above me, and the wind blowing, causing goosebumps on my skin, and all the laugher. So much laughter. Coming from so many different people who I didn't even know but for some strange reason felt a camaraderie with. *Was this what it was like?*

Having friends? Having fun? Throwing all your worries and cares out the window, I was beginning to think it was. And this made me feel two things. Whilst I was happy, exhilarated even, it was also making me sad. A deep sadness in the knowing of all the things I had lost growing up and missed out on in my life.

I shivered and felt something wrap around my shoulders. It was Noah, laying a dry, warm towel over my wet body. We were seated in a circle around the fire, and once all the laughter and chatter had died down, we all stared into the flames, watching them dance and curl in front of us. There was something so primitive about watching the flames like this. Probably a throwback from the time we lived in caves. As I watched the dancing flames, I was sure I could see pictures forming and twisting. A bottle of something was being passed around the circle. It went from mouth to mouth, hand to hand, in a kind of easy rhythm, a predictable relaxed rhythm so that, when it came to me, I didn't hesitate to take a gulp and then offer it to Noah. He shook his head and passed it to the next person, mouthing an "I'm driving" at me.

No one said a word; it was as if we'd agreed to keep silent and listen to the sounds of the waves and the flicker of the flames. The bottle went around again and I took another sip and passed it over Noah this time, to the person sitting next to him. The guy gave me a huge smile and then a small high-five. So this was what it was like being young?

Going from park, to club, to beach. Going where the wind blew you. Ending up somewhere, anywhere. Dancing and drinking and swimming in the sea. I was so lost in thought that when the cigarette came around, even though I didn't smoke, I took a long, deep breath and then coughed.

"NO!" Noah shouted, and pulled it from my hands. "What are you doing?"

"I've never tried a cigarette," I said. "You said to embrace things."

"That is not a cigarette," Noah said, giving it to the next person.

"Wh-what is it?"

"Dude, it's weed, man," one of our hooded friends said.

"WHAT?" I sat up straight and held my hand to my chest. "Did I just do drugs?" I looked at Noah, a rising sense of panic bubbling up inside me.

The whole circle burst out laughing. "Man, you are, like, so funny," one of the twins said to me.

"Totally," someone else echoed.

"Oh my God, what's going to happen to me? I can't feel it yet. I think I feel normal. Am I normal? What will happen to me?"

The people in the circle laughed even more, and Noah put his arm around me and pulled me closer. "You'll be fine. You only had one drag. And anyway, I'm here."

"You sure?"

He smiled at me. "You'll be fine."

The twins leaned forward and grabbed me by the hands.

"Totes fine," they said at the same time.

"Although, dude, that was the strong stuff. That's the shit I get from Barry's hydroponic greenhouse, man. His stuff is bomb—he uses his own urine to grow it!"

"Ssshhhhh." The twins looked at Hoodie One then back to me and smiled. "Just chill, babe. Go with it. It's all good."

* * *

"I am, like, soooooooooooo hungry!" I pushed my way into the store with our three hooded companions and the twins, who were now tagging along with us. The store had an old-school bell on the door that rang when we entered. The man in the store looked up as we stumbled in, giggling.

"Don't mind them. They're harmless," Noah said, trying to placate the man, who was *really* staring at us now.

"No shoplifting!" The man pointed at a security camera on the ceiling. "I know all about you lot, coming in here in the early hours of the morning, stuffing food up your sleeves."

"I have no sleeves." I turned around and showed the man my outfit, then burst out laughing. The twins and the hoodies also laughed, as if I had just made the funniest joke in the world. Who knew I was a joker?

"I'm being serious," the man said. "I will call the police if so much as a pack of chewing gum goes missing."

"No shoplifting!" I yelled, then whipped out my credit card and slapped it down on the counter. "All snacks on me!" I said, which was met by a loud *whoop* from our party companions.

The man looked unconvinced, so Noah leaned across the table and whispered, "She's good for it, trust me."

The man scanned me from top to bottom with skeptical eyes. "Suuuure," he said, but pulled my card towards him anyway. And then we got to work raiding the shelves. It felt like we shopped for hours. The shapes and colors and textures of everything seemed so new and unique, as if I'd never seen them before. It felt like an hour before we stumbled back out of there, bags bursting with late-night snacks. We staggered through the parking lot, passed our car and all instinctively sat down on the sidewalk together, shoulder to shoulder.

I reached into the shopping packet and ripped the closest things I could find open and shoved whatever they were into my mouth. "Oh, my flipping, holy hell," I said, my mouth full. "I have never tasted anything so good in my entire life!" I shoved another handful of salt-and-vinegar chips and Jelly Tots into my mouth. "Mmmmm," I moaned, as another burst of sweet, salty stuff filled my mouth. "This is amazing. Like, why don't they make this, you know? Like, this flavor, and sell it in a bag. Salt, vinegar and Jelly Tot."

"Dude, totally," Hoodie Three said, reaching into the bag and grabbing a handful of chips and Jelly Tots himself. He put them in his mouth, followed by some peanuts and raisins. The food combinations made so much sense to me. Of course, that would all taste perfect together. And this was confirmed when Hoodie Three let out a long, loud moan.

"Dude, this is better than . . ." He paused and squinted, as if he was looking into the distance to try and find the word.

"Sex?" I offered, and they all burst out laughing.

We sat there on the sidewalk, eating and watching the cars pass. Every time one did, Hoodie One would make the loud noise of a racing car—"Vrrooooom"—and we would all laugh. I don't know why this was so funny, and why it was so funny after all the times that he'd done it, but it bloody was.

"Oh my God, you guys." I jumped up off the sidewalk and held a

Galaxy Bar in one hand and the Ritz crackers in the other. "This—
this—is the best!" I put another Galaxy-Ritz combo in my mouth.

"I know what would make it better," one of the twins said. I was
still unable to tell them apart. "This!" She took a bite of the Galaxy
bar, added some Ritz cracker and then sucked two Hula Hoops off
her fingers.

"Oh my God, Noah, you have to try this!" I said, bending down
and balancing a Ritz cracker on top of the chocolate and then pushing it towards his mouth. He blocked it with his hand.

"Uh . . . no, thanks," he said with a smile.

"But it's a taste explosion in your mouth," I pressed.

"I'll take your word for it. Besides, I haven't exactly taken anything to make these flavor combinations work for me."

"What do you mean?" I fell back onto my bum, ripping a bag of
Smarties open as I did.

"You're stoned," he said.

"What?" I looked at him, and then at our travel companions. "No,
I'm not. I feel perfectly normal!" I emptied the whole box of Smarties
into my mouth then filled my mouth with orange juice and chewed.

Noah laughed. "Uh, I have some news for you: you are totally stoned."

"Nooooo," I said, little bits of orangey chocolate shooting from my
mouth as I spoke.

"Totally," Hoodie Two said, and soon all the others nodded in
agreement.

"But I don't even feel anything!"

"Yeah, but you also think that Galaxy chocolate and Ritz crackers
are a good flavor combination. Definite sign that you are stoned."

"Really?"

"In real life, this probably tastes like crap," one of the twins said,
sipping on a green-and-purple-mixed Slush Puppie.

"Wait, is this not real life?" I asked, going wide-eyed and looking
over at Noah.

He laughed. "Definitely not."

"But if this isn't real life, then what is it?" I stared at everyone, feeling like I was having some deep epiphany, as if I was tapped into something big and far off that was telling me things. Noah laughed even more, and so did everyone else.

"Are we, like, living in a parallel universe or something?"

The question stopped the laughing and Hoodie Two came closer and whispered, "Sssshhhh. Don't let them know that we know that." He looked dead serious.

"Who? Who mustn't know?" I asked.

But Hoodie Two didn't say a word, instead he simply looked up and pointed at the sky. We all gasped in unison and gazed up, staring into space.

I heard a loud laugh. It was Noah's, and it sounded like he was laughing in a totally different voice now.

"Have you always laughed like that?" I asked him.

Everyone's head swiveled around, and soon they were staring at me in a way that made me uncomfortable.

"Uh . . . what language are you speaking?" one of the twins asked.

"English."

"No, you're not," Noah said.

"*Uhleka ngalendlela njalo?*" I repeated the question, and that's when I realized I was speaking isiZulu.

Everyone looked at me again, and then they burst out laughing.

"Uh . . . I think that's our cue to leave." Noah stood up and held his hand out for me to take.

"Where should we go?"

"Let's mission back to my place and play some video games," Hoodie Three said. Or was he Hoodie Two? It was even harder to tell now. All of their hoodies looked the same. Mind you, everyone was beginning to look similar. Wait . . . were they swapping faces? Because one second Noah looked like Noah, and then he looked like someone else. Someone familiar, someone younger, someone that I was sure I had met . . .

Maybe I was stoned after all?

CHAPTER 57

~

"Where are we?" I sat up. The place we were in looked like a train had come through it. Bodies lay strewn across the floor, some sleeping, some playing video games, some swaying from left to right to some invisible beat that I couldn't hear. To my left, Noah was fast asleep next to me, clutching a cushion to his chest. And then two big feet stepped over him. I looked up to see who the feet belonged to, and it was our friend with the big cap from last night, who we'd met. He was a friend of the Hoodies, which made sense, since they all seemed to really care about what they wore on their heads.

"Morning, dude," he said, looking down at me.

"Morning, d-dude," I said back, and he gave me a lazy smile, followed by a big yawn. Oh God, this was so awkward. I was almost thirty years old and I was waking up on the floor of a house party full of teens! I nudged Noah in the ribs and he rolled over and moaned. He opened one eye and then smiled at me.

"Hey." His voice sounded croaky and sleepy. He raised himself up onto his elbow. "How did you sleep?"

"Uh . . ." I scanned the room again. One of the other girls from last night, also someone new we'd met, had fallen asleep clutching a bottle of vodka, while another one had fallen asleep with half her body on the couch, the other half on the floor. "Is that a rhetorical question?" I reached up and rubbed the back of my very stiff neck.

Noah sat up and did the exact same thing, adding a back stretch to the move. "I am way too old to sleep on the floor like this."

"We are way too old to bloody be here," I said, as two guys high-fived each other over a video game they were playing.

Noah watched them for a while and shook his head. "Ja, I think we should retire from this party. It looks like it's probably going to go on for another two days or so, and I'm exhausted!"

"Me too! But I did have fun!" I added.

Noah gave me a sweet, playful smile. "Me too."

"WHAT THE HELL?!?!" A door swung open and a voice ripped through the room, causing everyone to sit up straight and look in the direction of the noise.

"WHAT THE BLOODY HELL? TREVOR! TREVOR! WHAT THE HELL HAVE YOU DONE?"

I knew who the voice belonged to the second I saw her standing there in the doorway with a suitcase.

"Uh . . . Mom . . . uh . . ." Hoodie One replied, looking sheepish as hell. Trevor—that was his name! Suddenly, like reverse dominos, bodies starting jumping to life, grabbing bottles and clothes and general party debris. One of the twins shoved a joint down her pants and crawled across the floor to hide behind the sofa. Noah and I also jumped to our feet.

"Mom . . . I thought you were coming back tomorrow." Trevor sounded quite desperate.

"SO YOU HAD A BLOODY HOUSE PARTY???? AGAIN!" She looked furious. Her face was growing redder by the second and a big vein in her forehead had started to throb. "OH MY GOD, TREVOR!"

"Mom . . . I'm . . . uh . . ." Trevor looked terrified. Gone was all his teen bravado, now replaced by something else entirely: scared little boy about to be grounded.

"RUN!" someone yelled.

"YES, GET OUT! GET OUT! GET OOOOUUUUTTT!" Trevor's mom screamed, and we all scrambled for the door. "Not you!" She grabbed Trevor by the back of his hoodie and yanked him as he tried to make a red-faced run for it. "Get out of here before I call your moms and dads!" she bellowed, and this—*this*—seemed to be the thing that struck sheer terror into everyone there. Noah grabbed me by the hand and suddenly we were rushing towards the door with the rest of the frantic gang.

"Let's get out of here!" Noah hissed at me as we dashed for the door.

"Uh . . . thanks for having us, uh, sorry for the mess . . . uh . . . Mrs. . . ." I momentarily paused at the door, but quickly realized I'd made a terrible mistake when Trevor's mom glared at me.

"Get out NOW, young lady!" she reprimanded, striking icy-cold terror into my veins. I looked at her and blinked. I didn't know what to do. I'd never been in trouble with a parent before. Noah seemed amused by this and ushered me out of the door.

"If you're not all gone in one minute, I am calling your moms, and the POLICE!" Trevor's mom sounded angrier than I'd ever heard anyone sound before.

"Run!" Noah said, picking up pace as we burst out the front door and ran towards our car. The party crowd all followed us.

"Can we come with you?" one of the hoodies shouted.

"Cool." Noah flung the car doors open and we all flew in. The hoodies—what was left of them—the twins, and some other people I didn't know.

We slammed the doors closed just as I thought I heard Trevor's mom say she was going to send him away to a military boarding school in Papua New Guinea if he ever did this . . . *again!* Noah put the key in the ignition and we sped off down the road. When we were several blocks away, he pulled over and turned in his seat to look at everyone.

"That was close," one of the Hoodies said. "Trevor's mom is hectic. She's like an advocate or something like that."

"No way," one of the twins said.

"Hey, do you guys want to come to my house now?" Hoodie Two asked. "I've got some weed there."

"Uh . . ." I looked over at Noah. I was exhausted, and he gave his head the tiniest of shakes.

"No, it's cool," I said to our friends.

"And you guys?" Hoodie Two turned to the twins and the others in the car and they all nodded their heads.

"It's just around the corner. We can walk. Thanks, dude." And then he pulled out his phone, and the twins did too. "What's your number? We should hang out again. It was sick."

I pulled my phone out too and, once again, swapped numbers with all these new people. When they were gone and only Noah and I remained, we turned to each other and then, as if we were both thinking the exact same thing, began laughing. Our laughter was loud and hysterical and it escalated until it felt quite uncontrollable.

"Why are we laughing?" I asked, in between snorts.

"You know what just happened to us, don't you?"

"What?"

"We went to a very dodgy club. You climbed up onstage and sang with the band. Then we party-hopped. You got drunk and smoked weed and then we got kicked out of a house party by an angry parent. That is the quintessential teen experience. And you've just had it. All in one night."

"Oh my God! I did, didn't I? And I kissed a girl!!"

"Yeah, there was that too," Noah continued to laugh.

"And the lead singer of a rock band!" I added, feeling quite pleased with myself now.

His laughter stopped abruptly. "Yeah, that too."

"It was a wild and crazy night!" I said, but stopped laughing too when I noticed how Noah was looking at me. I was going to open my mouth and say something, but I didn't know what to say, because I don't think I'd ever been looked at like that before and I didn't know what the correct response was to it. That same feeling started to bubble up inside me again, that fizzy, warm, champagne feeling that I only got around Noah. We stared at each other now, neither one of us blinking, and with it came this crackling, screaming, zapping energy that I was sure I physically felt in the air around us. I wondered if Noah could feel it too. Or was it just me? It reminded me of a line in my favorite book, though:

A raging fire ignited deep inside me then seemed to climb out of me and ignite the space between us, as Amanda's eyes left mine and drifted down to my lips.

I quickly looked away. This was so overwhelming it was hard to know what to do with it. These were feelings that I'd only ever read about in books and had been sure I would never actually experience.

"I don't know about you, but I could do with some breakfast," Noah said, pulling off onto the road again.

"Me too." I tried to force a smile into my voice, but suddenly I wasn't feeling very smiley.

CHAPTER 58

~

*W*e found a diner by the beach and ordered waffles with bacon and syrup and strawberries, a breakfast that Zen wouldn't eat in a million years. But here I was eating it, and scooping the last remaining splotches of syrup up off the plate with the edge of my fork and pouring it into my mouth. When we were both done, syrup and coffee and enough stimulants in us to forget we'd spent the entire night out, Noah put his elbows on the table, cupped his face in his hands and looked at me.

"So, we did the teen years last night. What about re-living something a little earlier?"

I pushed my plate to the end of the table and copied his body language. "What?"

Noah looked out over the sea and started thinking. "I'm trying to remember what I was up to at age twelvish."

"Well?"

"Mmmm . . . Paintball, laser tag, movies, first dates, theme parks, waterslides—"

"Like that." I pointed to the poster on the wall behind us.

Noah swiveled round. "Yes! Exactly like that," he said with a grin on his face, and stood up. "Come on!" He slapped some notes down on the table and stood up.

I looked at the poster for a while and then turned my attention back to Noah.

"Okay, but we're going to need to buy swimwear. I'm not doing that in the bikini Sindi gave me," I said, imagining bikini bottoms and tops being ripped off by the force of all that water.

Noah nodded. "Let's go."

* * *

"I don't know if I can do this," I said, looking up at the massive waterslide in front of us. We'd found a surf shop, bought some swimwear and were now at uShaka Marine World, Africa's biggest aquarium and water park.

"Of course you can." Noah slipped an arm through mine and gave me a little pull as he walked us towards the waterslide, which seemed to reach up into the sky. "You have to, anyway. No childhood is complete without waterslides. Besides, when you've done them once, you'll want to do them over and over again. It's the law of waterslides: they're addictive."

I reluctantly walked towards it and stared up. I doubted this would be addictive. I was sure I would do this once and never again. But I was determined! "Okay," I said. The whole point right now was to try and live the parts of my life that I'd missed out on. To throw off the heavy chains of fear and anxiety that had weighed me down for so long, to throw caution to the wind and, and . . . I faltered.

"Can't we do a smaller one first?"

"Nope! Where's the fun in that?" Noah's grip on my arm tightened and he started pulling me a little quicker now.

"You're right! Let's do it," I said, trying to psych myself up. "Sure. Why not! Yes!" But the more I said that, the less it actually made me feel psyched.

The staircase up to the waterslide was absolutely terrifying, and it quickly became evident that I hated heights. Something I wouldn't have known, since I'd never been up anything so high before. I grabbed onto the railings on the side and crouched down as I walked, making myself as low to the "ground" as possible.

Noah chuckled.

"What? It's not funny. It's terrifying . . ." I said, getting even lower to the stairs now.

"It's all part of the experience. You'll be okay," he said, and then, my heart stopped, and it wasn't from the height, it was from the feel of his hands on my waist as he reached out and placed them there.

"You're safe," he said softly. And I did feel instantly safer, but I also felt something else, something . . . *wow!*

No one, no man—no one—had ever put their hands on my body before. Not like that, anyway. Hands that felt protective and caring but also hands that made me feel like Amanda had felt when Sheik Khalifa had pulled her into his bed. When he'd put his hands on her and . . .

Something that had being lying dormant for long inside her, maybe even forever, had been ignited. A passionate fire that blazed with the intensity of a thousand suns. She'd never felt the heat of a man like this, as it pulsed through her entire body.

That's how I felt right now, as Noah and I climbed. I forgot about the height! I forgot everything that I was afraid of. His hands had a way of dulling that. His hands seemed to be a cure for everything that was bad and scary in this world.

"Almost at the top," he whispered. His voice had taken on a different tone now and I wondered whether he was feeling something too. But I had no way of knowing. I had no idea how to interpret anything at all. I'd never had to interpret a man's feelings before and figure out if there was a spark between us. I'd only been with two men my entire life, and it had been nothing like it had been in my romance book.

Instead, it had left me feeling that sex, in real life, was not even the slightest bit worth pursuing. But now I was starting to wonder if that was really the case. I was starting to think about sex. With Noah, and well, that was a very unusual thought for me!

CHAPTER 59

$\mathcal{W}$e finally reached the top of the slide, and I think I was starting to feel a little better about the whole thing, until I looked down.

"Oh my God!" I slapped my hands over my eyes and shook my head. "I can't do this!"

Noah pulled my hands away from my face, but I kept my eyes closed. "Look at me," he said. I opened my eyes and looked at him. "*We* can do this!"

I tried to nod, but I think my head actually gave a shake instead, which had not been my intention at all.

"Turn around, sit down and I'll sit right behind you."

"Okay." I lowered myself nervously, immediately getting wet as I sat down. And then I felt Noah come up behind me. I felt a pressure on my lower back and then saw his two legs come out on the sides of me. I felt his breath on my neck as he leaned forward.

"Can I put my arms around you?" he asked. "Like this?"

I nodded. I didn't think I could speak. He brought his big arms around the front of me and, before he had a chance to wrap them around me, I grabbed them and pulled them close, tightening them and holding on.

"You ready?" he whispered.

"Yes!"

And with that, I felt him push our bodies forward into the spray of the water and then I felt like I was flying. I opened my mouth to scream, but no sound came out. The wind was rushing into my mouth and pushing the sounds back down, and so was the water. The water that was flying up off the slide and spraying into my face. I grabbed onto Noah tighter as the slide turned sharply, and we went riding up the side of it, lifting towards the sky, as if we were about to take off into the blue above. My heart pounded out of my chest. But it didn't pound with nerves or anxiety, it pounded because it was alive. Adrenalin rushing through my veins alive. My senses were sharp and awake and I was terrified in the best kind of way possible, a way I didn't even know you could be terrified in. I let go of Noah's arms and threw mine in the air and was finally able to scream.

"Whoooo-hooooooo!" We picked up pace as we went around and around and then, a tunnel. We were plunged into darkness and my shouting turned to laughter, which echoed in the tunnel. It smelt of warm chlorine, fiberglass and coconut sun cream. I think it was the best smell I'd ever smelt before. This was the smell of all the things I had missed growing up. This was the smell of hot, sticky summers spent by the pool, of friends' birthday parties and eating too much cake, of running through sprinklers laughing and going on merry-go-rounds until you're so dizzy that you fall over. This was the best smell in the world and I wanted to bottle it and keep it because it now reminded me of joy. Pure, unadulterated joy as we burst back into the sunshine, flew up into the air and crashed into the pool below. I allowed my body to fully submerge, and stayed there for a while. Enjoying the feel of water surrounding me and holding me up. I was in another world down here, a world I hadn't visited in the longest time. And I loved it. I finally bobbed back up and looked at Noah.

"AGAIN!" I screamed, and raced out of the water as fast as I could. I think we did it another four times, and each time it got better and my courage grew until I was flying headfirst down it. My eyes and nose burned from the chlorine and my skin stung from the friction of the slide, but it was the best feeling in the world. Well, that's not true, the best feeling in the world was when Noah grabbed me by the hand and ran me to the next slide, called the Tornado.

We raced up the stairs together. I was taking them two at a time, all previous fears of heights gone. Heights took you to fun places. Places of rushing water and giggling and splashing and all those good things. We reached the top, and I didn't even hesitate. Instead, I threw myself down the slide and laughed as the spray struck me in the face once more. The slide curled around and, this time, instead of a tube, it became a massive disk and, like its name, my body went around and around and around until my stomach flew up into my head and my toes tingled. I finally slowed down, and then, just when I thought I had stopped, I fell through the eye of the tornado and into the pool below. I waited for Noah to come through, and when he did, I couldn't help myself. I threw my arms around him and pulled him into a wet, tight hug.

"Thank you," I said against his shoulder.

"For what?" he asked, wrapping his arms around me too.

"For this. For everything!"

"I should be the one thanking you," he said into my ear.

"Why?"

"If I hadn't met you, I would have sat on my butt watching TV series."

I giggled and hugged him tighter. "Noah, I wanted to say—" But before I could finish a frantic scream filled the air around us.

"MOVE! MOVE! MOVE!" The lifeguard at the top of the slide screamed as someone flew out of the tube and into the tornado disk. We hadn't moved far enough away from it and, any moment now, they would fly out of that opening and onto our heads. I felt myself being lifted up in one quick move as Noah raced us out of the way. It was only once the body had fallen and stood up again that I realized I now had my legs wrapped around Noah's waist and he was carrying me.

CHAPTER 60

~

$\mathscr{I}$ turned my head slowly, acutely aware that Noah's face was so close to mine now. Closer than he'd ever been to me before, except for that ill-fated almost-kiss in the field, but I was trying to forget that. Our noses almost touched, like the echo of an almost-kiss. I could feel his breath on my face; it was warm against the cool wetness of my skin. I'm sure he could feel my breath too, because it was coming out fast and jagged, in time to the beating of my heart. Fast, because I'd just been down a tornado slide, and fast because of something else. Because I was suspended in a man's arms, my arms around his neck, our faces almost touching, our eyes meeting and locking and like a million lines I'd read before in my book: *earth moving, stars exploding, fault lines cracking open and shaking the ground beneath my feet and relentless quivers and breath hitching . . .*

It was happening.

All of it.

All the things from all the pages of my book were happening as I looked at Noah and he looked back at me and the water lapped around us and the screams and the laughter of people disappeared into the silence that engulfed us as we seemed to slide into our own little world. Noah's blue eyes looked even bluer now, reflecting back the sky and the rippling water. They seemed to be as deep and vast as the entire ocean, and you wanted to dive right in and discover every treasure that was hidden beneath their surface. But I'd tried to dive once before, not in an ocean, but in a field of flowers, and that hadn't exactly gone well.

"Sorry! Sorry!" The words I heard just as Noah and I fell backwards into the water. For a second, we were both under water, still looking into each other's eyes, and then we came up to the surface and looked around to see what had happened. A large guy, well over six foot, was rushing towards us.

"Sorry, man, I didn't know I would fly out like that!" he said, pulling up his swimming trunks, which were now dangerously low.

"It's okay," Noah said. "It's a crazy ride."

"Crazy," the guy agreed, tying his swimming trunks tighter in the front. "Anyway, sorry I knocked you guys over. Keep well."

"No worries," Noah replied, and just like that, we were back in reality and back in the pool and back with our feet on the ground. Bubble burst. Like someone had come and just stuck a pin into our own private inflatable.

There was a slight awkwardness after that, as we walked out of the pool together, me lagging behind. We grabbed our towels and moved to a sunny spot, out of the shadow of the massive slide. It was still warm in Durban, but still there was the lightest cool breeze in the air that made the hairs on your arms prickle.

"I'm exhausted," Noah finally said, breaking the persistent silence between us.

"Me too!" I smiled at him, despite the feelings inside.

"I feel quite lazy all of a sudden," he said, his straightened shoulders slumping a little and his posture changing. "I could seriously do with a change of pace."

"Me too," I agreed. The exhaustion from the night before was catching up with me.

"What about that?" Noah said, pointing at a sign.

"The Lazy River ride," I read. "Kind of sounds perfect."

CHAPTER 61

~

$\mathscr{W}$e floated down the river on the big inflatable ring. It was just big enough for the two of us to rest our backs against, our legs trailing off the sides into the water. Our bodies were pressed together, and I was hyper-aware of every part of him that was touching every part of me. We moved slowly down the man-made stream, the gentle movement of the water creating this relaxing sound. The walls of tropical plants on both sides made you feel like you were in a river in the Amazon or something equally adventurous and exotic. It reminded me of the tropical atrium inside Sheik Khalifa's Desert Palace, the one where he and Amanda had shared their first kiss, and I thought how amazing and fortuitous it would be if Noah and I shared our first kiss here.

"This is amazing. Like being in a jungle," Noah said.

"Did you know that half of the world's animal and tree species live in a jungle?"

Noah smiled at me. "No, I didn't know that."

"Well, now you do," I declared as we floated underneath a wooden bridge. The ring touched the side of the wall, and the motion made us spin around slowly in a full circle, before we continued on our way down the lazy river. I touched the water with my fingertips, and let them trail there languidly, along the top of the slow-moving river. This really was a lazy river; the gentle movement of the inflatable was making me feel more relaxed than I had in days. I threw my head back and looked up into the bright, blue cloudless sky illuminated by the warm autumn sun. It wasn't too hot; it was just perfect. I was having a Goldilocks moment here: not too hot, not too cold . . . *just right*.

That was the thing about this moment, everything just seemed so damn right, and there was a part of me that was genuinely scared by this. My life had never been "just right," and this was a new feeling to me. And, as much as I liked it, I was terrified because, in a few days' time, Noah and I would go back home. Him to his house and his new career, and me to my—well, I don't think I had a career anymore, but I did have a dull as hell apartment. And then it would all be over. *Just right* would be gone, and now that I'd tasted it, the metaphorical porridge one could say, I don't think I ever wanted to feel that things were not *just right* ever again.

* * *

We climbed into the car, still damp from our excursion. I pulled the car mirror down and looked at my face. It was sun-kissed. My cheeks were slightly red, and a spray of freckles had appeared, freckles I never knew I had. The old me wouldn't have gone into the sun like this, but the new me, Zoe, went into the sun and into the water and did all sorts of things she was no longer afraid of.

"What are you thinking about?" Noah asked, while I silently looked at myself.

"How perfect everything feels." I turned away from the mirror to face him.

Something moved over his face, a look of confusion. "Then why do you sound so sad when you say that?"

"I guess I don't want it to end. But I know it will."

"Why would it end?" he asked.

I shrugged, but didn't answer him. Instead, I watched a crowd of schoolkids disembark from a bus and assemble in the parking lot. A loud beep made me glance back at Noah. He was looking down at his phone now, fingers sweeping across it, and a strange, solemn look swept across his face.

"What?" I asked, sensing a very definite shift in the mood between us. I didn't know if it was a good shift, or a bad shift. It was hard to tell, because it had been so sudden.

Noah shook his head, as if in disbelief. As if something in the message he was reading had thrown him.

"What?" I pressed, feeling something coming.

"It's just . . . my last pay check came through." He held his phone up and I briefly saw a notification from a bank. "That's it, then. I'm no longer a paramedic. It's official. It's over." He looked up at me and I understood why he was reacting like this.

"You're closing a chapter of your life. It's a big deal," I said.

Noah looked at me intently, zoning in on my eyes, and then dropped the phone from his hands onto his lap, like a dramatic exclamation mark.

"And opening another chapter," he said, staring at me as if he wanted something in return.

"I . . . I . . ." I shook my head. I had no idea what he was saying, what his words meant, but he was looking at me like that. *Like that!* Like Sheik Khalifa had looked at Amanda in the tropical atrium just before they kissed. I knew this look! And this time I was sure Noah was looking at me like that! My palms began to sweat, my heart raced and butterflies flapped so hard that I was sure I would take off out of the seat. Go flying up into the air, and Noah would have to pull me down by my ankle. *So this is what it felt like!* To have a guy, and not just any guy—Noah—look at me like this.

"I have a confession to make," he said, all husky and whispery.

"What?"

"I was jealous when you kissed Douche Klaw Asshole last night."

"Douche Klaw?" I smiled.

"Yeah, that's what I've been calling him in my head."

I swallowed hard. My throat felt a little tight. "It didn't mean anything. Besides, it was only a tee—"

"Teeny bit of tongue. So I've heard. A lot. More than enough, actually." He looked at my arm and then traced his finger down it. I shivered.

"Truth be told, I'm kind of thrilled that his number has almost washed off." He was right. The black phone number was more of a smudge now, but still he took my arm and rubbed his fingers across it.

"Almost gone!" He was smiling as he rubbed even faster now, and I laughed as more and more of the ink blurred, and all signs of Klaw disappeared from my arm.

"Looks like you really want it off."

"Oh, you have no idea." He kept rubbing until every last trace of Klaw was gone, and then, when it was, he looked back up, our eyes met and I swear I could hear them colliding. As if looking at someone like this had a sound.

"Don't worry. I don't taste him anymore either," I said.

"Well, Lila kind of made sure of that." His eyes darkened as he said that.

"That also meant nothing. Also just a teeny bit of tongue," I teased.

His lips parted and stretched into a smile. "You and teeny tongue . . ." He leaned ever so slightly, but it felt like the whole world shifted. "And what if I wanted to kiss you now?"

"Do you?" I asked.

"Yes," he said.

"Why didn't you kiss me back yesterday, in the field?" I asked.

His eyes drifted down to my lips and they burned. Actually burned. This was not fictitious. This happened in real life. People's lips could feel like they were actually on fire.

"It didn't feel right." His voice was husky and I couldn't believe this was happening to me. "I mean, it did *feel* right. But it wasn't the right time."

"And now?" I asked, equally husky.

"Well, you're no longer my patient." He leaned closer to me. "And you have all your memories back."

"Yes, I do," I whispered. This leaning was stealing the volume straight out of my voice.

But he didn't say anything. He didn't need to. My burning lips parted, my eyes fixed themselves on his mouth and the space between us quickly disappeared as our bodies got closer and closer, until the last tiny bit of space vanished and his lips came down on mine. They were warm, that was the first thing I noticed. They were soft, softer than I could ever have imagined. He was so masculine, but yet he had these lips that felt like wispy cotton candy against mine.

I'd never kissed a man before—well, I had, but not in any meaningful way—and this felt so full of meaning that I was bursting. I panicked for a second, unsure of what to do with my lips and my tongue and hands, but when Noah put his hands on the sides of my face, and whispered against my lips that he'd wanted to do this so badly, something instinctive kicked in. Something that I don't think can ever be taught. Something that just moves and flows out of you, from this place that comes alive when someone like Noah looks at you like *that* and kisses you like *this*.

Soft. Slow. As if he was easing me into it, as if we were both easing into it. As if this was just the appetizer and there was so much more to come. And there was. I had read about this kind of kiss. The kind that is deep and wanton and hungry and filled with a sense of urgency and lust. Hands traveling, tongues meeting and heat burning. But until now, I never knew what it really felt like, that is until Noah pushed my body back against the door and pushed his way deeper into my mouth.

I heard myself moaning. My hands reached round to the back of his head, my fingers found their way into his hair, where they tangled and tightened and pulled him closer. His hands also found things to tangle into and pull at, like my waist, which he was now gripping as he pushed me even further into the door with the weight of his body, as his lips crushed mine in a way that was both painful and pleasurable. I couldn't get enough. All those years of reading the same book over and over again and never thinking I would ever have this, never having the courage to try and have this, and I was having it. Damn, I was having it! And as if someone had opened something that couldn't be closed again, a frenzy was building up inside me that was making me feel quite wild and dizzy as my hands left his hair and began tugging on his shirt. I dug my fingers into his hard back the second it was exposed. He let out a moan, which only caused this feeling inside me to build even more, as I slipped my finger through the belt loop on his pants and pulled him closer to me.

But a loud knock on the window made us both jump. Noah scrambled off me and back into his seat and I went about straightening myself. We both looked up at the source of the noise.

"Shit!" Noah whispered.

"Oh crap!" I echoed his sentiments as the man in the police uniform leaned down and looked at us. He pointed to the window, and Noah opened it.

"Hello." The policeman looked from me, to Noah and back again.

"Uh . . . Officer. Hi!" Noah sounded sheepish.

"Hey." I lifted my hand and gave him a half-hearted wave. He did not look impressed.

The policeman pointed to the bus behind us and we both turned. A group of schoolkids were laughing and pointing at the car and two teachers looked like they were trying to hurry them away.

Noah face-palmed and I thought I heard him mumble "shit" again.

"License, please," the policeman said in a tone that was as terrifying as Trevor's mom's.

"Sure, here." Noah pulled out his wallet and handed his license over. The policeman began scrutinizing Noah's photo and I noticed that something had fallen out of the wallet and tumbled to the floor, but I dared not point it out now.

"It's an old picture," Noah said. "My hair was different and I haven't shaved." He pointed to the card. "In case I don't look the same."

The policeman handed the card back to Noah without saying a word and then turned his terrifying attention to me.

"ID, please." I shivered; he had a very penetrating gaze. Once he'd examined me and my card thoroughly, he made a long, slow walk around the car. Checking the license disk and the plates. He looked through the window into the back seat, as if he was expecting to see something dodgy there, like a body bag. Finally, after his inspection, he was back at our window again.

"You know that is a bus full of kids over there." He was, of course, stating the obvious.

"Uh, would it help if I told you that I'm a paramedic and that this lady over here was experiencing breathlessness and I needed to administer mouth-to-mouth?" Noah asked.

The policeman looked at Noah with a deadpan expression for a while. "Would you have something to verify that?"

"Yes! YES! I do," Noah scrambled for his wallet again and pulled out a card that identified him as an EMS.

The man looked at the card for the longest time now, and then his face softened.

"Man, I was just called out to a possible domestic violence case. Turned out the kid was just having a tantrum, but I had to climb over the fence, and I scratched myself, and it's very red today and my wife told me to go to a doctor, but I don't have time for that, and I don't know if I need to."

The policeman rolled his sleeve up, revealing a very red-looking cut.

"May I?" Noah reached out, and the policeman nodded. Noah pressed the skin next to the wound and the big, burly officer winced.

"Well, I'm afraid your wife is right. The skin around the wound is tender, swollen and warm to the touch, which means an infection has set in. You're probably going to need a course of antibiotics, so you're going to have to go to the doctor."

The policeman rolled his sleeve up and then glared at us again for a while, and then he tapped the roof of the car a few times. "Do not—*do not*—let me catch you doing that again in public, you understand?"

"We totally understand," Noah said.

I leaned over and made eye contact with the man. "We won't. I promise."

"Go on, get out of here. And don't come back."

"We won't. I swear," Noah reiterated as the policeman turned and walked away.

Noah slipped his ID back into his wallet and suddenly his head jerked up.

"What?" I asked.

"My . . . card, I usually have a . . ." He swiveled his head around frantically. "Something very important . . . I keep it in my wallet and I . . . uh . . ." He continued to look. He looked panicked now as he opened the car door and checked the ground outside.

"Is it that?" I pointed to the place at his feet where the folded piece of paper had fallen.

Noah's demeanor changed in a second. He let out a massive sigh as he picked it back up and slipped it into his wallet with care. Whatever that was, it looked really important to him. It also looked old. Like it had been there for a very long time. The stretched credit-card slot in his wallet told me so.

"What's that?" I asked, unable to contain my curiosity.

"It's just something I've had for a very long time. Something that was given to me by someone special."

I nodded at this very vague description. He wasn't telling me something, and I couldn't help but wonder what it was, and who had given it to him. I didn't want to pry. It was clear that, whatever it was, it wasn't something he wanted to share with me, and I didn't really know how I felt about that.

Soon we were driving again, rather aimlessly, it seemed. But the drive didn't feel comfortable. I squirmed in my seat, still feeling the warmth of Noah's lips on mine. And then I looked down at my leg, as Noah slid his hand onto it.

"You know what that was?" he asked, smiling.

"What?"

"We just got into trouble with the police for making out in a car, another quintessential teen experience!"

I reached down and slid my fingers through his. "Really?"

He nodded. "In the last two days you've re-lived your teens and, today, we re-lived childhood."

I smiled. He was right. And I'd had more fun in the last few days than I'd ever had before.

"I'm having so much fun!" It was uncanny, but Noah and I had said it at the exact same time, and then found ourselves smiling at each other.

"Me too." Again, we said it at the same time.

"These last few days with you have been . . ." I wanted to say *the best of my life*, but maybe that was too much?

"I know," Noah said. "It's been amazing."

"It has." I wanted to say more, only I didn't. *How much did I say to him?* That from the moment he'd held my hand in that ambulance, something inside me had felt so comfortable with him. That even though we'd only known each other for nearly two weeks, it felt like he'd been in my life forever. It felt like we were old friends, meeting once more. And everything about that just felt right. Everything about him and me felt right. But I didn't say any of that to him. *Not yet anyway.*

CHAPTER 62

~

$\mathcal{W}$e drove a little longer and soon we were going in circles.

"Do you know where we're going?" I asked.

He squeezed my hand. "No. Do you?"

"No," I admitted.

"Well, I don't know about you." Noah sounded tentative now. "I could seriously do with something more . . . adult, in my life right about now." He dragged his eyes away from the road momentarily and glanced at me. A bolt of lightning seemed to rush through me. Splitting me in half like an atomic bomb, only for me to crash back together again with this internal force that made me jump out of my chair a little.

"Like what?" I crossed and uncrossed my legs; the word *adult* had conjured up all sorts of images in my head. His hand moved up and down my leg in a sweeping motion . . . *yes, that was very adult*. This was getting adult. We were moving away from PG and I had no idea what to do.

"What about a date?" he asked.

"A date?"

"Dinner?"

"But we've had dinner before, and lunch, and breakfast, and strange midnight snacks at a garage."

"Those weren't dates." He said it in this tone. Rough and masculine and, my God, the tone made me feel like the chair was a hot frying pan and I was the bacon. And then the clincher, the thing he said that turned the sizzle into a downright burn.

"I'd like to take you on a real date, Zoe. Real."

I flushed. I blushed. "I've never really been on a . . . well, I mean, I did internet dating for a while and it was horrible, and they weren't really dates, you know?"

"I know what you mean. There's seldom anything romantic about meeting someone online and going to a restaurant to eat food with them."

"No," I said.

There was a pause.

"So, let me take you on your first real date then, tonight." His thumb ran up my leg in a way that told me he was thinking about more than *just* a date. What came after the date, perhaps. This made me feel two things: excitement and utter terror. Because I'm sure he had no idea how sexually inexperienced I really was. Sex had always terrified me. Being so close to someone. The germs. The possibility of sharing diseases. It was not something that had ever appealed to me, in real life, anyway. It appealed to me in books. But so far, my experiences had shown me that the real-life thing was very, *very* different to books.

My first sexual experience had been strange to say the least. It had been at the age of eighteen with a guy called Monty, a friend of mine who I'd been in and out of hospital with for a decade. We both had leukemia, his was worse than mine, but through it all we'd supported each other and become the best of friends. Even our parents had become friends. But the last time we were in hospital, things were very different. Monty's leukemia had progressed and the doctors had said there was nothing they could do anymore. Like me, he had been poked and prodded and operated on for years. The two of us had spent more time inside hospitals than outside. Monty got word that he was being transported to an "end-of-life facility" in the morning, and to all intents and purposes, this was going to be the last time I ever saw him.

Being a leukemia patient, you develop a strange relationship with death. At first you fear it, like everyone does, but then, over time, as your illness hangs around like an unwanted friend, for years, you kind of get familiar with the notion of death. Monty and I had both accepted long ago that this might not be something we would return from. But the night that I heard he was definitely not returning, I was still devastated.

We'd sat on his bed together, eating chocolate pudding cups late into the night, like we usually did. On this night, though, we didn't have to steal them. This night, the nurses willingly gave us more than we could eat. We didn't really say much while we ate, we just enjoyed the moment together, which we both knew was going to be our last.

"I only have one regret," I remember Monty saying.

"What's that?"

"That I'm going to die a virgin."

It wasn't only because he was dying that it happened, it was also because all my old friends were doing it now. In fact, it seemed that everyone was doing it, except me, and for the first time in a long time, I felt I could do something that was finally normal. And although I thought it was rather unusual to be having my first kiss and my first sexual experience all in one night, I guess nothing about my teen years had been usual anyway.

The kiss had lacked any kind of finesse. It was all hard tongues and grinding braces. The sex had also lacked finesse. It had been quick. Very quick. I hadn't expected that. And I hadn't really understood where all the pleasure was meant to come from either. Monty seemed to have enjoyed it, though. He'd told me that he could die happy now, knowing that he'd lost his virginity to the most beautiful girl he knew. I think he just didn't know that many girls outside of the hospital, because if he did, he wouldn't have thought I was pretty, with my bald head full of peach fluff hair and my collar bones that jutted so far out of my chest.

The next day he was transferred to the end-of-life facility and I never saw him again. I wasn't even able to go to his funeral. I'd experienced a lot of death growing up, so many friends from the cancer wards and support groups who I'd gotten to know over the years had died, but his death had been the worst.

My second experience had happened a few years later. I guess I was trying to remedy the first one, but it only served to further solidify the idea that "sex" was much better left for solitary moments with myself and my book and my lipstick. I'd tried the internet-dating thing. I'd met an IT engineer who was almost as set in his ways and paranoid about germs as I was. He was also a vegan, so we only ever went to the same restaurant for dinner, a place he could trust because he knew the owner and everything served was non-GMO. I'd appreciated that too, as someone who rarely deviated from the same food and routine. The conversation never really moved past the mundane, punctuated with long silences. There had been a kiss at the end of date three, and by date six . . . sex. It had seemed like the appropriate time, really. Date six felt like a date that could end with more than a kiss at the door. I should have got a sense of what the sex would be like from the kiss.

Sloppy, way too much spit and, what was worse, he kept asking if it was good . . . *the whole way through.*

I think if you have to ask that question, you probably already know the answer. Or maybe he asked the question so many times because I'd lain on my back, staring at the ceiling, drumming my fingers on the mattress while I waited for the whole ordeal to be over. Again, *nothing* like my book. I was starting to think that fictional sex was really not a good representation of what real sex was. And that's when I decided to watch porn. I mean, if anyone is going to show you what real sex is like, it's professionals. People who have sex for a living— surely they would be able to show me what real sex was like . . .

Only, when I Googled whether a woman could have a screaming orgasm every thirty seconds while her legs were in that position, the internet assured me it was highly unlikely.

So, if Noah was hoping for sex with me, chances are, he would be sorely disappointed, since I'm not sure I actually knew what real sex even was.

CHAPTER 63

❧

"**S**ure, a date," I finally said, after what had been a very long silence.

I heard Noah laugh next to me.

"What?"

"It's about time you said something. I've been sitting here waiting for you to say something for three minutes now. I thought I'd scared you off."

"You didn't scare me off," I said, even though that didn't sound very convincing at all, and there was a part of me that felt completely scared off.

"Okay, I'll try to believe you, but I'm not sure I totally do . . ." He turned and looked at me. "If you don't want to then, I mean, we don't have to . . . it was just a kiss. If you want it to end here, then that's cool. I won't pretend that I won't be disappointed, but if that's it and this doesn't go anywhere and there's no date . . ." He sighed. "Sorry. I'm rambling. What I mean to say it, it's totally up to you. Whatever you want to do, I'm fine with it."

"I'm cool with it," I quickly chimed in. "The date. Totally cool with it."

"You are?"

"Yes!" I said, feeling a little more self-assured now. This was a time to try new things, right? To live experiences I had never lived before, after all.

"Great." His cheeks and eyes brightened at the same time and he quickly looked back at the road.

"Where will we go?" I asked.

"I have no idea. We'll have to Google."

"Okay." I pulled my phone out.

"I mean, *I* will have to Google. I'm taking you out."

"I'll narrow some options down. Besides, you're driving and it's getting late, so we should probably find a place sooo—" And then something dawned on me, and I was so shocked I hadn't thought about it before. "Where will we stay tonight?"

"Well, I know where I don't want to stay," Noah said.

"Where?"

"In a teenager's basement again."

I laughed. "Me neither."

"We'll figure it out," Noah said casually. "Lots of places to stay around here."

"True," I said, looking back down at my phone and typing "Places to eat in Durban," and then adding the word "romantic" after it and blushing to myself as I did.

Something popped up on my screen, a place that I knew from living here for a while. It was the most expensive and, arguably, most luxurious hotel in the area. It boasted a beach-front cocktail bar and restaurant, which was supposed to be wildly romantic. It was a little way outside of the city, just down the coast. I tapped my fingers on the screen and brought up the pictures of the rooms. Gorgeous, opulent rooms facing the ocean. One room in particular caught my attention, the most beautiful bedroom I'd ever seen. It looked sumptuous, romantic, so unlike the bedroom in my apartment. It was bursting with plants, and the walls were covered in this intricately patterned green-and-pink wallpaper depicting a scene from a jungle. The bed had an ornate golden headboard with the fluffiest pillows that existed in the world, I thought. A private plunge pool on a deck surrounded by tall, elegant-looking palm trees, looking out over the sea below. I read about the room; this was the presidential suite at the Lighthouse Hotel in Umhlanga Rocks. Built on two levels with its own private elevator, two bedrooms, two bathrooms and a dining room for ten people. It was the ultimate in luxury and romance. My eyes followed the words and, when I came to the last line, I choked out loud as I read the price at the bottom.

"Oh my God." I held the phone up for Noah to see. "Look how expensive this place it. One night is, like, my entire month's salary."

Noah was driving, and when he stopped at a red light, he glanced at the phone and gave a shocked whistle.

"It is amazing, though," he said. "Although I'm not sure I'll ever stay anywhere like that."

"Me neither. I mean, you would literally have to be a millionaire if you wanted to st-stay . . ." I stared at the screen again. "I am a millionaire," I said out load, as if it were only really dawning on me now. "I'm literally a millionaire!"

"Oh. That's right. I keep forgetting!"

"Me too!"

I stared at the road in front of me, thinking about all that money I had sitting in a bank account somewhere. I had done *nothing* with it. All I'd done was save it for later, although I had no idea what "later" really meant, or what I was meant to do with it "later." I had used it to pay for my studies, I had used it to buy my apartment and I used some of the interest each month to live off, because that salary they paid me at the agency was not even enough to furnish me with one month of the organic, non-GMO, nutritionally balanced meals I got delivered. But other than that, and buying a club full of random people shooters, I'd never actually done anything with it. I'd never splashed out. Thrown caution to the wind and spent way too much on a handbag or a night in a luxury hotel. And God knows, I probably deserved to spend that money!

"You know what! Let's do it!"

"Do what?" Noah asked.

"Let's stay here! Let's live it up and stay here for the night, and who cares what it costs." I looked at the screen again and a feeling rose inside me. "And it has two bedrooms, so that's . . ." I paused.

"Good," he said.

"Yes. Good," I said, and for some reason it came out sounding like a question.

"Yup. Good. It is," he said back, and, strangely, his statement also sounded like a question. What was he asking?

What was I asking?

And what was the answer?

CHAPTER 64

"*N*ow this is more like it," Noah said, as we were escorted into the palatial room. And it was palatial. Gold-and-white marble floors. Crystal chandeliers and, the best part, that plunge pool on the deck overlooking the sea.

"I've never been anywhere so fancy before," Noah said.

"Me neither."

"And why do you think that is?"

"What do you mean?"

"Well, you have all this money, that you rightfully deserve, and yet you've never spent it on anything. You've never treated yourself to a night like this before, or an overseas vacation, or . . . *anything*."

His question floated through the room towards me. It seemed like a simple one. But it wasn't. It was very loaded, and it summarized the life that Zenobia had led in many ways.

"That's just who I was," I said softly.

"Was?" he asked.

I turned and smiled at him. "Well, the old me would never have smoked weed, even if it was accidental, the old me would not have gone down waterslides, and certainly wouldn't be staying in a place like that. So, yes, *was*. Or at the very least, *getting there*." I watched Noah, and his look seemed to draw me closer towards him. I reached out and took his hand. It felt so comfortable in mine. Like I'd been taking his hand forever.

"I like you like this," he whispered. "It suits you."

"Thanks, and I have you to thank for that," I whispered back.

"No. I had nothing to do with this. I was just there when it happened. You—*you*—did all of this. I'm just along for the crazy ride."

I smiled, and this time it was huge.

"You're incredible." He stepped forward and slowly placed a hand on the side of my face. This was exactly like the moment that Amanda Stone and Sheik Khalifa had shared . . .

Wait?

Why did I keep referring to that book? That book wasn't real. It was someone's else's made-up romance, it was not *my* romance, and I was no longer going to live inside the pages of someone else's bloody love story. I was going to live my own love story. I was going to experience it and feel it, not as Amanda Stone, but as me. Zoe! The new me who was more than capable of writing the words to her own *real* romance and feeling whatever she wanted to feel, not what some character had felt.

"You're the bravest, strongest, most adventurous person I've ever met in my life and, quite frankly, I'm a little in awe of you." He reached out and touched the other side of my face.

"You are?" I choked back the words, because I could feel that tears were so close to the surface now, and I didn't want to cry.

"Everything you've been through in your life—I can't even imagine what it was like. And look at you, not only did you survive it all, but you're thriving in your bright tie-dye clothes."

I giggled and put my hand over his. A tear slipped out of my eye, and I was unable to stop it.

"Are you crying?" Noah asked.

"Not bad tears, happy tears. Tears of 'I can't believe this is actually happening right now.' *It is happening, right?* This isn't a dream. We are standing here in the most beautiful room in the world and you do have your hands on my face and we did kiss, right? That wasn't some dream or a fake memory or . . . something?"

Noah smiled. Slow and seductive and so, so sure of himself. The certainty gave him this sexiness that oozed out of him. He had a glint in his eyes, dark, a little bit dirty. Dangerous, even. *God, it was so sexy.*

"I mean." He dragged the words out. "I'm pretty sure we kissed, but maybe we should do it again, to see if it's familiar, or not."

"Just to see if it's familiar?" I asked, playing along. I felt so euphoric right now. I'd never played along in a flirtatious, sexy game before.

"Exactly," he growled in a low, gravelly voice.

I closed my eyes and smiled, parted my lips and waited for him to kiss me. But when he didn't, I opened them quickly to see what was going on.

"Oh wait, you wanted me to kiss you, not the other way around?" He let out a chuckle.

I gave him a playful smack on the arm as he teased me.

"Fine, fine. I'll kiss you . . . *if I really have to*." He rolled his eyes and then pulled me close. I let out a giggle that was low and kind of sexy-sounding, if I do say so myself.

And then he kissed me again, soft and slow and short. He pulled away as soon as he'd done it and raised his brows at me.

"Does that feel familiar?"

I cast my eyes upwards and shook my head. "Not at all."

"Okay, let's try again."

He kissed me again, this time longer and slower and even sexier than the first, and when he was done, he pulled away and raised his brows at me.

"Mmmm, I don't know, I'm still not sure. Something about it is ringing some bells, but . . ."

"Oh, fine! You leave me no option then." And with that, he grabbed me and dipped me like you would do in *Strictly Come*

Dancing. This time, the kiss was not soft and slow. This time, it was something else entirely. He held me like that in his arms, kissing me hard and deep, and I'd never been so vulnerable before. The only thing stopping me from falling backwards onto the hard marble below were his arms around me. And even though he was physically stopping me from falling, I couldn't help but think I was falling for him in another way entirely.

CHAPTER 65

~

Three hours later, after the briefest nap in my room, which Noah and I had both agreed we needed, and a really long soak in my bath, I was getting ready for my first date with Noah. The sun had started setting, and the view out my bedroom window was stunning. The orange from the sun was painting the waves a warm caramel color that I was quite mesmerized by. I didn't have a large selection of clothes to choose from, only the ones Sindi had lent me, and they weren't exactly very "first-date-y." I was feeling excited and nervous, I'd never really been on a first date before—well, not one that meant anything, and this one meant something. I was almost done when my phone beeped and was lit up by a message from a number I didn't recognize. I clicked on it and read, and as soon as I did, I knew exactly who it was from.

Noah: So, I'll pick you up at seven.

I smiled to myself, walked up to my bedroom door and looked out. Noah was standing in the doorway of his bedroom, phone in hand, staring straight at me. We smiled at each other and then I looked back down and typed my reply.

Zoe: I can see you, you know.

I glanced up at him again, and couldn't stop the huge smile that spread across my face. His face too. He lowered his head and typed while I watched my phone with painful anticipation.

Noah: I can see you too.

Noah: You look good.

I felt a warm rush through my body, starting at my toes and ending in my cheeks.

Zoe: So do you.

Noah: Thanks. I've got a hot date now, so I needed to scrub up.

Zoe: You scrub up well.

Noah: Not as well as you . . .

I looked up again and our eyes locked across the suite. I felt myself bite my bottom lip, and his eyes immediately went there. So, this was flirting? So, this was what it felt like to be giddy, and swept up and tingly? I looked back down at my phone. I didn't want this moment to end, so I messaged him again.

Zoe: Who's your date with?

Noah let out a soft laugh, looked up at me briefly and then started typing again. It was taking forever, and the anticipation I felt as I looked down at the dancing dots was so overwhelming that, I swear, it made me feel physically itchy.

Noah: She's this woman I met recently. I didn't plan on meeting her, she kind of met me, you could say. And she's one of the most amazing people I've ever met. She's strong and funny and caring and gorgeous and brave and silly, in the best way possible. And I think she's probably totally out of my league, so I'm really going to have to impress her with this date.

I read the message and, I swear, my heart missed several beats. It started jumping back and forth in my chest, as if it were doing hopscotch. I lowered my fingers to the keyboard and was just about to start typing, but didn't. Instead, I put my phone down and looked up at him.

"She's not out of your league by the way," I said.

"Really? So, you think I stand a chance with her?"

"I do, actually."

Noah's blue eyes darkened, and his cheeks flushed just a tiny bit pink. "That's good to know."

"Does she stand a chance with you?" I asked, a pitter-patter of nervousness building inside me.

Noah tilted his head to the side and smiled. A sexy half-smile spreading across his face that I wanted to climb into and swim around in. "I would say she stands *more* than a chance." His words melted me instantly. I was chocolate and he was the microwave.

We both stood there in silence, staring at each other across the suite. We didn't need to say a word; the silence was speaking volumes. I felt a tug in my chest that made me pull away from the doorframe. I guess Noah must have felt the same tug, because he pulled away too. And then, like an invisible lasso had been thrown around us and was now being tightened, we started walking towards each other. Step by step, getting closer and closer, until we both arrived at the golden rose in the middle of the marble floor. He stood on one side, and me on the other. We both looked down at our feet. Only this pattern in the floor was separating us, and I didn't want to be separated anymore. We stepped straight into the rose and straight into each other's arms.

"So, shall we go?" Noah asked, his lips at my ear.

"Where are we going? I hope it's nowhere too fancy. I'm not really dressed for a date."

"Not too far." He took my arm and walked me in the opposite direction of the front door.

"Wait. I thought we were going out."

"We are, just not out that way." He walked us towards the sliding door that led onto the deck. He pulled the curtains aside and gestured for me to step through, and when I popped out on the other side and saw what he'd done for me, a small explosion went off in my heart.

"When did you do this?" I ran my eyes over the blanket and pillows, the flowers and candles and the bottle of champagne on the small table chilling in ice.

"When you were napping and bathing, I called the hotel and arranged it. Picnic by the beach."

"It's perfect," I whispered, watching the orange flame from one of the floating candles dance across the top of the water.

"I figured you would prefer this," he said.

"How did you know that?"

"I think I've gotten to know you better than you think."

I looked back at the romantic scene in front of me. This was so much better than any book I'd ever read. Perhaps better than any book that had ever been written. No writer could do this moment justice by putting words to it. Because there were not enough words in the universe to describe all the feelings rushing through me.

Noah helped me down onto the picnic blanket then reached for two other small blankets and spread one out across my knees once I'd gotten comfortable. I leaned back against the pillow and looked out over the dark sea in front of us. It looked so vast, spreading out from here all the way to the horizon, where it vanished into the night sky, joined it as if they were one. Noah popped the champagne and poured us two glasses. He passed one to me and then paused.

"What?" I asked.

"I want to say something, but it might sound strange." The warm orange glow from the candles made his eyes a completely different shade of blue now.

"Say it."

"I don't know if you believe in stuff like this, but I do."

"Believe in what?"

"You know I told you that it felt like Sindi was always meant to be my sister," he said.

"Yes."

"It's just that . . ." He shrugged and went silent for a moment. "You know, I wasn't meant to be on duty that day that you had your accident. I was meant to be on leave already. The only reason I came in was because two people got sick that day. Two people had to get sick on the same day for me to have to go to work."

"Really?"

"And if I had been on duty, I don't work that part of town. What I'm trying to say is that I feel like we were meant to meet each other.

That's all." He looked at me expectantly, but I didn't say anything. "Sorry, was that too much? Too deep? Did I get carried away there with meaning or—"

"No." I cut him off. "You didn't. It's just weird, because I was feeling the same way. I mean, what are the chances of getting stuck in an elevator, and then hearing you say your address so randomly, and then waking up and that being the only thing I really remembered?" I paused. "It's been a weird two weeks, that's for sure."

"It has. But really, really good."

"Really good," I echoed.

He held his glass up and I clinked mine against his. "To weird, fateful meetings," he said.

"To weird, fateful meetings," I repeated, taking a sip of the champagne. The bubbles burst against my lips and tongue, and each one felt like it contained a little magical possibility.

CHAPTER 66

*W*e didn't do much eating, we didn't do much drinking or talking, for that matter. In fact, we'd spent most of the evening doing nothing more than staring at each other in the dim, warm candle-light. The only sounds around us were the rhythmic breaking of the waves, and the sound of our breathing. When a breeze picked up, rushing through the palm trees and causing our candles to dance frantically, I shivered. Noah walked over to the edge of the pool and dragged his fingers over the water.

"It's heated," he said.

I didn't know much about the world of *real* romance and seduc-tion, but I knew enough to know that the fact the pool was heated wasn't really the pertinent point that Noah was trying to make. It being heated was almost irrelevant, the question and intention lay more in the *what* were we going to do about the fact it was heated?

"It's heated," I repeated.

Noah smiled. Naughty and flirty. "Do you want to . . ." He left the question open-ended and it hung in the air around us. We both knew what the question was. God, even that gray monkey sitting in the palm tree watching us knew what the question was.

"I'll get my swimsuit." I rushed back to my room and changed as quickly as I could. I wrapped a fluffy gown around me and, before walking back out, looked at myself in the mirror.

"*This is it!*" I whispered to myself. This was the moment. I could feel it. *It* was about to happen, and I was ready for it . . . *or was I?*

I smiled at myself and then ran my hand through my hair. It was weird how it looked different on me. When I was chicken-eating Zenobia-Phobia, it just looked like a non-hairstyle. The kind a momish-mom who was too tired to take showers might have. But when I was like this—*like me*—the me I should be, it looked totally different. Short and playful and a bit irreverent. Or was I just seeing myself in a different light? Was that it? I was no longer seeing the person I used to be a few days ago, but rather seeing the person I really was. And maybe that person had always been there, lurking just below the disinfected surface, waiting for something to bring her out, and that's what the elevator had done. Losing my memories, forgetting who I was, had allowed me to become who I was supposed to be. I smiled at myself and then turned and rushed back out to Noah, but when I got there he was already in the water waiting for me.

"I thought you weren't coming back," he said.

I shook my head. "I'm back. I was just having a moment in the mirror."

"Should I ask what that is?"

"It was nothing. Well, it was something. But it was a . . . *wait*. Are you . . . uh . . . naked . . . under the water?"

Noah laughed. "No!"

"So you're not . . . ?"

"No! Why, do you want me to be?" he asked, his laughter stopping and my cheeks suddenly going very hot. I put my cool hands over them in an attempt to bring the general temperature down, but it didn't work.

"I'm not very experienced in all this," I blurted, getting the words out of my mouth as quickly as possible.

"What?"

"This!" I waved my hand around, indicating the space between us. "Flirting. Kissing. Going on dates. Swimming in a plunge pool in a romantic setting with a bloody monkey with a torn ear watching us." I looked at the tree, and Noah followed my gaze.

"Yeah, I don't have any experience in that either . . . monkeys."

At that, the monkey bobbed his head from side to side and then shook the palm tree.

"The monkey agrees." Noah smiled.

"I'm not joking, Noah. I'm not, I have no . . . I haven't done this before. I know how lame that sounds. I'm almost thirty and I've hardly gone on any dates and my idea of romance is reading the same romance novel over and over again, highlighting the little bits I like and . . . uh . . . *putting on lipstick.*"

"You put lipstick on when you read?" he asked.

I cleared my throat. "You could say that, but that's not the point anyway. Point is, the only sex I've had is bad sex. The only dates I've gone on have been bad dates. When I was on a dating app, I never made it past the first few messages, which means I'm clearly not very adept at flirting either. Especially after they send me those pictures of their . . ." I cringed. "I mean, that's not exactly flirting is it? Send me a photo of your dick!" I shook my head rapidly, thinking about that one in particular where the guy had put a can of toilet spray next to it, obviously to show off his masculine prowess, but all I could think about was *why* one would use toilet spray in the first place. Very off-putting. "My point is, Noah, wait, I've already said that, but I'm going to make this point soon. Give me a moment . . ." I paused, feeling a little flustered now. I took a deep, long, slow breath and steadied myself. "I'm probably going to be useless at all this stuff. Sexual innuendos and seduction and . . . *why is the monkey still looking at us?*" I glared up at the little gray beast and he let out an almighty shriek.

"I thought animals liked you again," Noah said.

"Maybe it's you he doesn't like," I returned, and picked up a few strawberries and tossed them into the bush. The monkey made a run for them and disappeared. "Right, where was I?" I turned my attention back to Noah, and he was looking at me in a way that made me stop breathing. His lips were slightly parted, his pupils seemed bigger suddenly and it didn't look like he was blinking anymore.

"What?" I asked nervously. He took a step closer to me, and the water around him rippled and splashed against the sides of the pool. He climbed up the steps, then another one, and another, his body getting higher and higher out the water.

"What?" My "what" was so soft it was almost inaudible over the sound of my heart beating against my ribcage.

"I was just thinking how wrong you are about all of that." His voice sounded rough around the edges, not as smooth and polished as it normally was.

"You were?"

"Yes. You're totally wrong about not being good at it. You are good at it and I am totally seduced."

"Really? Did I? When? How?" I was genuinely shocked by this.

He didn't answer, though, he simply stepped all the way out of the pool and stood in front of me in his underwear. And truthfully, he might as well have been naked. I tried not to gape at the way the wet underwear seemed see-through and how it was now sticking to a certain part, creating a very detailed outline of the whole affair. And when it was clear I'd been looking for too long I quickly looked away and mumbled a "sorry."

"Wow, do I feel a little objectified right now!" Noah chuckled.

"No! I didn't mean to . . ." And then I stopped talking and looked at him. I wasn't going to fight these feelings any longer. "Actually, I kind of did mean to." My voice was seductive and I was pleasantly surprised to hear this version. It was foreign to me, but it sounded good.

"You did?" He lifted one of his brows at me, that sexy, cute signature move of his.

"Well, you're hot, I mean, look at you."

Noah shook his head. "No. Look at you." He said it in a way that made my head spin, made my arms feel like they were floating and made it feel like my feet were no longer on solid ground.

"No one's ever said anything like that to me before," I whispered.

"Then I'd better make up for that . . ."

CHAPTER 67

He wrapped a wet hand around my waist and pulled me towards the pool, towards him. I didn't object, I just let him lead me towards something totally new, exciting and also a little bit frightening. But one thing I'd learnt over the last two weeks was that the best things in life did seem a little frightening at first. But they were always, inevitably, the best things for you. The things that pushed you out of your comfort zone and took you to new, better places. And this, *right here*, Noah, the sea, the heated pool, the two of us, this felt like a better place.

He pulled me into the pool. It was so warm that I winced in surprise.

"I know," he said. "Warmer than you expect."

"Much." I slipped my shoulders under the water, slinking down into its heat until only my head was out. Noah did the same and we bobbed up and down like this together for a while.

"Why do you like me?" I found myself asking, a question I hadn't even thought of asking, prior to it coming out of my mouth.

"So many reasons. Some I can explain, some I can't."

"Try," I said.

"How do you explain the reasons you feel close and attracted to someone? I think those are a little inexplicable. They come from somewhere else inside you." He smiled. "I don't know, does that make sense?"

I smiled back. "It does. I felt so comfortable with you from the beginning, as if being with you in your house was just . . ." I tried to look for the word, but it escaped me.

"Right?" he asked.

"Right," I repeated.

"I felt the same way." He reached up and ran his thumb over my lips and then he moved it down, onto my neck, my shoulder, where he circled one of the scars I had. I put my hand over his.

"Don't," I said.

"Why?"

"They're ugly. I don't like them."

He pulled my hand away gently and laid his entire hand over the scar. "I like them."

"No, you don't. How could you?"

"They're you. They're what you've been through. They're what made you who you are. A survivor."

I laid my hand over his now and closed my eyes, and it wasn't long before I felt his lips on mine again. This time they tasted of strawberries and champagne and the slightest bit of chlorine. I loved the taste. I wrapped my hand around the back of his head and drew him in for a deeper kiss. Our mouths melted together, and I no longer knew where his ended and mine began. He walked me backwards, until my back collided with the side of the pool, hard. Water lapped around us, the feel of the warm water spraying across the cold parts of my face made the kiss intensify as drops of warm liquid trickled over our lips and onto our tongues.

He held me in place with two big hands on my waist. I didn't want to break free of the grip he had on me. Slightly possessive, so masculine and totally damn sexy. This was, by far, the most erotic, naughtiest, thing I'd ever done in my life. I let out a sharp sigh as his hands left my waist and trailed up my body and over my breasts. *So, this was what it was meant to feel like!* Every single one of your nerves connected and exploding all at the same time. I smiled and heard the tiniest giggle escape my lips.

"What?" he asked, pulling his hands away. "Is that . . . ticklish?"

I shook my head. "NO! No, not at all. It's just . . ." I grabbed his hands and put them back where they were. "Don't stop. Just. Do. Not. Stop."

"You don't have to tell me that," Noah said, his hands going right back to where they had been. But this time, he pulled the top of my bathing suit down, the warm water rushed at my naked breasts and there was no longer any kind of barrier between them, and him. They were his to do with as he pleased. And he did. He reached out, big hands smothering them completely. Cupping them and covering them like he was claiming them. I put my hand over my mouth to stifle a whimper as he squeezed them in his palms. Noah pulled my hand away and looked around.

"No one is going to hear us," he said.

"Except him." I pointed at the monkey again.

"Damn monkey." Noah pulled away and walked towards the other side of the pool. "Bugger off. Go!" He brought his hand down on the water, sending an enormous splash into the air. The water hit the monkey on the face and, for the second time that evening, it screeched at us and then ran into the bush.

"Okay, gone!"

"Gone!" I said in agreement, and then I laughed a little again.

"Right! Now, where was I?" he asked playfully.

"I think you were somewhere here." I pointed to my breasts. "With your hands, if I'm not mistaken."

Noah looked at them and then shook his head. "Maybe I'll use something else now."

And this time, I was unable to stifle the sounds coming out of my mouth as he lowered his mouth to my breasts and almost drew the whole thing in as he sucked. Stuff inside didn't just explode, they went supernova. I arched my body forward. I don't know how I knew to do this, but I did. This sexual instinct just came out of me, and it wasn't even hard to access, as if it had always been there, just below the surface, ready and waiting for Noah to bring it out. No one else. Just him. I laced my fingers through his wet hair and held on tightly to the strands as I pulled his head to the other breast. I wanted the other one to experience the same thing. And it did, as he ran a hard, flat tongue under it and around it, circling the fleshy part, but not going near the nipple, *yet*. He ran a tongue through the middle of them, running it all the way up my neck. I threw my head back to give him access to the sensitive underside, just below my chin. He traced my jaw, up to my ear, pulling my earlobe into his mouth and biting down on it ever so softly. And then he let go and his tongue trailed back down to my breast and this time, the tip of his tongue grazed my nipple. The feeling was too much to take, and my hands longed to be on him like his were on mine.

I put my hands on his body for the first time ever. On his chest first, then I moved them to his back, dragging my nails over it as his muscles seemed to move beneath my fingertips. He moaned at the feeling of my nails running the length of his back; they seemed to infuse him with a certain urgency that had him grabbing at my bathing suit, pulling it down even further. I felt it by my hips now, and I knew that in a matter of seconds I was going to be completely naked. It didn't feel right that I was the only one, though, so I dug my fingers into his shorts and pulled at the same time he did. We both gasped, pulled away and looked at each other, holding eye contact for one second before he fell forward again and pressed back into me. The weight of his body crushed me into the wall even more. I would not be able to get out from under him, even if I wanted to. This idea of a total loss of control drove me wild with excitement. And even more so when I could feel him, all of him. Hard, pressing against my hip and stomach. It pushed against me and I could feel the aching. In him, in me, in the very water around us even.

We were completely naked together now, and nothing about it felt uncomfortable. It felt natural, and right, as if we'd been building up to this moment since we'd met. This moment of wet nakedness in a pool, on a deck looking out over the sea with . . .

"Crap! He's back." I pushed Noah away as I locked eyes with the monkey in the tree.

"What?" Noah turned and glared at him.

"Oh my God, and he's bought reinforcements!" I pointed as little gray faces burst out of the bushes.

"You sure you don't have that watch of yours on this time?" Noah asked.

"No. What are they doing?" I asked, getting nervous, as they seemed to be holding some kind of psychic conference. Looking at each other over and over again, planning something in their little furry, primate brains.

"Is it me, or do they look like they're about to come for us?" Noah and I held hands and instinctively started crab-walking our way out the pool.

"They're coming for us," I said through the giant, toothy grin I was giving the monkeys. I was trying to look friendly and unperturbed and not show my fear . . . but that was all a lie.

"Run!" Noah hissed in my ear as we reached the steps of the pool. It all happened so quickly after that. Fast, blurry flashes of gray descending on the deck as we ran for the door. Frantic gray fingers reaching for the left-over picnic scraps, fighting over the bread sticks and bits of cheese and mashing strawberries between their teeth until it looked like they were bleeding out of their mouths. We made it inside and slammed the glass door behind us and stared out over the carnage that was now the once-romantic picnic on the deck. The sounds of them fighting over the scraps was almost earth-shattering. One of them picked up a champagne glass and polished off the liquid in the bottom and then threw the glass into the pool. Some of the younger ones were now playing on the top step of the pool, splashing each other, whilst young two males squared off around the picnic basket, fighting for dominance over this new container of treats. Another monkey was dragging our champagne bottle into the bush, another two were sucking on the ice cubes, one was ripping up one of the pillows and another two were using our picnic blanket as a convenient place to mate! Noah and I slowly turned to each other. Wide-eyed. Wet, naked, out of breath and dripping on the marble floor.

"Uh . . ." Noah finally whispered. "Only in Africa!"

"Yup!" We stared at each other for a while, in a silent, shocked daze and then . . .

"AAAAH!" I screamed and jumped back from the window, almost falling, but for Noah's quick arm around me, as a monkey charged the window.

"That's him! Look, the ear." I pointed.

"Bastard!" Noah hissed as the monkey who had started this whole mess. He was glaring at us through the glass now.

"Let's go!" Noah took me by the arm and rushed me to the bedroom, our wet feet sliding across the floor as we went. He slammed the door behind us, closed all the windows and then drew the curtains as quickly as possible and, when he was done, we collapsed onto the bed in naked fits of laughter.

CHAPTER 68

When our laughter finally stopped, I realized that Noah and I were lying on the bed together naked, and the implications of that, were, well . . . *sex*.

Because yes, we were going to have sex tonight! That was a given and, based on what had happened so far in the pool, it was going to be fantastic. We fell into a kiss as soon as our lips were no longer laughing and smiling, and this was the kind of kiss we hadn't shared yet. Because this one was filled with so much lust and longing that I knew it wouldn't be able to stay *just* a kiss for much longer. And it didn't. His lips left mine and soon they were traveling down my collar bones and my breasts and my stomach, and that's when it hit me.

"Wait!" I put my hand on the back of Noah's head.

He stopped what he was doing and crawled his body back up over mine. I looked at him and swallowed, hard. I stared into his blue eyes, and I wasn't sure I knew how to say this to him.

"Uh . . . ." I started and then looked away.

Noah sat up. "What?" He reached down and touched my cheek with his fingertips.

I lifted myself up onto my elbows and fixed my eyes to a spot on the wall, unable to make eye contact any longer.

"Tell me," he urged, taking my chin gently in his hands and tilting my face towards him. I kept my eyes down for a while, and then slowly lifted them back up to meet the blueness of his. The first color I had seen after my accident in the elevator. I pursed my lips together tightly. I didn't really want the words out. I knew they needed to come out, but . . .

"I'm not sure if I want to have . . . sex yet," I heard myself say. The expression on Noah's face didn't change at all.

"I mean, I do. Don't get me wrong. I *really* do, but I also don't. I know that probably sounds ridiculous, and it's hard to explain. The first time I had sex I just did it because everyone else had done it and I didn't even feel that way about the person, not really. And the second time, I did it because I thought it was something I was supposed to do after six dates. And I know this feels like the perfect moment in the romance novel where the characters are meant to have sex, like when Amanda Stone and Sheik Khalifa finally made love in the Bedouin tent and everything was perfect, with the candles and the roses. And I know everything is perfect now—well, except for the monkeys—but it's perfect and you're perfect and that means it's supposed to happen, but . . ." I took a deep breath, I needed one. I had been talking so fast that all the air in my lungs was almost depleted. I was just about to take another breath to continue when Noah stopped me.

"You don't need to say another word, Zoe." Noah brought his face all the way up to mine. "Not. Another. Word."

"You're not . . ." I couldn't quite bring myself to say it.

"No, I'm not," he said. "How can I be? Look where I am. I'm on a date with a gorgeous woman, in the most beautiful hotel room in the world, and we have a National Geographic Documentary happening right outside our window." He smiled, and I felt a sense of relief wash over me immediately. I could see he meant this. Every. Single. Word.

"You sure?" I looked at him and felt myself falling even more. Slipping down a waterslide, falling.

"Besides, we have to move onto season two of *Game of Thrones*."

"I thought you would have finished it by now."

"No. I didn't watch anymore."

"Why?"

He shrugged. "I was waiting to watch it with you."

I raised myself higher on my elbows. "Really?" I reached out and put my hand on his cheek. "Did you miss me?"

"Yes. I did. I missed you when you were gone."

I could relate to that feeling. "I missed me when I was gone too," I said. Because for those few days that I was away from Noah, I had been missing.

"Besides, it wouldn't have been fun to watch it without you," Noah said, laying his hand over mine.

"I don't know why, but that's the nicest thing anyone has ever said to me." I thought Noah would smile at this, but he didn't.

"Clearly, the bar has been set very low then. Because I think I could say a hundred things to you that are much, much nicer than that."

Falling . . . falling faster.

"You could?"

He nodded.

"Like what?"

Noah smiled at me and then leaned in close, putting his lips to my ears, and whispered in a low voice that tickled my skin.

"I'm falling for you."

I gasped at the sound of those words. The bloody gasp was so big, though, that it made me cough, which was a total mood killer, especially when I had to hit my chest a few times and push Noah aside to sit up.

"Uh . . . that either went down very well, or not well at all."

I shook my head and then nodded. Still unable to speak. Then I put my hand on his chest and patted him. "Well! Well! It went down well, just down the wrong pipe!" I finally managed. "It went down well."

"Okay. For a second there, I thought I might have jumped the gun."

"No! No gun-jumping." I smiled at him, I couldn't stop myself. This bubble of something big and warm and tingly seemed to expand from my heart and fill my chest. "You know how it felt when we went through the eye of the tornado today?"

"Yes?" Noah replied.

"It feels like that." The giddy, warm bubble that had filled my chest burst out of me and filled the room, wrapping us both up in it. We smiled at each other like giddy fools. Like we couldn't stop ourselves.

"So, you want to watch *Game of Thrones*?"

I shook my head. "Noah, when I said I didn't want to have sex, that's all I meant."

"Really?" he asked.

I nodded. "Just not sex. That's all . . . I didn't mean we should stop . . ."

"You didn't?"

"No," I said, and then lay back down flat on the bed, inviting him back.

CHAPTER 69

*W*e picked up right where we left off. With that kiss that seemed to have the power to shift entire continents, and I felt like I was being transported into the pages of my very own romance book and writing all the words myself as I went. And this was the big sex scene, even though I wasn't having sex, and that was okay, because this way *my* story, *my* scene, *my* moment and I was going to do it *my* way.

His hand slid down my body, and stopped at my breasts. He ran the tips of his fingers over my nipples. They hardly touched, like a breeze blowing over them, whooshing past, just grazing them. Grazing them enough, though, that when I closed my eyes and felt it, I wanted that feeling to never stop. Somehow if I could press pause on this moment, I would. Press pause on this feeling and live it in forever.

And then the fingertips weren't so gentle anymore. Suddenly it was a squeeze. I flicked my eyes open at the delicious shock of it. From soft to hard. I inhaled sharply, breath getting stuck in my throat as he played with my nipples between his fingertips. *Who knew this could all feel like this?* All these parts of myself that had been dead and dormant for so long, seemed to have awoken and roared back to life with this simple touch.

He let my nipples go, they felt his absence immediately, and wanted him back. But they were gone, and his warm, wet fingers continued down my stomach and then stopped on my hip bone. He traced a small circle around my hip with his fingers. Once, twice, three times, his tongue too, circling my tongue, following the slow, languid pattern of his fingers until I was shivering with anticipation. And then he lifted his fingers off me gently and stopped kissing me. He looked down at me, a question in his eyes.

I knew what the question was and I was so desperate for him now that I didn't think my mouth could form words. So I reached down, grabbed the back of his hand and pushed it between my legs. I heard myself let out a whimper as his hand cupped me there. Covering me completely. I tensed my muscles as he squeezed me. And then, when he eased the pressure, I let my legs fall open in total invitation. The cold air rushed over me and in me as everything parted for him. I watched him as his eyes went there. I watched as that stormy black cloud moved across his face, turning the blue of his eyes black as he stared at me, his lips parting slightly as if he wanted to taste. *Would I let him do that? Or would I do that to him?*

And then he pulled his hand away, and in a gesture that I'd only ever dreamed about, and read about, in a gesture that was without question, hotter than anything I'd seen so far, he raised his fingers to his mouth and drew them in, wetting them. My entire body arched up towards him, waiting for the feel of these warm, wet fingers on me. I watched them, stared at them, willing them to move faster as he lowered them. It felt like it took forever to feel him on me again. But when I did, I couldn't hold my body up anymore, and it flopped back down onto the bed. All my muscles melting and turning to jelly as his fingers moved over me, bottom to top. And when they reached the very top, he sped up and flicked his fingers upwards. I gasped. Loudly.

He did it again, this time the flick was faster and harder. More pressure, more pleasure. The gasp turned into a long moan, which became a pant as he did it over and over, relentlessly. With each flick the pressure seemed to get stronger. A coil felt like it was twisting and tightening in my belly. And it was going to tighten and twist so much, that soon it was going to reach its limit, and explode apart. That's what it felt like. I clenched my fists and my hands felt like they needed to grab a hold of. *Something.*

I reached down between us and without a moment's hesitation, I grabbed for him and wrapped my hand around him tightly and possessively like he had done with me. As soon as I did, the look on his face and the moan that escaped his lips urged me on. He lifted his body a little so I could get better access. That move caused all the muscles in his shoulders and arm to bulge and twitch. I ran my hand up his length, pulling it towards me. When I reached the top, I released my grip and let my fingertips trail over the soft skin there. And now I did what he had done. And I watched with pleasure as he also shivered with anticipation as I circled him there, once, twice, three times. His breath came out in little bursts, and then he moaned as I gripped him tightly again and worked my way down. His hips thrust, pushing hard against my hands, as if he wanted to make sure he felt everything. Every possible sensation that my hands could deliver. He pulled back and thrust again. Sliding in and out of my hand as I kept it quite still. His thrusting was slow, and hard. I looked down for the first time, to see what it looked like. To see what him moving through my hand looked like. I licked my lips as I watched how desperate and needy it all seemed. And when I looked up again and caught Noah looking at me while I watched him, I felt a completely new sensation that caused my head to slam into the bed.

His fingers were inside me now. They pushed in deep and slow and filled me. His thrusting stopped and I ran my hand up and down him with urgency as he pushed deeper into me. In and out, faster and deeper and then slower. He brought his lips back down to mine and kissed me deeply and slowly as his fingers explored every part of me. One second they were inside, and the next they were out, his thumb rubbing me and flicking me, before diving back into me again.

We rocked our bodies back and forth like that until I could no longer kiss him anymore, because I was panting. Because my chest was rising and falling faster and faster and my free hand was forced to grab a hold of the pillow and hold on tightly, as tightly as I was holding onto him. It felt like I was going to fly off this bed and into the sky as his fingers moved faster too. His thumb seemed to be drawing circles around me, while his other fingers seemed to trace the inside of me, twisting and turning and finding places in there I didn't know existed.

I was on the verge of totally losing control of my body now. And he was too. I could feel it in the way he could no longer kiss me either. Rather rest his open mouth on mine and pant. Pant in time to the movement of my hand. And then everything around me disappeared as I was forced to close my eyes. All I could feel, hear, smell and taste was him. Him and the pleasure making my body tense and my teeth clench and causing my lungs to hold the breath that was inside them. I was forced to let go of him as I came. As my body twitched and then slowly unfroze and melted back down into the bed. And when I opened my eyes again, he was looking down at me with a small smile. A satisfied, sexy smile. I smiled back at him, a small breathy giggle escaping my lips as the smile parted them. But then I realized something.

My eyes left his and drifted down. He was still hard and wanting and so was I. I wanted to give him the same kind of pleasure that he had just given me. I wanted that so badly, almost more than I wanted it for myself. I pushed him on his chest with my hands. He looked surprised, lost balance and fell onto his back. Without thinking, with just this instinct deep inside driving me, I crawled down the bed and reached for him.

"Wait," I felt fingers tangle in my hair and hold my head in place. Not allowing me to move. "You . . . you don't have to . . . uh . . ."

"I want to!" I said, and didn't even wait for a response from him as I opened my mouth and slid it over him. Noah flung his arms out to his sides and his hands grabbed at the sheets, tangling them between his fingers. As if he was desperate to grab a hold of something. As if, like me, he too felt like he might fly off the bed and into the air. I wrapped a hand around him too and I pulled him in and out of my mouth. The taste and the sounds and the way his muscles were clenching and unclenching spurred me on. All the sounds and sensations and smells combining into this thing that throbbed in me and around me and made me just close my eyes and let instinct take over. I used two hands now, I used my lips and my tongue. Sometimes I took him all in, sometimes I simply let my tongue dance over him. Sometimes I pulled with both hands, and sometimes they were just soft fingertips. And then he reached for me to pull me away.

"I'm going to come," he panted. He grabbed himself with his hand and moved it up and down once more before his entire body stiffened and froze. I watched, fascinated and turned on even more. And truthfully, if he hadn't pushed me away, I would have kept my mouth there . . . *maybe next time I would.* Because there was going to be a next time. I wanted there to be a next time already, even though this time hadn't even ended yet. I wanted to explore him even more and for him to explore me like that too, and for it all to eventually lead to sex, when I was ready for it.

But right now, I was perfectly content with this as I flopped back down onto my back. He reached for tissues and cleaned up and I'd never felt so sexy and powerful in my entire life. *I had done that to him.*

We both lay there, out of breath, the chlorinated water that had coated our bodies had been replaced by a thin layer of sweat and we held each other's hands while we looked up at the ceiling together, shoulder to shoulder on the bed.

"That was. . . ." Noah turned his head and I turned mine. We looked into each other's eyes. He didn't finish the sentence. He didn't need to.

"It was." I smiled and bit my bottom lip. "How can we top that?"

He laughed and reached out, pushing a wet strand of hair out of my face. "We'll have to see." And then he pulled me into his arms and my head came to rest on his big chest. He wrapped his arms around me and squeezed as I bent my leg and draped it over him.

And that's how we fell asleep that night. Tangled up with each other, in many more ways than just physically.

CHAPTER 70

~

$\mathcal{I}$ looked over at the sleeping Noah. He looked so peaceful with his head squished against the pillow in a way that made his cheeks puff and his lips press together like a cherub. I climbed out of bed quietly, careful not to wake him. I was still naked, and I picked up the nearest thing I could find, Noah's T-shirt, and popped it on. I walked out of the bedroom into the huge, luxurious lounge that sprawled out in front of me. I walked to the massive glass window that looked out over the deck. The monkeys were gone, but they had left their mark across the entire deck and pool. It was late, everything was dark, except for the smudges of light lined up on the ocean horizon. I wondered about the people on those ships. Were they on holiday? Going somewhere? And if so, where? Sleeping? Or was there someone standing at the window like me, wondering about the lights?

I looked back over at Noah to make sure he was still sleeping, and then gently pushed the doors open. The salty sea breeze hit me immediately and I shivered. It was cold, but the air felt so fresh out here, and alive. I walked over to the couch and grabbed the throw that was draped over it, wrapping it around my body, and that's when I saw the hotel stationery on the table. I glanced at Noah again. I wondered whether this was where our adventure ended. What would happen when Noah and I returned home? Him to his studies, and me to my—God knows what I would do now. But if it did end here, in this room, by this ocean, if this was where our story ended, I wanted him to know how much it had all meant to me. How special he was, and how much he'd changed me . . .

I picked the stationery up and went out onto the deck. I sat at the table and smoothed the paper out, ran my fingertips over it as I always do, as if I'm trying to pull the image out of it. The one that's already inside the paper, just waiting to come out. I folded the paper in half and was just about to start when I caught some movement out of the corner of my eye. The monkey who'd tried to carry the champagne bottle into the bush was lying on the grass, passed out over the bottle. Each time the wind blew, the bottle moved and the monkey startled, only to pass out again seconds later! I shook my head at him disapprovingly and turned my attention back to the paper. I lowered the pen and started.

The playful-looking font came to me immediately; writing the big thank-you across the front of the card also did. And then, with the greatest care and patience, I set about decorating the letters with elements from the last two weeks together. A little ambulance raced over the top of the "T," chilis grew out from behind the "H," I gave the "A" a tie-dye effect, I drew waterslides curling around all the letters, even a joint popped out from behind one, flames from the fire on the beach, champagne and the waves and monkeys hanging by their tails off the top of the "Y" and, finally, when I came to the last letter, I decorated it with a spray of cosmos.

The cosmos was where it had all gone wrong for me. The cosmos was where I'd stopped living the first time, but the second time in the cosmos with Noah, that is where I'd come to life again. Just like the flowers themselves in autumn. Once the design was complete, I opened the card and the words just flew out of me.

And when it was done, I signed my name at the end. I'd been signing my name on the bottom of my cards like this right from the first card I'd ever made all those years ago. The letter "Z" that looked like a little lightning bolt. And when it was all done, over two hours later, I quietly walked back into the room and placed the card on Noah's bedside table, before climbing back into bed and wrapping my arms around him.

CHAPTER 71

I woke up the next morning and the first thing I did was reach out and feel for Noah. But he wasn't there. The bed was empty, the duvet thrown open. The pillow had fallen to the floor. I looked at the side table, where I'd put his card. It was gone. I sat up straight and looked around the rest of the room. He wasn't there.

Shit!

I'd woken up with a strange feeling in the pit of my stomach, and I didn't know why, and the feeling had instantly grown at the realization that Noah was no longer in bed with me. I looked at my side table. Something was there, but I didn't know what. I scrambled out of bed and grabbed it, and when I did, my fingers knew what it was before my brain did. I froze.

"Wh-wha- ho——" I stuttered out loud, the words sticking on my dry tongue, unable to form or get out.

How was this even possible?

Why was this here?

Who had put it here?

I raised it to my face and touched my cheek with it, like I'd done all those years ago when I'd first made it. I opened it. The paper and writing were old and almost illegible, as if it had been read and opened and closed over and over again. I rushed through to the lounge and looked around. Noah was still nowhere to be seen and I had so, so, so many questions. A feeling of panic started building and just when I was about to rush out of the door and go looking for him, the curtain to the deck blew into the room like a white ghost. It flapped in the breeze, so hard that it came back on itself and cracked like a whip. I stood there and watched as Noah walked through the door, his eyes rimmed red, as if he'd been crying and, as soon as he saw me, he stopped and looked down at the card in my hands. And then, he raised his card in his hands, the one I'd made him last night.

Twenty years ago – the night before Christmas

The Christmas lights looked really pretty that year. Shiny and bright and red and green. It was cool that I was staying on the third floor. That way I could see them from my window all the way down the street. The pediatric oncology ward was usually on the first floor, but a burst water pipe that Cyril couldn't fix—Cyril is the nice man from maintenance who always comes to help me if my TV is broken or if my bed gets stuck in the upright position (he also smuggles me chocolates from the vending machine sometimes, which I am not really allowed to eat)—meant the whole ward got flooded. And when I say whole ward, I mean just Monty and me. Monty is the other leukemia kid. We hang out whenever we're allowed to. When our immune systems are so compromised that a tiny germ will kill us. His real name is Montgomery, which is so fancy-sounding. His parents are really fancy too. His mom wears these big strings of pearls and talks with a British accent, and his dad is like a baron or something . . . or is it a sir? A duke? I don't really know what he is. I just know that they all have British accents and say things like "Oh my" and "By golly." Monty is not really like that, he's pretty cool. We have this whole thing worked out where we have this code for communicating by knocking on the walls. It drives Sister Mary nuts! I guess that's part of the reason we do it. But I think she also secretly likes it a little, even if she will never admit that! She's always warning the other nurses about us naughty kids, but she always says it with a smile in her voice. She says it in isiZulu, so she thinks I don't understand it, but what she doesn't know is that I've been secretly studying it, so I can listen to the late-night conversations that the nurses have. It makes me feel less lonely at night, when the chair is empty in the corner of my room, to be able to listen to and understand someone else's conversation.

The only horrible thing about being on the third floor is that this is where the ICU is. Well, it's down the passage, and if I stand in my doorway I can see a lot of very scared and distressed-looking people in a small waiting area there. I guess they look like that because someone they love is in serious trouble. That's why they would be at the ICU. They almost—*almost*—look as distressed and scared as the moms and dads down at the oncology ward. *Almost.*

Although no one will ever look as distressed as Mr. and Mrs. Dlamini, when Sizwe died right in the room next door to me a few months ago. He got an infection after a bone-marrow transplant and it led to septicemia, which is the worst kind of infection you can get. That's what Sister Mary told me anyway. I didn't know Sizwe for very long, but he was cool and I was sad when he died. I couldn't go to his funeral, though, so we all had a little funeral here in the hospital. We lit candles and said a prayer, and I feel really bad sometimes about what I prayed for. I know I was supposed to be praying for Sizwe and stuff, like praying that he went to heaven and that. But I was really praying for myself. I was praying that I didn't die too like him, and that my mom and dad didn't have to scream like that and crumple to the floor, and they didn't have to call a doctor to give my mom a sedative like they had to give Mrs. Dlamini. Sister Mary always says that losing a child is unnatural. That you should never have to bury your own child. She says she cries for days when she loses a child in her ward. I wonder why she works in the pediatric oncology department then, if it upsets her so much.

Monty and I couldn't knock on the wall that night. He's feeling very weak today and is in a lot of pain. I hope he doesn't die either. I would be really sad if he died and it would seriously suck. We have been in and out of hospitals together for a while now. But I'm trying not to think about that. Instead, I'm thinking about the Christmas lights and how I wished I could go outside and see them for real. I don't get to see much stuff for real. I only get to see things from behind a window. Except that time we all went to the zoo together. This charitable organization arranged it for us all—well, for the cancer kids who were allowed out of the hospital. They even opened the zoo an hour earlier for us so that we could all see the animals without other people being there. It was very kind of the zoo people. The lady who ran the zoo lost her mom to cancer or something like that, and now she ran these things where cancer patients could come out and look at the animals. I got to play with a lion cub, which was pretty much the coolest thing ever. Monty and I joked that maybe we should steal it and smuggle it out with us. We could keep it as a pet in the ward and no one would notice. The only thing I didn't like about the zoo was the panda bear. He looked so sad and lonely. Panda bears are actually only found in China, and China is like a million miles away from South Africa, and I wondered if maybe he was missing his family back home. After that I decided that zoos weren't so cool. That no animal deserves to be locked up like that and look at the world through a pane of glass, like I do. For some reason I was thinking about that panda a lot when I looked at the Christmas lights. Maybe it was because spending Christmas, or my birthday, in hospital is literally the worst ever. But I guess I've kind of got used to it. The nights before Christmas and your birthday are usually the worst, because my parents can only come on the actual day, so the night before, it's only me. They used to take turns to sleep in the hospital with me when this first all started. But after a year of doing it, and me getting older, we all agreed it wasn't necessary anymore. I was used to being in the hospital, and now that I'd gotten to know all the staff and other kids, I kind of had a family here in a way.

I walked away from the window. Looking at the lights was

starting to irritate my eyes. But I couldn't go to sleep either. Mostly because there was a constant stream of business in the passage outside my room, and if you closed your eyes and listened really hard, you could hear the "beep beep" of all the machines in the ICU. And every now and then you would hear a very loud "Beeeeeeeeeeeep," followed by a lot of noisy commotion. That was the part I didn't like.

I walked over to the door and peered out. The small waiting room had been empty for a while, but now, it wasn't. I was shocked when I saw what I did, and at first it frightened me, so I quickly hid behind the door before he could see I was staring at him. My heart pounded in my chest. I'd never seen so much blood before, and I'd been living in a hospital for almost two years and had so many operations I couldn't even count them. When I'd mustered up the courage to look again, I peered around the doorframe, only my forehead and eyes looking out.

In the waiting room, all alone, was a boy. Maybe a bit younger than me. He was staring off into the distance at a spot on the wall, as if he was waiting for something to happen. I followed his eyes and looked at the wall, thinking I might see something there. But I didn't. He was staring at a blank wall with a faraway look in his eyes that made me feel scared. His shirt was covered in blood. It was everywhere. His pants too. It was dry, though. It wasn't like it was dripping on the floor or anything like that, but still, it was everywhere. And then I saw a man in a uniform, a paramedic, rush up to the boy and wrap a blanket around his shoulders.

"Your dad will be here soon," the man said to the boy, rubbing big circles on his back. But he didn't move, he just continued to look at the blank spot on the wall. It was actually a little creepy. Like he could see a ghost that I couldn't. I once read that animals, especially cats, can see ghosts that we can't, and when they stare into the distance at nothing at all, that it was actually a spirit that we are unable to see with the human eye. I wondered if he was staring at a ghost now too.

I watched the paramedic walk off a little way and then he started talking to a nurse. I got up and rushed to the other side of my room and pressed my ear up to the small window that never opens to listen.

"I have to get back on duty," he said. "Is there someone who can sit with him? Poor kid has been through the wringer. He's the one that called the police."

"Shame," one of the nurses said; I didn't know her. She was a nurse from this floor. "I'll make sure someone is with him."

"We spoke to his father. He's on his way. But will probably only be here in ten minutes."

"Sure, we'll keep an eye on him," the sister said, and then the paramedic rushed off, saying goodbye and good luck to the boy. I went back up to the door and stuck my head around again, just a little so I could see. The nurse had walked over to him now and sat down.

"What's your name?" she asked. But the boy said nothing. He just stared at the wall.

"Well, I'm Sister Esther, and I'll be waiting with you until your dad comes. Is that alright?"

This time the boy did move. He gave the tiniest nod of his head.

"Can I get you anything?" she asked. And then she leaned in more and whispered a little. "You know, I think we have some extra chocolate pudding cups left over from dinner."

Chocolate pudding cups . . .

The only tasty thing in the hospital. One night, Monty and I raided one of the food carts that had been left in the corridor unattended and stole six. We sat up all night stuffing our faces with them. The boy should have a pudding cup. They were super-tasty.

He looked up at her for the first time and gave her another small nod. She smiled at him.

"Will you be okay here alone for a minute while I go and fetch you one?"

The boy nodded again and the nurse rushed off down the

corridor. The boy moved his head and it looked like he was going to go back to looking at the wall, only he didn't . . .

"Oh no!" I gasped when he turned and looked straight at me, as if he'd known I was there the entire time. I jumped up and raced for my bed, quickly climbed in and threw the bedcovers over my head and waited there, hoping he wouldn't come into my room and be angry because I was listening.

I only climbed back out of bed when I heard a loud noise a few minutes later. It sounded like someone getting really sick. I crept out of bed again and saw the boy throwing up in the dustbin. The nurse was holding the pudding cup in her hand and rubbing his back . . .

I guess he shouldn't have eaten the chocolate pudding cup after all. It did kind of look like the blood on his clothes a bit. The blood had kind of turned brown and I wondered if maybe the chocolate color reminded him of the dried blood. Or maybe he was just so upset that he couldn't eat at all. I couldn't eat for a super-long time once and they had to put a tube into my stomach and pump in this gross-looking stuff that looked like a cross between soup and porridge. And then, for the first time since seeing him, I wondered who the blood belonged to. I couldn't believe I hadn't thought of that yet.

Perhaps he had also been in an accident, like me, although I couldn't tell you how much blood was at my accident, because I was knocked unconscious, so I never saw if there was a lot of blood or anything. But I guessed there must have been. Or maybe someone else had had an accident and he'd tried to help them. Maybe that's what the paramedic had meant when he said that he called the police! That was brave. I don't know if I could have called the police if there was an accident. Even when I had my accident my parents said that they were in so much shock that for a moment they didn't know what to do. And they are adults. So you can imagine how much shock he was in. Maybe that's why he was staring at the wall like that.

"Oh my God, son. Son!" I turned my head when I heard this huge noise coming down the passage. It was a man, and he was running so fast. He had this look on his face that made his eyes so big that they looked like they might fall out of his head. Like he was a cartoon character or something.

"Are you okay?" He rushed up to the boy and fell onto his knees and then pulled him into a huge hug. And that's when the boy started crying. He started saying over and over again that he'd tried to help his mommy, but there was so much blood. *There was so much blood!* His dad held him tightly as he cried and cried and cried and then his dad started crying too, and then I couldn't help it, I started crying too. Even though I didn't know the family, I started crying too. And when the doctor came through and told them that their wife and mother had to be rushed into emergency surgery and it didn't look good, I cried even more. When the doctor said that she'd lost a lot of blood, I cried even more. But that's when Sister Esther caught me eavesdropping and shuffled me back into the room with a scolding to mind my own business and closed the door behind me. I didn't hear the last part that the doctor said that caused the man to grab onto the wall and let out the loud cry, like he was wounded.

Only, I couldn't mind my own business. Because for some reason I felt that this *was* my business. For some reason, I felt like I needed to know what was going to happen, and it wasn't because I was just being nosey, but because I was really worried about that boy. I kept creeping to the door the whole night and peeping through the keyhole, trying to see if I could see anything. But nothing had really changed much. The dad was pacing up and down the small passage, and the boy was now curled up and sleeping on the chairs. If I never found out what happened, I wanted to let the boy know that someone cared and was thinking about him. Because I know that when people care and think about you, it makes such a difference to your life. It makes you feel less alone, and I bet the boy was feeling about as alone as I was right now. The night before Christmas.

And that's when I got the idea to make him a card. I had a million pens and colored pencils and paper. My mom had bought me lots so I could draw and color in. I climbed onto my bed and pulled the table across it and started drawing. I drew things that I thought were nice. Things that didn't remind you of a hospital. Like butterflies and sunshine and colored fishes that you find in coral reefs and all the things that I wanted to see when I left the hospital and maybe that the boy would want to see too. But because he was a boy, and I didn't really know that much about boys, other than I was guessing they weren't really into butterflies, I drew a lion on the card too. Because I think boys must like lions. I opened the card and stared at it for so long because I didn't know what to write in it. I must have stared for a really long time, because I hadn't noticed that it had started storming outside my window. The rain was hitting the glass and making such a loud sound that I could no longer hear the beeping machines, which I was happy about. I finally knew what I was going to say to him. The thing that I wished I felt more often. The thing that sometimes I didn't feel, even though I wanted to feel it more than anything else in the world. The thing I wanted to believe more than anything else in the world. Maybe if I said it to him, and really meant it, then maybe it would come true for me too. Maybe if I wrote it down on a piece of paper, the words would be real and then it would all become real.

You are strong, stronger than you know, and one day everything is going to be okay.

When I was finished writing, I looked at the words on the card. I'd written in a beautiful, scribbled font. I was really impressed that I'd done this, actually. I'd always loved creating letters and drawing and, for the first time ever, I was putting them all together. I wondered if I should sign my name at the bottom. After all, all great artists signed their names, didn't they? Only, I had no idea what my signature would look like. I didn't have one. I'd seen Mom and Dad sign a lot of papers over the last few years. Every time I was in and out of hospital, they signed a lot. Their signatures looked like scribbles, though. I suppose that's so no one can copy them, but I didn't want something that just looked like a scribble, I wanted something that looked like something. Something strong and bold and . . .

"Aah!" I jumped as lightning cut through the sky for a moment, illuminating everything outside as if it was no longer night time. It made all the darkness bright for just as second, and that's when I knew what my signature should be like. I brought my pen back down to my paper and in the corner at the bottom left, I drew a lightning bolt in the shape of a "Z." "Z" for Zen.

I held onto the card and crept back towards the door. I pushed it open just a bit. If Sister Esther caught me again I was probably going to be in a lot of trouble. Like, a lot. But there was no way I was going to be able to get the card to him, because his dad was still pacing up and down. So I sat there and waited by the door, peeping through and waiting for the perfect time. I waited for so long that my bum was getting cold on the floor. Hospitals always have such cold floors. You would think they would warm them up. So, I grabbed a pillow from my bed and sat on it to keep my bum warm. And then, after waiting for ages, I got my chance. The doctor came around the corner. He looked tired, like he'd been in surgery for a long time. I think he had. I don't know how these doctors stand on their feet for so long. I once had a surgery that lasted ten hours. I once tried to stand on my feet for that long too, to see if I could do it, but I only lasted three hours.

"How is she, Doctor?" the dad said, racing towards the doctor.

The doctor took his scrub cap off. They always do at times like these. It's like a sign of respect or something, I don't know.

"She made it through the surgery."

"She's okay?" The man asked, in tears now.

"Can we talk for a while?" the doctor said. Oh no, that did not sound good.

And the man could sense it too, I think, because he suddenly started asking what was wrong.

The doctor said that he wanted to talk to him and explain a few things. The dad looked back at the sleeping boy and asked if there was somewhere else they could go. I guess he didn't want to wake up his son, who was sleeping really peacefully now. You usually sleep peacefully after something traumatic happens to you—well, in my experience, anyway. Or maybe you sleep because you want to forget the traumatic thing. Perhaps that's why you sleep so much. I sleep a lot in the hospital. I stuck my head around the corner more and watched the doctor and the father walk up the corridor and then disappear into another small waiting room. I looked up the other side of the corridor to make sure Sister Esther wasn't watching and then, when the coast was clear, I realized that this was probably my only chance to give this note to the boy. I had to go now. Now or never. My heart thumped in my chest, not like it thumps in my chest before they stick a needle in my arm or before I have to have surgery. That's a scared thump. This was an excited thump, and I couldn't remember the last time I had felt an excited thump like this. I crept out and walked across the passage, on my tiptoes so I didn't make a noise, and when I was close to the sleeping boy, I stopped and held my breath. I was scared he was going to hear me breathing. Or maybe even hear my heart thumping in my chest. I reached down to put the card on the chair next to him. I was concentrating so hard on watching the card and making sure that it didn't hit the chair with a noise that I hadn't noticed that he'd opened his eyes. And by the time I noticed, it was too late to make any kind of a getaway. Suddenly, he was sitting up in the chair. I gasped and fell backwards, shocked and terrified that he'd seen me. I stared as he shook his head a little, rubbed his eyes with the back of his hands, and then, he saw the card next to him. I tried to scramble to my feet as he picked it up and opened it. But my stupid slippery slippers on the shiny hospital floors didn't allow for that.

Finally, I managed to pull myself up, using one of the chairs in the waiting area, and as soon as I was up, I made a dash for my room.

Only something stopped me. I looked behind me to see what it was. The boy had grabbed my hand and was holding it tightly in his. I looked at his hand. He looked at mine, and then at the same time, as if someone had told us to, big breaths came out of our mouths. I felt my whole body relax as I slowly raised my eyes and looked at him. It was hard to tell what his eyes really looked like. They were red and swollen from crying. I stood there, looking down at him as he looked up at me, both of us holding each other's hand. This was the first time in my life I'd ever held hands with a boy, and it was rather exciting, but also really scary. It made my heart beat faster in another kind of way.

I heard a voice behind me. It was Sister Esther. She was walking back to the nurses' station. I looked back at the boy, and then at my hand, and then I pulled it away and ran back into my room, closing the door behind me. I sat with my back to the door, pushing all my weight into it so he wouldn't be able to open it if he tried. Only he never did open it. Because when I looked out the door after about ten minutes, he was gone. He was gone, my card was gone, and I never saw him again.

CHAPTER 72

~

"What's going on? I don't un-understand? Why do you have this? How do you . . . ?" I scratched my head like I was trying to order my thoughts in a way that I was able to understand and process what was going on.

"You . . ." He pointed to the card in my hand. "You made that!" It was a statement, not a question. I looked down at the card in my hand, at the drawings on the front of it: butterflies and rainbows and a crudely drawn lion. I opened it again, looking at the signature lightning bolt, just to make sure I was seeing what I thought I was seeing. I looked back at the bed, almost imagining that I would see my sleeping body back in it and this was all a dream. Because if this was *not* a dream, if this was actually real, then this was perhaps the most serendipitous thing that had ever happened in my life. Perhaps even in anyone's life.

"I made this," I said flatly, almost to myself. "I made this card years ago. On Christmas Eve. In hospital." I was still trying to convince myself that this was real. If I said it out loud enough times, maybe I would actually start believing it, even though it seemed completely unbelievable.

"And you gave it to me." Noah stepped forward and held up the card I'd given him last night, and then pointed back at my card. "The signatures are identical. You made that and you gave it to me all those years ago in the hospital on the worst night of my life . . . you gave that to me and I've been carrying it around with me in my wallet ever since."

I shook my head. "Really?" I'd had no idea that the note I'd written all those years ago would have become imbued with such meaning, that it would have been kept like this.

Noah walked all the way up to me. "We met twenty years ago, in the hospital that night, and you gave me this card and you held my hand."

Tears prickled in my eyes. "You were the boy covered in blood. And that's why you hate Christmas," I said.

"I was the boy covered in blood," he repeated. I looked into Noah's eyes. They were shining, his lower lids twitching, as if he was fighting back tears. "I was the boy covered in blood and you were the girl who made me feel just a little better in that moment. One of the worst, most terrifying moments in my life."

"Like you did, in the ambulance," I whispered.

"You know, I can't tell you how many times over the years I've pulled this card out and read it when I'm having a bad day. If I lose someone at work, or I just don't feel great, I read your card over and over again. I must have read it thousands of times. That card changed my life."

And now a tear did escape my eyes. It trickled over my nose and dropped onto my chin. Noah wiped it away with his thumb, but instead of taking it away, he left it there. He stepped even closer to me, bringing his face almost all the way up to mine.

"Do you know how many times over the years I've thought about you? The girl in the hospital gown who gave me that card and held my hand. I wanted to find you so badly. I used to dream about finding you one day and telling you how much that card changed my life. When I was older, I went back to the hospital, but obviously they wouldn't give out your information. I even thought of creating a Facebook page and posting the card on social media in the hope that you would come forward so I could tell you how much it had meant to me. And now I can."

I nodded, feeling so overwhelmed with emotion.

"It wasn't an accident at all in that elevator. It wasn't an accident that you landed up on my doorstep at two in the morning."

"But how?" I asked.

He smiled. "I have no idea. I have no idea how the universe works, or why. I just know that you are the girl that held my hand and gave me this card and now you are standing in front of me."

Another tear escaped my eyes. "This was the first card I ever made." I clutched the card in my hands. "Since this one, I've made hundreds. I've given them, anonymously, to hundreds of people. But this was the one that started it all."

"Why do you make them?"

"It's been my only way of reaching out and trying to connect with people. Connecting without having to connect in person, because I've been too scared of doing that. It was always safer to communicate through a card. Not in person."

He nodded. "But you don't need to do that anymore."

He leaned in and kissed me. It was slow and soft and gentle, like it was last night. "You have me now," he said. "You've had me for twenty years, I just didn't know it was you."

"I have?" I asked.

He nodded, his face still pressed into mine. His lips dragged against mine as his head moved up and down. "You've been on my mind and in my dreams since that day you gave me this card. You've had me for longer than I think you know."

I let out a small sigh, and then wrapped my arms around his shoulders, the card still in my hands. I looked at the card and I couldn't believe it had come back to me like this. All those years ago, I'd sent that card out into the world, given it to a boy who needed it, and that card and that boy—*man*—had come right back to me. Like a perfect circle, curling around and completing itself.

Completing me.

CHAPTER 73

We didn't go back home after that night together in the hotel. *How could we?* It felt like our adventure together was just beginning and we had so much more to do before we both had to go back home, back to reality. Noah still had another few weeks off before he started nursing college and I, well, I didn't have a job to go back to, it seemed. Which was confirmed when I received that email officially firing me. I don't really blame my boss for that. I had sworn at him in front of the entire company. But strangely enough, I'd also gotten another fifty or so emails from the various staff members who I'd sent cards to over the years, each one of them thanking me for the cards and apologizing that they had never gotten to know me.

But I was glad they hadn't gotten to know me, because the person I had been when I was there wasn't really a person to get to know, and wasn't the real me anyway. Zoe was the person to get to know. She was the real me. She always had been, she'd just needed a little more time to come out. She'd taken a slight detour in life to get to this point, but now that she had arrived, she was living loud and bright and tie-bloody-dyed.

Instead of going back to Joburg, Noah and I chartered a yacht to Mozambique. The idea had come to me when we'd been having dinner at my parents' house the next day and they'd told me about the cruise they wanted to take when they retired. As soon as we'd left, I got in the car and Googled and booked a holiday for the following week. So what if I was a few years late with the cruise that my parents had encouraged me to take? It might have been late, but as it turned out, it was exactly the right time for me. In fact, everything that had happened to me had happened at just the right time, and in just the right way. Like living my teens and childhood in only a couple of days at the age of almost thirty, and then only having my first real love story now. And that was okay. My life had been put on pause by the accident, and then the illness, and then by me. I'd pressed the pause button out of fear, but now I'd picked the damn remote back up and had pressed play! And I was playing in full HD color right now.

Noah and I spent a week on the yacht, winding our way around the six islands off Mozambique and, on the last night on the yacht, we *did* make love. And it was that, by then. Love. Because we'd fallen in love with each other and I was so glad that we'd waited to do it this way. And when we disembarked the next day and walked off hand in hand, we both knew that this was it for us. There was no him and me anymore, *there was us*. And we had a whole life spread out in front of us, a life where everything and anything was possible . . .

Two weeks later

"Happy birthday," Noah said, pulling the chair out for me to sit.

"Thank you." I sat down and looked around. My eyes immediately went to the photo of myself on the wall. I was smiling, red-eyed and red-lipped and with just the tinest bit of chili saliva on my chin.

"Hello! Happy birthday!" the waiter who'd brought me that chili just a little over a month ago said. God, it was amazing to think about how much my life had changed in such a short time. "Welcome back, welcome back," he said happily, placing the menus down on the table.

I looked around the restaurant and suddenly noticed something. "Are we here early?"

"Why?"

"It's empty. Apart from us. Is this place open?" As I said this, the waiter's face scrunched up into a strange shape and he pursed his lips together tightly and started shaking his head. He looked over at Noah, who seemed to shoot him some sort of warning look.

"What's going on?"

"Nothing! Nothing going on. No! Nothing wrong here. Nothing! No!" He looked back at me and started squeaking in a high-pitched, nervous-sounding voice.

"Obviously something is wrong. Or you wouldn't be so red in the face and talking in such a high-pitched voice."

He pursed his lips together even tighter and his face went red, as if it was about to explode.

"Noah, what is going on?"

"I'm so sorry, señora, I just couldn't. I know I said I could, but I can't. I'm no good at it."

"Good at what? What can't you do?" I looked between Noah and the waiter.

"What?" I asked, feeling a little desperate now.

"It was supposed to be a surprise," Noah said.

"What was?"

"SURPRISE!" the waiter suddenly yelled, and then slapped his hands over his mouth again.

"It's kind of early for that." Noah shook his head at the waiter.

"Sorry, I know. I know you said they were all going to come in at exactly seven, but I just couldn't wait. I'm sorry."

"Who's coming in? What?" I looked around, my head snapping back and forth, trying to make sense of this all.

Noah hung his head.

"Noah?"

He finally looked up at me. "I organized you a surprise birthday party with some friends and family. At exactly seven, everyone was going to burst through that door over there and surprise you."

I looked at the door. "They were?"

"But the waiter over here has kind of ruined it! I might as well go and tell them."

"I'm so sorry. I'm not good at secrets. I was too excited. I just can't keep a secret, you know. I've always had this problem. If a secret goes in, it has to come out."

"You haven't ruined it! I've never had a surprise party before. Wait . . . don't tell them. Don't. I'll just act surprised."

Noah laughed. "You sure?"

"Yes!"

"So this hasn't ruined it? You're not disappointed?"

"No, oh my God!" I reached out across the table and grabbed him by the hands. "How could I be disappointed? No one has ever done anything like this for me before, and I love it! What's the time?" I asked the waiter.

"Three minutes to seven!"

"Great, right, I'm ready to be surprised. Pass me a menu and I'll pretend to study it."

Noah laughed at me. "You, you."

"Me what?"

"Just you." He grabbed my hands again and pulled me across the table and into a kiss. "Just you, the way you are. You're perfect!"

I kissed him back. I had kissed him hundreds of times over the last few weeks, but each time it still had the power to melt me. I pushed Noah away now.

"No more kissing. I need to act surprised." I picked the menu up and stared down at it happily. I was excited to see my parents, Maxine and Sindi again. But when the door did finally open and people started streaming in, I didn't need to act surprised at all, because I was. So surprised that I couldn't help but cry when I saw who came through that door.

Mom and Dad, Betty, Tiaan and Mienkie, Cynthia, The Hoodies, the twins, Zamantha and Lila and Ntethelelo and Beauty and

Maxine and Sindi and Andi. Every single person who'd given me their number in the last few weeks was here with me. For years, I'd been reaching out to people anonymously, never wanting to get too close or let them in. But now they were everywhere and they were reaching for me and I was letting them. And for the first time in my life, everything felt full. So full it was bursting at the seams with people and laughter and happiness and . . .

"Klaw!!" I gripped Noah as the dark crooner slid up to me again, looking every bit the lecherous Lothario.

"Heeyyyyya," he hissed at me seductively.

"Hi!" I blinked at him and was just about to ask him what the hell he was doing there when Lila came up and slipped an arm around him.

"Oh, I didn't want to tell you on WhatsApp because it's such big news, but Klaw and I are official!" she said, and threw her arms around me. "And it's all thanks to you. You're a matchmaker!"

"So glad I could help." I patted her on the back and grimaced over at Noah.

"Great news! Great news!" Noah said overly enthusiastically, and then he wrapped an arm around Klaw and gave him a manly hug. "How 'bout we get a drink? I feel like we might have gotten off on the wrong foot," Noah said, and dragged Klaw away. He shot me a look over his shoulder and I burst out laughing. I was so happy right now, and I didn't know how it was possible to be even a little happier than I was. Only it was. I just didn't know it yet.

CHAPTER 74

〜

One year later

"*D*o you want to go to my place?" I said, walking out of the coffee shop with Becca and Frankie in tow. The day I'd figured out who they were, it had hit me like a bolt of lightning. They and that day was the last memory to come back to me, and when it did, it was almost as though I'd known it all along, but just wasn't able to access it.

It happened to me when I went to Vast Investments again. I passed that bookstore once more, and then the pharmacy and then the elevator, and it had just dawned on me. What was weird, now that I thought about it, was that both Becca and Frankie had been in my life that entire time. Lurking in the background constantly.

"Sure," Becca said, following behind me. She looked so different from the photo in the back of her last book. That photo had been in black and white and didn't capture her at all. But the photo of her in her new book, *You, Me, Forever*, looked so much more like her. She'd showed us the book, and it was due to hit the shelves in a few weeks' time. Frankie too seemed very, very different. For one thing, she was no longer blonde and there was no longer anything perfect and polished about her. The little bits of dog hair on the back of her shirt told me that. We all crossed the road together and then walked through the park that was directly opposite the café we had just been in. Our new house was right across the road from this park, in a treed suburb full of bright jacarandas that bloomed in summer, leaving the road coated in a soft purple carpet. We arrived at the bright pink door in the bougainvillea- and ivy-covered wall. Another reason I loved this house.

"Is this you?" Frankie asked, looking back at the coffee shop.

"It is. I chose the coffee shop because I didn't want to go too far away from my house. I haven't really been out much lately, and certainly not too far."

"Oh," Becca said a little flatly, and I wondered what she was thinking, that maybe I was back to my old ways of not leaving the house much, and whilst that was in fact true at the moment, it wasn't for the reasons they might be thinking.

"I want to show you something," I said to them both. "That's why I brought you here."

I eased the door open and we walked into the front garden. It was big and sprawling, full of flowers and bright rose bushes, which I'd planted. Having a big garden had been a non-negotiable for me when we'd bought this house, and I'd splashed out quite a bit when buying it.

"This is beautiful," Frankie said. "So green. I've been living in a desert for a while. I haven't seen this much green in ages."

"It's gorgeous," Becca added, looking at the house in front of us. And it was. And unusual. I'd chosen a modern house full of glass to let as much light in as possible. A house with strange, cool angles that reminded you of a piece of art. I loved living in this unique house with the green, rolling lawns and more plants than I could have ever wished for.

"Who's this?" Becca stopped at the massive aviary that we'd built under and around the massive oak tree.

"That's Chloe." I ran my hands over the cage and Chloe rushed up to it and stroked my finger with her beak.

"Naughty girls. Naughty girls," Chloe said, and then whistled at us.

Frankie laughed. "Reminds me of a parrot from back home, except this one has a little more manners than the other one."

We walked up to the entrance of the house and I pushed the massive glass door open and walked in.

"Wow!" Frankie said. "I love this. So much color."

"Thanks," I said, scanning the walls and floor of the house. I'd spent so much time decorating this place, to make it feel like a home. A colorful, bright home that was bursting with life. The floors were covered in intricate black-and-white tiles, the walls in colors and paintings and photos and ornaments that I'd collected over the last year.

"Reminds me of the floors back home at Mike's and my house," Becca said, looking at the floors and running a foot over them.

"This way." I walked across the hall, through the huge sunken lounge, past the tropical atrium with the skylight and then up to the glass stairs that led to the upper level.

"What do you want to show us?" Becca asked, sounding excited.

"Wait," I said, equally excited to show them. To show them the miracle that had come of that moment in the elevator just over a year ago. I stopped at a door and pushed it open ever so slowly. My mom and Sindi were sitting on a couch, and smiled at me as I walked in. My mom and dad had been staying with us for a week already, and Sindi was practically living here now—*well*, that is to say she visited every day.

"He's just woken up," my mom said, standing up and moving over to the cot. "Hi," she said to the others. "I've heard so much about you guys."

"Me too!" Sindi said, also standing.

"This is my future sister-in-law, Sindi," I said. "And this is my mom."

"Future sister-in-law and best aunt in the world," she added quickly, and then I think they got it. They knew what I'd brought them here to show them.

"You've . . . oh my God, you have a baby!" Frankie said suddenly from behind me.

"I do." I turned and smiled at them. "He's only one month. I'm still a very new mom and I still totally freak out when I have to leave him. In fact, this might have been the longest I've left him so far."

"Oh wow!" Becca said as we all walked up to the crib and peered in.

And there he was. Lying there, looking up with those big blue eyes, just like his dad's. Noah and I hadn't exactly planned on this, at all. We'd only been together for a few months, and I didn't even think I could have kids. He'd just started nursing school and I'd just started my online card shop, Noah's brilliant idea. "To give others the same joy that you have me," he'd said. And then one morning, when I got sick after breakfast and went to the pharmacy, Andi and her strange psychic abilities had just known instantly and given me a pregnancy test, even though I'd insisted it was impossible! Turns out nothing is impossible it seems.

And although I say Zack wasn't planned, that's actually not entirely true. I think Zack had been planned since that day in the hospital that I'd given a card to a crying boy, and the plan was further actioned the day I stepped into the elevator with Becca and Frankie.

"He's gorgeous," Frankie said.

"I know!" I squealed in pure delight. I still wasn't used to looking at his little face and feeling the love that rushed into me when I did. A love that was so vast and big that it felt like it might make my heart explode right out of my chest. I could stare at him for hours, and sometimes I did. I reached into the crib and picked him up. He made that cute cooing noise that he always makes when I pick him up, and then, like he always does when I hold him against me, he tangled his chubby fingers into my hair and pulled on it in the sweetest way.

"He's so tiny." Becca reached out her hand, but stopped momentarily. "May I?"

I nodded and she brought her hand down onto his. He curled his fingers around her finger, and she laughed. "Wow, this is amazing. You have a baby."

"I have a baby," I said, as Frankie laid her hand on his tiny back and rubbed little circles around it.

"And I would never have had this baby, if I hadn't gotten stuck in that elevator with you guys that day."

We all looked up at each other and something passed between us. This strange knowing. This knowing that those few moments together in the elevator had changed everything for each one of us. It was as if the hand of destiny had chosen us specifically and put us there together, because each one of us, in our different way, needed to change.

Our lives had needed a shake up, and that elevator had done just that, sending us off into different directions. *The right direction.* And for me, I had arrived at the right place. The perfect place. The only place I ever wanted to be. With Noah, Zack and Chloe, living in a house that was literally bursting with color, overflowing with life, and plants, and chilis and chocolates and everything that I loved in the entire world.

ACKNOWLEDGEMENTS

I'd like to thank Dr. Kim Nash for helping me with the medical elements, although I'm afraid I may have taken some creative liberties with them, so don't blame her if some seem a little "less" medically inclined.

It all started with a love letter . . .

It all started with a love letter...

You, Me, Forever x

Jo Watson

THE SMASH-HIT EBOOK BESTSELLING AUTHOR

HEADLINE
ETERNAL

Truly, Madly, Like Me

**She's used to faking it.
Now it's time to get real.**

HEADLINE
ETERNAL

Don't miss Jo's glorious,
laugh-out-loud standalone
office rom-coms!

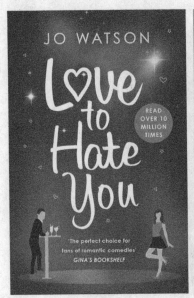

HEADLINE
ETERNAL

For laugh-out-loud, swoon-worthy
hijinks, don't miss Jo's
Destination Love series!

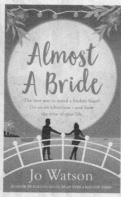
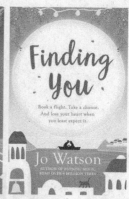

HEADLINE
ETERNAL

HEADLINE
ETERNAL

FIND YOUR HEART'S DESIRE...

VISIT OUR WEBSITE: www.headlineeternal.com
FIND US ON FACEBOOK: facebook.com/eternalromance
CONNECT WITH US ON TWITTER: @eternal_books
FOLLOW US ON INSTAGRAM: @headlineeternal
EMAIL US: eternalromance@headline.co.uk